HE002689

Shake Hands
with a Connaught Ranger

John Michael Doyle
BA Hons IEng MIED

John Doyle was born at Beaufort, Co. Kerry, the son of an Irish father and English mother and lived in Ireland until moving to England at the age of 17.

He served three years in the British Army and then worked in the aerospace industry for over twenty years.

In 1988, John graduated from the Open University with a Bachelor of Arts degree and achieved BA (Honours) three years later. He then joined the staff of the Institution of Engineering Designers with responsibility for Continuing Professional Development. In 1998, he was appointed as Associate Lecturer at The Open University in the field of Professional and Career Development in Engineering. He retired in 2005 but continued to work for the OU in a consultancy capacity.

On final retirement, John took up writing and his hobbies also include walking and photography.

He lives in Wiltshire, is married to Shireen, has one daughter, two granddaughters and a dog.

Shake Hands
with a Connaught Ranger

John Michael Doyle

Shake Hands with a Connaught Ranger

Olympia Publishers
London

www.olympiapublishers.com
OLYMPIA PAPERBACK EDITION

A CIP catalogue record for this title is
available from the British Library.

ISBN: 978-1-84897-286-5

First Published in 2013

Olympia Publishers
60 Cannon Street
London
EC4N 6NP

Printed in Great Britain

Dedication

For my wife, Shireen

Published works

The Last Coachman (2010)

978-1-84897-088-5

This Bitter Land (2011)

978-1-84897-173-8

Prologue

Even the noisy Christmas Eve gaiety and festive hubbub of the crowded public bar failed to force it out of his consciousness. Even here, the sound of the rifle volley still haunted him. Strange that it should, because he had recently been, and to all intents and purposes still was, a British soldier; a man who had served with distinction in two theatres of war. He had heard the sound of rifle fire on the Western Front and in Mesopotamia, but this was different. Perhaps the difference revolved around the fact that this was a single volley fired by a small squad, and not the ear splitting cracks of thousands of rifles firing at will, accompanied by the rattle of machine guns and the terrifying boom of artillery. He was well used to the cacophony of battle, but the volley that caused him such pain had been fired at dawn, not on a battlefield but on an orderly parade ground, and it had been aimed at a single target.

Before the volley rang out an almost reverential silence engulfed the entire prison. The officer in charge quietly gave the order to fire. The sharp crack of the rifles broke the silence and his best friend, Private James Daly of the Connaught Rangers, fell dead: executed by firing squad for mutiny.

That had been less than two months ago, yet half a world away in the heat and dust of India. The guards at Dagshai Military prison had been increased in anticipation of a riot among the other imprisoned mutineers, but the precaution proved to be unnecessary. Rather than riot, the men in the cells knelt and prayed as the fatal volley rang out. Among the officers, too, there was a strained silence. Although they could to some extent understand the reasons for the mutiny they could in no way condone it. So began the blackest day in the history of one of the oldest and proudest regiments in the British Army, The Connaught Rangers.

The man whose friend had faced the firing squad had also been sentenced to death, but his sentence had been commuted to twenty years hard labour. That did little, however, to ease the pain of losing the friend who had stood by him through thick and thin. He resolved that one day he would set the record straight.

The heat and dust of India were now behind him, and he had arrived in the cold and damp of an English winter. Although he had managed to wrap up relatively well, he was still not used to the change in climate, and had risked coming into this Weymouth pub to try and enjoy at least a brief period of warmth before looking round for somewhere to spend the night. He was hoping that, as it was Christmas, vigilance at the harbour would be lax and he might be able to discover an unsecured cabin on one of the many fishing boats; or, at least, find some relative warmth and comfort in a pile of nets, or in the shelter of a deckhouse.

He had already made some plans for tomorrow, Christmas Day: he had located a Catholic church and although he had for many years been less than diligent in the practice of his religion, he was determined that he would go to Mass in the morning and offer up a prayer for the soul of his friend. It had never been in his nature to beg but survival was paramount, and he knew that if he sought charity from the priest, who in all probability would be a fellow Irishman, on this of all days he would not be refused.

Chapter 1

Michael Flynn held firmly on to the rail for security as the *SS Celtic* pitched and tossed its unsteady way through the angry North Atlantic towards its home port of Liverpool. His tall, lean companion followed suit. They had braved the bitter December weather to come on deck for a short break from the stifling atmosphere of their cramped quarters below. The voyage was proving to be extremely uncomfortable, but both men were more than ready to endure the most rudimentary living arrangements on a vessel not designed to carry passengers because the ship was, albeit by a circuitous route, taking them home.

'Home', thought Michael. Home for him was the family farm at Beaufort in County Kerry. There he would find his parents and, more importantly, his infant son. But in order to see them again he would have to tread extremely carefully. For although completely innocent of anything that could reasonably be called a serious crime, in Ireland Michael Flynn was a wanted man. If his presence back in his native land became known to the Royal Irish Constabulary or the regular British Army, he was confident that he would be left in peace, but should he be discovered by the dreaded Black and Tans, he would be shot down without the slightest hesitation. The irregular 'Tans, introduced to support the hard pressed RIC, were something of a law unto themselves and terrorised local communities in their efforts to suppress the Irish fight for independence. Together with another mercenary force, The Auxiliary Police, they literally got away with murder.

So, Michael could not return to his former position as a legally elected Kerry County Councillor because the 'Tans would certainly be watching for him in Tralee, the county capital. The family farm, newly repaired following its burning by those same irregular cut-throats acting in the name of Great Britain, would also be watched. It would be difficult, but return to Beaufort he must. He simply had to see his six-month-old son again. Thoughts of the son he hadn't seen since the baby's christening immediately brought back the painful memory of the child's mother. Maureen Flynn had died in childbirth following harsh treatment by the Black and Tans, or at least by one particular Black and Tan officer. But that officer had paid dearly for his crime – he had been shot and killed by Maureen's brother, Michael's brother-in-law, Kevin Ryan. As a consequence, Michael had become a marked man and been forced to flee to America.

Salty spray splashed his face as he glanced up at his rain-coated and woollen-capped companion. Eamonn de Valera was *Priomh Aire,* First Minister, of the *Dáil.* Described as 'The Parliament of The Republic of Ireland, the *Dáil* was as yet unrecognised and was regarded as an illegal assembly by Great Britain. But in spite of his position, 'Dev', had, in fact, spent little time in Ireland over the previous four years. Imprisoned for his part in the Easter Rising of 1916, he was, together with the other rebel leaders, sentenced to death for treason; but in his case, because of his American birth, the death sentence was commuted to life imprisonment. He was later released in a general amnesty. As the most senior of the 1916 Republican leaders to survive the British reprisals, he was, while still in prison, elected president of Sinn Fein and then *Priomh Aire* when the *Dáil* was established. He was, paradoxically, also an elected Member of the British House of Commons but, in common with other Sinn Fein members, he refused to take his seat at Westminster. Not that he would have had the opportunity to spend much time in Parliament, as shortly after his election, he was back in a British prison. Ostensibly his latest arrest was due to his highly vocal opposition to British attempts to impose First World War conscription in Ireland; but in reality, it was because of his part in establishing the fledgling Irish Republic.

De Valera eventually escaped from Lincoln Jail in an operation organised by the Republic's Minister of Security, Michael Collins; and in which Dev's current travelling companion, Michael Flynn, had played a leading role. Immediately after his escape, de Valera fled to the United States where he spent eighteen months drumming up support and raising money for the struggle for independence in Ireland.

Following his tragic encounter with the Black and Tans, Michael joined Dev in America and had spent the last several months helping the *Priomh Aire* raise funds and political support for The Cause.

The weather worsened and soon the wind and spray drove them back below. They went to the makeshift passenger lounge and shrugged out of their wet coats. When they were seated, Dev said, "Are you still set on following a peaceful path to Irish independence, Michael?"

"I am," Michael answered, "I think it's the only way."

It was the answer de Valera had expected but he persisted. "After what happened to your wife, no one would blame you if you joined an IRA flying column, and I think that it might be as well for you to do so. Personally, I don't see any way of gaining recognition for the Republic other than a military one, especially after the way Michael Collins has been running things while I was away."

"Oh I wouldn't be too sure of that," Michael said. "Did you see where the Galway County Council called on the *Dáil* to sue for peace?"

Michael suspected that de Valera would not be pleased to be reminded of that. "I did," was his testy response, "but I doubt if they'll get much support, and I can't see overtures for peace coming from your own home county. Kerry will always remain steadfast to The Cause."

They lapsed into silence, both lost in thought. In his mind, 'Dev' reminded himself that his decision not to tell Michael about the consignment of Thomson sub-machine guns hidden in the *Celtic's* hold had been the right one.

Not for the first time on the voyage, Michael considered his position regarding his travelling companion. This was a different Eamonn de Valera to the one he remembered from his first contact with the man. That first meeting had occurred on a boat taking Irish internees to the camp at Fron-goch in Wales. Michael had not taken part in the Easter Rising; indeed, at that stage in his young life, he had not given much of a thought to the Irish Nationalist cause. But that had not prevented him being picked up and thrown into an internment camp along with hundreds of other innocent men and women in the reprisals that followed The Rising. Now, here he was again on a ship with the 'Long Fella', a nickname de Valera had picked up from his students at Maynooth College.

During their time in the United States, Michael had come to realise that far from being Ireland's best hope for a peacefully negotiated separation from the United Kingdom as he had first thought, de Valera, was in fact, an extremely able but devious politician ready to use anybody and any method to achieve his dream of an Irish Republic. On several occasions while in America, 'Dev' had allowed his enormous ego to come to the fore and in the process had made as many enemies as he had friends. Michael suspected that de Valera's decision to return home was influenced by the fear that his position as Ireland's leading Republican was being usurped by Michael Collins, who had been responsible for carrying on the armed struggle in Dev's absence.

Internment had drastically changed Michael's life and, more significantly, his attitude towards the Irish cause. At Fron-goch, he met Michael Collins and on his release he was determined to do everything he could to help make Ireland free. He had joined the remnants of the Volunteers left behind after the disappointment of the failed Easter Rising and then training in the remote south western hills for yet another attempt at armed resistance. During this period, he was thrown into close contact with Maureen Ryan, a Dublin girl from a staunch Nationalist family. They fell in love and both seemed destined to follow the growing number of young Irish men and women into what was soon to become known as the Irish Republican Army. But then Michael killed a man. Although he had done it in the process of saving Maureen's life, and the life of his friend, William Quinlan, it did not sit easily on his conscience. The man had been a senior Republican activist and in order to avoid being hunted by both the authorities and 'the boys', as the Republican insurgents were generally known, they had unceremoniously buried the body in a lonely bog. As far as Michael was concerned this compounded the sin and, from then on, he had vowed to do his best for Ireland without recourse to violence. Somewhat to his surprise, Maureen, who was soon to become his wife, supported him. It was then he met Collins again and was recruited to help free de Valera from Lincoln Jail, a feat which he accomplished without the necessity of him carrying a gun.

Even after Maureen had died in childbirth following her rough treatment in a Black and Tan prison cell, a tragedy which could easily have been avoided had any of the 'Tans cared enough, Michael's resolve to seek a peaceful end to the killing had not been weakened.

They left the Atlantic behind and immediately the ship docked in Liverpool they were met with news of yet more examples of the bitter violence he feared might put an end to hopes and dreams of peace. A group of Auxiliaries were ambushed at Kilmichael in County Cork by an IRA Flying Column led by Tom Barry, and eighteen of the British irregulars were killed or wounded. A week later, a grenade was thrown into the back of a lorry carrying 'Auxies', which resulted in the death of one man, and several others were badly wounded. The inevitable reprisals followed and the Auxiliaries demonstrated their total lack of any form of military discipline by going on a drunken orgy and setting fire to Cork City Centre.

It looked as if the Irish War of Independence, with its never-ending cycle of atrocities and reprisals, would go on.

Chapter 2

Jack Quinlan threw down the newspaper with an uncharacteristic show of exasperation. "Sure weren't you always a bloody hot-headed eejit, Jim Daly, but all the same, may The Lord have mercy on your soul."

From her seat by the fire, his mother, Annie Quinlan, looked up in surprise at this sudden and unexpected outburst from her eldest son. She glanced across to where he sat at the kitchen table fully prepared to admonish him, but he had quickly regained his composure and as she watched, a look of sadness replaced the anger on his face.

"What's up, Jack?" she asked gently.

"It's Jim Daly, Ma," he replied. "They shot him for mutiny in India, and after all he did for them in the war too." The anger returned briefly. "Why would they want to do that to the likes of him?"

Annie crossed herself. "May the Good Lord have mercy on him," she said devoutly. She lowered her eyes and Jack could sense that she was saying a silent prayer for his friend. And he knew that she would certainly add one for Daly's mother, it was typical of her that she should. Although Annie didn't know the woman, she felt an affinity with all mothers whose sons were involved in the never-ending circle of violence that seemed to beset the world in this, the first year of the nineteen-twenties.

Jack stood up. He went over to the mantelpiece and took down the photograph in the silver frame which stood there among the collection of trinkets and the holy statues. It showed three soldiers in tropical dress against a bleak desert background. He himself stood in the centre of the trio wearing the badge of the Royal Field Artillery and he was flanked by two infantrymen, Privates James Daly and Patrick Coughlin of the Connaught Rangers. The picture had been taken during a lull in the fighting in Mesopotamia where all three had served in the Great War, a war which had ended two years before almost to the day.

Annie finished her prayer, crossed herself again and watched Jack, clearly lost in memories, gazing at the photograph.

"God knows what the world is coming to, Jack. I prayed to God that after the war all this murdering would stop, but will you look at what's happening in Ireland these days? And it's all round us, even here in Beaufort. Is there to be no hope for us at all?"

As if to emphasise the horror of what was happening in Ireland, there had been an ambush on a party of Black and Tans, the irregular force introduced by the British authorities to combat the IRA, just outside Beaufort village last evening. Four men had been killed: three of the 'Tans and one of the attackers. It was not known how many others had been hurt; both sides took their wounded away from the scene of battle as soon as possible because neither side was too particular about taking prisoners. But, as usual, there had been casualties among innocent civilians, if such a term could be applied to anyone in Ireland in 1920. Several local people had been hurt and at least one was not expected to live. Harsh reprisals by the Black and Tans, in the name of enforcing law and order, could be expected before long. And again, it was the blameless who would suffer most. This was the second such ambush to have been staged in Beaufort by the IRA. Earlier in the year, an attempt had been made on the life of Jack's employer, the aristocratic owner of Beaufort House, who was then a high-ranking British government official. The attack had failed, but the reprisals had been harsh.

After a quiet moment, in which Annie again remembered the dead, she had a sudden thought: "What about poor Patrick Coughlin? Does the paper say that he was shot as well?"

"No, Ma, thank God there's nothing at all in the paper about Pat. I know that he would have followed Jim Daly anywhere, so I suppose he was put in jail with the rest of them, but as far as I can see Jim was the only one to be shot. But there's some talk here about the prisoners being brought back to a jail in England."

Jack stood to replace the photograph. His mother reached up and touched his arm. "God knows it must be hard for you to bear, Jack, after you saved their lives out there in that terrible desert."

"Yes, I suppose you could say that I helped to save Pat's life, Ma, and it's a sad thing to see them end up like this. And sure they were sound men the pair of them, and good friends too."

Annie wiped away a tear. "How in God's name did it come to this Jack?"

Jack thought for a few minutes before answering her. "I'd say that it's all down to what's happening here in Ireland," he said. "Even though he was a British soldier, and a good one at that, Jim Daly was always an Irishman first and foremost and he couldn't bear to be out there in India doing the same things to the Indians as the Black and Tans are doing to his own people here at home. And sure Pat Coughlin would follow Jim no matter where he led him."

"Do you think that they will bring poor James Daly's body home to his mother?"

Jack felt that he should have anticipated the question, and he instantly realised that there was nothing he could say that would ease the pain that crept into his mother's eyes as she asked it. He knew that she was thinking not of his friend in India, but of his father, her husband. Michael Quinlan had died at an enormous munitions factory in Scotland during the Great War. He had suffered a fatal heart attack brought on by becoming inadvertently involved in an Irish rebel plot to sabotage the factory. As this had happened during the Easter Rising of 1916, his body could not be brought home for burial. And so he lay interred in a pauper's grave in England, a fact which pained Annie as much as his actual death.

As gently as he could, Jack told her the truth. "No, Ma," he said, "they won't bring Jim's body home. He'll join the thousands of British soldiers buried all over the world."

He spared her further grief by not mentioning the fact that, having been executed by firing squad for mutiny, it was highly unlikely that Private Daly would be buried in one of the special cemeteries reserved for the British war dead.

Jack sensed what was coming next. "God help his poor mother," she said sadly. Then she brightened up a little. "At least James and William are still alive, although I fear for the pair if them and I have a terrible feeling that I'll never see either of them again."

James and William were Jack's younger brothers. James, who had been with their father at the munitions factory in Scotland, had fallen foul of the rebel saboteurs and been forced to emigrate to America. William, who had become disillusioned with what he saw as a dead end life in Beaufort, and was looking for a way to enhance his prospects for a better future, had joined the British Army and was currently serving in the Royal Tank Corps.

"Ah sure of course you'll see them again, Ma," Jack reassured her. "As soon as things settle down here in Ireland, James has promised to come and see you, and there's every chance that William will be here for Christmas."

Annie was sceptical. "Do you honestly think that William can come home for Christmas, Jack? The way people feel about the British these days he won't get much of a welcome in Ireland outside of this house."

"Well, now, that's the funny thing, Ma. Since the Black and Tans and the Auxiliaries came and started terrorising the whole country, sure a lot of people have changed their minds about regular British soldiers. I'd say that Bill has nothing to worry about, even if he comes home in uniform."

His mother did not look convinced, but Jack knew of one sure way of cheering her up. "But whatever happens, Ma, isn't young Michael sure to be here for the Christmas."

Annie smiled. 'Young' Michael, named after his father, was her youngest son and a joy to her heart. It was not that she loved him one jot more or less than she did her other children, but he had been the one to fulfil her lifelong dream; like every Irish mother, she had prayed that at least one of her sons would become a priest, and Michael had just begun his training at the seminary in Maynooth.

Seeing her more settled in her mind, he rose and reached for his coat. "Anyway, Ma, I can't stop here all day, I have a job of work to do. I'll look in on Mary while I'm up at the house."

Mary was the eldest of Jack's two sisters, both of them younger than the four boys; she had just left school and gone 'into service' as a very junior maid. The last and youngest member of the Quinlan family, Elizabeth, was still attending the local school.

As he left the cottage, Jack said, "Her Ladyship will be going out any minute now and you'll have to open the gate for her."

'The house' was Beaufort House, the Irish seat of an aristocratic former British government official. 'Her Ladyship' was the owner's wife and in spite of the Irish War for Independence currently ravaging the country, with its ambushes, atrocities, reprisals and counter reprisals, she insisted on carrying on as if nothing whatsoever was amiss. Even though His Lordship had been fortunate to survive the IRA attempt on his life, she insisted on carrying on with her full social calendar; to her mind it was her duty as Lady of the house.

The Quinlans lived in a cottage close by Beaufort Bridge, which spanned the river Laune. Jack's father had been coachman at Beaufort House and the cottage came with the job. After the war, Jack, in recognition of his war service, had been employed as 'steward', in effect, Beaufort Estate Manager, and the cottage was passed to him. Situated at the bottom of the long drive which led up to the house itself, the cottage doubled up as a gatehouse and, even some four years after the death of her husband, Annie still saw it as her duty to open and close the ornate wrought iron gates.

Jack left the cottage and set off for the house. He turned up his coat collar and pulled down his cap against the chill late November wind. Overnight the first dusting of winter snow had fallen on the MacGillicuddy's Reeks mountain range to the south of Beaufort. As he walked up the drive, his thoughts turned to the events leading to the recent mutiny of the Connaught Rangers in India, and how he first came to know the two mutineers he had just been talking to his mother about. He had first met them at the rest area near Basra during a lull in the fighting in Mesopotamia when, as one of the few Roman Catholic Irishmen serving in an artillery battery, he had gone over to the Connaught Rangers lines to attend Mass. There, Jack and Private Patrick Coughlin had become good friends and Coughlin had introduced him to Private James Daly. Coughlin was a largely carefree, easy going young man from County Galway in the west of Ireland, the traditional recruiting ground of the Connaught Rangers. Daly, from the neighbouring county of Mayo, on the surface exhibited the same devil-may-care manner as Coughlin, but underneath, Jack soon found him to have a much more serious side to his nature. Both men had joined the British Army before the war when taking the 'King's Shilling' provided a way of escape from the abject poverty in Ireland. Although a brave soldier who was extremely proud of the long history and tradition of his regiment, Daly was first and foremost a staunch Irishman. He had served the Empire well in India and had fought bravely both in France against the Germans and in Mesopotamia against the Turks. But his heart remained in Ireland and he longed for the day when his native land would be free of British rule.

At the height of the fighting, Jack helped Daly to get a seriously wounded Coughlin off the battlefield and in effect saved his friend's life. The bond of friendship between the three men had been cemented back in Ireland. While recovering from his wounds, Coughlin had visited the Quinlan family and been made to feel completely at home by Annie and Jack's brother, William.

After the war, Jack had been 'de-mobbed' and went home to Beaufort while the two 'Rangers, who were regular soldiers, stood by for posting with their regiment to India. James Daly became increasingly concerned about the deteriorating situation in Ireland and particularly about the tactics adopted by the British authorities to suppress the growing Republican movement. The introduction of the Black and Tans made Daly seriously question his loyalty to The Crown. Home on embarkation leave prior to being sent to India, Daly and Coughlin were falsely arrested on suspicion of being IRA gunmen. This was the final straw as far as Daly was concerned and he would have deserted there and then to join the IRA, had he not been persuaded by Jack and another friend, Michael Flynn, to return to his unit. Daly eventually went to India, but Jack feared that it would not take much to drive him over the edge, and the loyal Coughlin, although not caring as deeply about Irish independence, would follow his friend anywhere.

In India, other members of the 'Rangers also became increasingly concerned about their families at home. As news of atrocities committed by the Black and Tans reached them, they, like James Daly, became increasingly disturbed at being ordered to carry out what they considered to be similar tactics against the local Indian population. Things eventually came to a head when the 1st battalion, stationed at Julundur and Solan, refused to carry out orders until something was done about Black and Tan atrocities in Ireland. The mutiny was soon suppressed but the consequences would be felt for years to come.

News of the mutiny of the Connaught Rangers reverberated around the world, and quickly became an acute embarrassment to the London government. By the time the courts martial began in August 1920, a great deal of sympathy had been generated, especially in America but also across the British Empire and, indeed, in Britain itself. And some, particularly the traditional factions of the British Army, while they could never condone mutiny, felt as uneasy as anyone about the tactics of the Black and Tans in Ireland. So, while they had little time for the mutineers themselves, they recognised that they had acted under extreme provocation. The army in India however, far removed from the situation in Ireland, was not prepared to be so lenient. Conditions in Dagshai prison where the mutineers were detained were extremely harsh. The heat and the sparse rations began to take their toll and several mutineers became ill. At one point, six men managed to break out but instead of making a clean getaway, they broke into the stores and stole a large stock of food. One man volunteered to make a run for it and while the guards gave chase, his comrades crept back into the prison with the food.

Public opinion in Britain was beginning to take effect and some of the men deemed to have played a minor part in the mutiny were given light prison sentences of one to three years, and a few were even acquitted. Those thought to have been more heavily involved were not treated so leniently. Fourteen death sentences were handed down and the remainder given gaol sentences of twenty years. But eventually all but one of the death sentences, including that handed down to Patrick

Coughlin, were commuted to life imprisonment. The only man to face a firing squad was Private James Joseph Daly.

Jack determined that he would write to his old friend Coughlin. But he would first have to find out if the mutineers were still detained in Dagshai gaol, or whether they were being shipped back to Britain to serve out their sentences, as the newspaper report had indicated. Obtaining information on which prison they were to be held in could prove to be difficult, and he wondered if he dared approach his employer for help.

As he reached the top of the drive, Jack noticed His Lordship exiting the house with someone he had not seen before, probably another of his employer's frequent official visitors. Since His Lordship's brush with the IRA, it was not unusual for old friends from the Ministry of Munitions to visit him at Beaufort House rather than risk him having to travel to London. Although Jack did not recognise the tall figure in the smart dark suit, his army experience told him that this stranger was a military man. He noted the manner in which the man kept his left hand in his jacket pocket with the thumb hooked over the edge, and he immediately identified his employer's guest as a naval officer.

Jack kept a respectful distance between himself and the two men as he made his way round to the stable yard but to his surprise, His Lordship called him back.

"Ah, there you are, Quinlan, there is someone here I should like you to meet."

Chapter 3

At noon, Kevin Ryan left the local train that had brought him out to Clontarf from Dublin city centre. He exited the station, turned up the collar of his coat against the light drizzle, and limped down the road to his lodgings. Beneath his feet lay the ancient battlefield of Clontarf where Brian Boru had defeated the Vikings in 1014. The ancient battlefield was to all intents and purposes now a suburb of Dublin, but as a member of the Irish Republican Army, Kevin would have been well aware of the events of that momentous Good Friday when the Danes had been finally driven from Ireland. He would have been imbued with the 'Spirit of Clontarf' and the words spoken by Brian Boru before the battle nine hundred years ago would have been familiar to him:

'...The barbarians have impiously fixed, for their struggle, to enslave us, upon the very day on which the Redeemer of the World was crucified. Victory they shall not have!...'(Annals of Innisfallen)

His limp was genuine, the result of a wound received in the abortive IRA ambush on the important British government official living at Beaufort House in County Kerry, and he had discovered that if he exaggerated the limp he was less likely to be stopped and questioned by the police. Should he be stopped, however, the forged British Army discharge papers he carried, which showed that he had been wounded in the Great War, would make it extremely unlikely that he would be searched. Should he be searched by the Royal Irish Constabulary, he would be arrested and tried before being hanged or shot; if, on the other hand, it was the Black and Tans or the Auxiliary Police – the second irregular force employed by the British Government to help subdue the IRA – who searched him and found the Webley revolver jammed in the waistband of his trousers, he would probably be shot there and then. These men would not bother to observe the formalities of either arrest or trial. It would be said that he had been shot attempting to escape, and no one in authority would have questioned it. But he had every confidence that, since the events of a few short hours ago, the RIC, the 'Tans, and the 'Auxies' would all be too busy in the city to worry about a seemingly innocent war veteran limping through the suburbs. He could feel the weapon against his body. It was still warm from having been extensively used earlier on this grey November Sunday morning.

Ryan was not simply a soldier in the IRA; he belonged to Michael Collins' elite murder squad known as 'The Twelve Apostles', and that morning he had taken part in the assassination of several members of 'The Cairo Gang'.

The Cairo Gang, so called because they often met in Dublin's Cairo Café and because several of them had served in Palestine during the war, was a group of officers from the various British intelligence services. Their purpose was to infiltrate the Irish Republican movement and gather intelligence for use against the IRA. They worked closely with the RIC, the Auxiliaries and the Black and Tans, and they were proving to be a thorn in Michael Collins' side. As head of security for the IRA, Collins knew that if he could eliminate 'The Gang' he would severely cripple British intelligence activities throughout Ireland, and especially in Dublin. The IRA's own intelligence organisation had learned the addresses where the gang members lodged, the information having been passed on by sympathetic hotel maids, boarding house proprietors and informers within the RIC. The operation was set for a Sunday morning when most Dubliners would be at Mass and the gang would be at their least vigilant. In all, eleven British agents were gunned down, some of them in front of their families, and several more were severely wounded. Two Auxiliaries who had been alerted by the sound of gunfire and tried to intervene were also shot and killed.

Swift and severe reprisals by the authorities were to be expected, but Collins knew that these would only serve to generate further public support for the Republican Cause.

At his lodging in an IRA 'safe house', Ryan changed his clothes and had his lunch. He then set off back into the city. That afternoon Tipperary were playing Dublin in a Gaelic football match at Croke Park and the city would be crowded with supporters. He reasoned that the safest place in Dublin that afternoon would be at the match so he decided to go and mingle with the crowd. He considered leaving the revolver at home but knew that he would feel vulnerable without it, so he risked taking it with him.

As the game got underway, a convoy of British security forces from the RIC and the Auxiliary Division approached with orders to surround the ground and search everyone there for arms. It was the custom at Croke Park for authorised ticket sellers to sell tickets outside the gates, but when these saw the approach of a dozen lorry-loads of police, 'Auxies' and 'Tans, they bolted into the ground. The police in the leading lorry gave chase and fired indiscriminately into the crowd with rifles and revolvers. In the ensuing panic, some of the badly overexcited policemen continued firing from the pitch while others opened up on people trying to escape over the walls, and a machine gun fired over the heads of the escapees from an armoured car parked in the road outside. By the time the officer-in-charge had regained control over his men, seven people had been killed outright and five more had suffered fatal wounds; dozens more were injured. Among the dead were a young woman, two small boys and one of the footballers. Two people were trampled to death in the panic.

When order was restored, the men leaving the ground were searched for arms, but Kevin Ryan had already made his escape. He threw the revolver over a garden wall as he fled. It was the only weapon found by the police that day.

There followed claims and counter-claims and there was outrage in the press on both sides of the Irish Sea. However much they were provoked by the events of the morning, it was generally agreed that the police had opened fire without authority.

It was nine hundred and six years since Brian Boru's victory at Clontarf, but Ireland was still as troubled as ever. November 21st 1920 would go down in history as 'Bloody Sunday'.

Chapter 4

Commander Wilson RN felt a sense of déjà vu as the owner of Beaufort House called Jack Quinlan over to meet him, and it brought on a feeling of anxiety unbecoming of an officer in the Royal Navy. It was not an anxiety engendered by renewing his acquaintance with members of the Quinlan family, that was something he had always planned to do at the earliest opportunity, but he would have much preferred the meeting to have taken place under different circumstances. What troubled him was the thought that his duty might require him to once again involve a member of that family in an undercover operation.

Wilson was a British intelligence officer, but a rather reluctant one. He would have been much happier, and in his opinion far more useful to King and Country, serving aboard one of His Majesty's ships.

Jack, who in the first place had been surprised to be called to meet a visitor to Beaufort House, was further surprised to learn the man's name.

"Quinlan, this is Commander Wilson of the Royal Navy," his employer informed him. "He wishes to have a word with you."

Jack immediately recognised the name and, even two whole years after the end of the Great War, his military training was still having its effect, so he drew himself to attention before answering, "Yes, sir."

The Commander offered his hand, something Jack would not have expected from either a serving officer or a visitor to Beaufort House, but he nonetheless accepted the firm handshake.

Wilson cleared his throat and came as near as a naval officer dared to shuffling his feet. "I've been anxious to meet you for some time, Quinlan. You see I knew your father, knew him quite well in fact. I can't begin to tell you how sorry I was when he died."

Jack felt that the concern was genuine. He knew that Wilson had been the security officer at the great wartime munitions factory in Scotland where his father, Michael Quinlan, and brother, James, had worked. James had laboured there as a navvy, but Michael had worked directly under Wilson as a member of the factory's internal police force and had died during an operation run by the Commander to foil the Irish rebel plot to sabotage the factory in conjunction with the 1916 Easter Rising in Ireland. Michael had actually died of heart failure but James had told Jack that Wilson still felt that, as the man in charge, he should shoulder some of the blame. Although not on active service at sea, and even though Michael Quinlan was a civilian, the naval man still considered Jack's father to have died under his command.

"Thank you, sir," Jack replied. He was at a loss for anything else to say but he suspected that there was more to come from Wilson.

There was. "I should also like to pay my respects to your mother, if she could possibly bear to see me. I realise that it might bring back some unwelcome memories and I should hate to cause her any further distress; and I fully understand that your family may well hold me responsible for your tragic loss."

Jack was touched by the man's obvious concern and attempted to put him at ease. "Ah sure we don't blame you at all, sir. Didn't my brother, Jim, tell us all about it. He said that you couldn't have done more for Da, and for Jim, too, after what happened. I'd say that Ma would like to meet you, sir, but I'd like to have a word with her myself first if that's all right with you?"

At that point Jack's employer chose to join the conversation. "I think that would be for the best, Commander." He turned to Jack. "Perhaps you would be good enough to bring her up to the house, Quinlan. You can talk to her on the way and then she can meet Commander Wilson over a cup of tea."

On his way down to the cottage to fetch his mother, Jack had ample opportunity to collect his thoughts. He knew that his mother would recognise the name and be eager to meet Commander Wilson, even though it was bound to bring back painful memories. In Jack's opinion, his employer's suggestion of holding the meeting up at the house was indeed the best way to handle the situation, and he suspected that His Lordship had thought it through carefully beforehand. He would have known that Annie Quinlan's world still revolved around the firmly established social conventions that had been part of her life since childhood. Having an important visitor to Beaufort House coming to see her on a personal matter in her own home would go against these conventions and make her feel uncomfortable. Being summoned by the master of the house would, however, seem to her to be in the natural order of things.

It was these same conventions that had caused Jack to volunteer for service in the Great War. Answering Kitchener's call of 'Your Country Needs You' was simply something that would be expected of the coachman's eldest son. But four years of war in a far distant corner of the world had changed his perspectives on what had been the accepted social order. He did, however, understand his mother's feelings and was glad that his employer had recognised them too.

The meeting with Commander Wilson took place in a small room off the large entrance hall where visitors waited before being escorted in to meet the aristocratic owner of the house. In this case it served as a kind of halfway house between the working areas around the kitchen and 'the family's' private apartments. It was another example of His Lordship's careful stage management of the affair to provide an environment where Annie Quinlan and Commander Wilson would both feel most at ease. Wilson, who had been briefed by His Lordship, invited the Quinlans to sit, and then sat down himself to avoid intimidating Annie. He lit a cigarette and offered his case to Jack who accepted. Tea was served by Annie's daughter, Mary, rather than one of the more senior maids. She was briefly introduced to the Commander and then ushered out to carry on with her duties. Annie was grateful to have Jack present for support but would not have wished Mary to be there. It would not have been proper to have allowed a very junior member of the household to hear what was being said; and the impulsive Mary, who had been still a child when her father died, would certainly have embarrassed her mother by asking questions.

The Commander opened the conversation by saying, "It's good of you to meet me, Mrs Quinlan, and I should first like to offer my sincere condolences on the death of your husband. I realise that this comes somewhat belatedly but it is the first opportunity I've had since the tragic events at Gretna."

"Thank you, sir," was all that Annie felt it appropriate to say.

"Your husband was a fine man, Mrs Quinlan, one of the finest I have served with." Under some pressure, the Commander couldn't help speaking as if Michael Quinlan had actually been serving in the Royal Navy.

He went on to tell Annie about her late husband's work as a member of his factory police force, how well liked he had been and how well he had performed his duty. Much to Jack's relief, he did not go into the details of his father's death but merely said, "His heart attack came as a shock to us all, we had no idea that he was so ill."

"Ah sure it was just like Michael not to complain at all, sir," Annie replied.

She wiped away a tear and Wilson judged that he had said enough. He changed the subject. "Of course I knew your son James too. He was a fine young man and you must be quite proud of him, I know that his father was. He is now in America, I understand, you must give him my regards when you write to him."

This brought a smile. "I will so, sir, and sure I'm proud of all my boys. As well as James in America, Jack is the steward here, William is in the army, and young Michael is training for the priesthood."

The Commander judged that this would be a good note on which to finish. He rose and Annie immediately followed suit. "Thank you again for coming, Mrs Quinlan, I'm glad to have met you at last."

As they made their way back down the drive, Annie said: "Ah sure he's a real gentleman that Mr Wilson and it was grand that he took the trouble to tell us all about your father. But I don't think that he told us the whole story, and neither did that young tinker, James. I think there's a lot being kept from me but God knows, maybe it's for the best."

Jack remained silent; he had to admit to himself that there was indeed a lot being kept from her and he sincerely believed that it was for the best. When he returned home after the Great War, James had given him a full account of the events leading to their father's death and Jack agreed that his brother had been right to keep many of the details from their mother. It would only have added to her grief, and it served no useful purpose to tell her that her husband and son had been taken hostage by the saboteurs and would have been shot, had it not been for the intervention of an undercover British security operative.

After Jack and his mother left, Commander Wilson breathed a sigh of relief and went to join the owner of the house in his private study, where his host handed him a glass of Irish whiskey. His Lordship had not met Wilson before this unexpected visit to Beaufort by the security man, but he certainly knew him by reputation. As a government official responsible for wartime munitions production, he was fully aware of Wilson's part in foiling the Irish rebel plot at the Gretna factory. And, as Michael Quinlan had served as his coachman before the war, like Wilson, he took a special interest in the Quinlan family.

"Mrs Quinlan will have appreciated your taking the time to talk to her," he said.

"It was the least I could do as I was already here in Beaufort," Wilson answered.

"When are you going to bring up that other business with Quinlan," His Lordship looked closely at his visitor, "or have you not as yet decided on a course of action?"

Wilson took a sip of whiskey. "I sincerely hope that it doesn't come to that, I'd much prefer not to have to involve him in this, especially after what happened to his father." He paused and drank again, then went on with some feeling. "God how I hate these infernal cloak and dagger operations."

He did indeed hate 'these cloak and dagger operations'. After the war, he had tried his hardest to be transferred out of the security service and returned to duty at sea. But to no avail. Following his success in overcoming the Irish rebels at the factory, he was considered by his superiors to be an expert in all things Irish, and so he was retained in the security service and given special responsibility for helping to resolve the 'Irish problem'. He didn't like it, but naval tradition demanded that he would do his duty, however distasteful.

"But what is so special about this man, Flynn?" his host asked. "I realise that he is, or was, a Sinn Fein councillor, but according to local gossip he is no IRA killer, although after what happened to his wife it wouldn't surprise me if he were to become one. I also suspect that he was the one who passed the warning to Quinlan about a possible plot against me. In any case I've heard that he went America."

"Yes, following his affair with the irregulars," like most serving officers Wilson had little time for the Black and Tans and the Auxiliaries and usually referred to them as 'the irregulars', "he did go to the United States where he met with Eamonn de Valera. But de Valera is currently is on his way home and I shouldn't be at all surprised to find that Flynn is accompanying him. I believe that you're right about him not being a terrorist gunman; in my opinion he may well be the direct opposite and be seeking a peaceful end to this war. But his former brother-in-law, Kevin Ryan, certainly is such a killer. We believe that he took part in the murders in Dublin the other week, and he is one of the IRA men we really would like to get our hands on. Among other things, I'm hoping that Flynn might lead us to him."

His Lordship thought for a moment and put down his glass. "Ah, I see it now, if Flynn comes back to Ireland he will certainly come to Beaufort to see his family and, as a good friend of his, Quinlan will know about it when he does. But you said 'among other things, Commander."

"That's right," said Wilson. "There is more to it than that. My orders are not merely to help catch IRA gunmen; there are plenty of others working on that side of things. The directions I have been given are far more complicated and have to be handled much more delicately." He looked directly at his host. "So, I'm sure that what I am about to tell you will remain in the strictest confidence?"

"Of course," His Lordship assured him.

Having got that assurance, Wilson went on to outline what was contained in his orders; orders that had come from the highest level, and included making contact with the former wartime government minister who was, at this moment, his host at Beaufort. When his visitor had finished, His Lordship was silent for some minutes while he thought over the implications of what he had heard.

Eventually, he was ready to comment. "It seems, Commander, that, at last, some factions within the government are beginning to show some basic common sense. I don't know how you are going to achieve this, but I wish you well and I am certainly willing to help in any way I can. In that respect may I suggest that should it become necessary, you allow me to personally handle the approach to Quinlan."

Wilson smiled. "I was hoping you might say that," he said with some relief.

From somewhere in the house there came the sound of a telephone ringing, followed a few minutes later by a polite knock on the door. The butler informed them that there was a telephone call for Commander Wilson. When the naval officer returned he was wearing a frown.

"I'm afraid that what we've been discussing will have to wait," he said. "I've just been handed a different problem. It seems that one of those mutineers brought back from India has managed to escape and is on the loose somewhere in the south of England. Some fellow called Coughlin. It seems that the 'powers that be' want him caught as quietly as possible so that the rebels here aren't handed a propaganda opportunity, and it seems that I'm to be the one to carry it off. But God knows how. Anyway, I'll have to shelve what I'm doing here for the moment and get back to London."

He turned to leave but His Lordship called him back. "Just a moment, Commander, it's quite a coincidence, but if this chap Coughlin is who I think he is then your two assignments may actually be connected. You see, Coughlin, too, may well be a good friend of Quinlan's."

Chapter 5

Kate Steele was bored. With several weeks still to go until Christmas the bar in the out-of-the-way inn was almost empty. Business would pick up nearer to the festive season but at the moment she had little to do but think. She went over in her mind the events of the last couple of years.

After three years spent experiencing the excitement and danger of working in a wartime munitions factory in Scotland, life in peacetime had proved to be decidedly dull. She spent the first months after the war at home in Bristol where she tried her hand at several menial jobs, including helping out in local cafés and bars. Days and nights spent waiting on tables and serving behind bars could not begin to compare with days and nights working with the dangerous material euphemistically nicknamed the 'devil's porridge'. This highly volatile mixture of gun-cotton and nitro-glycerine formed the basic ingredient of the cordite propellant the great factory produced in enormous quantities. The years of wartime living and working with the women and girls known as the 'Gretna Girls' had transformed Kate from a naive teenager into a worldly, and extremely attractive, young woman; but one who had soon become totally dissatisfied with what she saw as a humdrum peacetime existence.

She went out to the cinema and to dances with young, local men, dates which, although enjoyable in themselves, never led to anything approaching a meaningful relationship. Men who had served in the war wanted nothing more than to settle down and live a quiet life with a girl who would be happy to marry and take up the duties of a housewife; and Kate Steele was far from ready for that. Those few young men who had not been in the forces felt intimidated by her accounts of the dangers she had faced as a Gretna Girl. When she contacted old school friends she found that they had little in common any more. Many of them also asked for nothing more from life than to find a suitable husband and several had already fulfilled that ambition. The only way Kate would have contemplated following their example was if the man had been extremely rich. At her mother's insistence she went 'into service' as a live-in maid in a wealthy businessman's home, but she only managed a couple of weeks before having a blazing row with her mistress. Her failure to settle down caused friction at home and by the early summer of 1919 she had had enough.

Life was returning to normal after four bleak years of wartime austerity and people were again beginning to enjoy seaside holidays. Kate lied her way into a job in a large hotel in Bournemouth on England's south coast by exaggerating her experience as a waitress and barmaid. Working in the hotel with its ever-changing stream of holidaymakers and constant supply of new faces was more to her liking, and she found that going out with men who were either on holiday or working away from the constraints of home to be more satisfying than being courted by the young men in Bristol; at least they were not in search of a 'nice girl' eager to become a wife. She worked hard and at the end of the season was invited to return the following summer.

Her second winter at home after the war was no more successful than her first, but it gave her an opportunity to consider her position. She recognised her need to add some excitement to her life and thought that she might satisfy it by going abroad. She looked into the possibility of emigrating to America where some friends from her factory days had gone after the war and she decided to try and contact them. This gave her a sense of purpose, but joining the stream of emigrants leaving Europe for a better life in the New World, and travelling across the Atlantic as a steerage passenger in an overcrowded ship, held little appeal. If Kate Steele was going to go to America she was determined to do it in some style. In order to achieve this, however, she would have to raise a considerable sum of money.

When she returned to Bournemouth in the spring of 1920 she was given a permanent post as a barmaid. Her plan to save enough from her pay and tips to fund her passage to America was, however, proving difficult to achieve; even with a permanent job she soon realised that it would take time, probably several years, to save up enough to travel in the grand style she had in mind. Then she met a man called Mark.

Older than Kate, she estimated that he was in his mid-thirties, he was a relatively handsome man of medium height and build and well, if quite plainly, dressed. When she first saw him in the hotel foyer she took him for one of the guests but this proved not to be the case. He came into the bar, which was open to the general public, ordered a half pint of beer and struck up a conversation. After this had been repeated on a few occasions, some of the hotel staff began to jokingly remark that he had his eye on her. Kate, proud of her pretty looks and trim figure, was flattered, and when he eventually asked her to go out with him on her next night off, she readily accepted. Their first date, a trip to the cinema, was a success and led to several more. Soon, she was spending virtually all her free time with him. He was a bit vague about what he actually did for a living, but he seemed to be available whenever she was free, and she certainly found him much more interesting to be with than any of the other men she had known since the war. On one occasion he told her that he had been abroad during the war on 'official business', but didn't go into exactly what that meant, and he didn't seem at all intimidated by her own wartime experiences in the munitions factory. In the end, Mark was the first, and as it turned out the only, man to be invited to sneak up the fire escape to her room in the servants' quarters high up under the roof of the hotel.

When she told him of her ambition to go abroad, he said that he too had had been thinking of emigrating and, like her, he would prefer to have an adequate stake to do it properly. But that kind of money would not be easy to come by. This surprised her, for when they went out together he always seemed to have sufficient cash with him to be able to spend freely. But, although he said nothing definite, the intimation was that they could go together and Kate knew that should the offer be made, she was ready to accept. When she thought about it, she admitted to herself that in spite of there being something interesting and even intriguingly mysterious about him, she was not in love with him. But she regarded him as providing her with the best opportunity of achieving her ultimate goal.

In July, the beginning of the busiest part of the holiday season, he finally broached the subject of raising the necessary cash to take them to America and outlined his plan for obtaining it. She didn't hesitate to go along with it.

Over the following weeks money and valuables began to disappear from some of the best rooms in the hotel. From her vantage point behind the bar, Kate could see enough of the reception desk as guests registered, and Mark had coached her on how to identify the most suitable 'targets'. She would then stroll round and find their room numbers. In the early hours of one morning, Kate had sneaked down and taken wax impressions of the spare keys to the most expensive rooms from which Mark had produced a set of duplicates. In the quiet period after lunch, he would enter a room posing as a guest, a repairman, or even a waiter. He would search for loose cash and jewellery carelessly left lying around, and anything else of value he could lay his hands on while she kept watch outside. To avoid suspicion she carried a tray of drinks as if delivering a room service order. Mark kept some of the cash for himself, 'for expenses', and gave the rest to Kate. This she deposited in a Post Office account for safe keeping and he warned her that she must not be seen to have suddenly come into some extra money. The jewellery and other valuables were hidden in a small suitcase under her bed to wait until they had enough for him to take to a 'fence' he knew in London.

Kate was in her element. The affair provided her with the excitement she had been craving since the war, and the thought of the loot under the bed added spice to her love making. She knew that they couldn't expect to get away with it for long, but she didn't care.

To begin with, the hotel management tried to keep a lid on things, news of the thefts from their rooms would seriously damage the hotel's reputation. But the complaints from angry guests increased and there was no option but to call the police. Mark seemed to sense when this would happen: he sneaked the loot out of the hotel in her suitcase to take to his 'fence' in London. Kate, however, retained a few items for herself which she kept securely hidden in a rarely used storeroom. If they were discovered she could easily deny any knowledge of them.

Early on it had become obvious to Kate that this was not the first time Mark, if in fact that was his real name, had been involved in breaking the law. But it didn't bother her in the least; it added an element of danger to her life that peacetime had deprived her of.

It was not the first time that the Bournemouth police had been called on to deal with thefts from local hotels and they knew that the thieves invariably had inside help. All members of staff were interviewed and their rooms were searched but to no avail. As it was Kate's second season at the hotel and, as she had not previously come under suspicion of doing anything remotely illegal, in her case the questioning and search were cursory and nothing was found. So, she sat back and waited for Mark to contact her and take her to America on the proceeds of their crime. What happened after that she would think about later. Then things began to fall apart. A local reporter got wind of the thefts and began his own investigation. He learned from a colleague on a London paper that a known thief had been arrested trying to fence a consignment of stolen valuables which were thought to be the proceeds of thefts from hotel rooms, and the prisoner had a long record of committing such crimes. But the only clue to the origin of the haul was the initials 'KS' plainly displayed inside the suitcase the thief had been carrying it in. It was a long shot but the reporter thought that it might be worth his while checking with the hotel in Bournemouth and went to see the manager.

By a stroke of good fortune a waitress overheard snippets of the conversation when she took tea into the manager's office. She realised that Kate's initials were 'KS' and, not for a minute thinking that Kate was actually involved, jokingly gave her the news straight away.

Kate knew that the game was up; she quickly packed as many of her things as she could get into a small bag, collected the rest of the loot, and left the hotel for good. Stopping only to collect the money from the Post Office, she dashed to the station, caught the first train out and got off in the small Dorset town of Wareham. In the pleasant market town with its ancient earthen walls, she booked into a small bed and breakfast and sat down to consider her options. She had money in her purse and the thought of getting as far away from Bournemouth as it would take her was an attractive one. But on reflection, she decided that finding somewhere to hide locally would be more to her liking. At least the danger such a plan entailed appealed to her. She found a job as a barmaid at a remote country inn at Cold Harbour in the desolate heathland just north of Wareham, and well away from the main south coast holiday areas. Although it promised to be boring, she would wait out the winter there and resurrect her dream of going to America in the spring.

The inn was called 'The Silent Woman'. It had acquired the name in the eighteenth century when the local smugglers found that the innkeeper's wife had been informing on them to the excise men and they cut out her tongue to silence her. As far as Kate Steele was concerned, the story added to the inn's attraction.

Chapter 6

It was raining: a cold and sleety early morning December rain as the *SS Celtic* docked in Liverpool. Michael Flynn stood in the shelter of the deckhouse and watched the tall figure of Eamonn de Valera being spirited away by a couple of men dressed as labourers, while the attention of the dock police was diverted by a rowdy confrontation between several obviously drunken men some distance away. Michael also noted the two coffin-like wooden crates being surreptitiously loaded into the back of a covered lorry. From the careful way that the crates were being concealed, it was obvious that they contained some contraband and he guessed that it was arms for The Cause in Ireland. It was also clear that de Valera knew about the shipment but had not seen fit to tell him. Michael thought that it was typical of the man to keep things to himself and he doubted if any of the senior leaders in the IRA had been told of the shipment either. If the crates did contain arms then they were for some private scheme being hatched by Dev. Michael was not at all sorry to be seeing the back of the *Priomh Aire*, at least for the time being; but it was inevitable that their paths would cross again.

When he disembarked, Michael was met by a man he didn't recognise with a message from Michael Collins: arrangements had been made for de Valera to travel to Dublin via Belfast and an elaborate scheme had been devised which involved him going first to Stranraer in Scotland, and then being taken secretly aboard a fishing boat to Larne. He was too recognisable, and too important to The Cause, to risk travelling aboard a scheduled passenger ferry. Should he be arrested and imprisoned again it would prove extremely difficult to arrange another escape for him. Having allowed the Irish leader to escape once, when Michael Flynn had smuggled some duplicate keys into Lincoln Jail, the authorities would now be more alert and it was highly unlikely that they would make the same mistake twice.

Not being as notorious, or as recognisable as 'Dev', Michael had much more freedom of movement and could travel openly on the steamer from Holyhead to Kingstown. But as a precaution he would travel disguised as a priest. It was not the first time that he had masqueraded as a clergyman; it was by playing the part of a priest that he had gained access to Lincoln Jail to make contact with de Valera, and he had travelled to America similarly disguised. He was getting quite competent at playing the part and could carry it off with a high degree of confidence, but that did not mean he was altogether happy with the pretence. It went against every aspect of his strict catholic upbringing. But it had proved to be a most effective way of avoiding being questioned by the authorities who were wary of handing the IRA a propaganda opportunity by harassing a priest, and so he viewed it as just one more necessary compromise he had to make between his religious belief and his determination to help achieve Irish freedom. Ireland, he thought, was fast becoming a land of compromises and only when his native land was at last free would he and countless others be able to put the need for such compromise behind them. There was one thing, however, that he was resolved to avoid at any cost: his mother must never know about him having committed what she would certainly have regarded as a mortal sin.

On arrival in Dublin, Michael was met and told that he was 'under orders' to report immediately to Michael Collins. Although de Valera was *Priomh Aire*, and as such, leader of the Republican Movement, Collins, known as 'The Big Fella', was the man who carried on the day-to-day struggle for independence. He had gained a well-deserved reputation for ruthlessness, but in spite of this, Michael had a deep respect for the man and so he had no hesitation in answering the summons.

He was conducted to a house in a quiet Dublin suburb where Collins greeted him warmly. "It's good to see you again, Michael, although, in my opinion, it would have been much safer for you to have remained in America. But I suppose your family ties, and particularly your young son, proved to be too powerful an incentive and you simply had to return home."

As always, Michael marvelled at how well-informed Collins was and how he invariably managed to grasp the essence of a situation. And he knew that it would be futile to be anything less than completely honest with the rebel leader.

"You're right there," he said. "But I'll have to call in on the Ryans' first, although I'm not sure how much of a welcome I'll get. They'll still be in mourning for Maureen and I wouldn't blame them if they held her death against me. Will it be safe to go there? I don't want to add to their troubles by bringing the 'Tans down on them."

"I would prefer you not to go to the house, Michael. It's being watched in case Kevin turns up there. They probably wouldn't arrest you here in Dublin but we don't want them to know that you're back in Ireland if we can help it." 'The Big Fella' thought for a moment. "But leave it with me and we'll find a way of arranging a meeting for you."

"I suppose Kevin had a hand in what happened a few Sundays back?" Michael regretted the question the minute he asked it. It contravened one of the movement's most sacred commandments and in any case, he already guessed that his brother-in-law would almost certainly have been involved.

Collins seemed to let it pass but pointedly changed the subject. "You've been out of Ireland for a while. In truth, I never really believed that you would leave us for long, Michael, and you can take that as a compliment."

This did surprise Michael; in his experience it was not like the man who was responsible for the conduct of the vicious guerrilla war against the forces of the British Empire to hand out compliments.

There was a knock at the door and a maid brought in a tea tray. After she had poured and departed, Collins said, "Tell me now, how did you find working with the bold Mr de Valera over there in the States?"

Michael had anticipated the question as soon as he heard that Collins wanted to see him. He had worked out an honest if somewhat inadequate answer. "Well for one thing, I found that he's not entirely the man I used to think that he was."

He expected Collins to press him on the point, but instead his host asked a different question. "Do you have any idea why Dev insisted on leaving the safety of the 'States and taking an unnecessary risk by coming home at this particular time?"

Again Michael had anticipated the question and had his answer prepared. "All I can say is that he never told me exactly why, but I suppose that he wasn't too keen on being over there while the real fight is going on here. The truth of it is, though I'd say that there's more to it than that, he might have the notion that he's being left out of it and he doesn't like the idea of someone else getting all the credit for carrying on the fight."

He didn't say that it was Collins who was 'getting all the credit' but his meaning was clear.

'The Big Fella' laughed. "Didn't I always say that you had the makings of a fine politician, you're getting to have quite a way with words. And you're right, of course, Michael, Dev hates the thought of anybody else, and me in particular, getting what he sees as all the glory. Did you know that he's pushing for me to go to America while he stays here?"

"No," Michael replied, "he never said anything to me about it. You're not thinking of going, are you?"

Collins shook his head. "Not for a minute, and what really makes Dev mad is that he can't make me. He knows very well that if he were to take the idea to the *Dáil* they'd turn him down, and having been away from Ireland for all this time, he can't afford that. But I'm afraid he'll do his level best to cause trouble for me."

Michael thought over the ramifications of what he had just heard. "Sure that won't do The Cause one bit of good," he said.

Collins agreed. "No it won't. But I'm afraid that's how things stand."

Again he changed the subject. "Are you still dead set on working for a peaceful end to all this, Michael?"

"I am so," was the immediate reply. "Is there any chance at all of that happening?"

The candid nature of Collins' reply yet again took Michael by surprise. "One day soon there has to be an end to it, Michael. No doubt you will have heard that some of your County Council colleagues have called on the *Dáil* to negotiate a cease-fire. And my information is that a significant faction in the British Government would also welcome such a move. But they face grave difficulties. For one thing the British generals would be totally against it. They are doing their level best to convince their political masters that they can gain a military victory in Ireland and that it is only a matter of time before they achieve it. And God knows they may well be right. We certainly have our backs to the wall at the moment; we're running short of everything, arms and ammunition, and between casualties and arrests, we're even running short of men. So from that point of view the thought of a cease-fire has its attractions. But the problem is that if we were to agree to a secession of hostilities, we would lose our greatest advantage: secrecy. We have built up a most efficient undercover network, far better than anything the British have managed to put together, and a cease-fire would mean us losing that advantage. We would never be able to regain it."

"I see," said Michael, not at all sure why he was being allowed access to Collins' innermost thoughts.

"But as I have already said," Collins went on, "it has to come some day. Neither side can hope to put it off forever. And that is when men like yourself will come into their own, Michael. So, it is essential that you keep yourself out of trouble. I know that it would be futile to ask you not to go back to Beaufort, especially with Christmas coming up, but please be careful. I can arrange travel arrangements for you and I could alert the local Flying Column to look out for you, but that might only draw attention to your visit. Have you given any thought as to how you might manage to see your son without alerting the 'Tans?"

"There is a man down there that I would trust with my life," Michael told him. "I was thinking of getting in touch with him."

Collins smiled. "Ah, that would be the steward at Beaufort House, if I'm not mistaken."

Again, Michael could only wonder at how well-informed 'The Big Fella' was.

Chapter 7

It was with some apprehension that Jack Quinlan answered the summons to come up to 'the house'. He suspected that it had something to do with Commander Wilson's visit, and he wondered if news of the letter he had just received from Michael Flynn had reached his employer's ears. When he was ushered into His Lordship's private study and invited to sit, an almost unheard of break with social convention, his suspicions were confirmed.

It was typical of the master of Beaufort House that he should come straight to the point. "Now, Quinlan, I want to speak to you about this friend of yours, Michael Flynn. I know that he has returned from the United States, and if even half of what I've learned about him is true, he will certainly try to come to Beaufort to visit his family at Christmas. In this respect I strongly suspect that he may well get in touch with you."

Jack's heart sank. His worst fears were confirmed. He was aware that His Lordship knew of his long-standing friendship with Michael Flynn and he fully expected to be warned about associating with known rebels, or worse still, be asked to 'inform' on his old friend.

But His Lordship's next remark, while coming as something of a relief, gave Jack quite a shock. "If, or rather when, Flynn comes to Beaufort I should like to meet with him."

While not surprised by his employer's direct approach, Jack was certainly taken aback by the fact that he would want to have anything whatsoever to do with a man like Michael Flynn. As a member of an old aristocratic English family with a country seat in Ireland, His Lordship was naturally opposed to the principle of Irish independence, but unlike many of his fellow British landowners living in Ireland, he had never become actively involved in the complications of Anglo/Irish politics. And in Jack's experience it would be most unlike the man to set any sort of hidden trap, even for a known Nationalist sympathiser. It would be even more out of character for him to take advantage of one of his employees by forcing him to help in the plot.

His Lordship's next remark set Jack's mind at rest. "Let me assure you Quinlan, that I have no intention of laying a trap for your friend in order to have him arrested. As far as I can see he is not really guilty of anything other than falling foul of these irregulars; and I have been led to believe that he is basically against the use of violence as a way of solving this country's problems."

In common with many, including the regular British Army, His Lordship had no more time for the terror tactics used by the Auxiliaries and Black and Tans than he had for the equally murderous methods of the IRA.

He went on to say, "The only problem I can see with Flynn concerns his brother-in-law, Kevin Ryan, who from what I am told, is a horse of an entirely different colour. But that aside, I am convinced that Flynn is a decent fellow and I have been approached by someone to talk to him in strict confidence on a matter of grave importance; and for the moment, at least, merely as an exploratory exercise."

Jack quickly put two and two together. He already suspected that there had been more to Commander Wilson's visit than to meet the widow of a man who had worked, or to use the navy man's term 'served' under him. It seemed to be a long way out of his way for the Commander to go, especially after a lapse of over four years.

"Would this someone be Commander Wilson, sir?" he asked.

His Lordship smiled. "I'm not at liberty to say at this stage, Quinlan," he replied. "But again, let me assure you that I mean your friend no harm. On the contrary I am prepared to offer him some protection from the irregulars. If he were to spend Christmas at your cottage I could see to it that he is not bothered by them and it would also be safe for him to meet with his family there. On that basis would you be prepared to arrange for me to meet him?"

Jack was still at a loss to know what business his employer, and more to the point, Commander Wilson, could possibly have with

Michael Flynn. He was well aware that Michael was dedicated to the Republican Cause, but apart from the fact that he was a Sinn Fein County Councillor, Jack was not at all sure of how deeply, or in what capacity, his friend was involved in the fight for Irish independence. Of one thing, however, he was certain: His Lordship was right in assuming that Michael was not a frontline soldier and did not belong to an IRA 'Flying Column'. He knew the story of how Michael had been forced to kill a man in order to save several lives, including William Quinlan's, and how the event had changed Michael's views on bloodshed. And although they had not spoken since the death of Maureen Flynn, he was sure that his friend's resolve to seek peace would have remained unshaken.

While Jack had complete faith that his employer would keep his word, he was not so sure about Commander Wilson. But after a little thought, he decided that because of His Lordship's involvement, he could place his trust in the naval officer as well.

"All right, sir," he said. "I'll see what I can do, but it will be up to Mick Flynn himself to decide what he does."

"I fully understand that, Quinlan," His Lordship said, "and I don't have to tell you that this must be kept strictly between ourselves. I am aware that news of Flynn's arrival will soon be common knowledge locally, but if it became known that he had a private meeting with me, it would seriously compromise some extremely high level and important moves to put an early end to this conflict."

Jack also realised that if the story came out Michael would certainly lose His Lordship's protection.

"Oh, I can see that, sir," he said. "And sure you can trust me to keep my mouth shut."

"I'm quite certain that I can." After a pause His Lordship went on, "Now there is something else I have to discuss with you, which also requires your complete discretion and – " he gave Jack a knowing look before continuing – "I'm sure you won't be surprised to learn that this too originated from the good Commander Wilson. It concerns that other old chum of yours, the mutineer from the Connaught Rangers, Private Coughlin. You may or may not be aware that the convicted mutineers have been brought back to complete their prison sentences in England, and it appears that Coughlin has somehow managed to escape from custody. I must say that you certainly have a peculiar way of choosing your friends, Quinlan, but knowing you as I do, I feel sure that you always try and do the best you can for them."

Jack's heart sank; if Patrick Coughlin had escaped and been recaptured, there could only be one fate awaiting him: execution by firing squad. "Has Pat been taken, sir?" he asked anxiously.

"Not yet, Quinlan, but in my view it is only a matter of time before he is. There is, however, one ray of hope for him, but it depends on whether or not he tries to make contact with you; something which both the Commander and I believe he might attempt."

By now nothing about Commander Wilson came as a surprise to Jack. For an officer in His Majesty's Navy, Wilson seemed to have his finger in a great many pies and, because of some long-standing friendships, Jack was being caught up in whatever it was the Commander was up to. More worryingly, and although His Lordship would be extremely reluctant to say so, his employer, too, was being drawn into the plot, whatever it was. And that could have serious consequences for Jack's position as 'steward' at Beaufort House. It was yet another example of how no one, irrespective of rank or personal beliefs, could avoid being touched by Ireland's 'troubles'.

Before resuming the conversation, Jack cast his mind back to the events that had taken place when Privates Patrick Coughlin and James Daly of The Connaught Rangers had visited him in Beaufort before departing with the regiment for India. Because of the situation in Ireland, they had worn civilian clothes and, as a result, when they arrived in Killarney they were suspected of being members of the IRA. They were arrested and roughly handled by the RIC. That had been enough to send the already volatile Daly, who was extremely unhappy about the repressive tactics of the British authorities in his homeland, and uncomfortable about being expected to help suppress the nationalist movement in India, over the edge. His frustration at being unable to do anything about the situation eventually led directly to his taking part in the mutiny in India and his eventual execution. Coughlin, although not as deeply moved as Daly by events in Ireland, had been through the war with him and so stood by his comrade-in-arms. Now, it seemed that Coughlin's death sentence had been commuted to life imprisonment, but Jack wondered what effect Daly's execution would have had on Patrick's attitude towards the happenings in Ireland. He feared that Patrick Coughlin would no longer be the jovial, carefree professional soldier he had served with, and whose life he had helped to save in Mesopotamia. And if his old 'Ranger friend had risked escaping, it could only be to come to Ireland to take up the fight Jim Daly had been so anxious to join.

"After what happened the last time he was here, I'd say that there is no chance at all of Pat coming back to Beaufort," Jack said. "But you were saying that there might be a way out of this fix for him, sir?"

"You are probably right about him not coming to Beaufort, Quinlan," His Lordship said, "but the odds are that he will still try to contact you. And it is true that there is a way for him to avoid his death sentence being reinstated. But before I go on I must insist on having your word that you don't tell anyone about the man's escape. If one word of that gets out then your friend will certainly face a firing squad."

Jack could see that his employer was deadly serious. He had no hesitation, however, in giving his word: he was certain that it was Patrick's only chance of avoiding the same fate as James Daly.

"Good," His Lordship said. "Now, if he does contact you, Quinlan, you can tell him this: if he gives himself up quietly he will simply be returned to prison with the other mutineers to serve out his current sentence and no further action will be taken against him. It seems that the powers that be want to keep news of his escape under wraps. They wish, quite wrongly in my opinion, to avoid any further publicity regarding the mutiny. I am convinced that it amounts to your friend's only chance."

"So I could tell Pat that this comes straight from Commander Wilson himself, sir?"

"You can, Quinlan, and you can also tell him that if he goes into any police station in England and asks them to contact Commander Wilson, he will be treated as I have described, that is returned quietly to prison; but you must also inform him that if he is caught trying to make his way over here to Ireland then his original death sentence will be reinstated and carried out. I realise that this places you in something of an invidious position, Quinlan, but I do again strongly suggest that the best way of helping your friend is to put your faith in the Commander. It is entirely up to you."

Being told that it was 'up to him' did little to ease Jack's dilemma. Persuading Patrick Coughlin to turn himself in would be no easy task. Jack had no idea of what the state of Patrick's mind would be following his recent traumatic experiences, but he could guess how he would react to Wilson's offer. Having made the effort to escape it was highly improbable that Pat would be prepared to simply give himself up and, in Jack's opinion, it was much more likely that he would try to make his way to Ireland and join the IRA, as Daly had wanted to do. He would see it as a way of avenging his friend. And that could lead to fatal consequences.

His Lordship could see that Jack was having difficulties in coming to a decision and was prepared to wait.

When Jack eventually spoke he knew that he was stepping close to the line, but he was determined to be truthful. "If Pat does get in touch with me, I'll pass on the Commander's message, sir," he said. "But," he added, "that's all I'll do."

His Lordship nodded, he quite understood what Jack had left unsaid. His steward was not prepared to 'inform' on his friend by revealing his whereabouts. He knew enough about what happened to people even suspected of being informers, and he had no intention of placing Jack, and his family, in that kind of danger.

"All right, Quinlan," he said, "that is all that can be reasonably asked of you."

"It won't make any difference anyway, sir," Jack answered, "Pat won't give in now. I'd say that he'll try to come home to join 'the boys' because that's what Jim Daly was all set to do before Mick Flynn talked him out of it."

His Lordship showed some surprise. "You mean to tell me that Flynn actually persuaded them not to join the rebels? Now that is interesting, it rather confirms what Commander Wilson and I have been hearing about him."

"Oh Mick persuaded them to go back to their regiment all right sir, but only because he didn't want to see them hunted down as deserters," Jack assured him. "Not that it ever did poor old Jim Daly any good at all, Lord have mercy on him," he added with sadness in his voice.

Then something else occurred to him. "It might help if I could tell Mick about Pat, sir. He persuaded him to go back to his regiment once and he might be able to do it again. In any case two of us would have more chance of doing it than one."

In spite of his position and background, the former British government minister felt an almost admiring respect for both his steward's and Michael Flynn's integrity. It seemed to him to provide some glimmer of hope for the future.

"You may be right, Quinlan, but I would have to discuss this with Commander Wilson before agreeing to it," he said. "Leave it with me for now." And in yet another departure from the accepted social norm, he added, "I'm sincerely sorry that you have been dragged into this affair. But if it's any consolation to you, it will not have any detrimental effect on your position here at Beaufort. I don't intend to let the current situation here in Ireland interfere with the running of this house." He laughed. "For one thing, 'Her Ladyship' would never stand for it."

As he walked back down to the cottage, Jack took time to collect his thoughts. He tried to guess what Patrick Coughlin would do now that he had escaped from prison. Unlike Jim Daly, Pat had always been apt to think things through before acting and Jack reasoned that, even in his current predicament, his old comrade would plan every move with care. There was a good chance that he would consider it safer to lie low in the south of England for a while before making a run for Ireland. In which case, Jack could see a way of at least trying to contact him first and letting him know about the offer Wilson was making. But, in the unlikely event that Patrick did manage to reach Ireland and join the IRA, there would be nothing Jack or Michael Flynn would be able to do to help him.

"So," he said to himself, "for Christ's sake sit tight for a while, Pat, until I get a chance to do something about getting you out of this fix, you bloody eejit."

But first, he had to cycle to Killarney to send a telegram to Michael Flynn's in-laws in Dublin, from where he hoped it would be passed on to Michael.

Chapter 8

The man in the public house in Weymouth wondered whether he should spend his last few precious coppers on another pint of beer. The money was all that remained of the two shillings he had earned by helping a woman tidy up her garden in a small village somewhere between Blandford Forum and Dorchester. But it was Christmas, and he felt in need of some diversion. He went to the bar, bought a pint of bitter and returned to stand in a relatively quiet corner to consider the events of the past few weeks.

He had always planned to make an attempt to escape when, with the rest of the imprisoned mutineers, he was brought back to England; but he had not expected the opportunity to present itself quite so soon after their arrival back in 'Blighty'. But it had, and he had carried it off with seemingly ridiculous ease. The ship docked at Southampton from where the prisoners were scheduled to be transferred, in irons, by train to prison on the Isle of Portland. But there were delays in getting the transfer under way and some slipshod work by the guards. Not enough military police were available to guard such a large number of mutineers, and neither the officers nor the soldiers of the makeshift unit, hastily assembled to reinforce them, had any experience in transporting prisoners by rail. To compound the problem, the officers in charge of the reinforcements came from different units and there was no central command structure. Several of the mutineers had gone out of their way to make life difficult for the guards on board the prison ship, and continued to do so after they had docked. These were considered to be the ringleaders and were placed under the direct supervision of the military police, and in the event they were the only prisoners to be actually put in irons. The ordinary soldiers were left to cope with the other mutineers as best they could.

At the docks the prisoners were crowded onto a special train which, not being a scheduled service, continually stopped and started on its journey to Portland. As it stopped at the goods yard in Dorchester waiting to be signalled through, Patrick Coughlin simply slipped out of a toilet window and hid among some blocks of Portland stone on the flatbed wagon of a goods train travelling slowly in the opposite direction. He didn't know how far the prison train would travel before he was missed, but there seemed to be no early signs of pursuit. After what he judged to be an hour or so he jumped from the goods train and spent two days hiding in the New Forest without daring to move very far.

He realised that he could not remain hiding in the forest forever. He could drink clear water from a stream but eventually hunger forced him to take a risk. He approached a pair of foresters enjoying their dinner break who, to his immense relief, proved to be friendly and taking him for an ex-soldier down on his luck, gave him some tea and bread. They gave no indication of knowing anything about an escaped prisoner being on the loose in the area. One of the foresters gave him a copy of a daily newspaper and he failed to understand why, while there was an article about the Connaught Rangers mutineers being brought back from India and imprisoned at Portland, there was nothing about one of them having escaped. Surely, he thought, he must have been missed by now and an extensive search for him mounted? But it seemed that the countryside had not been aroused and the population alerted to keep a watch for him. He dared not ask the foresters if they had heard anything about one of the Connaught Ranger mutineers having escaped because that would only arouse their suspicions, so he thanked them for their generosity and left to consider what to do next. His military training told him that he needed to find out more about what level of danger he faced, so he took a chance and walked openly through a small village on the edge of the forest. Forcing himself to walk boldly and trying not to appear wary or furtive in any way, but being ready to bolt at the first sign of recognition, he passed through without incident. There was no doubt in his mind that the army would be making strenuous efforts to re-capture him, and they would certainly have alerted the police and security services; but he failed to understand why the pursuit was not highly visible.

Years of army service in various parts of the world had equipped him with a sense of direction, and some time spent stationed in the south of England had given him a feel for the geography of the area. Now he had to use this knowledge and training to help him decide which direction to take in order to make good his escape. By going east he would be moving towards London and consequently into more densely populated areas, which would mean a larger police presence; to the south lay Bournemouth and the busy port of Poole and he could expect the authorities to be watching the ports; to the north lay Salisbury Plain which he felt he should avoid at all costs because of its extensive military training grounds; that left west which, if nothing else, would take him closer to Ireland and home. But his pursuers would guess that he was trying to reach Ireland and concentrate a large portion of their resources in that direction. There were problems whichever direction he took, so in the end he decided that his best option was to remain in the Dorset area for a while, effectively hiding in plain sight.

After a period of extreme caution he began to travel around the countryside with more confidence. At first he was conscious that the army uniform the prisoners had been issued with on arrival at Southampton to replace their tropical kit would, although assembled from an assortment of regiments, attract too much attention, but he need not have worried. Many former soldiers still wore remnants of military uniforms, either their own or purchased cheaply from one of the many army surplus stores. He had managed to discard and replace the khaki blouse; the woman in the village yesterday had given him a heavy Arran sweater along with his wages, but he had decided to retain the greatcoat and boots. After the heat of India and the stuffy atmosphere of the confined quarters on the prison ship, he was, at first, finding the damp chill of an English winter hard to bear but he gradually became acclimatised.

He had been on the move for a couple of weeks, surviving on charitable handouts and by doing odd jobs, without seeing any sign of a concentrated search for him. But he knew that he was being hunted and the fact that the hunt was seemingly being carried out in some secrecy made it all the more dangerous; he had no way of telling friend from foe and could easily miss seeing the danger signs before it was too late. So he stuck to his strategy of keeping on the move, avoiding the main roads, the towns and larger villages and, even in an English winter, for a man who had served in the trenches of the Western Front and in the desert of Mesopotamia, living rough did not present any unsolvable problems.

Christmas came and gave him some hope that the authorities might have reached the conclusion that he had managed to slip through their net and had got away from this part of southern England. In which case the main hunt for him would have moved on, but he could not afford to think too optimistically. In any case, he reasoned the search was bound to be scaled down over the holiday. So he deemed it worth the risk making his way down to Weymouth. It was time to consider going home and the only possible way of reaching Ireland was by sea. He knew that there was little chance of getting on a boat sailing directly to Ireland from what was mainly a fishing harbour; and even if there were ships crossing the Irish Sea from Weymouth they would be watched. But there might be a coaster bound for Bristol or one of the Welsh ports which might not attract the attention of his pursuers. With any luck the watch on the larger ports would be more visible and therefore easier to avoid. At a larger and busier port he might just be able to slip undetected aboard a vessel bound for Ireland and home.

But to make this plan work properly he would need to earn some money. Stealing was not only against the moral code still lingering on from childhood, it also carried the possibility of being caught in the act. That would certainly put an end to his break for freedom. It was much more preferable to find a way of earning some cash and he hoped that the priest he intended to visit after Mass tomorrow would have some ideas. It all sounded straightforward enough but that, too, worried him because he still didn't quite understand why there were no signs of a highly concentrated pursuit.

As he stood with his pint in a corner of the crowded public bar however, he felt secure enough to exchange Christmas greetings with the revellers milling around him and was glad to do so. The worst part of being on the run was the feeling of being alone, and loneliness was something he was not used to. He had been raised in a large family supported by a small patch of rented land in County Galway, and privacy had not been an option. As soon as he was old enough he had 'taken the King's shilling' and joined the British Army to relieve the pressure on his poverty-stricken family. In the army his life had been lived in the company of soldiers and now he missed the companionship of men like Jim Daly and Jack Quinlan. Once he had made his final plans for getting home, he would write to Jack in the hope that they could someday raise a glass to James Daly's memory.

He changed his mind about sneaking around the harbour and spent the night in an unsecured woodshed. On Christmas morning the priest more than lived up to his hopes and expectations. He was invited in to the presbytery, and before dinner he enjoyed the rare luxury of having a hot bath and a shave. After dinner he felt uncomfortable about the possibility of getting the priest into trouble and so he reluctantly declined an invitation to stay the night. He did, however, accept the offer of some money and a parcel of food.

While in the priest's house he had noticed an article in a local paper which he thought might possibly provide him with a way of earning some money.

Chapter 9

It was raining heavily in the small town of Ballymahon in County Longford. In a public house halfway down the wide main street, one of the broadest in Ireland, Christmas Eve 1920 was beginning to warm up nicely. As was common in Irish public houses of the day the premises served as both grocery shop and bar, and with the time approaching 8.30 p.m. the women had finished their last-minute Christmas shopping in the grocery section and left the entire house to the men. So what food remained was removed from harm's way and the counter commandeered as an addition to the main bar. In spite of the weather the crowd of drinkers was steadily growing, determined in spite of the War of Independence, to celebrate in the traditional way.

Officially there was a curfew in place, imposed by the authorities as a reprisal for recent IRA raids and ambushes across the county, but not even the Black and Tans could hope to enforce it at Christmas. So the hooley went on uninterrupted. There would be some sore heads in the morning, but not a man there would miss going to Mass for Christmas.

In a small room behind the rowdy bar, part of the innkeeper's private quarters, two men sat quietly at a table, each with a virtually untouched pint of porter in front of him. These men were taking advantage on the undeclared 'Christmas Truce' to hold a private meeting. The drinkers in the bar were well aware of the presence of the men in the back room, but they knew enough not to comment. Only an informed few knew that a third man was scheduled to join the meeting and these men had been warned to moderate their drinking; each carried a concealed weapon and was ready for instant action in case the authorities had got wind of these three men being in

Ballymahon that night. Neither the Black and Tans nor Auxiliary Police would hesitate to abandon their own Christmas celebrations to capture, or preferably kill, any one of the three.

"Are you sure that your man is going to turn up at all tonight, Sean?"

The speaker was Michael Reynolds from the village of Killoe and he was a member of the North Longford Brigade of the Irish Republican Army.

"Ah sure he'll turn up all right, just give him time," his companion, Sean MacEoin, assured him.

Known as 'The Blacksmith of Ballinalee' because of his former trade and his birthplace, MacEoin was the Commandant of the North Longford Birgade and he was quickly gaining a reputation for being one of the most able commanders in the IRA. His 'Flying Column' had enjoyed several recent successes over the forces of The Crown and his capture had been afforded a high priority by the authorities in Dublin Castle. In November, he had led his men in an attack on the British forces in Granard, just north of Longford town, and caused them to retreat to their barracks. The next day he held his home village of Ballinallee against a superior combined force of Regular Army, Auxiliaries and Black and Tans and forced them, too, to retreat, abandoning some of their arms and ammunition. As usual these successes brought about savage reprisals against the local population by the 'Tans and the 'Auxies'.

Reynolds was showing signs of becoming nervous. "This fella that's coming to give us a hand must be well up in the organisation if it's 'The Big Fella' himself that's sending him, but why did we have to come down to Ballymahon to meet him?" he said. "It was hard enough coming down here and it'll be murder going back without the 'Tans catching us. I'd rather be back in Killoe in a place I know like the back of my hand, and where I know who I can trust."

"I wanted to have a chat with some of the lads around here," said MacEoin. "I'm thinking that sometime soon we'll have to join up some of the Flying Columns into a real fighting force if we want to win this war, and I want to know what other people have to say about it."

"And what do they say?" Reynolds asked.

"To be honest with you, they have their hands full with what they're doing now, just like the rest of us," MacEoin answered, "and they can't see any further than that. Anyway, we're safer down here for a while. Even the bloody 'Tans know that it's Christmas, but they're more likely to be off their guard around here than up in Ballinalee. I wouldn't put it past them to be looking for us at Mass there tomorrow morning."

Reynolds caught on and his respect for MacEoin as a guerrilla leader went up yet another notch. It was easy to see why the North Longford Brigade was one of the most successful in the country; their Commandant was a man with the ability to look at the broader picture and plan for every eventuality.

They fell silent and drank sparingly from their porter.

"I hear that this fella from Dublin is a good man in a fight, but sure if that's true why would Collins be sending him to us? You'd think that he'd want to hang on to him up there in Dublin," said Reynolds.

MacEoin was thoughtful. "I think that maybe he's too much of a fighting man. It strikes me that this is more to do with Dublin wanting to get shot of him than it is to be giving us a hand. We'll have to watch out for ourselves with him around."

There was a quiet knock on the door and Kevin Ryan was ushered in.

Chapter 10

It was almost opening time and Kate Steele was helping the landlord of 'The Silent Woman' prepare for the expected Christmas Eve rush when she heard a car pull up outside the pub. She glanced out of the window and what she saw caused her to drop the pint glass she was cleaning. It shattered into smithereens as it hit the floor.

"I'm sorry," she said to the innkeeper, "I'll clear it up." She almost tripped as she beat a hasty retreat through the door behind the bar.

In the back room she almost collapsed with shock and for several seconds had to lean on a table for support. Seeing the uniformed police inspector had given her cause for concern, he was the first policeman of any rank she had seen since she arrived at the inn. But it was the sight of the man with him that had thrown her totally off balance.

She had instantly recognised the tall figure of Commander Wilson, the security officer at the Gretna munitions factory. And she was certain that he would recognise her.

Her first thought was that the policeman had come to arrest her, and had brought Commander Wilson along to identify her. She was about to dash up to her room to grab as many of her belongings as she could before making a hasty getaway, but as her nerves began to settle she realised that it was Christmas and there was nowhere she could go for at least a couple of days. So she would have to brazen it out. As she collected her thoughts further it dawned on her that it was extremely unlikely that the local police would have even heard of Wilson, so there must be another reason for his visiting 'The Silent Woman' with a policeman on Christmas Eve. But she felt that she must not let the security man see her because that could well lead to some unwelcome complications. She waited until she heard them leave before going back into the bar with a dustpan and brush.

"Where have you been, Kate?" the innkeeper asked.

"I looked in and saw you having a conversation with two policemen and I thought that I would only get in the way clearing that glass up. What were they doing here on Christmas Eve anyway, reminding you about the closing time?"

The innkeeper grinned. 'The Silent Woman' was known not to be too particular in its observance of the licensing laws. "No, he said they want us to keep our eyes open for some Irishman they're looking for. They didn't say what he's done, just that they are anxious to interview him, but it must be something serious for them to send an inspector out to look for him. And I don't think that the civilian gentleman with him was anything to do with the police. All I can think of is that the man they're looking for must be a spy or something."

Kate had to stifle a sigh of relief; if they weren't looking for her then she had a breathing space to think of how to handle the situation.

"How will we know him if we see him, and why would he want to come here?" she asked.

"Well," the innkeeper told her, "all they said is that he is an Irishman, probably wearing some odd bits of army uniform, and keeping very much to himself. But we are to report anyone who seems remotely suspicious, especially among the new gang of navvies due to start work around here any time now."

Kate had heard about an influx of labourers to the area to work on the heathland surrounding the inn, but she did not know what the work entailed. The innkeeper had already mentioned that he was looking forward to a consequent increase in trade. As she had not come under any suspicion, and had heard nothing of the affair in Bournemouth during her time at the inn, she had decided that it was safe for her to remain there for at least a little longer. But now it looked as if there could be policemen visiting the pub on a regular basis, so a degree of caution was called for.

"That could be anybody," she said, "but I'll keep my eyes open."

Chapter 11

In Beaufort, the Christmas Morning Mass passed without incident. There were no indications that the Black and Tans knew about Michael Flynn being back in the area, and there was no open hostility directed at William Quinlan.

As was customary, people gathered to talk after Mass and today Michael's baby son was the main attraction. While he held the child in his arms a crowd gathered around them, the women coo-eed and the men remarked that he was 'a fine looking fella'. A painful interlude had occurred during Mass when prayers were said for the soul of Maureen Flynn, and now there were many heartfelt expressions of sympathy. One well-meaning neighbour did mention that the baby 'took after his mother' but, in spite of these unwelcome reminders, Michael's joy at being re-united with his family was plain to see. His mother seemed most affected by the mixture of joy and sadness and she had to be comforted by Annie Quinlan.

Given the situation in Ireland, it was inevitable that along with the condolences came a few pointed assurances that Maureen's death would be avenged. Had he wished, Michael could have reminded them that the Black and Tan officer responsible for his wife's murder had already paid with his life: Kevin Ryan had extracted a deadly revenge for the death of his sister. But Michael felt that this was not the time to be thinking of revenge and so he merely nodded to indicate that he understood. He noted that even his closest friends were careful not to question him about his time in America with Eamonn de Valera; it had become the way of things, and people had learned to not enquire too deeply into what 'the boys' were doing. Michael was glad not to have to go into lengthy explanations because at the moment he had more important matters on his mind. It was quite obvious, however, that he had become something of a local hero and he was learning that being regarded as a hero also meant having heroic deeds, both real and fictional, and in which he had not played a part, ascribed to him.

William Quinlan was glad that it was Michael who was attracting all the attention. He stood rather self-consciously with his sister, Elizabeth and his brothers, Jack and 'young' Michael who was home on holiday from the seminary at Maynooth. His other sister, Mary, was on duty as a maid at Beaufort House. Although in civilian clothes, he was aware of the fact that he was known to be a serving British soldier, and it was a relief to him to have received a friendly welcome from a few old friends and to be treated cordially by several acquaintances. There were, however, a few men he knew to be members of the IRA who, whether for political reasons or simply through embarrassment, chose to avoid him. But it could have been much worse: many local families, including the Flynns, had suffered at the hands of the 'Tans and he might have expected to be confronted by some of these. There were no outward signs of animosity, but he was conscious that much of this could well be in deference to his mother. One thing in his favour, he realised, was that he was a personal friend of Michael Flynn's. It was known that Michael was staying with the Quinlans for Christmas, and local people, William thought, would feel that if he was good enough for Michael Flynn he was good enough for them. There was also the fact that he was a British regular; had he been even suspected of being a member of the Auxiliary Police or the Black and Tans, he would have been lucky to escape with his life, irrespective of who his friends were.

William had thought long and hard before deciding to come home for Christmas, but circumstances had dictated that he must: it would be his last opportunity to see his mother for several years. At some stage over the next couple of days he was going to tell her that he had volunteered, and been accepted, for a new armoured car company being established for duty on India's Northwest Frontier Province. He was excited about the prospect of seeing some of the world, but it was going to be difficult to explain this to his mother.

Both Michael and William had arrived in Beaufort on Christmas Eve, but by very different modes of transport. When his employer had mooted the possibility of arranging a meeting with Michael, Jack had already received a letter from his friend telling him of his arrival back in Ireland and of his intention of visiting Beaufort for Christmas. He also wanted Jack's advice on the best way of coming home without causing further trouble to his family. Jack had replied – to what he assumed was an accommodation address in Dublin – and passed on His Lordship's proposal. At first, Michael had been sceptical but, on reflection, he felt that although Jack was not one of 'the boys' he could be trusted implicitly and so he accepted the invitation to stay at Jack's home and agreed to meet with the owner of Beaufort House. Events were to prove that his confidence was not misplaced. He had been picked up from the railway station in Cork and brought to Beaufort in a chauffeured car. His Lordship's cars were known to the authorities, but they were still stopped at the frequent military roadblocks and a mock inspection was carried out for the benefit of prying eyes. Had they been waved through, the IRA would have noticed and perhaps ambushed the car in expectation of His Lordship being aboard.

William, on the other hand, had been met at the station in Killarney by Jack with a pony and trap. Before leaving for Beaufort, however, he took the precaution of reporting to the local police station to avoid any repeat of what had happened several months previously. On that occasion Jack's two Connaught Ranger friends, James Daly and Patrick Coughlin, had been mistaken for IRA gunmen and arrested by the RIC, a mistake that eventually have led to tragic consequences. On the way home William told Jack about his imminent departure for India.

After Christmas Mass, and greeting friends and neighbours, both families paid a visit to Maureen Flynn's grave. They said a communal prayer and then Michael and his son were left alone to grieve in private.

In spite of the overcrowding, Christmas dinner at the Quinlan's cottage was a grand affair. Annie Quinlan, aided and abetted by Mrs Flynn, had really pushed the boat out. Although she took a minute to say a silent prayer for her dead husband, and she missed her other son James who was now settled in America, it was Annie's happiest Christmas for years. After dinner the Quinlan family went up to 'the house' where, by tradition, all members of the staff and their families were invited to take tea with 'the family'. This year the tradition served a dual purpose in that it allowed the Flynns to spend some time together for a few hours and it gave Michael his first opportunity to be alone with his parents since his escape to America.

In the evening Jack drove the Flynns home to their farm in the trap. Michael would have liked to accompany them, but couldn't risk causing them yet more suffering because of him and his problems. He felt that they had already been through enough on his account when the Black and Tans had ransacked and burned the farm while searching for him. According to his father, the farm was completely restored and was working normally, thanks to the help of their neighbours. Michael was aware that these neighbours also risked being harassed or worse by the 'Tans in retaliation for having helped his parents, but he knew that local people would also see helping the Flynns as a way of demonstrating their defiance. This attitude on the part of the population would, he hoped, eventually lead the British government to recognise the fact that the terror tactics of the 'Tans and 'Auxies' were ultimately doomed to failure.

That night the three men sat by the fire long after the others had gone to bed and caught up with what each had been doing since they last met. It was inevitable that the discussion should turn to the current situation in Ireland. Michael told them about his travels in America with Eamonn de Valera and Jack filled them in on recent happenings in Beaufort. His account of the war in the Beaufort area mirrored what was taking place all over the country: IRA attacks followed by Black and Tan and Auxiliary reprisals. That this was happening close to home and to people they knew, including Michael's family, it had a much more immediate effect.

William did not take part in this discussion but sat and listened in silent thought. Jack noticed his brother's mood and guessed that William's excitement at the prospect of going to India had been dulled by what he was hearing.

"What's up, Bill?" he asked. "Maybe you were thinking that you were wrong to join the army and you should have stopped at home to fight for Ireland."

"I was so," William answered. "I'm only home since last night but God knows I've seen and heard nothing so far except the trouble caused by these bloody Black and Tans. We heard about them over the water, and most of the fellas in the army wouldn't give them the time of day. To be fair to the lads not one of them has a bad word to say about me or any of the other Irishmen in the mob. But all the same, when I see things for myself, I'm thinking that I should be at home here giving the boys a hand."

Jack understood his brother's dilemma; even during the Great War many Irishmen, while believing on the one hand that it was right and even their duty to join the fight with the rest of the British Empire, still suffered pangs of conscience about not supporting their brothers at home.

"Sure didn't I feel the same myself stuck out there in Mesopotamia when 'The Rising' here was on in 1916," he told William. "But there was nothing I could do about it. I couldn't come home even when Da died."

William still felt that he had a valid argument. "But you were in a war, Jack, it's different for me, there's nothing to stop me from staying here and joining the IRA."

Jack was alarmed. "For Christ's sake Bill, take your time and think things over before you made an eejit of yourself. What do you say, Mick?"

Michael looked directly at William. "Look, Bill, things are a lot different now to what they were when you left, so I'll tell you the same thing that I told Jim Daly and Pat Coughlin: if yourself, or any other British soldier, was to desert and come home to join in the war here sure you'd never get anywhere near the fighting. Even if you could get the IRA to believe that you weren't working undercover for the Brits, Michael Collins wouldn't let you join 'the boys'. He'd think that you'd be a lot more useful to him as a propaganda tool, and he'd have you in America in no time at all telling the Yanks how your conscience wouldn't let you stay in the British army while the same army was oppressing your countrymen in Ireland."

William was not fully convinced. "But sure I'm a fully trained soldier, and they must have some better use for me."

"I can see why you might be thinking that," answered Michael, "but look at it this way, Bill. Aren't you in the Tank Corps? So what good would you be in a guerrilla war? The IRA has no use for tanks or even armoured cars, what would they do with them? For one thing they couldn't afford to run them, but more to the point those big awkward things would only let the 'Tans know where they are and they'd spend all their time trying to hide them. The boys always know when the 'Tans are around because the eejits make a show of driving around in those Crossley tenders, and the IRA are not going to make the same mistake."

Jack could see that Michael's words had stung William. He knew that this had not been his friend's intention, but he feared that his brother might react angrily. Michael's next statement, however, served to mollify William.

"But listen, Bill, the day is coming when all that will change. It won't be long before the British government are forced to try other ways of dealing with the situation here in Ireland. You said yourself that there is no sympathy across the water for the tactics of the 'Tans and 'Auxies', so the government will soon have to listen to public opinion. They know in their hearts that there is only one way to sort out the mess and that is to grant us some sort of independence, and when that happens we'll have our own Irish Army. Then we'll need men like you to help us get started and train us to use tanks and armoured cars. So go to India, Bill, and learn all you can about modern, mechanised weapons; when you come back you'll have the chance to be of real service to this country."

William was ready to accept this argument. While he enjoyed life in the army his conscience had been bothering him, but Michael's words went a long way towards satisfying it.

Jack marvelled at the changes the last few years had brought about in Michael Flynn. It was obvious that time and experience had developed the carefree youth of their schooldays into an astute thinking man. That those experiences, especially the loss of his wife, had not had the opposite effect and turned him into a bitter revenge-seeker was a mark of Michael's character. Little wonder, Jack thought, that this was the one man in Ireland singled out by Commander Wilson and His Lordship for whatever it was they had in mind.

Michael decided that it was time to lighten the tone of the conversation. "Sure won't we make you a general the minute we have our own army, Bill."

The use of the 'we' was not lost on Jack.

Michael looked up at the photograph of Jack Quinlan, James Daly and Patrick Coughlin taken in Mesopotamia. "Have you heard anything at all from Pat Coughlin, Jack?" he said. "I was reading that after they shot Jim Daly, Lord have mercy on him, they brought the rest back to England, and I suppose Pat was with them."

"It must have been hard for him when Jim was executed," William said. "I never met Jim Daly, but Pat talked about him a lot when he was here."

Jack knew that this subject was bound to come up sometime and he had been struggling to find a way of dealing with it. He had given his word to his employer that he would not mention Patrick Coughlin's escape to anyone, and he had yet to hear from His Lordship about telling Michael. Commander Wilson had explicitly said that the British wanted the escape kept under wraps, but that could only be achieved if the escapee gave himself up. For that to happen, however, Wilson's offer had to be communicated to Coughlin. Both Michael and William had met the Connaught Ranger when he visited the Quinlan family while he was in Ireland recovering from his war wounds. Jack knew that both had liked the easygoing 'Ranger, and he was sure that if they knew the situation they would agree that Coughlin's best chance rested in accepting Wilson's offer.

In his heart Jack didn't really believe that Patrick would agree to go back to prison; the manner of James Daly's death would certainly have had an unsettling effect and changed his attitude to the world. He worried that his friend could well have been embittered to the point where he felt that the best way to honour his dead friend was to join Ireland's fight for independence; something James Daly had always been eager to do. While he didn't hold out much hope, Jack felt that he had to try, and he believed that Michael and William could help. He had hoped that Coughlin would have contacted him by now but that hadn't happened so he would have to proceed as best he could.

He felt sure that if he explained to His Lordship and Commander Wilson that by enlisting the help of Michael and William there was a better chance of contacting Coughlin and persuading him to accept the Commander's proposition, his employer would agree that it was worth trying. Besides, he had a sneaking suspicion that this could possibly be one reason why His Lordship and Wilson had chosen to confide in him in the first place.

He answered Michael's question. "No, Mick, I haven't heard a word from Pat, but I do know something about what happened to him."

He went on to tell them what he knew about Coughlin's escape and Wilson's offer. They already knew about the Commander's visit to Beaufort: Jack had told William on the way home from Killarney and Michael had heard the news from Annie who had been full of it all day. Both men, however, agreed that it was important to keep what Jack had told them to themselves.

They sat in silence while Michael and William digested what they had heard. Then Michael voiced his opinion. "I'd say that Pat's best course is to take your man Wilson's deal, but there's not much of a chance of that after he took the trouble to break out."

"I'm sorry to say that you're likely to be dead right there, Mick," Jack said. "But God knows I want to do all I can for Pat. After all that happened to him in the war and in India sure I'd hate to see him killed by these bloody Black and Tans at home here in Ireland."

"Maybe he's home already," William said.

"No, Bill," Jack told him. "Whatever he's up to, Pat Coughlin is no eejit. I think that he's clever enough to stay where he is until he thinks that the hunt for him over there has died down."

"What do you want us to do Jack?" Michael asked.

Jack didn't give him a direct answer. "Look, lads," he said. "It's nearly morning and if we're not in bed soon we'll have Ma after us, so I'll tell the two of you all about what I have in my mind tomorrow after Mick meets His Lordship."

Chapter 12

December 26th, Saint Stephen's Day, was the day for 'Hunting the Wren' in Ireland. This ancient ritual is said to have its origins in Celtic folklore when the wren was held to be sacred by the Druids. But in Christian times it is associated with Saint Stephen, the first Christian martyr, and it is meant to commemorate the occasion when the saint, hiding in a bush from his enemies, was betrayed by the singing of a wren. Another story told about this tiny bird is set in the eighth century and concerns a group of Irish warriors being betrayed by a wren while trying to sneak up on a Viking camp. But it is Saint Stephen who is most often associated with the tradition which involved groups of 'wren boys' hunting and stoning the wren to avenge the stoning to death of the saint. By the nineteenth century, however, the tradition had taken on a more social aspect and young men and boys in a variety of disguises, some even dressed as women, went around the local areas playing music, dancing and generally having a good time. Hunting an actual wren was not considered necessary, although the 'wren boy's' equipment usually included a holly bush. It was considered to be bad luck for householders not to contribute something towards a 'wren party' held in the evening. Gradually, the contributions became mostly cash donations and the wren parties became unruly drinking sessions. These were not always peaceful affairs and there is a record of one developing into a full scale riot between two bands of 'wren boys' in County Clare in 1827.

In Ballymahon, Saint Stephen's Day in 1920 dawned clear and frosty and there were more bands of wren boys than usual abroad in County Longford. Apart from a few local bands of small boys most of them were grown men, and their activities had been carefully orchestrated. The purpose of all the activity was to cover the passage of Sean MacEoin, Reynolds and Kevin Ryan from Ballymahon to Ballinalee. The trio had spent Christmas in relative safety in the Ballymahon pub, but MacEoin was anxious to get back to his duties of Commandant of the North Longford Brigade, and he thought that the traditional 'hunting the wren' festivities would provide an excellent disguise.

Kevin Ryan, a Dubliner and a city man born and bred, did not see the point of this 'country culshie' nonsense and objected to having to dress up in a collection of colourful rags. He was even less pleased when MacEoin ordered him to hand over his revolver. They would be travelling unarmed in case they were stopped and searched.

"For Christ's sake, MacEoin," Ryan said with feeling, "is this the way you country mugs go about fighting the war? It's small wonder that the bloody 'Tans have you on the run. You wouldn't catch the boys in Dublin going around in fear of being searched. If we're stopped by the 'Tans we shoot the bastards."

"Up in Dublin the 'Tans don't shoot innocent farmers or burn their houses and crops, and kill their horses and cows," MacEoin told him. "Sure I know very well that they cause all kinds of devilment there as well, but here everybody knows everyone else and it's always friends who get hurt."

Ryan was not pacified. "I was told that the Longford Brigade were real fighting men MacEoin. But now I see that all they're good for is running home to their mammies."

There was a hostile stirring among the other seven members of the party and MacEoin could see that one man was primed to confront Ryan.

"Easy, Mike," he said quietly. He turned to Ryan. "I couldn't care less what you think of us, Kevin, and anyway, you'll find that Longford men are as good as any in the country when it comes to fighting the 'Tans. In any case while you're here you're under my orders, so give me that gun before I tell these fellas to take it away from you. You'll get it back the same as I'll get mine when we're at home in Ballinalee."

"For God's sake why can't I keep it?" Ryan wanted to know. "What are we supposed to do if the RIC or the bloody 'Tans stop us? We'll be up to our arses in shit if we leave the guns here."

With some difficulty MacEoin held his temper. "There's only three of us armed," he said, "and we'd stand no chance in a fight with the 'Tans, all we'd do is get these other lads killed along with us. The guns are coming with us but we won't be carrying them. And don't worry about the RIC, they won't bother us at all; sure haven't most of them hunted the wren themselves, and they wouldn't feel right about interfering with an old Irish tradition. Anyway, from what I can see, in this part of the country they're fed up with the war and are happy to leave it all to the 'Tans and the 'Auxies'. We haven't seen hide nor hair of them for weeks."

"And what about the 'Tans," Ryan argued, "sure they don't give a shit about your stupid culshie traditions."

"If them or the army stop and search us, we'll pretend to be a bunch of eejits with too much drink in us. They'll laugh at us and call us names, but as long as they don't find any guns they'll have to let us go. But our day will come and we'll get our own back. Now, for the last time, give me that gun."

Ryan could see that this was an argument he wasn't going to win, but he promised himself that he would one day settle an account with this high-handed bloody country mug, and anyway, he still had a trick up his sleeve. So he grudgingly handed over the heavy Webley British Army revolver. MacEoin placed it in an empty milk churn with several others. They were protected with a specially made tight-fitting metal disc and the churn was topped up with milk. It was loaded onto a cart with several others. A woman led a horse out of the stable behind the public house and harnessed it between the shafts. She clambered aboard and took the reins. Two of the men also climbed on the cart, one with a fiddle and one with a tin whistle, and they set off on their tuneful way while the rest followed on bicycles. As Ryan wobbled along on his unfamiliar mode of transport, made more difficult because of his limp, he had to reluctantly admit that these country culshies did know something about planning; but this did nothing to lessen his anger at the way he felt he had been slighted by MacEoin.

It had been decided that they should travel by the main roads and through several small towns and villages. They would have felt more comfortable in the narrow country boreens they usually frequented in their cat-and-mouse games with the forces of the Crown, but on Saint Stephen's Day wren boys were much more likely to be seen in populated areas. To lend authenticity to their ruse, they stopped in the villages and towns along the way where the musicians entertained the onlookers. They were surrounded by dancing, laughing children, which served to disguise the fact that at each of the villages some men left the colourful party and other local men took their places. Members of the Royal Irish Constabulary looked on without attempting to impede their progress, some even put coins in the collection tins, verifying MacEoin's opinion that a large number of them were becoming weary of the war and were happy to leave the fighting to the British forces. Kevin Ryan was the only one who was not enjoying the festivities: he kept sullenly to himself, muttering about 'country culshies'. The newcomers to the party knew where the roadblocks were sited and how to circumvent them, but MacEoin knew that not all of them could be avoided. The test of his tactics for dealing with them came in the afternoon.

The block was cleverly sited at a bend in the road with a solid stone wall on one side and a large tract of bog on the other. It was manned by a ten-man squad of British regulars supported by a group of six members of the Auxiliary Police, and the road was blocked by a Rolls Royce armoured car armed with a .303 Vickers machine gun in the turret. The bend in the road and a couple of blackthorn bushes concealed the block from anyone approaching from the north, the direction from which any attack by the North Longford Brigade would come; but to the south it was clearly visible for several hundred yards and acted as a deterrent to any approach by foolhardy locals.

The local guides knew that the roadblock was there and that there was no way round it. They could turn back and find a completely different route home, but that would mean hiding up for the night and resuming the journey tomorrow. By then, however, their wren boy disguise would be rendered effectively useless. Waiting until dark and trying to travel at night was fraught with danger because of the curfew. If they were caught after curfew they would be arrested without hesitation and once they were taken to a barracks, they would be closely questioned and, stripped of their disguise, MacEoin, Reynolds and Ryan would almost certainly be recognised. By now it was getting late in the afternoon and the sun was dropping over the expanse of bog but there was still almost an hour of full daylight left, enough to get them near enough to home for members of the North Longford Brigade to give them covering fire if necessary. But MacEoin didn't want to fight on ground of the enemies choosing: his success was based on taking on the British forces on his own terms.

He had, however, already decided what he was going to do: they would try and bluff their way through, and well before they could be seen by the men at the roadblock he put his plan into action.

They each took a bottle of Irish stout from a crate and opened it. They drank enough to ensure that their breath smelled, and they splashed some on the cart and churns to add to the effect. Several unopened bottles were left in plain view. It was the first thing he had seen all day that Kevin Ryan seemed to approve of.

MacEoin gave them a last reminder: "Don't forget lads, if they find us out run for the bog. The ground there is too soft for the armoured car, it'll soon be dark and they know nothing at all about bogs and bog holes so they'll never find us there. But keep down low and scatter in all directions like pigeons so that machine gun can't fire on us all at the same time. You'll have to make your own way home on your own, but sure you all know the way from here. You stay close to me, Ryan, because I don't suppose that you know any more about bogs than they do."

They made sure that the men at the roadblock heard them coming before they saw them. As soon as they heard the music and tuneless singing the soldiers came alert, but when the cartload of apparently drunken clowns came into sight they relaxed and regarded them with great amusement. The Auxiliary sergeant, however, saw this as an opportunity to assert his authority. He was disgusted to see the machine gunner come down from the turret to get a better view of the fun and he decided to show the young regular army lieutenant how to handle drunken Irishmen. As the cart approached he made his men stand in the road with rifles levelled. The regular army lieutenant thought that he had better follow suit, so he ordered his men to fix bayonets and cover the seemingly drunk and incapable revellers.

The Auxiliary sergeant ordered the musicians to get down from the cart and the rest to get off their bicycles. They were lined up along the wall while the woman driver was told to stay where she was. The lieutenant recognised that the Auxiliaries had more experience at this sort of thing than he had and, for the time being, allowed them to get on with it. The 'Auxies' roughly searched the 'wren boys' for weapons while the drunken singing still went on. MacEoin reeled around and offered one of his tormentors a drink from his bottle. The bottle was roughly knocked out of his hand and he was pushed back into line. As no weapons were found the treatment grew more heavy-handed, some of the 'wren boys' were punched and one was doubled up by a blow from a rifle butt.

The regular army officer was, however, becoming uneasy about this treatment of civilian prisoners, but as there were no protests from the 'wren boys' – in fact they seemed to regard the whole thing as a joke – he decided not to act. He failed to notice that one of the 'prisoners' definitely did not see the funny side of the situation: Kevin Ryan stood silently and glared defiantly at his tormentors.

Then the Auxiliaries turned their attention to the cart. It was searched and nothing was found. The remaining beer was confiscated and the sergeant ordered his men to empty the milk churns.

Fortunately the first two churns emptied contained nothing but milk, which flowed out of the cart and ran all over the road. As the Auxiliaries took hold of the third churn the woman, who had been watching the regular army officer, leapt down from the cart and ran up to him. She fell to her knees with tears flowing down her face.

"For pity's sake, Your Honour," she pleaded. "Please don't let them ruin all the milk, 'tis all I have in the world, sir. Sure aren't I a poor widow woman trying to run the farm all on my own." She pointed to the 'wren boys'. "These grand fellas gave me a hand with the milking this morning before they got drunk and started acting like eejits. I'm on my way to Longford now to sell it to the creamery and if I have nothing to sell I won't be able to buy a crust for the young ones."

The sergeant jumped down from the cart and marched across the road. He hauled the woman to her feet and slapped her hard.

"Don't take any notice of this bitch, sir," he said. "I've seen this bloody act too many times to be taken in by it now."

He grabbed the woman by her shawl and proceeded to search her as they had the men.

This proved to be too much for the regular officer. "That's enough, Sergeant," he snapped, "I won't allow you to search a woman like that."

The sergeant let the woman go and turned on the lieutenant. "Leave this to me, I know how to deal with these buggers. This isn't the parade ground at Sandhurst, so just stand back and let me do my job. Sir," he added with some sarcasm.

Somewhat to his surprise the officer stood up to him. "I'm in charge here, Sergeant, and you will do as I say. These people obviously have nothing to hide and have done nothing wrong. So just let them go on their way."

The sergeant bristled. "You stupid young whippersnapper don't you know when you're being had? These buggers are only playing at being drunk and in my experience they are definitely up to something."

He turned to his men on the cart. "Turn the whole bloody thing over."

"No!" shouted the lieutenant. Rightly or wrongly the die was now cast and he could not allow his authority to be flouted by an Auxiliary Police sergeant. He turned to his own senior NCO. "Sergeant Smith, turn those people loose and if these Auxiliaries give you any trouble, place them under close arrest."

The regular soldiers were only too happy to comply; they were fed up with being lorded over by the Auxiliaries and Black and Tans and were delighted to have an officer who was prepared to stand up to the 'irregulars'. They turned their bayoneted rifles from covering the 'wren boys' and pointed them at the Auxiliaries.

The officer helped the woman to her feet. "God bless you sir, I'll say a prayer to Saint Patrick for you," she said.

"Thank you, madam," he answered. He turned to MacEoin and his men. "On your way you lot, and be quick about it." He signalled for the armoured car to be moved out of the way.

They needed no second bidding; the woman jumped up on the cart and took up the reins, the musicians joined her and the rest retrieved their bicycles from the ditch. The armoured car was moved and they set off up the road.

But the Auxiliary sergeant wasn't finished yet. He stood in front of Ryan and barred his way. "We can't possibly let this one go. He's no more drunk than I am and I don't like the look of him one little bit. Sir."

The officer was having none of it. "I'm sure there are a lot of people who don't like the look of you, Sergeant. But that doesn't mean you are guilty of anything. Now just let him be on his way."

By now the rest of the party had gone around the bend in the road and were waiting for Kevin to catch up. He set off to join them pushing his bicycle and exaggerating his limp as he went. But the 'Auxie' sergeant still wasn't satisfied and followed. He walked beside Kevin and grabbed his arm.

"I'll remember you. I'll have your balls off you cocky Irish bastard."

Kevin Ryan snapped. He reached down and drew a tiny Remington, double-barrelled pistol from its hiding place in his sock and shot the 'Auxie' twice at point blank range. Before anyone could react he jumped on the bicycle and pedalled furiously off to join the others.

Sean MacEoin was the first to recover. "Scatter lads!" he yelled. "Make for the bog."

He slapped the horse on the rump to get it moving and grabbed Ryan. He dragged the gunman into the bog with him. "Come on, quick, and if we lose one man because of you, Ryan, I'll be the one who'll have your balls, you trigger-happy madman."

At the roadblock one of the Auxiliaries was the first to react. "After them!" he yelled.

He pushed the regular gunner out of the way and climbed into the turret. By now dusk was falling but from his lofty position he still had a clear view. He grabbed the handles of the Vickers and opened up. The woman driver and two men on the cart never stood a chance; even the horse died as a result of the prolonged lethal burst of fire.

He traversed the gun towards the bog, but couldn't find a target. He spotted a couple of the escaping IRA men, but was unable to open fire because the troops and Auxiliaries following them were in his line of sight. The soldiers followed a little way into the bog but could make no headway in the unfamiliar terrain. After a couple of men had to be rescued from water-filled bog holes, the officer called a halt and they withdrew to the roadblock.

Later, the Auxiliaries took out their fury at the death of their sergeant by beating up a local farmer and shooting several of his cattle.

Chapter 13

The busy Christmas and New Year season was over and the lunchtime trade at The Silent Woman Inn had all but dried up. Winter was traditionally a bad time for the inn with business usually limited to a trickle of farm workers, but in January 1921 there were high hopes that things were about to improve. The expected influx of labourers into the area had begun and the landlord believed that many of them, particularly the Irish among their number, would be ready to drop in for a quick dinnertime pint. And in the evenings the newcomers were expected to have worked up a thirst which they would have to quench at The Silent Woman, the only public house between Wareham and Bere Regis. Apart from the newcomers and the local farmers, the pub's only other potential winter customers were soldiers from the army training camp at Wareham and the large Tank Corps depot at Bovington. But these men were more likely to be found drinking at weekends in the local towns. At times, however, one or two would drop in for a 'skive' and have a drink while on some duty or other from either one of the two camps, especially if they were not accompanied by an officer or an NCO.

Kate Steel had been seriously thinking that it would soon be time for her to move on. The police had not visited the pub again, although some of the local men mentioned having seen police cars patrolling the area, something which was generally agreed to be out of the ordinary. She judged that the Dorset force had been obliged to put the trouble in Bournemouth to one side for the moment while they concentrated on finding this mysterious Irishman; but she feared that as soon as he was found they would have time on their hands and would revive their interest in finding the barmaid who had provided the 'inside' information for the thief at the Bournemouth hotel. And in truth she had experienced enough of life in a quiet country inn. It was time to look for a more exciting occupation.

In anticipation of the expected increase in trade, however, the innkeeper had persuaded her to stay on, at least until he had found a suitable replacement. Not that he seemed to be putting much effort into finding one. But that was not what really tempted her to stay at The Silent Woman for a little longer. It was expected that there would be a strong contingent of Irish labourers among the new workers, and she remembered some exciting times with the navvies at the Gretna munitions factory. And the thought that one of them might be wanted by the police added an element of intrigue that she simply couldn't resist.

The work being carried out by the influx of labourers involved clearing the ground in preparation for planting trees. The First World War had wreaked havoc with Britain's ancient woodlands. Whole forests had been stripped bare in order to meet an insatiable need for timber to fuel the war effort. Trench warfare in particular swallowed up copious amounts of lumber. Something had to be done to redress the balance and in September 1919 the Forestry Act came into force. In response to the Act, the Forestry Commission was set up and given responsibility for all woods and forests in the United Kingdom. The Commissioners were charged with replanting Britain's devastated forests and building up and maintaining a strategic timber reserve. The heathland north of Wareham was deemed suitable for planting with conifers and work began in clearing the ground early in 1921. Such a labour-intensive programme required a workforce which could not be met locally, hence the need to recruit manual workers from wherever they could be found. Many of the labourers who came to South Dorset had served in the war. They had returned home to find that the future they had fought for had failed to materialise and they found themselves either unemployed or experiencing difficulties settling back into civilian life. Working in gangs in the open air provided at least some semblance of the comradeship they missed from the war years. Those who could not find cheap lodgings were accommodated in hastily constructed wooden huts, and indeed several of the old soldiers preferred life in the huts to living in lonely lodgings.

Having two large army camps nearby, the local population paid little attention to yet another influx of newcomers, but the proprietor of The Silent Woman regarded them as a valuable addition to his winter trade. A few of the newcomers had already discovered the isolated inn, but the rush had not yet begun in earnest and Kate was becoming impatient.

She was on her own in the bar, the innkeeper and his wife having taken advantage of the lull to go into Wareham on business. As she stood idly gazing out of the window an army lorry pulled into the rough car park. Two soldiers, whose faces she could not see, sat in the cab and seemed to be hotly debating something. Experience told her that they were in transit between Wareham and Bovington and had decided to leave the direct route between the camps in order to skive off for a quick pint in this out-of-the-way public house. Kate's mood lightened as they got out of the vehicle and the passenger came toward the entrance, at least she would have some company for a short while and she would be able to have some fun flirting with them. But as the driver came around the back of the lorry she gasped in surprise.

She went to the door to get a better look at him. "Good God!" she exclaimed. "James Quinlan. What on earth are you doing here, James, and in uniform too?"

The soldier stopped and looked up in surprise. She had clearer sight of his face and realised she had made a mistake. It was not like Kate to be thrown out of her stride, but the likeness was remarkable.

"Oh," she said, "I'm sorry but you look the spitting image of someone I knew during the war."

The soldier regained his composure and grinned. "The name is Quinlan all right, miss," he said, "but sure it's not James at all, it's Bill."

Even the Irish accent sounded familiar. "That's strange," she said. "The James Quinlan I knew when I worked in a munitions factory had a brother called William. He came from a place called Beaufort in Ireland."

The soldier thought for a moment. "Sure don't I come from Beaufort myself," he said. "And if it's the munitions factory up in Gretna you mean, you must be talking about my brother, Jim."

Kate was dumbfounded. "Well I never," she said. "My name is Kate Steele. James may have mentioned me to you."

"Jesus Christ!" William exclaimed. "Sure didn't Da and Jim tell me and my mother all about you." He laughed. "Ma had high hopes for yourself and Jim."

Kate smiled inwardly as she remembered the two shy teenagers she and James Quinlan had been when they first met. She wondered where their courtship would have led had they not been overtaken by some tragic events.

"We were all so sorry about what happened to your father, William," she said. "I only met him a couple of times, but he was a really nice man. I know that James thought the world of him. How is James and what is he doing now?"

William told her about James going to America to be with some other friends from the factory. Kate knew them and they chatted for some minutes in the open doorway.

The second soldier had entered the public bar and was standing impatiently waiting for William. "For Christ's sake, Paddy," he said. "Are you going to stand there talking all bloody day? We only have time for one quick drink before we have to be back in camp. I don't know what the bloody hell we're doing here in the first place."

Kate couldn't help but hear so she went to the bar and began pulling two pints of bitter.

While she was busy doing that, the second soldier carried on irritably, "I can see that you'd be in there if you played your cards right, Paddy. But we don't have time for chatting up birds, mate, if we're not back in camp sharpish-like that bloody sergeant will have out guts for garters. So just ask her if she's seen this old pal of yours and we'll be on our way."

Kate overheard and something clicked in her mind. "What's this about you looking for an old friend, William?"

William was swallowing a mouthful of beer, so it was his friend who answered. "He's looking all over bloody Dorset for some old Irish mate of his, and it's going to get him into trouble if he's not bloody careful. And then I'll be right in the shit with him."

Kate was becoming increasingly interested. "Who is this friend you're looking for, William?"

"He's an old friend of Jim's," William replied, "and I have an urgent message for him. He might be working with the fellas planting the trees around here, so if you see him would you tell him that Bill Quinlan is looking for him? He's a bit older than me and he'll have the look of an old soldier about him. You'll know him if you see him because he's the kind of fella that keeps himself to himself. His name is Pat."

William's friend gave an exasperated snort. "And there you have it, miss. Would you believe than since we came back from Christmas leave this silly bugger has been looking all over the place for a bloody Irishman called Pat, as if there's only one of them with that name. I wouldn't mind but I'm supposed to be his driver's mate and he's dragged me into it with him. If they check out our mileage and the time we spend on the road, there'll be hell to pay. It's a damn good job everyone is running around like blue-assed flies getting the company ready to go to India or we'd have been rumbled already."

"All right, Bert," said William, "we'll drink up and be on our way." He turned to Kate. "I'll look in again on Saturday night, and if you see Pat before that will you tell him to meet me here?"

Kate felt a thrill of excitement. Seeing Commander Wilson and James Quinlan's brother in the space of a couple of weeks could not be a coincidence, there was obviously a connection. As they left the bar she beckoned William back while Bert carried on out to the lorry.

"Is this the same man that Commander Wilson was looking for, William?" she asked.

It took William a moment to recover. "Jesus Christ, has Wilson himself been here looking for Pat?"

"He came here with a policeman and I remembered him from the factory," said Kate. "I know that he would have remembered me as well so I kept out of his way. He must still be something to do with the security services. They were asking the boss to keep his eyes open for an Irishman just like the one you described. What's going on, William?"

William thought fast. If Wilson found Patrick Coughlin before he had a chance to give himself up then he would be returned to gaol immediately. And that could change everything: Commander Wilson had specifically said that his offer depended on Patrick turning himself in, so if the escaped 'Ranger was arrested, would that offer still stand? Jack was sure that Coughlin would remain in hiding in the Dorset area for a while before attempting to make his way home to Ireland, and he had asked William to do what he could to try and find his old friend. But now it looked as if Commander Wilson had reached the same conclusion, so they would have to move fast.

"I haven't time to give you the whole story now, Kate. Bert is right, we have to go back to camp quick. But I'll tell you all about it when I come back, and if you do see Pat in the meantime, tell him to watch out for Wilson."

"I will," Kate assured him. She was impatient to know the whole story but William obviously wasn't going to tell her now, so she let him go without further questioning. But things were looking up and promised to be more interesting than she had imagined in the country inn after all. She decided that it would provide her with an exciting diversion to try and find this fugitive Irishman before Commander Wilson did.

Chapter 14

"I certainly think that there might be much to gain from at least listening to what this man Wilson has to say, Michael." The speaker was Michael Collins and they were in the secret headquarters of the Irish Republican Brotherhood in Dublin.

"But the question is: can he be trusted? What exactly do we know about him? Or for that matter what do we know about the former British government man living at Beaufort House?"

This was something that Michael Flynn had thought deeply about since his meeting with the owner of Beaufort House. Prior to the meeting, all that he had experienced over the last few years told him that he should suspect a trap, and had anyone other than Jack Quinlan passed on the invitation then he would certainly have refused. In the event, however, he was glad that he had accepted.

The purpose of the meeting proved to be relatively straightforward: Commander Wilson had been asked by a group of high ranking members of the London government to try and make contact with people within the Irish Republican Movement with a view to exploring the possibility of arranging a truce; or at least to try and determine what would be required to facilitate such a move. For the moment this was to be kept on a strictly unofficial basis, and Wilson knew that he had to tread carefully. To begin with, he had to try and gauge for himself the true situation in Ireland because most of the information available to him in London was either ill-informed or totally biased. Then he had to find someone prepared to give him a hearing, and it had to be somebody with access to one of the few people in the Nationalist Movement with the authority to discuss a truce. He couldn't go through official channels but he thought that his old wartime superior in the Ministry of Munitions, now living on his country estate in Ireland, would be able, and indeed willing, to help. Together they made some discreet enquiries and the name of Michael Flynn came up as a man who might be approachable.

The Commander's plans had been interrupted when his official duties required him to deal with the problem caused by the escape of the imprisoned Connaught Ranger, but the former minister in Beaufort had agreed to make the initial approach to Michael.

"I don't know all that much about this Commander Wilson, but from what the Quinlans have to say about him, he might be a man to be trusted." Michael suspected that Collins already knew what he was about to say next. "They tell me that he's a Royal Navy man with the traditions of the service close to his heart; he was pushed into the intelligence service in the war and now they won't let him go back to sea."

"Yes," said Collins, "once a British Intelligence Officer, always a British Intelligence Officer. As you well know, Michael, we operate a similar policy ourselves, although the penalties for failure might be more severe."

Michael knew that this was 'The Big Fella's' subtle way of reminding him to be extremely careful about who he talked to and what he said.

"Anyway," he went on, "it confirms what I have been able to find out about him. But what about the Englishman at Beaufort House? What is your opinion of him and what is his interest in this business?"

"I'd say that he badly wants to see an end to the war," Michael answered, "and he was honest enough to say that it's nothing at all to do with Ireland being independent. He doesn't want to see that happen, but for a man in his position a peaceful end to the war would make life a lot easier. He said nothing at all about what this Wilson fella wants to see me about, but one thing did come out: he definitely doesn't like the way the Black and Tans are carrying on, and I don't think that Wilson does either."

Collins nodded. "They are not alone there, Michael," he said. "There is growing unrest over the water about the tactics of the Black and Tans and the Auxiliaries. There have been articles in the

Manchester Guardian, The Times, and the *Daily Herald* all condemning what they call the 'policy of frightfulness'; and as you would expect, the Labour opposition are up in arms and have been speaking out against it. All of which is making the general public over there stop and think."

"Maybe that's why Wilson was sent over here, they're frightened of what the papers are saying. If it is, sure there's hope for us yet." Michael's voice carried more of an element of excitement than he had intended.

Collins looked thoughtful. "I know what your feelings are on the subject Michael," he said. "And on this occasion I think you may get your wish, because I believe that there is more to this than the power of the press. My information is that certain senior figures close to the government have been feeling distinctly uneasy about the situation here for some time, so it doesn't surprise me that someone like Wilson has been sent over to quietly make an unofficial assessment for them before they make their feelings public."

"Is there any chance that all the men high up in the British Government might be thinking the same thing?"

"Not at the moment I'm afraid, Michael." Collins' words carried an element of annoyance, "and as I was telling you the last time we met, we only have ourselves to blame for that. The well-publicised proposals for the *Dáil* to call for a peace conference by those county councillors in Galway and Wexford have been seen as a sign of weakness in the British Cabinet. Consequently the generals in the British Army have been able to persuade their political masters that they can achieve a military victory in Ireland. And, of course, Michael O'Flanagan's personal letter to Lloyd George saying that the Irish people would be willing to make peace hasn't helped the situation."

"I heard nothing about that." Michael was surprised that someone as senior as Father Michael O'Flanagan, Vice President of Sinn Fein, would write a personal letter to the British Prime Minister.

"No," said Collins, "Lloyd George is obviously keeping it up his sleeve for the time being in case it comes in useful later. But it will be interesting to see if Wilson brings it up: if he does it will mean that this goes a lot higher up in the government than we think. What exactly did you say to the man in Beaufort about meeting Wilson?"

"I said that I'd think about it, and that I'd have to have a word with someone else before I made up my mind," Michael answered.

Collins nodded. "That was wise. Did you tell him exactly who you were going have a word with?"

"Not at all," said Michael, "but I got the notion that he thought it might be Eamonn de Valera because he knew that I was in the States with Dev."

Collins sat up in alarm. "Good God, you haven't said anything to de Valera yourself, have you Michael?"

"No", said Michael. "I knew you wouldn't want me to do that. But I didn't tell your man in Beaufort that it wasn't Dev either, because I didn't want to give anything at all away."

"Very good, Michael," said Collins. "I'm afraid that our leader is still up to his old tricks. His latest move is to ask the *Diál* to hold an enquiry into my handling of our funds. But this means that we'll have to move quickly. I don't believe that it would help the situation if Dev were to hear about an unofficial approach by the British. Do you feel confident about going back to Beaufort House to meet Wilson?"

"Ah sure I have nothing to fear down there," Michael answered. "There could be a lot to this that we don't know about yet. And if it was me they were after, they could have taken me anytime over Christmas."

"I can see that, Michael, but your greatest danger could come from our own side. What will the local boys think of you spending so much time at Beaufort House? Someone could get the idea that you're up to no good, and the way things are I certainly can't tell them what's really going on."

"Everybody down there thinks I'm stopping with Jack Quinlan so that I can see my son without the 'Tans being able to do anything about it," Michael said. "They know that nobody can touch me there because your man up at the big house won't let the 'Tans anywhere near the place."

"All right then, Michael, set up the meeting with Wilson. I can't tell you what to say or do, but I'm prepared to trust your judgement."

Chapter 15

"Do we have anybody here called William Quinlan?"

The burley foreman in charge of the forestry workers showed every sign of being a former NCO of at least sergeant's rank, and his voice carried clearly in the frosty January air. Nearby on the heath a group of about twenty men were taking a well-earned break from preparing the rough frozen ground for tree planting.

"Who?" came a reply from among the resting labourers.

"William Quinlan," the sergeant/foreman yelled again. He lowered his voice and turned to Kate who was standing by his side. "That's right isn't it miss? I'm sorry that I can't point him out to you, but these men have only just joined us and I haven't had time to get to know them all personally."

When she nodded his voice recovered its parade ground volume. "William Quinlan, if he's not here does anybody know him, with a name like that he's probably a Paddy."

The former sergeant's question was met with shrugs and blank faces. But Kate's keen eye had spotted the momentary look of surprised alarm that crossed the face of one of the men, a look that was accompanied by a tensing of his body; and she knew that she had found the right man.

***

For Kate things had taken a sudden and disturbing turn, and she realised that she would have to move quickly when the police inspector visited The Silent Women for the second time. Although on this occasion he had not been accompanied by Commander Wilson, it was of little consolation to Kate. The forestry workers had discovered the pub, and the bar was crowded when he came in, and Kate, who was in the middle of serving two of them, hadn't seen him. Even if she had, she would not have had time to beat a hasty retreat into the back room. The inspector elbowed his way to the bar, refused the drink on the house offered by the innkeeper, and turned to carefully scrutinise the rough-looking and obviously thirsty clientele. The room went quiet, and while he received several surly looks and a few uncomfortable sideways glances, he was satisfied that the man he sought wasn't there. He turned and asked the proprietor of the establishment if he had seen the man he described the other day but the innkeeper shook his head. They chatted for a few minutes and then, much to her consternation, he turned to Kate.

"What about you, miss, have you seen anything of him? I'm sure that your employer will have described him to you."

Kate held her nerve. "No sir," she said. "I haven't seen anyone who looks like that."

"You weren't here that last time I came in, have you just been taken on to help with the extra business?"

Had her employer not been present Kate would have lied, but in the circumstances she had to be truthful, although she made sure her reply was as vague as possible. "No sir, I've been here for some time."

The proprietor butted in and gave the policeman the exact date he had first employed her at The Silent Woman, and remarked that it had been his lucky day.

"I see," said the inspector, and the deeply concerned Kate had the impression that the date meant something to him.

There were drinkers waiting and, glad of the diversion, Kate turned to serve them. By the time she finished the inspector was leaving, but she heard him tell the innkeeper that he would call back in a couple of days; and his parting shot included something about remembering that the licensing laws were still in force.

It was the busiest night since Christmas and she had little time to dwell on how she would deal with the problem of the police making frequent visits to the inn. She knew that they would be back because that inspector showed every sign of being a man who took his duty seriously, and even if the fugitive Irishman were to be captured, he would make sure that his men kept an eye on how well closing time was observed at The Silent Woman.

Later that evening they had difficulty removing the last of the forestry workers from the bar. Most of them were extremely reluctant to leave the warmth of the inn to go back to their frozen makeshift lodgings. But they finally managed it, and she helped the innkeeper to tidy up before going to her room. What disturbed her most was the thought that this particular policeman was definitely the sort who would check up on her. The timing of her arrival at The Silent Woman had certainly triggered something in his mind, and even with that mysterious Irishman still on the loose, he would want to find out exactly what it was that kept playing on his mind. And it wouldn't take him long to put two and two together and make the connection between Kate's arrival at the pub and the events at the hotel in Bournemouth where the jewel thief's inside helper had still not been apprehended.

It was time to go, or at least it was becoming much too risky to stay. She couldn't do much in the middle of the night so she lay down to consider her options, and she came to the conclusion that she would do this properly. A panic-driven flight like the one from Bournemouth was not something she wanted to repeat unless it became absolutely necessary, but she packed a few essentials just in case. It would, however, be much better to have a legitimate reason for leaving. She needed to invent an excuse that would prevent suspicions being instantly aroused and give her at least a few days' grace before a search for her was begun. After a further period of thought, she worked out that she probably had at most two days in which to formulate a plan and put it into action; after that it could well be too late. But what plan? Firstly, she needed to find an acceptable reason for leaving the inn; secondly, it would be helpful if she could get her hands on a bit more money than she had managed to accumulate so far. A possible solution occurred to her, however, when she heard the innkeeper mention that because of all the extra business he would have to increase his once a week trips to the bank. He usually visited the bank in Wareham on Monday mornings to deposit the week's takings, most of which were generated over the weekend.

It didn't take her long to come up with a workable solution to her first problem, but to solve the second she felt that she would have to rely on opportunity. She was finally satisfied that she had the situation under control, but she had to admit that, the police inspector apart, she had another compelling reason for not wanting to leave in too much of a hurry: her curiosity had been thoroughly aroused by the puzzle involving Commander Wilson, the police and William Quinlan all searching for the same fugitive Irishman, and she was extremely loath to leave before finding out how the mystery unfolded.

Tomorrow, Thursday, was her day off and she decided to spend some of it searching for Patrick Coughlin herself. When she first heard about him she had imagined a ghostly shadow gliding through the mist on the heath; but now, having seen the forestry workers, she was convinced that he would regard the tree planting gang as providing him with an excellent hiding place. The police inspector obviously had similar thoughts but she reasoned that she had a better chance of success than either the cumbersome police force, or William Quinlan, who was constrained by his army duties. The biggest danger she could see was running into Commander Wilson, but she determined to give it a go. Gradually she developed a plan that might just help her find the fugitive in the time she had available before leaving the area for good.

Next morning she borrowed the landlady's bicycle and set off to find exactly where on the heath the men were working. She had a rough idea where they were from listening to them talking in the bar and it did not take her long to find them. They were working close to the Bere Regis road, clearing firebreaks prior to burning off the thick gorse, just a couple of miles from The Silent Woman. Having located them, she turned and cycled back down to Wareham. She caught a local train into Poole but returned in time to cycle back to the forestry men by lunchtime.

***

The foreman had been more than willing to help a pretty girl, but when Kate explained what she wanted, to her amusement he had instantly jumped to the wrong conclusion.

"Leave you in the lurch, did he miss?" he asked. She assured him that she hadn't been 'left in the lurch', but he still gave her a quizzical look.

When his shouted enquiry to his men drew a blank, he said, "I'm sorry miss, there doesn't seem to be anyone of that name here, but I'll make sure that we keep an eye out for him."

She thanked him and told him that she could be reached at The Silent Woman Inn. As she walked away she could sense their eyes on her. The foreman's voice rang out again. "Right then, haven't you ever seen a girl before? Get back to work you lazy lot," and the sense of being watched faded.

When she reached the bicycle, however, she turned and found that the man who had reacted to the foreman's shout was still gazing in her direction. She caught his eye, pointed down the road towards the pub and raised her other arm to mime lifting a glass to her lips. He gave a slight nod and she cycled off, confident that she had aroused his interest and had made it clear where he could find her. It seemed so easy and she couldn't understand why the police hadn't managed to catch him yet.

When she got back to the inn she found an extremely worried-looking innkeeper's wife waiting for her with a telegram. Kate knew that the wire would be there – she had sent it herself that morning from Poole – and she was glad that it was the lady of the house who had accepted it on delivery. Even two years after the end of the Great War telegrams were still regarded as harbingers of tragic news, and women in particular still dreaded the thought of receiving one; so the innkeeper's wife stood by anxiously while Kate opened the envelope.

"Is it very bad news, Kate?"

"It's from my sister," Kate answered. "My mother has been taken ill and she wants me to go home for a few days."

The woman was sympathetic, as Kate had guessed she would be. "Oh dear, is it very serious?"

"My sister doesn't say what the matter with mum is. You can't put much in a wire, but I don't think she would have sent one unless it was urgent."

The poor woman was almost in tears. "Then you must go home right away, Kate, before it's too late."

The innkeeper, who had heard the exchange, had more practical matters on his mind but was loath to appear unfeeling. "When would you want to go, Kate, and how long do you think you might be away? We can manage during the week for a while at least, but when that lot get paid on Saturday, I'll have to find someone to help out over the weekend."

His wife gave him a look which presaged trouble later.

Kate made a show of thinking things over. Eventually, she seemed to have come to a decision. "I can't do much today," she said. "I'll work tonight as usual, but if you can manage Friday night I could leave in the morning and be back again in time for the rush on Saturday night, if that's all right?"

The innkeeper was about to say something but his wife had now taken charge and she pre-empted him. "Of course that will be all right Kate." She turned to her husband. "You were talking about going to the bank in the morning so you could give her a lift to the station."

It was taken for granted that her husband would agree, but Kate wanted to reassure them that she was definitely intending to return without delay. "Oh, there's no need for you to do that," she said. "You'll be busy getting everything ready on your own, and I can easily catch the bus. I'll only be taking a few things, just enough for one night, so it will be no trouble." Something seemed to enter her mind. "It will be all right if I leave the rest of my things here, won't it?"

The innkeeper's wife nodded. "Of course it will, Kate."

The proprietor was feeling that he needed to regain at least some control. "There is a lot of loose cash lying about that I really should take to the bank. I don't like the look of some of those navvies."

Kate immediately sensed an opportunity. "Oh I could do that for you," she said. "Just put the money in a bag with the paying-in slip. I'll pay it in for you and bring the receipt back on Saturday."

Her employer looked doubtful, but knowing that he would be overruled, he raised no objection.

That evening, the bar was not quite as crowded as it had been the night before, but still busy enough to give Kate and the innkeeper plenty to do. The vast majority of drinkers were forestry workers with just a smattering of local men. A few of the forestry workers had been in the night before but most of the faces were new. This was, in the innkeeper's opinion, due to the fact that the men there the previous night had run out of cash. He again pointedly remarked that on Saturday night, when everybody had been paid, The Silent Woman would be filled to overflowing and Kate, aware of what he was getting at, assured him that she would be back in plenty of time.

When William Quinlan came in halfway through the evening, he was breathless from having cycled the twelve miles from Bovington on a borrowed bicycle. He received a few curious glances but was otherwise ignored. He came to the bar and Kate made sure that it was she who served him. She quietly gave him a brief account of what she had managed to do regarding finding his friend.

"That's grand, Kate," he said. "Is there any chance at all that he'll come in tonight?"

"I don't know William," she answered, "but I hope he does."

They had similar reasons for hoping that Patrick Coughlin did in fact come in that night. After the effort Kate had made in finding the fugitive she was desperate to find out how the affair developed before she left in the morning. But she knew that whatever happened this would be her last night at The Silent Woman; everything was in place for her departure and there could be no altering her plans.

It would also be William's last chance to visit the inn. In two days' time the advance party of the 7th Armoured Car Company were due to embark for India, and Private William Quinlan was a member of that party. After that, there would be nothing more he could personally do for Private Patrick Coughlin. The only thing he could think of was to give Jack's letter, which contained some money, to Kate and ask her to try and deliver it. But he fervently hoped that it would not come to that.

As the evening wore on it looked very much as if neither would get their wish. William began to look anxiously at the clock. He shouldn't really be here. He had persuaded his long-suffering mate, Bert, to cover for him, but he couldn't afford to stay much longer or he would be late back to camp and instead of going to India he would end up in the cooler. Kate was resigned to the fact that her curiosity would have to remain unsatisfied.

William had given up and was on his way to the bar to give Kate the letter when the door opened quietly and Patrick Coughlin sidled in.

Chapter 16

Commander Wilson was waiting for him with the owner of Beaufort House when Michael was shown in. He remembered the small waiting room just off the impressive entrance hall from his preliminary meeting with the former government minister at Christmas.

They stood as he entered. His Lordship made the introductions and then withdrew. Commander Wilson extended his hand and Michael accepted the firm grip.

"I'm glad to meet you, Mr Flynn, and I'm delighted that you have agreed to see me." Wilson then came straight to the point. "I understand that you have a strong desire to see an end to this misguided war. Let me tell you that having seen something of the situation here in Ireland for myself, I am happy to apply the term 'misguided' to both sides. There must surely be a way of putting a stop to this nonsense."

"I'm glad to hear it, Commander," Michael told him, "and if you can see any chance at all of putting an end to these troubles, I'd definitely like to know what it is."

"Good," Wilson said. "Please do sit down."

They sat on either side of the small table bearing the almost compulsory tray of tea things. Neither seemed anxious to take the conversation forward, so Wilson poured some tea and, as they drank they sized each other up. To Michael, Commander Wilson fitted the description he had been given to a 'T'. Although wearing a smart civilian suit he looked every inch a naval officer, and his formal manner reinforced the impression. For his part, Wilson had only His Lordship's description of Michael, gained from their brief preliminary meeting, to go on. He noticed that while his opposite number also wore a smart suit and tie. Michael Flynn made no attempt to hide the fact that it was being worn by a born countryman. It demonstrated an aspect of Michael's character that Wilson silently approved of.

They knew something of each other's backgrounds: Michael knew about the Commander's work as a wartime security officer in the Ministry of Munitions, and about his previous involvement with the Quinlan family. Wilson knew about Michael's false internment following the 1916 'Rising', and about his tragic encounter with the Black and Tans. He felt a genuine sympathy for Michael, and again wondered at the character of the man who, having suffered the death of his wife and the necessity of leaving his baby son to escape to America, had not been driven to abandoning all thoughts of working towards a peaceful solution to Ireland's problems. Both men understood the need for secrecy and neither felt the need to bring the matter up.

Commander Wilson decided to use his knowledge of Michael's past to break the deadlock. "I should like to express my deepest sympathy for the loss of your wife, Mr Flynn, and for what you had to sufferer at the hands of the irregulars. I have no hesitation in telling you that they are proving to be something of an embarrassment to many of us on the British side. And I must say that I'm most impressed by the way you have dealt with the situation. You don't appear to be bitter about your treatment and are still able to commit yourself to seeking a peaceful solution."

Michael appreciated the compliment. "Thank you Commander, but to tell you the truth I do feel bitter about things all right, make no mistake about that. But sure I'm not the first to suffer at the hands of the 'Tans, and unless people on both sides of the water show some sense and put a stop to this war, I definitely won't be the last."

Wilson nodded. "Point taken," he said. "But I suggest that as we are here to talk about finding a way forward, it would serve no useful purpose to dwell on the past, whatever our personal views might be."

"Fair enough, Commander," Michael agreed. "So, tell me now, what do you think should be the first move towards making some kind of peace?"

"In my opinion, the most immediate requirement is to try and arrange an effective cease-fire," Wilson answered. "Without that, nothing else can move forward. And to that end I should tell you that I know of the calls several people in the Irish Nationalist movement have made on your leaders to negotiate a truce." He paused before playing what he considered to be a trump card. "And then of course there is the personal letter from Father O'Flanagan to the Prime Minister."

Michael struggled to conceal his surprise. Surprise generated not by the fact that Wilson knew about the letter from Father O'Flanagan to Lloyd George, but by the thought that for once, Michael Collins' information was less than completely accurate. It seemed that the British Prime Minister was not 'keeping it up his sleeve' after all, and more importantly, it seemed that Lloyd George knew about Commander Wilson's mission and had presumably sanctioned it. So the British approaches to the Irish Republican Movement were not as 'unofficial' as was first thought, and Michael realised that he was playing in a completely different game.

But he was determined not to let this show. "I'd say that you're right about some of us wanting a truce, Commander," he said. "And it's true that plenty of people here would like to see an end to the war, if only to see the back of the 'Tans and the 'Auxies'. But sure from what I hear, your man in London, Lloyd George, will have nothing at all to do with it. And the British military are telling him that they can beat us easily."

He used the term 'military' instead of 'army' to see how the Commander would react to the implication that the Royal Navy, and indeed, the Royal Air Force, were regarded as being just as deeply involved in Ireland as the British Army.

Wilson smiled but didn't take the bait. "As you well know, Mr Flynn, nothing in politics is ever as clear cut as that, which, by the way, is why I've always sought to avoid it. A British Prime Minister cannot afford to put all his eggs in one basket as it were, and what passes for public knowledge does not always tell the complete story."

Michael took his time before replying. The meeting was not going in the direction he had expected it would; but in spite of that he thought that it could have the potential to deliver more than he had originally hoped for. He felt that if he was able to realise that potential, he could help to make some real progress towards achieving at least a pause in the endless cycle of attacks and reprisals.

"So, you're telling me that Lloyd George himself would be ready to talk about a cease-fire?"

"Not quite," answered Wilson. "But I can say that he has authorised a representative to discuss the situation with a senior figure in Sinn Fein and report back directly to him. The only condition would be that the meetings are held in absolute secrecy."

"And that person would be yourself, would it, Commander?"

Wilson looked horrified. "Good Lord no," he said emphatically. "This is a job for an experienced politician not a naval intelligence man."

"And who would that be?" Michael asked him.

Wilson changed the subject. "I understand that you are quite close to Eamonn de Valera. And it is said that you have his ear."

"I spent a lot of time in the States with him," Michael said. "But sure nobody can say that they're close to Dev. And I couldn't exactly say that I have his ear."

"But do you think that he would be willing to meet a personal emissary from Mr Lloyd George?"

This placed Michael in an uncomfortable position. It was, in his view, vitally important that every effort was made to take advantage of Lloyd George's overture, but he was not at all sure that de Valera was the right person to be involved at this stage. Dev was too prone to turn events to his personal advantage.

"Is de Valera the only one Lloyd George's man will talk to?" he asked.

"Well de Valera does style himself as being head of the so-called Irish Republic," said Wilson. "But why do you ask, do you have someone else in mind?"

Michael thought carefully before replying. "To be very honest with you, Commander, I don't think that Dev would be very keen about talking to emissaries. Between you and me I think that he'd want to talk to Lloyd George himself, and he'd make sure that everybody in the whole world knew about it."

While he knew that what he was about to say might end the meeting there and then, Michael took a deep breath and went on. "I think you'd be a lot better off talking to Michael Collins."

"Collins?" Wilson looked shocked at first and then decidedly sceptical. "That could prove to be extremely awkward. If it ever came to light that the British Prime Minister had sanctioned a meeting with the man regarded as our greatest enemy here in Ireland, there would be the very devil of a row. The Unionists, among others, would be up in arms. It could possibly even bring the government down."

"Well I'll tell you this, Commander," Michael explained. "If it's secrecy you're after, you'll stand more of a chance with Collins than you ever would with Dev. Sure don't they say that he even keeps secrets from himself. And these days he has more of a say in the *Dáil* than Dev. And on top of that he has the Republican Brotherhood in the palm of his hand. All things considered I'd say that Collins is definitely your man."

"But I should have thought that Collins would be the last person on earth to countenance a cease-fire."

Michael grinned. "Sure didn't you say yourself, Commander, that nothing is ever as clear cut as people think."

Wilson rose and walked around the small room with his hands behind his back, in the manner of a captain pacing the bridge of his ship. He definitely did not like the idea of recommending that Michael Collins should be the man to be approached regarding a cease-fire. Collins' reputation was such that even the members of the British press, who were calling for a solution to the 'Irish problem', would be totally against it. But, having met him face to face, Commander Wilson felt that he could trust Michael Flynn's judgement; and the Irishman obviously had inside knowledge of what was happening in the Nationalist Movement.

With some trepidation the Commander eventually reached a decision. One which he realised could lead to serious repercussions, and not least for himself.

"Do you have access to Collins?" he asked.

"I do so," Michael replied.

"Very well then," said Wilson. "Please ask him if he would be prepared to meet with Mr Alfred Cope, who is a senior civil servant in Dublin Castle, and the personal representative of Mr Lloyd George."

Chapter 17

In spite of Patrick Coughlin having gone without shaving for several days, William instantly recognised Jack's old comrade the moment the fugitive entered the pub. He was older and thinner than William remembered and in his rough clothing he looked nothing like the smartly turned out Connaught Ranger he had been when he had last visited Beaufort. But even so, there was no mistaking Patrick Coughlin and William went across the room to meet him.

"Jesus, Pat, you're a sight for sore eyes, sure wasn't I thinking that you wouldn't show up at all."

"What's going on Bill?" Patrick asked him. "Christ Almighty, sure I nearly died of fright when that woman turned up at the bog looking for you."

"I'll tell you all about it, but sit down here while I buy you a pint." William handed Patrick a bulky envelope. "There's a letter there from Jack and some cash to see you all right for a while."

"Good man yourself, Jack Quinlan," said Patrick with feeling. "God knows I'll never be able to pay that man back."

William went to the bar while Patrick read Jack's letter. The pub was gradually emptying and Kate had been left to tend the bar on her own while the innkeeper went to attend to the cellar. She had noticed Patrick come in and was impatiently waiting to see what happened next. Then suddenly, a subtle addition to her plans for leaving the inn occurred to her.

"Tell him not to leave before I've had a chance to talk to him," she whispered urgently. "I'm going home to Bristol tomorrow for a few days." She quickly explained to William what she had in mind.

William returned with Patrick's drink and found him reading Jack's letter. When he had finished reading he threw the two sheets of paper on the table in exasperation.

"Jesus Christ!" he said with feeling. "Haven't I spent all bloody winter trying to hide from the army, the cops and everybody else, and all the time it was only this one fella Wilson looking for me." He calmed down and broke into a laugh. "I couldn't work out why there wasn't lorry loads of soldiers and the whole of the police force out hunting for me. If I knew that they were trying to keep the whole bloody thing quiet it would have saved me a lot of trouble. I tell you, Bill, it makes me feel like a bloody eejit."

Knowing the reason behind what had been puzzling him came as a welcome relief and lightened his mood. It was with a profound feeling of thankfulness that he took a deep draught of beer.

"What do you think about Wilson's offer, Pat?" William asked. "I know that Jack put in his letter that he thinks you'd be better off handing yourself in or stopping here in England instead of going home. With the way things are in Ireland that wouldn't be easy, and Mick Flynn thinks the same. According to Mick, you might have a hard time being trusted by 'the boys' over there if you have a notion to join them."

"I read what Jack and Mick have to say," Patrick said, "but what about yourself Bill, what would you do if you were in my shoes?"

"To be honest with you, Pat," William replied, "it's hard for me to know what to do. Sure doesn't half of me think that I should be over there in Ireland fighting for freedom, but God knows the other half of me wants to go to India and see the world."

"Didn't I think the same myself at one time," said Patrick. "But I'll tell you this. Bill, it was only because of Jim Daly that I took part in the mutiny. If it wasn't for Jim, Lord have mercy on him, I'd still be soldiering in India. But after all the things the two of us did together, when the time came sure I couldn't let him down. He stayed with me when I was wounded in Mesopotamia, and if it wasn't for Jack we'd both be dead. So you go to India with your regiment, Bill, and serve out your time. You can take it from me that being a deserter is no fun at all."

William digested this and it came as a relief to have what he saw as Patrick's approval. "So you're not going to turn yourself in, Pat?" he said.

"I am not," answered Patrick. "I'm going home. But the only reason why I'm going back to Ireland is because I owe it to Jim Daly's memory, and not because I'm mad at the British Army. Being a soldier is all I know, and being out of favour with the British as it were, I suppose the only thing to do is to give the lads at home a hand; I have this notion that Jim will rest easier in his grave if I do that. Did Jack or Mick Flynn think that I'd do anything different?"

"No, I can't say that they did," William told him. "That's why Mick gave me another letter for you. He told me not to give it to you until I knew for certain that you're going home."

He handed over a second letter and Patrick read it. "My life on you, Mick Flynn, he's telling me not to do anything when I land in Ireland before he fills me in on the whole situation, and sure he's even letting me know how to find him. I'd say that this is one bit of advice I'd be an eejit not to take."

William was glad to see elements of the Patrick Coughlin he had once known coming back to the surface. But he was becoming increasingly worried about the time.

Patrick noticed him casting anxious glances at the clock on the wall. "Christ, Bill, you'll have to run like hell to get back to camp before 'lights out', don't I know well enough what happens if you're late in. But before you go, tell me about that girl there behind the bar. Why would the likes of her want to be mixed up in this?"

"Her name is Kate Steele," William answered, and he went on to tell Patrick about Kate being a friend of his brother, James, from the wartime munitions factory, and of his own surprise meeting with her at The Silent Woman. But Patrick looked extremely worried when told that Kate had recognised Commander Wilson and had warned William about the security man.

"Jesus, Bill, if she knows this fella, Wilson, she could be in it with him, and the pair of them are setting a trap for me."

"I thought about that too, Pat," William answered, "but sure when she found you today she tipped you the wink about where to find me instead of calling Wilson or the cops on the spot. But there's something queer about her all right, and I don't know what it is. She told me to tell you that she's going home tomorrow and that a man and a woman travelling together wouldn't be half as likely to alert the cops."

"That sounds like a good notion all right," Patrick agreed, "but I still don't know how far I can trust her. Anyway there's one thing I know for certain, I can't stop around here any longer. And with the money from Jack, God bless him, sure I might as well head for home."

He stood up and extended his hand. "Well, Bill, it's time you buggered off back to camp or you'll be in the cooler before you can scratch your arse. And you'd be better off out of the way if the cops are waiting for me outside."

They shook hands and William left.

There were only three other drinkers left in the bar, sitting together on a bench at the back of the room and obviously spinning out their last drink. Patrick rose from his lone seat and went to the bar to order a second pint of beer. The proprietor himself served him with a remark about drinking up quickly as it was almost closing time.

When Patrick returned to his seat the innkeeper turned to Kate. "That fellow looks a lot like the chap the police are looking for," he said. "I think I'd better telephone that inspector." He rummaged through the bits and pieces on the shelf behind the bar looking for the number he had been given.

Kate sounded sceptical. "I thought that it could be him as well, but he seemed to be very friendly with that soldier, so now I'm not so sure."

"Perhaps I should call the inspector anyway, just to make certain. The sooner they catch that bloke the sooner they'll leave us alone and we can get back to normal."

Kate knew that 'back to normal' referred to the non-observance of the lawful opening hours. "I don't think they would thank you for calling them out at this time of night, especially as we're not sure it actually is the man they want," she said. "Anyway, it would be the early hours before they got here and you would have to wait up for them."

He thought about that for a moment. "Perhaps you're right," he said.

Kate pressed home her advantage. "Tell you what, I'll sneak out the back and try to see which way he goes when he leaves. Then you'll have something definite to tell the inspector when you telephone him in the morning."

The innkeeper accepted her suggestion. "Time, gentlemen, please!" he shouted and the trio of forestry workers drank up and made for the door.

Patrick too drank up and joined them. He turned as he reached the door and caught Kate mouthing "wait outside" at him. When she knew that he had got the message she left the bar and went to get her coat. "I'll see which way he goes," she told the innkeeper as she left.

Even though there was a full moon there was no sign of Patrick Coughlin. The three other men were making their noisy way back towards where Kate had found them working on the heath, their breath steaming in the frosty air. She walked up and then down the road for a minute or two in each direction, but he was nowhere in sight. Disappointed at not being able to see the affair through to a conclusion, she made her way back to the pub. As she passed by one of the outer buildings a strong arm reached out and dragged her into the shadows. A second hand went over her mouth to stifle any sound.

"I don't want to hurt you, miss." Patrick forced as much menace as he could into his voice. "But I want to know what your game is. If you're all set to bring this fella, Wilson, and the cops down on me, I want to know where and when and how it's set up."

Kate quickly got over her initial shock. She shook herself free. "Me bring the cops down on you?" she hissed. "It was you that brought the police down on me. I had a good thing going for me here until they came around looking for you and now I have to leave before they come back."

It was not the response Patrick expected. "And sure why would the peelers be after you?"

"That's a long story," said Kate, "and there's no time to go into it now. But I'm leaving Wareham on the nine-thirty train in the morning and if you are leaving here as well it would be safer for us to travel at least part of the way together. There is nothing to connect us, and the police won't be looking for a couple."

"I'll think about it," was all Patrick was prepared to say.

"Well, if you do decide to come with me, you had better smarten yourself up a bit," she said. "There's a market in Wareham tomorrow and you can get some cheap things there, and a shave wouldn't hurt you either. Now then, are you going to come with me or not?"

"I'll think about it," he said again and was gone.

Kate felt her temper rising, she felt as if she had somehow lost control of the situation to this Irishman, and she wasn't used to being treated in the offhand manner that Coughlin had employed. But there was no one to vent her spite on so she forced herself to calm down and returned to the pub.

"He went up the road towards Bere Regis with the others," she told the innkeeper. "So it looks as if he is working with them and will still be there in the morning for the police to find him."

He seemed satisfied, so they cleared the bar and closed up for the night.

In the morning Kate managed to convey the impression that she was in no hurry to be on her way home. After breakfast she collected the small canvas bag of money from the obviously still reluctant innkeeper who, conscious of still being under the eagle eye of his wife, handed it over without comment. Kate again assured them that she would be back tomorrow and left.

She caught the bus into Wareham. But instead of visiting the bank she made straight for the railway station, wondering if Patrick Coughlin would be there waiting for her.

Chapter 18

It was Friday afternoon and raining heavily in Beaufort. Annie Quinlan had just finished clearing up after the midday meal when there was a quiet knock at the cottage door. She was surprised and not a little flustered to find Commander Wilson standing in the rain. The Commander had already taken the trouble to offer her his condolences for the death of her husband and the thought that he wanted to speak to her again, especially at her cottage and not up at 'the house', threw her totally off-balance.

It took Annie several seconds to collect her thoughts and she wondered if inviting him in would be the proper thing to do.

Even in the rain, Commander Wilson removed his hat. "I'm sorry to trouble you, Mrs Quinlan," he said. "I wonder if I might have a quick word with your son?"

"Jack?" Annie managed to reply. "I'm sorry sir, he's not in. But sure he'll be back any minute now; he's only gone up to the post office to send a letter to William." Her face clouded over as she continued. "William is off to India any day now with the Tank Corps and I wanted to send him a miraculous medal so that Our Lady will protect him."

Wilson felt that he should say something comforting. "You can be very proud of your sons, Mrs Quinlan."

"Oh, I am so, sir," she said, "but with Michael at the seminary and James in America, and now William going to India, sure there's only Jack left at home."

Annie's discomfort at having to receive such an important visitor struggled with her innate Irish sense of hospitality. The hospitality won. "But will you look at us standing in the rain, come in, sir, and

I'll make you a cup of tea, and sure Jack will be here in no time at all."

This time Wilson accepted; he took off his coat, hung it behind the door where Annie showed him, and entered the cottage. Annie was still flustered and hurried around clearing things up. "We had Michael Flynn here for a few days," she explained as she removed some things from one of the 'best' chairs and invited him to sit.

"It's a terrible thing, sir, when a man can't go home to see his child without the fear of being arrested by them Black and Tans."

"It is indeed, Mrs Quinlan," Wilson agreed with some feeling. He sat and crossed his legs.

While Annie busied herself making tea the Commander looked absently around the room, his mind focused on how best to approach the matter he wanted to raise with Jack Quinlan.

Wilson had successfully completed his meeting with Michael Flynn and reported back to London via telephone from Dublin Castle. Michael Flynn had now gone back to Dublin to relay the proposal for discussions regarding a possible truce to Michael Collins. In Wilson's opinion the only question mark involved was whether the Prime Minister would be prepared to risk sanctioning a meeting with someone as notorious as Collins. Having spoken with Michael he had, however, formed the opinion that Collins was, after all, the best person for Alfred Cope to negotiate with. Collins was the Republican leader responsible for conducting the war against British rule, and therefore in the best position to negotiate a cease-fire. And he had recommended as much to his superiors in London. Michael Flynn had agreed that, although remote from the capital, Beaufort House would be more acceptable to the Republican side than the official British administrative centre in Ireland. The owner was only too happy to co-operate with Commander Wilson and, up to a point with Michael Flynn, but Wilson very much doubted if this level of hospitality would be extended to Michael Collins.

While he waited for information from both sides, Wilson turned his mind back to his other unresolved problem, the escaped mutineer, Private Coughlin. So, he had returned to Beaufort from 'The Castle'. One thing he felt he urgently needed was a better description of the escapee than had been provided by War Office records. And he also wanted to gain an insight into the man's character. He had learned something about the man from the police inspector who had interviewed Coughlin and Daly following their arrest in Killarney; but he would like to know more, and Jack Quinlan, who had served with Coughlin in the war, was the best source that he could think of. But interviewing Quinlan on the subject of Coughlin was not something that sat comfortably with the naval officer; it represented the 'cloak and dagger' aspect of security work that he loathed, and it would inevitably place the Beaufort House steward in an invidious position. If Quinlan refused to co-operate fully with Wilson, it would look extremely bad for him, especially if his employer learned of his refusal; if on the other hand, Quinlan told the Commander everything he needed to know, then Jack would feel that he was betraying an old friend. Wilson had already decided that he would not inform His Lordship if Quinlan refused to help him, but it did not make his task seem any easier.

As he gazed vacantly around the room his eyes rested on the photograph that stood in its frame on the mantelpiece. He stood and asked Annie if he might have a closer look. She took the photograph down and handed it to him.

"That's Jack in the middle there," she said proudly. "And that's Patrick Coughlin."

"And the other man?" Wilson asked. "Do you know who he is?"

Annie crossed herself. "That's poor James Daly," she said sadly. "He was executed for mutiny in India."

"Yes," said Wilson, "that was a sad business."

"It was so," Annie replied. "And Jack tells me that Patrick is in jail. He was a grand boy too and a good friend of Jack's, and he was very nice to me when he was here."

Wilson was surprised. "You actually met Private Coughlin, Mrs Quinlan?"

"Sure of course I did, sir," said Annie. "Didn't he come all the way to Beaufort to see myself and William when he came out of the hospital in Tipperary. And a nicer man you couldn't wish to meet. Didn't he go fishing with William and Michael Flynn." Annie paused to wipe away a tear. "I don't want to talk ill of the dead sir, but I don't think Patrick would have got into all that trouble if James Daly, God rest him, hadn't been dead set on joining the boys fighting here in Ireland. I don't know what gets into men to make them do things like that."

Wilson looked at the photograph. Due to the fact that the bright Indian sunlight cast a heavy shadow from the pith helmet across the upper half of his face, the image was not quite clear. But it was, in Wilson's opinion, good enough to allow him to recognise the Connaught Ranger should he manage to locate him. He was also impressed by what Annie had said about Coughlin as a person. She obviously thought highly of him, and Wilson guessed that it was not just because he was her son's friend. In his opinion it went deeper than that and it told him more about the real Coughlin than the bland War Office records ever could. And, much to his relief, he thought that while he would still have to talk to Jack Quinlan, he would not be obliged to subject the Beaufort House steward to the intense grilling he had at first feared would be required. He was confident that with just a little more information and a copy of the photograph he would be much better equipped to return Private Coughlin to his prison cell.

But actually obtaining the photograph could, at best, prove to be embarrassing, and he was not at all sure that he was prepared to demand that the Quinlans hand it over. He thought about asking Annie if he could borrow it, knowing that in her mind it would not be proper to refuse, but this would involve behaviour unbecoming of a naval officer and he dismissed the idea. It would be more seemly to ask Jack for it, even though Quinlan would know the purpose of the request.

He handed the picture back to Annie and they sat and drank their tea in silence. They had just about finished when Jack came in via the back door having hung his wet coat in the wash house at the back of the cottage. He showed some surprise at Wilson's presence in what passed for the cottage parlour.

The visitor stood. "Ah, Quinlan, I came down to see if I could have a private word with you and your mother was kind enough to make me some tea."

Jack was well aware that it would take a highly unusual set of circumstances to warrant the Commander calling on him at the cottage, but he could think of two obvious reasons for the visit: in short, either Michael Flynn or Patrick Coughlin.

"That's grand, Commander," he said, and waited for Wilson to make the next move.

Annie had heard Wilson's remark that he wanted to talk to Jack alone. In her mind there was nothing unusual about someone wanting to talk to the Beaufort House steward in private, so she went up to her room and left them to it.

Wilson came straight to the point. "I'm sure that you have already guessed Quinlan that I wish to speak to you about the escaped mutineer, Private Coughlin. And I felt that it would be less onerous for you if we held this conversation away from Beaufort House. For what it is worth I can assure you that nothing you say will get back to your employer."

Jack was grateful for Wilson's foresight. He had been expecting to be asked about Pat Coughlin and he realised that the Commander could quite legitimately have opted to interview him in front of His Lordship, which would have placed him in an extremely awkward position. He determined that he would try to answer all Wilson's questions as honestly as he could, but he would not volunteer any further information, especially about William's search for Patrick in the south of England.

"I take it that Pat is still on the loose, sir?"

Wilson looked keenly at him. "You don't seem surprised that he hasn't yet been apprehended, I sincerely hope that it is not because he has been in touch with you."

"No, sir," said Jack, "I haven't heard a single word from him, and to tell you the honest truth I don't think for one minute that I will. Like I told His Lordship, Pat Coughlin isn't the sort of a fella who would drag his friends into his troubles if he can help it."

Wilson digested this for a minute. "That seems to fit with several opinions I've had of the man. The police inspector in Killarney seems to think that he conducted himself extremely well when he and Daly were mistakenly arrested. But the fact remains that he took part in a mutiny and then escaped from custody, although I'm having difficulty in understanding why a soldier with his fine record would become involved in crimes like these. Can you shed any light on that?"

Jack knew exactly why his friend had joined the mutiny and thought that, as a serving officer, Wilson would accept his explanation. "I'd say that Pat never wanted to get mixed up in any mutiny, sir, but Jim Daly did, and sure Pat would die before he'd let Jim down. They saw too much action together for either of them to do that to the other. So with Jim dead, Pat would still think that he still owed him something. God knows I'm no expert sir, but I think that Pat's loyalty will be to Jim's memory now, and not to the army, or to even the Connaught Rangers, any more."

It was an explanation that Wilson could, indeed, understand. "I sense that you think that he will try to return to Ireland?"

"I hope to God that he doesn't, sir, but I think he will. He'll be thinking that he owes it to Jim's memory to do what his friend wanted to do but can't. Anyway, if he joins the IRA he won't be fighting for Ireland but for Jim Daly."

To Wilson this made perfect sense and he felt that he now had a clearer insight into what made Coughlin act as he had. But although he could understand the man's reasons, he could not bring himself to have any sympathy whatsoever for a mutineer.

"I don't think that I need to bother you further, Quinlan, and I thank you for being candid with me. But I must tell you that I am determined to recapture Coughlin and return him to prison."

He decided that the best course of action was to come straight to the point. "To that end, Quinlan, I have to ask you to lend me that photograph. You have my word that it will be returned."

Jack was taken aback. The picture on the mantelpiece was something that had not entered his head. But there was nothing he could do but remove the photograph from the frame and hand it over. If he told his mother the truth and said that Commander Wilson had borrowed it she would not question why.

***

Shortly after his return to Beaufort House there was a telephone call for Commander Wilson. Michael Flynn informed him that Michael Collins had agreed to meet with Alfred Cope. Collins was prepared to talk about possible ways of arranging a cease-fire, but there would be conditions attached which he would only discuss with Cope. And he wanted an assurance that the man from 'The Castle' actually did speak for Lloyd George himself. The only other condition Collins imposed before meeting Alfred Cope was that the meeting be held in Dublin. He was not prepared to travel to Beaufort, for although he accepted Wilson's assurances that he would be under his protection while he was at Beaufort House, he could not be adequately protected on the journey there and back.

Wilson knew that this last demand merely represented Collins trying to present the British with as many difficulties as possible – in spite of being 'on the run', Collins seemed to be able to travel at will throughout Ireland. But in any case, it was a relief for the Commander not to have to try and persuade His Lordship to allow Collins into his home.

By far the greatest difficulty, however, would be persuading Lloyd George to give Collins an assurance that Cope was, in fact, his personal representative. To do this Wilson needed to return to Dublin Castle.

Chapter 19

Patrick Coughlin was nowhere to be seen when Kate arrived at Wareham railway station on the Friday morning, but this did not come as a great surprise. She had already seen enough of him to know that a man who had avoided capture by the authorities for so long was not likely to take any unnecessary chances at this stage. Having purchased two single tickets to Dorchester, she sat on a bench to wait. Although there was a severe frost, she chose to wait in plain sight rather than enjoy the warmth of the heated waiting room. When he arrived, and she was confident that he would, she wanted him to be able to spot her immediately. She had chosen to buy tickets to Dorchester because the town boasted two railway stations operated by two separate railway companies, so as well as having the opportunity of changing trains, they would also have the opportunity to change lines and further confuse any pursuit that might result from their leaving Wareham. As she waited in the cold she removed her gloves to breathe some warmth into her hands and as she did so she looked again at the ring on her wedding finger. It was a small lady's signet ring, part of the loot left unsold from the last Bournemouth haul, and which when turned round on her finger with the seal on the inside would pass for a plain gold wedding band.

The Dorchester train pulled into the station in a cloud of smoke and steam. She looked anxiously round for Coughlin but he was nowhere in sight. A few passengers had come out of the waiting room to board the train, but at this time of day the station was sparsely populated. Bitterly disappointed that he had decided not to come with her, she was about to board the train when a firm grip on her arm pulled her back. She knew instinctively that it was him.

"Hurry up," she said angrily. "This is our train, I've got two tickets to Dorchester."

"I know that," he said. "Sure isn't that why I bought two tickets for Portsmouth. If you're thinking of travelling with me, that's where we're going."

Kate was taken aback. She turned round to argue but hardly recognised him. Gone were the remnants of old army uniform and in their place he wore a long raincoat, which although of good quality, had seen better days; on his head was a dark trilby hat and round his throat a heavy woollen scarf; below the coat several inches of grey trousers were visible; but he still wore his heavy army boots although they had now been well cleaned. He looked every inch the working man wearing what passed for his Sunday best. He had spent some time, and as much of Jack Quinlan's money that he felt he could afford, at Wareham market and in the town's second-hand shops, never buying more than a single item from any one vendor. During the night he had broken into a stable and, in spite of the near freezing temperature of the water, he had shaved in the horse trough.

"Why on earth did you get tickets to Portsmouth of all places?" she asked crossly. "And how did you know where I bought tickets to?"

"Sure didn't I say to your man in the ticket office what a grand looking woman you were. He told me that I was out of luck because you had just bought two tickets to Dorchester so you must be travelling with somebody else. I bought tickets to Portsmouth so that he'd know you weren't with me, and anyway, to tell you the truth, I have a notion that I'd be an eejit to trust you too far."

For a moment Kate thought he was joking, but then the guard blew his whistle and waved his flag and the Dorchester train left the station. "There," she said, "now you've made us miss the train and there isn't another for an hour. And I'm definitely not going to Portsmouth, that train goes through Bournemouth and I'm not going anywhere near there."

"Suit yourself." He walked away and crossed over the footbridge to the opposite platform without looking back.

Quite incensed, she shouted at his retreating back, "Go on then, you arrogant sod."

Kate was livid: this was supposed to be all her show. She was the one who had suggested that they travel together; she was the one who was doing him a favour, and yet here he was trying to take everything out of her hands and treating her as if she didn't matter. In her anger she blamed him for making it necessary for her to leave The Silent Woman in such a hurry, but in the process she completely forgot the fact that it was her own curiosity which had enticed her to take an interest in him and to postpone her departure in the first place. And what really frustrated her was that she had still not learned a single thing about him or why he was on the run. Had she taken a moment to think about it, however, she might have admitted to herself that the days since William Quinlan had turned up at the inn looking for Coughlin had been the most exciting since her flight from Bournemouth. And her suggestion that they travel together had been prompted not by any thoughts of security, but by a desire to extend that period of excitement. She had even entertained the thought that she might travel all the way to Ireland with him; if that was in fact where he was going, but she was learning that you never really knew with him. At least in Ireland she would not have the Dorset police to worry about. She had read something about there being some sort of trouble over there but did not believe that it was anything very serious, and it certainly was not serious enough to prevent him from planning to go there.

But now, all that no longer mattered; he had the temerity to ruin her carefully worked out plan and then to simply turn his back on her. And if he thought that she would go after him he had another think coming.

She was heading for the waiting room when she noticed the policeman. He was marching purposefully up the platform towards her. Her first thought was that the innkeeper had contacted the bank and discovered that she had not deposited his money. If that was the case he would have immediately alerted the police. The cash began to weigh heavily in her bag. Patrick Coughlin was standing on the opposite platform unconcernedly reading a newspaper and in her anxiety she forgot how angry she was with him. Travelling in his company suddenly regained its attraction and, as calmly as she could force herself to, she walked to the footbridge and crossed over to him. When she looked the policeman had gone from sight.

They stood in silence until the Portsmouth train arrived, he held the door open for her and she got in without acknowledging him. In an otherwise empty compartment they sat on opposite sides. The ticket collector accepted both tickets from Patrick and grinned, obviously thinking that they were a married couple who had just had a blazing row. Although neither was prepared to admit it, they both recognised the incident as providing clear evidence of the advantages of travelling together. When the train stopped at Bournemouth, Kate fidgeted anxiously, worried that someone from her time there would recognise her. She tried to keep out of sight as best she could until the train began to move out again. Patrick, who had already noted her reaction to seeing the policeman at Wareham, saw her anxiety as further evidence that her reasons for wanting to travel in his company had more to do with her wanting to avoid the police than with any connection with Commander Wilson. At Southampton he stood up, obviously intending to leave the train.

By now nothing surprised Kate. "I thought we were going to Portsmouth?" she said when they were on the platform.

"And why would we want to be going there?" he asked. "Sure wouldn't we only have to come back this way again to go to Bristol. When we're there you can go home and I'll be on my way."

"I'm not going home," Kate said. "I can't, they will be looking for me there."

Patrick thought about this. "I'd say that it's about time we put some of our cards on the table."

Rather than risk being seen at the station, where any search for them would be concentrated, they went into the city and found a small café. He ordered tea and, not having had breakfast, some buns similar to the 'wads' he had become accustomed to in army canteens.

"So," he said when they were settled. "You can't go home to Bristol because the peelers might find you there. I don't know why they're after you, and sure I don't want to know, but you'll have to tell me where you do want to go so that I can work out whether we can stay together for a while longer."

Kate felt a pang of disappointment. She had been hoping that he would want to know why she was wanted by the police, partly because she would have enjoyed sharing her experiences with someone, but mainly because it would have somehow given her a right to know more about him.

"It really doesn't matter much where I go," she answered. "But I did think that I might go wherever you're going."

Patrick was adamant. "Jesus no, you can't go where I'm going, it'd be too bloody dangerous for both of us."

"You're going to Ireland, aren't you," she said quietly. "I've heard that there's some trouble there but it can't be all that serious."

His reaction startled her. "Trouble you call it! Jesus Christ woman there's a full scale war on over there." He calmed down and continued with all the seriousness he could muster. "I'm for Ireland all right, and it's on the cards that I'll join in the fight. But listen to me now, Kate. If I show up there with an English girl they'll shoot the pair of us on the spot. And if the IRA don't do for us sure the bloody Black and Tans wiii."

It was not the tone of his voice that impressed Kate but the fact that, for the first time, he had actually called her by name. It was, however, plainly evident that there would be no changing his mind, so they fell silent and drank their tea.

Eventually Kate broke the silence. "Well then just how far can I come with you?"

He thought for a moment. "Well as you can't go to Bristol we might as well head for London. I'll get the Irish boat train, and you'll be able to go anywhere you like in the country from there. Or you could even stay there for good, sure the place is big enough for you to be able to hide from the cops."

But Kate's inherent need for excitement had again been aroused. The thought of continuing the journey with a man evidently bent on taking part in something dangerous in Ireland held much too strong an attraction to resist.

"If you're going to Ireland," she said, "you'll have to go to somewhere called Holyhead. I know that because that's where the Irishmen at the munitions factory used to go to catch the ship to take them home. And you saw for yourself the way the ticket collector on the train acted, he thought that we were a couple who were in the middle of having a row. So if I go as far as Holyhead with you nobody will pay us any attention, especially if we pretend to be married."

She removed her glove and showed him the reversed signet ring.

"And why, in the name of God, would you want to come with me instead of stopping in London?" he asked.

"I don't really know," she answered with some honesty. "But I can go to London anytime I want, and this might be my only chance I'll ever get to go to Holyhead. And you don't have to worry about the cost I have enough money to pay for myself."

Patrick was inclined to believe that she didn't know exactly why she wanted to go with him, but he was sure that she was being driven by something he recognised as a natural need for excitement. He had known plenty of eager young men who had volunteered the moment war broke out in 1914 not because of any real patriotic fervour, but fired by a desire to join in what they imagined would prove to be a great adventure. It would be, he assumed, an unusual trait to find in a woman but the signs were all there. There was always a danger that she might be inclined to be foolhardy in a crisis but, so far, she had seemed capable of keeping a cool head. And the advantages of travelling as a couple were obvious.

"Tell me," he said, "exactly how much trouble would you be in if the peelers take you?"

"Enough to put me in prison for some time," she answered.

Again he believed her. "All right," he said, "we'll go to London and look up the times of the boat trains to Holyhead and the steamers to Kingstown."

"Where is Kingstown?" she asked. "I've never heard of it."

He explained that Kingstown was a port just outside Dublin where the packet steamers from Holyhead docked.

At Waterloo Station they checked the timetables for a journey to Ireland and, in another small café, they sat down to plan the journey over platefuls of fish and chips. Kate's excitement at the prospect of the journey was such that for once she was content to let him make all the decisions.

It was now late on Friday afternoon. They would spend the night in London and take the boat train for Holyhead in the morning. That would get them on the overnight steamer for Kingstown. He wanted to arrive in Dublin early on Sunday morning when the only people up and about would be going to an early Mass. And he did not deem it necessary to tell Kate of his arrangement to meet Michael Flynn in Dublin on Sunday morning. After some argument he reluctantly agreed that it would be better if 'his wife' accompanied him all the way to Kingstown, but only after he had extracted a solemn promise that she would return to Holyhead on the next return crossing. And to this end he insisted that she buy a return ticket. Her resentment briefly returned at what she saw as a demonstration of mistrust, but again she knew that it would be futile to protest and let it drop.

Nothing had been said about exactly how they would spend the night. Kate wondered if he would make a pass at her, and knew just how she would react if he did. Underneath the rough exterior she found him to be quite an attractive man, and the excitement generated by the thought of travelling all the way to Ireland with him had aroused a sexual desire in her; just as the excitement generated by robbing hotel guests in Bournemouth had aroused her sexual interest in her partner-in-crime there. But she had to admit that Patrick Coughlin was no habitual criminal like Mark, with his eye on the main chance.

Becoming sexually involved with her was, however, something that Patrick was determined to avoid even though he sensed that she would raise little objection. He was only human and his life as a regular soldier had been far from a celibate one, but the caution he had been forced to practise during his time on the run could not be easily shaken off, and he could not afford to allow anything to divert him from what he had set out to do. He was also still a long way from trusting her completely, especially as she now knew something of his plans, which itself presented him with something of a dilemma. In his current position he could not, he felt, afford the complications that sleeping with her would inevitably bring. On the other hand he was reluctant to let her very far out of his sight.

The clear sky heralded another night of severe frost. On his own he could easily have found an adequate shelter and survived the cold, as he had been doing since his escape. But he could not reasonably expect her to do the same. In the end they found a cheap hotel not far from Euston Station from where they would be leaving in the morning. They registered as a married couple and the woman at the desk made no comment. The room contained a double bed and an ancient but comfortable armchair which was, he assured her, a better bunk than anything he had been able to sleep in recently. He visited the bathroom while she got ready for bed. From force of habit she placed the stolen money under the mattress.

Alone in the double bed she found it difficult to drop off, but he seemed to have little difficulty in sleeping. She thought about him and wondered if she would ever be able to satisfy her curiosity about him, although she was beginning to suspect that solving that problem might well lead her into trouble. Her common sense told her that she would be well advised to leave him in the morning and remain in London, but she knew that her sense of anticipation for the coming journey wouldn't allow her to. In the early hours she considered waking him and inviting him into bed with her, but she sensed that it would be useless to even try.

After breakfast on Saturday morning they boarded the boat train for Holyhead.

Chapter 20

When Commander Wilson arrived back in Dublin at midday on Saturday he managed to contact Alfred Cope who, when he heard that Michael Collins had agreed to meet him, immediately left for London to talk to the Prime Minister in person. At 'The Castle', Wilson found a message waiting for him from the police inspector in Dorset. Someone resembling the man they sought had been seen drinking in The Silent Women Inn near Wareham, and according to the innkeeper, the suspect had been in the company of the men working in the area for the Forestry Commission. As soon as he heard the news, the inspector had immediately visited the worksite and was told by the foreman that one of his men had not turned up for work that morning. When questioned by the policeman, some of the workers told him that the missing man had indeed been drinking in The Silent Woman the previous evening and had seemed in perfectly good health. None of them could, however, confirm that he had returned to their hut that night, but he certainly wasn't there in the morning.

When the foreman checked his records, he found that the man had given his name as 'Daly' when he was first employed by the Commission. Thinking that it was not relevant, the foreman failed to mention that a girl had been asking about a man called Quinlan two days previously.

The workmen, who knew the missing man only as 'Paddy', said that he kept very much to himself to such an extent that in the pub the previous evening he had not associated with them, but had sat apart talking to a soldier with whom he seemed to be on very friendly terms. As former servicemen themselves they recognised the soldier as being in the Tank Corps. The inspector was not sure what all this meant but hoped that the Commander could make some sense of it.

The Commander could indeed make sense of it. His instinct told him that the man in question was indeed the escaped mutineer, Private Coughlin. Working for the Forestry Commission on the deserted heath was a perfect place for an experienced soldier to hide, and he could have kicked himself for not thinking of this before; and the soldier in the public house was almost certainly Jack Quinlan's brother, William. Mrs Quinlan's remark about William 'going to India with the Tank Corps' confirmed that he was definitely serving in that particular army corps, and as such he could well be stationed at one of the camps in Dorset. And as he was about to embark for India, that could only mean the depot at Bovington. At first he thought that Jack Quinlan had lied to him and that Coughlin had, in fact, contacted his old comrade, and the thought saddened him. But then he realised that the Beaufort House steward had been much more subtle than that. Quinlan had answered truthfully when asked if Coughlin had been in touch, but had failed to mention that he had decided to try and contact the escaped mutineer himself, and had enlisted his brother to help. How the Quinlan brothers had managed to locate Coughlin before the police was something of a mystery, but it was obvious that they had. That, however, was something that would have to wait until he was next in Beaufort and could question Quinlan about it.

His most immediate concern was to alert the police inspector that the man missing from among the forestry workers was almost certainly the escaped prisoner and that every effort should be made to apprehend him. He telegraphed the Dorset police headquarters but was not hopeful that they would have any success in trying to arrest Coughlin. The Commander was sure that by now the bird would have flown. By now his quarry could, in theory, be making for anywhere on the British mainland, but given everything that had recently transpired, Wilson was convinced that Coughlin would now head for Ireland and home.

While he waited for Alfred Cope's return to Dublin he turned his attention to the photograph he had commandeered from the Quinlan cottage. The obvious course of action would be to have the photograph copied and circulated to the police at all the ports where the steamers from the British mainland docked. The embarkation ports on the mainland were being watched by the Military Police, but Wilson suspected that, given the time that had elapsed since the escape, vigilance would have become lax; a factor which could well have been included in Coughlin's plans. There was always the possibility that Coughlin would not travel on one of the scheduled services but try to land secretly on any one of hundreds of places on the Irish coast. Wilson, however, doubted if the escapee would have either the time or the resources to arrange for the skipper of a fishing boat or other small private vessel to ferry him across the Irish Sea in the depth of winter. That reduced the number of possible arrival ports to a handful: Larne near Belfast, Kingstown in Dublin, Rosslare, Waterford, and Queenstown in Cork.

The Commander still faced one major problem: he needed to keep Coughlin's escape under wraps. Even though the original plan had been to mount a full scale search for the fugitive should he avoid capture on the mainland and manage to escape to Ireland, recent events would, Wilson reasoned, require him to revise that position. With negotiations aimed at arranging a cease-fire now a distinct possibility, it would not do to hand the Nationalist side an easy propaganda coup. There would inevitably be diehard Republicans who would oppose a truce, however favourable the conditions might be, and who would make every effort to hamper the negotiations. So the need for caution was paramount and it would not help the British cause if their army were held up as something of a laughing stock for being incapable of hanging on to a prisoner, especially one of the Connaught Ranger mutineers. The worldwide interest in the mutiny would be rekindled, much to the further embarrassment of the British government.

With this in mind Wilson was extremely reluctant to enlist the help of the Royal Irish Constabulary. The RIC was riddled with Republican spies and, once they came on board, all hope of secrecy would be lost. The 'Tans and 'Auxies' would regard the hunt for Coughlin as an opportunity to exercise their favourite tactics of coercion and terrorising local communities, while making no secret of who they were looking for.

What Wilson required was a small force of trusted men, armed with Coughlin's photograph, to mount a watch at the main disembarkation points. He had a word with one of the senior men at 'The Castle' and was directed to 'G' Division of the RIC, the section responsible for all intelligence matters in the war against the IRA. The officer-in-charge of the division was at first reluctant to release any of his hard-pressed officers for what he considered to be a routine police matter, especially as Commander Wilson wasn't exactly forthcoming in explaining the real purpose behind the request. But eventually, he had little choice other than to cooperate with the man from the Security Services, and he decided to view the operation as an opportunity to give at least a few of his men some much needed relief. Because of their role at 'The Castle', the 'G Men' were a particular target of the IRA. They and their families were constantly harassed and threatened; they were left under no illusion of the consequences of not passing on information to the IRA, and inevitably several had succumbed. As an extra incentive a few had actually been 'executed', and the memory of what had happened to members of the 'Cairo Gang' on Bloody Sunday was enough to convince most of them.

Wilson was well aware of the fact that there was a constant stream of information being passed from 'The Castle' to Michael Collins' undercover intelligence organisation, but this was the best he could do over the weekend. He had already got some copies of the photograph made by the well-equipped technical department at 'The Castle', and he organised his men to cover the four ports outside Dublin. The men chosen were only too glad to leave the threatening atmosphere of the capital behind, if only for a few days.

As there was nothing else he could do until Monday he decided to keep watch at Kingstown himself.

Chapter 21

It was cold and damp when the steamer from Holyhead docked at Kingstown soon after six o'clock on the Sunday morning. It was late arriving due to foul weather in the Irish Sea, which was something of a regular occurrence during the winter months. They stood by the ship's rail prior to taking their places in the far from orderly queue of fractious passengers waiting to descend the gangway. The vast majority of the people on board were men, many of them still suffering from the effects of either seasickness or a night spent in the ship's bar; and all of them impatient to be off the steamer and on to dry land. A couple of RIC men stood on the quay showing little interest in the routine arrival of the steamer from Holyhead. At the other side of the quay by some warehouses, a train stood by with steam up ready to convey the passengers off the steamer into Dublin city.

Kate suddenly tensed up as she noticed a familiar figure standing at the bottom of the gangway and pulled Patrick back from the rail in alarm. "Good God," she said anxiously. "That's Commander Wilson down there checking people as they get off. He's obviously looking for you."

"So, now is your chance to inform on me." Patrick had, by this time, reached the conclusion that she was definitely not in league with Wilson, but he was not yet disposed to tell her so.

Kate flushed with anger. "You know very well that I couldn't turn you in, even though I would very much like to, without getting myself into trouble with the police as well. I'm beginning to think that even being seen with you would be enough to put me in prison."

After spending some forty-eight hours in his company on the long and tiring journey her temper was, not for the first time, becoming frayed.

"Sure won't you be telling me next that you're sorry you stuck your nose into my business." Even though he was, on balance, quite glad that she had, he was not about to admit it.

Travelling together had in fact worked out very well, and had helped them to avoid arousing suspicion on their somewhat roundabout journey from Wareham in Dorset to Kingstown on Dublin's doorstep. But he still did not really know very much about what her motives were, and certainly not enough for him to trust her completely. He also suspected that she would like to continue with what she still seemed to regard as nothing more than an exciting diversion and try to stay with him after they disembarked. But no matter what she might think, that would definitely not be possible: it would be much too dangerous for both of them. So he feared that if he were to offer even a slight degree of friendliness, it would make it all the more difficult to persuade her to return to England by herself.

"You can say that again," she retorted tartly, "but I'm stuck with you for a little longer and we have to find a way of getting you off this horrid smelly ship without being caught."

The journey from London, which until now had been largely uneventful, had been spent in silence, with each of them content to dwell on their own private thoughts. What words that had passed between them being largely confined to the requirements of the journey. But as the steamer corkscrewed its unsteady way through the Irish Sea towards Kingstown, Kate became more and more impatient to find out exactly why Patrick Coughlin was being hunted by Commander Wilson. When she tried to coax him to talk, however, the only response she got was to be told that knowing the whole story would only serve to get her into far more serious trouble than she was in already. All of which had the effect of increasing her curiosity, and by the time they reached Kingstown she was seething with frustration.

But the sight of Commander Wilson standing at the bottom of the gangway, and the sense of danger that his presence there aroused, served to calm her down and helped to focus her mind.

"I'll go down first and distract him," she said. "I'm sure that he'll remember me from the munitions factory and I can keep him busy while you slip off with the others. I'll meet you again over by that train."

Patrick considered this. "From what I hear he's not a man to be distracted by a pair of lovely brown eyes and a smile, but sure I can't think of anything better. But listen to me now, Kate, if he shows any sign at all of catching on, you look out for yourself and forget about me. You never laid eyes on me before now."

"Never mind about all that now." Kate was anxious to put her plan into action and didn't stop to consider the possible consequences. "We have to be quick or everyone else will be off the ship."

He thought that he should make some attempt at saying goodbye, but before he could say anything she had pushed her way to the gangway and was using her elbows to move down to where Wilson stood. The Commander was holding things up by checking every male passenger as they reached the bottom of the gangway, and he had enlisted one of the RIC men to help him. This served to increase the restlessness among the passengers still on board, especially those on the crowded gangway, but they grudgingly allowed Kate to jump the queue. Patrick followed her but with less aggressive tactics, so that when she reached the bottom of the gangway, he was perhaps half a dozen passengers behind.

Wilson was busy trying to match faces against the photograph when a female voice broke his concentration. "Good gracious, it is Mr Wilson isn't it? I thought I recognised you from up on the ship but I wasn't sure."

The Commander looked at Kate in some surprise as she held out her hand. "Perhaps you remember me from the Gretna factory, Mr Wilson. My name is Kate Steele, or at least it was then."

Wilson had little choice but to accept the offered hand. "Why of course I remember you, Miss Steele, what on earth are you doing here?"

Kate thought quickly. "Actually it's Mrs Kelly now," she said. "I've come over with my husband to visit his family for a few days. He's around somewhere but we seem to have been separated in the crush. I've been feeling a little unwell and had to go to the toilet so he may have got off before me." She stood directly in front of the Commander and looked around on the pretext of trying to find her 'husband'.

By now the impatient crowd waiting to leave the ship were becoming increasingly belligerent. The man immediately in front of Patrick shouted. "For Jesus' sake hurry up or we'll be here 'till Patrick's Day!"

Patrick saw this as his chance. He gathered his strength to give the man in front a hefty push and send the front of the queue barging into Wilson and Kate intending to leap over the tangled mass of bodies and make a dash for freedom. But this proved to be totally unnecessary: a voice shouted, "Stop there!" A man ran from behind the stationary train. He turned and fired a revolver at an unseen target. His fire was answered by several rifle shots and he fell to the ground. Two Auxiliary Policemen ran into view and cautiously approached the prone figure with their rifles held at the ready.

Pandemonium broke out among the passengers. At the sound of the first shot, Commander Wilson instinctively yelled, "Get down!" He grabbed Kate and forced her to the ground; the RIC man needed no encouragement to follow suit. For a few minutes they were in grave danger of being trampled by the panic-stricken stampede off the steamer. Patrick was one of the first to reach the quay. He ran for the shelter of the train fearing with every step that the 'Auxies' would open up on him. But with everybody running in all directions they were obviously at a loss to know who to shoot at, so they held their fire.

Gradually, the situation calmed down. Wilson helped Kate to her feet and, still clutching her bag with the stolen money, she looked frantically round for Patrick. He was nowhere in sight.

"Are you all right, Miss Steele, excuse me, Mrs Kelly, I should say? I'm sorry to have been so rough with you. Unfortunately this is all too frequent an occurrence in Ireland these days. You have been here before I take it."

As he spoke he tried to shelter her from the sight of the Auxiliaries, who had been joined by three more, as they carried the body of their victim away leaving a dark red stain on the quay where he had fallen.

"Oh yes," she answered, "with my husband. I'll have to go and find him. He's probably waiting for me at the train." She still held some hopes that Patrick might actually be where she had asked him to wait.

The two RIC men stood idly by the train trying not to become involved, but Wilson noticed that a few of the Auxiliaries were still in evidence on the quay. "I think that I had better come with you," he said. "I'm afraid that not even a lone woman is immune from harassment by these irregulars after an incident like this."

Kate's first thought was to refuse. The last thing she wanted was Wilson to be present if she actually found 'her husband'. But witnessing the shooting had made her stop and think. Perhaps the situation in Ireland actually was more serious than she had imagined, and she was beginning to feel distinctly uneasy about the whole affair. So, she accepted his offer, but as they made their way towards the train she desperately tried to think of a way of getting rid of him without arousing his suspicions. The guard was already checking the doors indicating that the train was about to leave, but Wilson caught his eye and signalled for him to wait.

"Have you got much further to go? Where in Ireland do your husband's family live?" The Commander knew that there was no longer any point in searching for Coughlin among the passengers on this particular crossing, and he was merely making conversation.

Kate, who was afraid that the situation was rapidly slipping away from her, blurted out the only place in Ireland that she knew, "Beaufort."

Wilson stopped in his tracks. "Beaufort?" he repeated. His mind raced and he remembered that she had been friendly with James Quinlan at Gretna. The Quinlans lived in Beaufort and were somehow in league with Coughlin. There was something happening here that required further investigation.

He held Kate by the arm. "When we find your husband I will require both of you to come with me to answer some questions."

Kate knew that something had gone drastically wrong. She did not know exactly what, but she was not going anywhere with Wilson to answer his questions. Without further thought, she broke away from him and sprinted as fast as she could after the departing train. She realised that she couldn't catch it but she continued to run along the quay and out of the dock area into the surrounding streets.

Wilson's first thought was to yell at the RIC men to go after her, but he feared that if they gave chase the Auxiliaries would follow suit and he had already seen enough of their methods for one morning.

Chapter 22

There was still a good ten minutes to wait before the Mass began. He knew he was early but felt it would be safer to wait inside the church rather than hang around outside. He went in, sat in a pew at the back, and settled down to wait.

***

On Sunday morning Michael Flynn was walking along a Dublin street with Kevin Ryan, their progress slowed by Ryan's limp. The brothers-in-law joined the crowd making their way to nine o'clock Mass. In the distance the bell pealed to remind the worshippers that they only had a further five minutes before the service began. But there was no sign of anybody hurrying; those people anxious to get there in time were already at the church.

"Christ, Mick. Do you get the notion that 'The Big Fella' has it in for me?" Kevin asked.

"Not at all, Kevin," Michael assured him. "Sure I'd say that he's only sending you back to Longford because he thinks you'll be best placed to help The Cause there, like he always does."

This was only partially true, but Michael knew that he couldn't possibly tell his volatile brother-in-law the truth behind why Michael Collins was sending him out of Dublin and back to the North Longford Brigade. Kevin would find it difficult to accept and was liable to react violently. He might even disobey orders and remain in the capital.

"And sure what good will I be doing down there in bloody Longford?" Kevin argued. "I'll tell you this Mick, that North

Longford Brigade are a bunch of lazy bastards, and the great Sean MacEoin is nothing but an arrogant eejit. God knows where he got his reputation as a fighting man from, but it wasn't from fighting the bloody Brits. Sure all we did while I was there was to run away from a bunch of regulars and a handful of 'Auxies'. He had us dressed up like clowns out of a circus doing something they call 'Hunting the Wren', for all the good that did. A woman and a couple of local fellas and even a horse got killed because of it."

His mood lightened. "But anyway, I did for one of them bloody 'Auxies' myself. A mountain of a sergeant he was who thought he could get the better of me. But I showed him and he's not so big or so bloody smart now."

"I heard about that, Kevin," Michael said.

"And that eejit, MacEoin, sent me back to Dublin because of it. I was glad enough of the chance to come home, but sure wasn't it up to 'The Big Fella' himself to bring me back and not that bloody Longford man. I told Collins all about what was going on, I even advised him to give MacEoin the sack and send me back there to show the buggers how to fight. But sure he wouldn't listen; and me being one of the 'Apostles' and all."

Kevin was referring to Collins' elite group of assassins which had become known as 'The Twelve Apostles'.

"But didn't he tell me last night that he's sending me back to Longford, and under MacEoin's orders too," Kevin continued. "I tell you, Mick, something is up that I'm not being let in on. Did you hear anything yourself?"

"Not a word," answered Michael, surprised that someone with Kevin Ryan's knowledge of Michael Collins would even think of asking such a question. "But sure don't you know very well that Collins always has something in mind that he keeps to himself. He'll tell us when he's ready like he always does, if it has anything at all to do with us."

"True enough." Kevin still didn't sound convinced.

Michael, however, did know what Collins was up to. The previous evening he had been called to meet 'The Big Fella'. At first he thought that it was to discuss the situation regarding the proposed meeting with Alfred Cope. But that was only partially true.

***

Collins had obviously been giving the prospect of meeting Lloyd George's emissary considerable thought. He told Michael that when he met with Cope, and he seemed confident that the meeting would actually take place, it would be helpful if the IRA were to mount a significant raid or ambush just to 'give the other side a reminder that a truce would be as much to their advantage as it would to ours'. He had earmarked the North Longford Brigade to plan and carry out an appropriate operation because, in his opinion, they had by far the best chance of success.

"Isn't Kevin Ryan with Sean MacEoin's brigade?" Michael asked.

"He was," Collins replied, "but Sean sent him back here." He went on to tell Michael about the incident with the Auxiliaries on St Stephen's Day. "The trouble is that I have two versions of what happened. I've given you Sean's official version, but I'm afraid that Kevin's is completely different."

He gave Michael a brief account of Ryan's version of events and said, "I know that he is your brother-in-law, and there's no better man in a fight, but I fear that Kevin Ryan is becoming too ready to shoot first and think afterwards. What do you think, Michael?"

Michael knew Collins well enough to understand what he was really getting at. While 'The Big Fella' was perfectly happy to arrange assassinations, he liked to keep his assassins under strict control.

"I'd say you're right," he said. "Kevin isn't the same man he was a few years ago, I think that Maureen being killed made him want to kill every British soldier he comes across. And I'd say that he'd be the last man in Ireland that would want to have anything to do with a truce."

Collins agreed. "That's why I want him out of Dublin. He's getting to be too unpredictable, and if he got wind of the fact that we're talking to 'The Castle' about a cease-fire he'd be liable to do something to rash. He certainly won't be the only one to take that view, but Kevin is the one most likely to react violently. So I'm sending him back to Longford. I realise that Sean MacEoin won't like it, but once he and Kevin know that there's going to be some action they might put aside their differences."

Michael felt a pang of disappointment. It seemed ironic that the prospect of talks about a cease-fire should only lead to an increase in the fighting.

***

They walked on in silence until they reached the church. As Michael was about to enter Kevin drew him back. "Jesus, Mick, I didn't know we were going to Mass. I haven't seen the inside of a church since Maureen's funeral. You're not trying to convert me are you? Sure won't the whole place fall down if I walk in the door."

Michael noted that he had failed to cross himself or issue a traditional Irish saying like 'Lord have mercy on her' when mentioning his dead sister's name.

"I told someone that I'd meet him inside," Michael said. He drew a deep breath. "The thing of it is, Kevin, I was kind of hoping that if he turns up you might do me a bit of a favour and take him over to Longford with you."

Kevin gave him a hard look. "Are you telling me that this is something else 'The Big Fella' was keeping from me?"

"Not at all, Kevin," Michael answered. "Between you and me this is personal. I'm trying to help out an old friend who got into a bit of trouble over the water."

"Personal? Christ Mick, what sort of shenanigans are you mixed up in? Who is this fella and what sort of trouble is he in?"

"His name is Pat Coughlin from the County Galway," said Michael seriously. "He was put in jail over there for something he didn't think was a crime. The same way you and me were arrested after the 'Rising. But he broke out and the cops are after him over there, so he wants to come home and join the boys here. And I think that you're the man to show him the ropes."

Michael knew that mention of their internment in 1916 would serve to grab his brother-in-law's attention. They had first met in the Fron-goch internment camp in Wales where the insurgents captured after the failure of the Easter Rising had been imprisoned. Kevin had actually taken part in the fighting but Michael had merely been one of hundreds of completely innocent men and women swept up in the countrywide British reprisals after the rebel surrender in Dublin.

But Kevin was still far from happy. "For God's sake, Mick, you know very well that I haven't the time to train somebody to fight the Brits. Unless he's a good fighting man already he's no use at all to me."

"Ah sure he's a fighting man all right, Kevin," Michael said. "Didn't he fight the Germans and the Turks in the war."

Kevin was incredulous. "He was a bloody British soldier! Jesus Mick, have you lost the little sense you were born with? You can't trust any of the bastards who fought for the Brits in the war. The chances are that he could be a spy."

Michael had been hoping that he would be able to persuade Kevin to take Patrick Coughlin under his wing without telling him the whole story, but he had known that it would be difficult. Now it was impossible, but he was resolved not to disclose any more about Patrick than was absolutely necessary. And it would serve no good purpose to mention Commander Wilson's involvement. He would have to trust Kevin to keep what he did tell him to himself, which, in his brother-in-law's present state of mind, could prove to be problematic. But if he was to help his, and Jack Quinlan's, old friend, he felt that he had to take the risk.

He held Kevin's eyes. "Listen, Kevin," he said. "I'll tell you the whole story, and I'm trusting you not to let on to a single soul no matter who it is. If you do, it'll be the end of me. Do you hear me now?"

Kevin's first instinct was to be indignant that his discretion should be called into question, but he knew Michael well enough to see that he was deadly serious. "All right, Mick, you have my word," he said.

"The truth of it, Kevin, is that Pat Coughlin was one of the Connaught Rangers that mutinied in India. He was given life, but when the Brits brought the prisoners back to England he got away from them. Now he wants to come home and I'm helping him."

"Jesus Christ!" Kevin was dumbstruck. After the mutiny, the Connaught Rangers had achieved hero status in Irish Nationalist circles. "But sure I never heard anything about one of them breaking out of jail."

"No", Michael said. "The Brits are keeping it quiet to save being embarrassed even more than they were during the mutiny itself."

"But why isn't 'The Big Fella' letting the whole world know all about it? Sure this must be a godsend for him?"

Michael knew that this was where he had to be extremely careful. He tried to couch his reply in terms that Kevin would understand. "Michael Collins doesn't know anything about it," he said. "Look at it this way, Kevin, if he got to hear about it, sure wouldn't he have Pat over in America talking about the mutiny and raising money for The Cause. Isn't that what he did to me after Maureen, Lord have mercy on her, was murdered? But that's not what Pat Coughlin wants at all. He didn't go to the trouble of breaking out of jail just to be sent to America to entertain the Yanks with stories about what happened in India. He'd rather join the IRA and fight the Brits so that he can get his own back. Jim Daly, the fella that was executed in India, was his best friend."

Michael's gamble that in his present state of mind his brother-in-law would be far more receptive to talk of action than he would to the concept of propaganda paid off, and Kevin was convinced.

"You're dead right Mick," he said. "Sure a fella like that will be a hundred times more use with a gun in his hand here in Ireland than he would be taking his ease in America. Leave him with me. Sure won't I take him down to Longford and between two of us we'll show them country culshies how to fight."

Michael slapped his brother-in-law on the back. "Good man yourself, Kevin," he said. "But don't let on to Sean MacEoin who Pat is either."

"I'll tell MacEoin nothing," replied Kevin. "But sure there's no need for the pair of us to go to Mass to meet him. You go in and I'll hang around across the road until you come out."

Michael didn't argue: he welcomed the opportunity to talk to Patrick in private before introducing him to Kevin. But that depended on Patrick Coughlin actually turning up. William Quinlan had managed to get a message to Jack to let him know that he had contacted Patrick, and Jack had informed Michael by telegram. But that still left the escapee with the problem of getting to Kingstown on the Saturday night crossing and then making his way to the designated church without being captured. And he'd heard a worrying rumour that a man had been shot by the Auxiliaries at Kingstown that morning.

When he entered the crowded church Mass was well under way, and the congregation were on their feet for the Gospel. He dipped his fingers in the holy water, crossed himself, genuflected towards the altar and joined those worshippers, all men, standing at the back. With a few exceptions the pews were mostly occupied by women and children. At the end of the Gospel the people in the pews sat for the homily while the men at the back remained standing. Having established that Patrick Coughlin was not among them, Michael inched his way forward to search for the fugitive and soon spotted him in the last pew on the opposite side of the aisle. He heaved a sigh of relief and offered a silent prayer of thanks that Patrick had arrived safely back in Ireland.

He turned his attention to the remainder of the Mass. He was aware that since his internment in 1916 he had committed several grievous sins in his work for The Cause, not the least of which had been killing a man and hiding the body in a Kerry bog. The fact that he had killed in defence of not only his own life but also the lives of his future wife and his best friend did nothing to ease his conscience. He knew that one day he would have to seek absolution in the confessional, but for the moment he felt that he could do no better than offer a sincere act of contrition, and a promise to do his best to avoid similar serious transgressions in the future.

It was then time to pray for the soul of his dead wife, and for a peaceful and happy future for his infant son; a future he was convinced could only be made secure when Ireland was at last free.

The congregation stood for the blessing, and then began to file out of the church. As everybody genuflected as they vacated their places and dipped their fingers in the font as they reached the door, there was a considerable crush. In spite of this Michael managed to catch Patrick's eye and make his way over to where the fugitive 'Ranger was waiting.

He greeted the former soldier with a slap on the back and spoke quietly in deference to their surroundings. "It's grand to see that you finally made it home, Pat."

Patrick's first thoughts though were for Michael. "I was sorry to hear from Jack about what happened to your wife, Mick. If it's any consolation at all, I just said one for her along with the one for Jim Daly."

Michael was touched. "Thanks, Pat," was all he could say.

They stood quietly for a moment each lost in their private thoughts.

Patrick eventually broke the silence. "You're a sight for sore eyes, Mick, God knows there were times there when I thought I'd never see Ireland again. And sure if it wasn't for yourself and Jack Quinlan, I wouldn't be here now, that fella Wilson was getting too close to catching me. Did you know that he was waiting at Kingstown when the boat docked this morning? If it wasn't for some poor fella getting shot by the Auxiliaries, I'd be on my way back to jail."

Michael was taken by surprise. "I knew that he was in Dublin, but sure I never thought that he'd come looking for you himself like that. He's no eejit that Commander Wilson, so the sooner we get you well clear of this city the safer you'll be."

He explained what he had arranged with Kevin Ryan and concluded by saying, "Sean MacEoin is one of the best and you can trust him with your life. He knows you're coming from me but he thinks I'm sending you down there to keep an eye on Kevin. The truth is, Pat, that Michael Collins knows nothing at all about this and if he finds out that you're one of the Connaught Rangers he'll have you in America before you know it; and he'll have me up against a wall for not letting on to him about you."

Michael knew that Collins would eventually discover what he was doing, but he hoped that a negotiated truce would be in effect before then.

"Fine, Mick," said Patrick. "But what about this fella, Kevin, does he know all about me?"

"He knows a bit," Michael answered, "but don't tell him any more than you have to. And watch out for him, Kevin is my brother-in-law but I'm afraid all the fighting has gone to his head and the way he is now, he'd shoot you as soon as look at you if he took a notion to. He's waiting for you across the road."

Patrick nodded. "I knew fellas like him during the war."

The church was now almost empty. Michael held out his hand. "I'll see you across the road to meet Kevin but I'll say so long now, Pat, but sure won't we be having a good yarn over a pint along with Jack Quinlan before the year is out."

Patrick hesitated and shuffled his feet in obvious embarrassment. "Jesus Christ, Mick I hate to ask you for another favour, but I wouldn't be here if it wasn't for someone else."

He told Michael about Kate Steele finding him in Dorset and about their journey to Kingstown together. "She was supposed to go back to England on the next boat, but with Wilson turning up and that fella getting shot, anything could have happened to her. She might even be left high and dry in Ireland. I'm still not sure about what her story is, but she stuck her neck out for me when she had no reason to, and I'd like someone to help her out now if she's in trouble because of it."

Michael knew that Patrick would not have asked unless he was deeply concerned about this girl. He remembered the circumstances under which he had first met his wife, Maureen, and resolved to help if he could.

"Leave it to me, Pat," he said, "and I'll let you know what I find out."

"My life on you, Mick Flynn," said Patrick with some feeling. For the first time that morning he grinned. "Jesus, Mick, and there was me thinking that things would be as straight as a rifle barrel as soon as I landed in Ireland. But sure wasn't I the biggest eejit in the world for thinking it; nothing is that simple in Ireland these days."

Michael led him across the street to where Kevin stood. "Here he is Kevin, Private Patrick Coughlin himself," he said. "And sure isn't this your chance to shake hands with a Connaught Ranger."

He left them to it and made his way back to his lodgings with mixed feelings. He was no more comfortable about sending Patrick Coughlin off to fight with someone like Kevin Ryan than he was about Michael Collins planning to mount an operation against British forces as a prelude to truce talks. But helping Patrick was the least he could do for Jack Quinlan. Ryan had probably dismissed the incident by now, but Michael remembered that it was Jack who had saved Kevin's life after the botched IRA ambush in Beaufort.

Chapter 23

Commander Wilson spent the remainder of Sunday checking both the arrivals and departures at Kingstown. He was no longer confident of apprehending Private Coughlin at the port, and he couldn't shake off an uneasy feeling that his bird had flown during the panic caused by the shooting earlier that morning. He had no solid basis for his unease but there were too many things which did not add up; Kate Steele, or Kelly, if indeed that was what she was now called, for instance. He cursed himself for allowing her to get away from him when there were so many questions he needed her to answer.

It was too much to suppose that she was making her way to Beaufort, if that was where she was actually going, for any reason other than to visit the Quinlan family. James Quinlan, the man she had been friendly with at Gretna, was now in America; William Quinlan was on his way to India; so that left only Jack; and Jack, he was now certain, was in contact with Coughlin. That led to the inevitable conclusion that the girl was also somehow involved. In any case the fact that she had run off when he had challenged her certainly meant that she had something to hide. He wondered if having been discovered, she might well decide to abandon whatever scheme had brought her to Ireland and return to England immediately. So he kept up his watch at Kingstown. He waited until the last sailing of the day had left before eventually having to concede that both fugitives had, for the moment at least, managed to give him the slip.

On arriving at Dublin Castle on Monday morning his first task was to telephone the Dorset police. Although they could be reasonably certain that Coughlin had left the area, Wilson asked the inspector to make further enquiries. He wanted to know how the escapee had managed to avoid capture for so long, and he was particularly interested in whether Coughlin could possibly have received any assistance from a young woman called Kate Steele, but she might also be using the name 'Kelly', and he gave the policeman a detailed description of her. The inspector replied that he was pleased to do what Wilson asked, but it would take a little time to complete his enquiries.

Wilson would have liked to return to Beaufort. There were things he needed to clear up with Jack Quinlan and he wanted to return the photograph in person; but he could not leave 'The Castle' in case there were developments in the attempts to arrange cease-fire negotiations. Alfred Cope could be returning from London at any time and until then the Commander was constrained to remain in Dublin. As far as looking for Kate Steele was concerned, however, he did not see any problems attached to arranging a full scale police search for her. An exhaustive and highly visible hunt for her did not have the same problems of security attached as did a similar hunt for Coughlin. As far as he could see, her capture could have no possible bearing on the delicate matter of arranging a cease-fire, and she might be able to shed some light on Coughlin's whereabouts. The only obstacle that Wilson could envisage was a lack of solid evidence, and he hoped that the Dorset police would soon be able to supply that. So for the present all he could do was wait.

Michael Flynn was not tied down by the same constraints. When he left Kevin Ryan and Patrick Coughlin after the Sunday Mass, he started out to return to his lodgings but changed his mind and decided to go to Kingstown instead. There he hoped to find out what had happened to the woman called Kate who had helped Patrick reach Ireland. At the dock he was lucky not to bump into Commander Wilson who was standing by the gangplank, watching passengers going aboard the steamer for Holyhead. It wouldn't do for him to be seen in public with the British security man so he avoided Wilson and asked around the dock workers, who were much more ready to impart information to him than they would be to either Wilson or the police. He soon learned that a young woman had run away from 'the fella watching the ships' and that after finding her way out of the dock area, she had caught a tram into Dublin; but where she went when she got there nobody knew.

Michael realised that once she was in the city, even though she was a complete stranger there, finding her would be next to impossible. He had a detailed description from Patrick, but trying to find her on his own in the crowded city would be akin to looking for a needle in a haystack. And he couldn't enlist 'official' Republican help because that would require him to supply some, at least partially convincing, explanations.

But he still had most of Sunday at his disposal, and it would be at least midday on Monday before he expected to hear anything from Wilson. He had time to travel to Killarney and back to find out if Jack Quinlan knew anything more about who Kate was, and more importantly, what game she was playing. There would not be time to make the complex arrangements necessary for him to go to Beaufort to visit his family and see his son without alerting the Black and Tans, but he knew that Jack would deliver a message to them. He checked the Sunday timetable and sent a wire to Beaufort. Without waiting for a reply he caught the next Killarney train.

They met in the spacious foyer of The Great Southern Hotel which stood opposite the station in Killarney. Michael experienced a deep sense of loss as he went inside. His wife, Maureen, had worked there before they were married and the memories came flooding back. It was, however, the one place in the town where the Black and Tans could not enter at will and throw their weight around in their usual manner. The hotel's clientele consisted of British and American tourists, businessmen and wealthy landowners, all of whom could wield considerable influence and none of whom would take kindly to being harassed by the 'Tans. As the steward at Beaufort House, Jack Quinlan qualified as an acceptable, if not especially welcome, visitor; the hotel management would not run the risk of turning away one of His Lordship's senior employees. It was extremely rare for Jack to take advantage of his position, but today there were extenuating circumstances. They sat and drank tea while he told Michael all he knew about Kate Steele, and gave him William's letter to read.

The letter was mostly concerned with Patrick's refusal to give himself up to Commander Wilson. Jack, however, confided to Michael that he was not at all sure about how strongly William had tried to persuade Coughlin to accept the Commander's offer, but there was nothing that could be done about that now. The only reference to Kate was that William had met her by accident at The Silent Woman Inn, where she had recognised him as James Quinlan's brother. She had also recognised Commander Wilson from the wartime munitions factory and learned that he was searching for Patrick Coughlin. There was nothing to indicate why the girl had decided to become involved.

"According to Pat, the police are after her for something she did over the water," Michael said, "but he doesn't know what it was. She blamed Pat for bringing the cops down on her and making her leave her job at the pub."

It seemed clear to Jack. "So the only reason she helped Pat out was because she had to go on the run herself."

"That's a part of it all right," Michael replied. "She told him that a couple travelling together would be less likely to alert the cops, and as far as Pat is concerned she was right about that. But he thinks there's more to it. She struck him as being the kind of person who is always looking for some sort of excitement and who doesn't stop to think about what sort of trouble it causes."

Jack nodded. "I knew men like that in the war, but I never came across it in a woman. But sure it's easy see how Pat would want us to try and look out for her after the way she gave him a hand. The only thing is, if she's that way inclined God knows what she'll do or where she'll go."

"The last Pat saw of her was Wilson pulling her down out of the way when the 'Auxies' shot some poor fella at Kingstown," said Michael. "I found out since that she ran away from him and went into Dublin on a tram. She could be anywhere in the city now."

Jack sighed. "So, there's nothing at all we can do about it."

"Nothing that I can think of," said Michael. "But here's something else we have to face, Jack. Wilson will be sure to have got the notion that there was something funny about the way she turned up at Kingstown, and after she ran away he'll know for certain that she's up to some kind of shenanigans. He'll check up with the police over in England and when he finds out what they want her for he'll have the RIC after her here. And it won't take him long to put two and two together and start thinking that maybe she has something to do with Pat. If he does that there could be some real trouble."

"How's that?" Jack asked.

"If the RIC start looking for her, Michael Collins will know all about it the minute they start," Michael replied. "And the worst of it is that if Kevin Ryan finds out anything at all about her and gets the notion that Pat Coughlin is friendly with an English girl, he'll think that she's a British spy and I wouldn't put it past him to shoot the pair of them on the spot."

He let Jack think about that for a minute before continuing, "And Wilson might start thinking that maybe you and me know all about her. I'd say that it won't be long before he starts asking questions of us, and it wouldn't do any harm at all to start thinking about some good answers."

They discussed the problem for some time before coming to the conclusion that their best course of action was to tell Wilson the truth, or at least as much as they could without putting Patrick Coughlin in danger of being taken by the authorities. Michael suggested that they should to try and pre-empt any immediate action on Wilson's part by approaching the security man before he had an opportunity of confronting them. He couldn't tell Jack about the proposed moves towards arranging a truce, but he felt that he could persuade Wilson that any inappropriate moves could have an adverse effect on the situation regarding a cease-fire.

Chapter 24

With time on his hands waiting for news from both London and Dorset, Commander Wilson spent all day Monday at Kingstown, again watching the comings and goings of the passengers crossing the Irish Sea to and from Holyhead. In the intervals between arrivals and departures he kept in touch with 'The Castle' by telephone from the Harbour Master's office. He was no longer hopeful of finding either Kate Steele or Private Coughlin, but he nonetheless kept up a watch which inevitably turned out to be fruitless.

The police inspector's call came through on Tuesday morning. It confirmed his suspicions, and relieved him of having to waste any more time at the Kingstown docks.

There had, indeed, been a young woman called Kate Steele who worked as a barmaid at The Silent Woman public house. The inspector's enquiries revealed that she was suspected of having been involved in a series of robberies at a hotel in Bournemouth, and now it appeared that she had absconded from the inn taking a large portion of the previous week's takings with her. Further to this, a girl matching her description had enquired about a man called Quinlan among the Forestry Commission workers engaged in tree planting on the nearby heath. There was, however, no solid evidence that she was in league with the escaped prisoner, Coughlin. But it was enough for Wilson; it was too much of a coincidence to suppose that the Steele girl was not involved with the mutineer. And in any case he now had sufficient evidence to organise a full scale search for her in Ireland.

Before he could begin to set the necessary wheels in motion, however, Alfred Cope returned from London with a tacit agreement from Lloyd George to meet with Michael Collins.

It was raining when Wilson met with Michael Flynn in Phoenix Park. With events now moving forward it was no longer practical for them to travel to Beaufort, so they were forced to adopt a less cautious approach and meet in Dublin. They walked briskly through the park giving the impression of men hurrying about their business and anxious to be in out of the rain. An open tender carrying a squad of Auxiliary Police drove past and for a moment Michael feared that they would stop. If they were questioned it would have put Wilson in the awkward position of having to vouch for Michael. As a member of the security services he would not be required to offer an explanation for meeting Michael Flynn, but the mere fact that they were seen together would in itself constitute a breach of security before the cease-fire negotiations proper had even begun. But the 'Auxies' were soaked to the skin and as anxious as anyone to be in out of the rain.

It took only a few minutes for Wilson to give Michael the news that Alfred Cope was now prepared to meet with Michael Collins at a venue of Collins' choosing, but with one proviso: it had to be clearly understood that Collins would be considered to be representing Sinn Fein, because at this juncture, the Prime Minister would not risk allowing Cope to negotiate with the IRA. Cope had also stressed that word of the meeting must not be allowed to reach the ears of the Unionists in the North who would be incensed at the thought of a British official talking to the Nationalists under any guise whatsoever. Lloyd George's Liberal/Conservative coalition needed Unionist support to survive, and alienating the Unionist faction risked bringing down the British Government.

It was not ideal but Michael thought, and fervently hoped, that Collins would consider it to be at least a starting point.

Before Wilson left to return to 'The Castle', Michael decided that this would be a good opportunity to raise the subject of Patrick Coughlin and the woman who had helped him escape. If the weather could provide cover for his 'official' meeting with the British security man, it could equally well provide cover for a more personal one.

"Maybe you could spare a minute to talk about the Connaught Ranger who escaped, Commander," he said.

Wilson stopped in his tracks and turned to Michael. "What do you know about that?" he asked sharply. "Have you been talking to Mister Quinlan?"

"I have so," Michael answered.

Wilson was aghast. If Michael Flynn knew about the escape then Michael Collins would almost certainly know and the IRA would be handed an excellent propaganda opportunity prior to any cease-fire negotiations.

He showed a rare moment of anger. "Damn Quinlan," he said with uncharacteristic anger. "I had a feeling that he has been looking for Coughlin. His Lordship asked me if Quinlan could discuss it with you and I have been considering it. But I'm surprised to learn that he has seen fit to talk to you before I came to a decision."

Michael looked the Commander straight in the eye. "That may be, Commander, but the only reason Jack Quinlan set out to find Pat Coughlin was to persuade him to accept your offer and he had to do it while his brother was home for Christmas. He asked me for my opinion and I agreed with him. We didn't think that there was much chance of Pat taking any notice of us, but we had to try. Jack has a letter from Bill to prove that, and he'll show it to you if that's what you have in mind."

Wilson considered this and it served to calm him down. "All the same," he said, "the secret is out now and I suppose Collins knows all about it."

"Michael Collins knows nothing at all about it, Commander," Michael told him. "And I hope to God he doesn't find out, or my life won't be worth tuppence for keeping it from him."

The Commander had by now learned enough about the way the Irish Nationalist movement operated to recognise the risk Michael was taking, and in other circumstances would have commended him for it. It helped him to regain his composure.

"I know that Coughlin has reached Ireland and I suppose you know precisely where in the country he is now."

"I do so," said Michael.

"But you won't tell me, will you?"

"No, Commander."

"You realise that I could, and probably should, have you arrested for this, Mr Flynn?"

"Sure don't I know very well that you could Commander, but I don't think that you will," Michael answered.

Wilson didn't pursue the matter, but he made a mental note to warn Alfred Cope about the nature of the people he would be negotiating with. To use an Irish expression he had picked up, they were certainly far from being 'eejits'.

There was, however, one thing still bothering him: "I find it difficult to understand how Quinlan and his brother managed to find Coughlin when the mutineer managed to evade the English police for so long."

Michael saw no point in holding anything back. "Pure luck, Commander," he answered. "Jack asked his brother to look for Pat, but sure they had no luck at all until a girl in a pub recognised Bill. She knew Jim Quinlan at the munitions factory, and when she recognised yourself from there as well, she knew that something was up. Bill took a chance and asked her to keep an eye out for Pat Coughlin and she got the notion that he might be working with a gang planting trees. It turned out that she was right."

Wilson again showed some alarm and interrupted Michael's account of how Coughlin had been found. "So she knows who Coughlin is and what he's guilty of. I find it hard to believe that of an English girl who worked in munitions during the war."

"No," said Michael, "she knows nothing at all about him. Bill Quinlan didn't let on to her who Pat really was, and Pat didn't tell her anything himself because he didn't entirely trust her. He thought that she might be working for you. All he knows about her is that she was on the run from the police over the water and she persuaded him that they would be safer running together. But he has no more idea about what the police want with her than she knows about what you want with him."

"Well, at least that's something," Wilson said. "She's wanted in connection with some robberies at a hotel where she worked, and she stole some money from that public house in Dorset. So as long as she doesn't realise who Coughlin is I can get the Irish police to mount a search for her and return her to England to face trial."

Michael nodded. "It's true that the safest place for her would be in jail over the water, Commander. An English girl on her own in Ireland will stand out like a sore thumb. Nobody will trust her and she won't have a friend in the world. But if you turn the RIC loose to look for her, Michael Collins will know all about it inside of five minutes, and he'll wonder what's causing all the ructions. Because it's an English girl they're after he'll get the notion that there is something queer about the whole thing and he'll start looking for her himself. And make no mistake about it he has a far better chance of finding her than the RIC. When he catches her she'll tell him about you and Jack Quinlan and more to the point, about Patrick Coughlin. He'll know about Pat from when he was arrested in Killarney, and then the game will be over."

Wilson thought about this and had to concede that Michael had a point. "So what do you suggest?"

"The best thing would be for us to find her ourselves if we can, but I have no idea where she is. She went into Dublin city when she ran away from you but sure she could be anywhere in the whole of Ireland by now."

Wilson remembered what Kate had said to him at Kingstown. "I think that there is a chance she might be making for Beaufort," he said. "She mentioned that it was where her husband came from and that's when I knew that she was lying to me."

"If you think there's any chance of that I'll send a wire to Jack to look out for her. But the first thing is to tell Michael Collins what Mr Cope has to say."

Commander Wilson was left with something of a dilemma: his duty required him to do everything he could to recapture Private Coughlin, and as an officer in the Royal Navy with little sympathy for mutineers, it was a duty he was keen to carry out. After what he had just heard, he was sure that questioning the Steele girl could help him achieve this goal, but acting too hastily could put the possibility of obtaining a cease-fire in jeopardy; or, at least, seriously undermine the British position in the delicate negotiations that would eventually have to take place. He realised that Michael Flynn had cleverly manipulated the situation and left him with little choice.

"Do that," he said eventually. "I can wait for a few days before I alert the police. Now perhaps we can get in out of this diabolical weather."

Michael laughed. "Ah sure a small drop of Irish rain never did anybody any harm, Commander."

***

Kate Steele was not overly concerned when the landlady at the Dublin lodging house where she had stayed for the last two nights asked her to leave. Neighbours were beginning to enquire about the English girl and questions were being asked about who she was, and what she was doing in Dublin. As a result, it would not be long before some of 'the boys' began to show an interest and the last thing the woman wanted was to arouse their curiosity. Although the money from renting the room was welcome, Miss Steele would have to go.

Two days previously, on the tram into Dublin, the shock of the shooting at the docks and the flight from Wilson had gradually given way to a sense of excitement at the prospect of exploring an unknown 'foreign' city. Kate knew little about Ireland; it was merely a part of Britain with a rather violent history that she vaguely remembered from her schooldays and what she had picked up from the Irishmen at the munitions factory. She had never been one for keeping up with the latest world news in the newspapers, but she remembered how friendly and boisterous the navvies had been, and felt a thrill at renewing acquaintance with more people of a similar disposition. It did not take long for the excitement to wear off.

The day was cold and damp and the gloom of the weather seemed to pervade the city; in the main streets the great Georgian buildings seemed grey and lifeless. It was Sunday and there were few people about on the streets. She noticed that their mood seemed to match the weather. The few who did extend a friendly greeting became withdrawn when they heard her West of England accent. In the café where she had lunch she was served with politeness but her attempts at making conversation were not met with any marked enthusiasm. Much more to her consternation, though, was the number of policemen in evidence on the streets. She found it impossible to avoid them, and unlike the police she was familiar with in England, they were all heavily armed. And there were also small lorries loaded with heavily armed men in strange uniforms driving past at regular intervals. As dusk began to settle the sound of gunfire and explosions could be heard and she suddenly knew why the people acted the way they did. She realised that this was a city at war. It frightened her and she began to worry about what to do next. Her first thought was to go back to Kingstown and return to England, but she was afraid that Commander Wilson would still be there in search of Patrick Coughlin, and now he would be on the lookout for her too. That posed a real difficulty because if she was to go back to England she would have to go quickly; by Monday it would become perfectly clear to the innkeeper that she had no intention of returning to her job at The Silent Woman, and that she had not deposited the money in the Wareham bank. Given that the English police would have been alerted by Commander Wilson, they could well be waiting for her at Holyhead.

She decided that she would have to stay in Ireland for some time to allow things to settle down, and although she was not happy about it, she realised that she had to remain in Dublin until she could learn more about this strange country she found herself stranded in. She knew the names of a few places in Ireland, including Beaufort, but she had little or no idea where any of them were in relation to Dublin.

Having made up her mind to stay in the city she needed to find some lodgings. She still had most of the money stolen from innkeeper at The Silent Woman, but it would not last long if she were to stay in expensive hotels. She plucked up the courage to enquire at the information office at a large railway station about possible lodgings and was given several addresses and directions on how to find them. She chose one in the suburb of Clontarf which, according to a map she obtained at the station, was on the other side of Dublin Bay from Kingstown and, she thought, would be far enough from the city to be safe from Wilson. She took a tram and managed to locate the address.

Much to her relief the landlady was quite friendly and agreed to let her have a room for a week.

After a restless night spent listening to the sounds of gunfire interspersed by dull explosions, some of them disturbingly close, she ventured back into the city on Monday morning. The streets were busier and the shops were open and her mood lightened. She asked at a bookshop and was advised to purchase a Michelin Guide with maps and general information on Ireland, enough to help her formulate a plan. Her second night in Clontarf was more restful and she looked forward to exploring more of the sights of Dublin; but the rain which had helped Commander Wilson and Michael Flynn to meet in relative secrecy also put a damper on her plans for sightseeing, and she spent the afternoon in a cinema.

She returned to Clontarf where her landlady broke the news that she wanted her out in the morning. Kate was not overly perturbed: her confidence had returned and she had decided on a plan of action.

Chapter 25

Although in late January there was little to occupy the steward at Beaufort House, Jack Quinlan still had some essential duties to perform and couldn't afford to spend all his time at Killarney railway station waiting for a girl he didn't know, and who might not even be on her way there. He knew that she had not turned up in Beaufort but she could easily have reached Killarney without him being aware of her arrival. Jack agreed with Michael Flynn that she was probably heading his way and, if that were true, to get to Beaufort from Dublin she would first have to travel to Killarney by train. So he spent as much time as he could spare in and around the station on the lookout for Kate Steele and desperately trying not to appear too conspicuous.

As he waited he went over in his mind the events of the previous evening when he had again been questioned by Commander Wilson about his part in Private Coughlin's success in reaching Ireland. Jack gave the Commander the letter he had received from William to back up his argument that, with Michael Flynn's help, he had tried to persuade Coughlin to accept the offer of a quiet return to prison as an alternative to being hunted down and having his death sentence reinstated. Wilson merely glanced at it before handing it back, grateful for the fact that it had not been necessary for him to demand to see it. He asked about the girl, Kate Steele, and was satisfied that Jack knew no more about her than what was in William's letter, and what his other brother, James, had told him about knowing her at the Gretna factory. Jack agreed with Michael Flynn that the safest place for Kate Steele would be in prison in England, and told Wilson so. But he knew that before she was sent back 'across the water' the security man would want to question her about Patrick Coughlin. And Jack felt that he still had a duty to look out for his old friend. The Commander sensed this and he decided that Quinlan was merely caught up in something beyond his control, and he could not help but feel some respect for the way the His Lordship's steward was dealing with the situation.

Wilson returned the photograph, and asked Jack to thank his mother for lending it to him. Although he knew that it was a waste of time, and not feeling at all happy about having to ask someone to 'inform', he warned Jack that if he received any further information, especially from Michael Flynn, it was his duty to pass it on.

The mention of Michael Flynn caused Jack a moment of anxiety: "What about Mick, Commander?" he asked. "What will happen to him, will he be arrested?"

"No," Wilson answered, "at least not by me. I've reached the opinion that if we go around locking up people like Flynn we shall never see an end to this war."

To Jack's relief Wilson was called back to Dublin before he could arrange his own watch for Kate Steele in Killarney. He returned to the railway station where he was further relieved to find that it was not Kate Steele who got off the next Dublin train to arrive, but Michael Flynn. They spoke briefly; just long enough for Michael to explain what he had in mind regarding the English girl, assuming they found her before Commander Wilson did. Jack nodded and went back to Beaufort, but agreed to return that evening. In the meantime Michael kept watch on the station from the safety of the Great Southern Hotel.

***

When forced to leave her lodgings in Clontarf, Kate decided to spend one more day in Dublin. Then she would go to Beaufort. She was aware that since their meeting at Kingstown, Commander Wilson would suspect that she would try to go to the village in Kerry and he might well be waiting for her there as he had for Patrick Coughlin at Kingstown; and by now he would certainly have alerted the English police. But she clung to the hope that by delaying her trip for another day he might think that she had returned to England. In her heart, she knew that her safest course of action was to do just that, and when she looked up all the possible crossings she thought that the easiest place for her to evade the police was Fishguard in Wales. From what she had seen so far it seemed that the Irish police had no interest in her whatsoever; they were she thought, fully occupied with what the Irish euphemistically called 'The Troubles'. So she managed to convince herself that for the moment, at least, it was safer for her to remain in Ireland. And besides, she had started something with Patrick Coughlin that she was determined to see it through to whatever conclusion it might eventually lead her to.

She counted up the stolen cash she had left and found that there was enough to buy some new clothes, including a coat, to confuse any description of her that Wilson might have circulated. And she decided to treat herself to a night in one of Dublin's better hotels.

Staying at the Dublin hotel brought back memories of the hotel in Bournemouth, and of the excitement generated by being involved in stealing from the guests. Since her dramatic arrival in Ireland, Kate had, for the first time since her flight from Bournemouth, to face the fact that she might eventually have to pay for her crimes. It was becoming more and more difficult to keep ahead of the police, and while she realised that this was largely her own fault for getting involved with Patrick Coughlin, she did not for one minute regret what she had done. Thoughts of Bournemouth inevitably brought with them thoughts of Mark, her former partner-in-crime, who was still in prison and would remain there for some time yet. It was also inevitable that she soon found herself comparing him with Patrick Coughlin, and it was clear that Mark did not stand up at all favourably when viewed alongside the Irishman.

Kate realised that the basic difference between the two men concerned their respective attitudes to life and how it should be lived. It had taken very little time after they first met for her to recognise that to Mark she was merely a means to an end, but he had brought some much needed excitement into her life and she had accepted him for what he was. Now that he was gone she had no regrets. Patrick Coughlin was, however, a man much harder to understand; his sole purpose in life was not simple self-satisfaction. No, to Kate it was evident that he cared deeply about something other than his own selfish desires, something which seemed to mean more to him than life itself. Whether he was driven by loyalty to a person or to an ideal she was not sure, but there was certainly something deep inside him that would not allow him to think only of himself. And it was certainly of greater significance than stealing from rich hotel guests. She might have thought that he, too, had used her, and that she had simply supplied him with a means of reaching Ireland, but she knew that this wasn't entirely true. With hindsight she realised that, in spite of his rough and often rude manner, there had been occasions during their brief time together when he had shown a genuine concern for her personal wellbeing, certainly more than anything she had ever experienced during the months spent with the glib, smooth-talking Mark.

On the train to Killarney she saw further evidence of the war going on in Ireland when they passed close by a thatched cottage with the roof ablaze. Men in uniform and carrying rifles were holding back an obviously angry crowd of country people. One woman broke through the cordon and ran towards the house, only to be clubbed to the ground by a rifle butt. There were angry mutterings among the other passengers and Kate was left in no doubt that the burning cottage belonged to the poor woman who had been knocked down. It had a sobering effect and, not for the first time since her dramatic arrival at Kingstown, she saw further evidence that Patrick Coughlin had not been exaggerating when he described Ireland as a 'dangerous place'. She had to admit that she had been much too hasty in thinking that he had simply been trying to get rid of her; instead, he had been genuinely concerned for her safety and she was beginning to understand why.

But the urge to seek adventure soon re-surfaced and the thought of the dangers involved were swiftly banished by the prospect of the excitement that remaining in Ireland offered; if only she could find Patrick Coughlin again.

He was still on her mind when the train arrived in Killarney, and when she saw the man in the long raincoat and trilby hat standing among the travellers on the platform she thought for a moment that it was him. When he approached her she felt a moment of anxiety but then realised that he was a complete stranger and admonished herself for worrying about nothing. He seemed not to notice her and started to walk past. Suddenly he bumped into her as if jostled by someone; he gripped her arm and forced her to walk along the platform beside him. She tried to break away but couldn't.

"Don't worry, Miss Steele, I mean you no harm," he said quietly. "I'm a friend of Patrick Coughlin's."

Kate was so taken completely by surprise that she couldn't think of anything to say. She allowed him to lead her out of the station and into the large hotel which stood opposite. Once inside The Great Southern, in the familiar surroundings of a large hotel, she recovered some of her composure.

"Who are you and why have you brought me here?"

"Sure didn't I tell you that I'm a friend of Pat's," Michael Flynn replied. "Sit down now, Miss Steele, and we'll have a cup of tea and I'll tell you a bit more. And for God's sake keep your voice down: there are people around here who'd see the both of us dead if they heard a single wrong word."

He led her to a quiet corner of the spacious foyer, sat her down and ordered tea from a passing waitress. Kate noted that he addressed the waitress by her Christian name and worked out that he must be a local man. While her surprise had abated, her curiosity had risen, and something about this man she had never met told her that he meant her no harm.

"Now, will you tell me who you are and why you were waiting for me at the station. And another thing, how did you know who I was?"

Michael waited until their tea was delivered. He looked her in the eyes and spoke quietly but firmly. "I'm not going to let on to you who I am, Miss Steele, because to tell you the truth from the way you've been carrying on I'm afraid that it might be more than my life is worth. I knew you at the station because from the cut of you any eejit could see that you're no Irish girl. And sure maybe you'd rather it was Commander Wilson and a squad of policemen who were waiting for you."

Michael could see that his words had struck home. Before she could say anything he went on. "I'm thankful for the way you helped Pat out, but it's time for you to get it into your thick English head that you're mixed up in something that could easily get a lot of people killed, including yourself. Haven't you seen anything at all since you landed in Ireland? And why in the name of God didn't you go back to England like Pat told you?"

"I couldn't go back because the police are looking for me there," Kate replied, still trying to maintain a defiant air.

"I know all about you and the hotel over the water, and about the money you stole from the pub, too." He noted Kate's startled look. "But sure I haven't the time to be thinking about that now. I'm not joking when I say that the safest place for you would be in the jail in England, and the biggest favour I could do you would be to hand you over to Commander Wilson. But you helped Pat Coughlin out and I'll help you in return, but only if I have your solemn promise that you'll do exactly what I tell you. Otherwise you're on your own."

By now Kate was in no doubt that for the moment, at least, she had bitten off more than she could reasonably expect to chew. She found herself believing every word this man said. She was in trouble, and although she couldn't yet fathom exactly what kind of trouble, she knew it was serious. But even so she felt her pulse race at the thought, and she decided that her only immediate option was to trust this man who claimed to be a friend of Patrick Coughlin's and who seemed to know so much about her.

"Well, Kate?" Michael said kindly. "What's it to be?"

"I'll do as you say," Kate answered. "There's just one thing I would like to know first, when will I be able to see Patrick again?"

"Not for a while," Michael answered. "You have to understand that Pat is in the middle of this war we're fighting to make Ireland free. He's in a lot more danger than the rest of us and sure you're not helping him one bit by running after him. If you do something stupid or say the wrong word in the wrong place, he could be captured by the Black and Tans, and that means he'll be dead. I'm not trying to frighten you, Kate, you were a friend of Jim Quinlan's and his father too, over there in Scotland, so I'm only trying to tell you the truth. If it ever came out that you caused Pat Coughlin to be taken or killed, you'd have the IRA after you. And believe me, they'd find you wherever you tried to hide. And then you could forget about the police; with these fellas there's no jail, no trial, no judge, no jury, just a bullet in the head and a bog hole for a grave."

Michael may not have deliberately set out to frighten Kate, but for the first time in Ireland she felt genuinely scared, not as yet, however, frightened enough to abandon all hope of finding Patrick again. Agreeing to go along with Michael Flynn seemed to offer the best chance of achieving that goal.

"What do you want me to do?" she asked.

"Just sit tight here for a while," Michael said. "A fella will come in looking for you. He'll travel on the night train with you as far as Mallow and from there you'll have to go on to Dublin on your own. When you get to the city in the morning, go to this address and wait there until you hear from me. They'll look after you all right there."

Kate looked at the slip of paper and put it in her coat pocket. "But why can't I travel to Dublin by myself?" she wanted to know. "If you're worried about whether I get on the train you needn't be. You've made my position quite clear, believe me."

For the first time since they met Michael smiled. "Sure wasn't it yourself that said that two people travelling together was the best way to avoid suspicion. He'd go all the way to Dublin with you but he can't."

"So if we have to wait here until this man comes we might as well drink some of this tea before it goes completely cold," she said.

"No," Michael said, "I'll have to trust you to wait on your own. I've been spending too much time hanging around Killarney, and if I'm not careful, the 'Tans will have me."

He left and Kate sat by herself, her brain still trying to assimilate what had happened over the last few days. For a brief moment she entertained the thought that she could say to hell with them all and simply walk out, but she knew that she wouldn't. She believed every word that the man had said about the perilous situation she was in, but it was what he had said about her putting Patrick in mortal danger that had sunk in deepest.

When the other man hurried in to fetch her she recognised him instantly as a member of the Quinlan family, and she stood to greet him.

"You must be Jack," she said. "You look very much like your brothers."

"Come on, Kate," Jack said, "we'll have to run to get the Dublin train."

She picked up her bag and followed him.

Chapter 26

The little village of Clonfin was on the road from Granard to Balinalee in County Longford, and was situated at roughly the half-way point between the two. Just below Clonfin, a stone bridge carried the unpaved road over a stream and this bridge marked the spot chosen by Sean MacEoin for the ambush. It was a site that any competent military strategist would have recognised as an excellent choice of ground. Surrounded by a landscape made up of small fields bordered by thick hedges and stone walls, it was a sparsely populated area dotted with a few small, thatched whitewashed farmhouses. The hedges and walls would give adequate cover, and the nearby Clonfin Woods provided a concealed assembly point and an easy escape route. With the weather being unseasonably mild and uncharacteristically dry, everything was in place for a classic IRA action against the forces of The Crown.

With his first meeting with Alfred Cope now definitely arranged, Michael Collins was keen for action against the British forces to be stepped up in order to remind the government in London that the Irish still had plenty of fight left in them. But this would no longer be the single spectacular raid Collins had first discussed with Michael Flynn. There had recently been a subtle change in Nationalist strategy when Collins, in conjunction with the IRA leadership in Dublin, had decided that in future, large scale attacks on police and army barracks were to be replaced by smaller but more frequent raids and ambushes. These tactics would be less wasteful of precious resources of arms and ammunition, not to mention men, and would prove to be equally effective in giving the authorities the run-around.

The loudest dissenting voice in the discussions was that of Eamonn de Valera, who advocated combining the existing Flying Columns into a large single force, and fighting a series of pitched battles in an effort to end the war once and for all. He argued that such an army would prove too strong for even the combined strength of the RIC, the Black and Tans and the Auxiliary Police. Such an enemy force would be sorely hampered by their vastly different tactics and command structures. If the IRA struck quickly, and in large numbers, they would also be more than a match for any units the regular British Army, scattered in bases throughout Ireland, could put into the field at short notice. It was evident to Collins and others that 'Dev' had little idea of the reality of the situation on the ground, and that the 'army' he proposed could never be properly equipped. Collins won the day, but the argument served to widen the rift forming between him and de Valera.

In County Longford, Sean MacEoin's local intelligence system alerted him to the fact that an army patrol was expected to pass through Clonfin on the morning of February 1st 1921, and he made plans to ambush them. Among the twenty-three men assembled to carry out the ambush were Kevin Ryan and Patrick Coughlin.

In truth, MacEoin would have preferred not to have selected either of these men for the action, but he feared that leaving the volatile Ryan out would probably cause more trouble than including him, and he had to concede that the Dublin man was more than useful in a fight. As far as Coughlin was concerned, MacEoin felt that there were still some questions to be answered; but he now knew the story of how Patrick had come to be in his command, and felt that the escaped Connaught Ranger deserved at least one chance to prove himself.

It was unusual for someone totally unknown and unproven to be immediately accepted into an IRA Flying Column, but Patrick Coughlin came with excellent references. MacEoin knew and respected Michael Flynn and the Kerry county councillor's word was good enough for him. There was also the fact that Coughlin seemed to be well-known to Kevin Ryan, and MacEoin knew that if Ryan had the slightest suspicion about the newcomer he would have shot Coughlin out of hand. For his part, the military astute former

Connaught Ranger immediately recognised in MacEoin the qualities of a true leader of men. It was soon evident, however, that the members of the Column had little or no time for Ryan and as such, were not overly disposed to befriend him, so rather than risk any problems with morale he decided to confide in their leader.

MacEoin's first reaction to Patrick's story was to urge him to return to Dublin and speak with Michael Collins. When Coughlin, however, explained that he had not escaped from British hands merely to be sent to America as a propaganda tool, the IRA man nodded his understanding and agreed, for the moment at least, to keep the news of the 'Ranger's escape to himself. But while he was content for Patrick to remain as a member of his Flying Column, he needed some further reassurances before he was prepared to risk including him in the forthcoming ambush. He was satisfied that someone who had fought with 'The Devil's Own', as the Connaught Rangers were known, could prove to be a valuable addition to his meagre force; yet he was not convinced that a man who had served all over the world as a soldier in the British Army would be ready and willing to fire on fellow regulars.

Now that he had safely reached Ireland and there was time to reflect, it was a question Patrick Coughlin had also begun to ask of himself; and when MacEoin openly posed the question, Patrick answered that whatever his personal feeling might be, he had come to Ireland to finish what his friend, James Daly, had started and it was too late to turn back now.

After some thought, MacEoin decided to include the newcomer in the ambush party as his personal runner, and not simply as a convenient way of keeping an eye on him; he felt that Patrick's experience might be invaluable and so wanted him close at hand.

In the event neither Coughlin nor MacEoin needed to question Patrick's willingness to fire on British soldiers. MacEoin's intelligence had, for once, let him down and instead of British regulars it was two lorries carrying a strong detachment of Auxiliaries, generally considered to be much tougher opponents than either regular soldiers or Black and Tans, who drove into the IRA ambush. And

Patrick, remembering the man shot down at Kingstown, had no compunction about opening fire on them.

As the Auxiliaries reached the bridge a bomb was detonated which overturned the first lorry, killed the driver and blocked the road. The second skidded to a halt; the men inside jumped out and took cover under the stalled vehicles and on the bridge itself. The battle which developed lasted for close to two hours and for the first hour or so involved both sides sniping at each other. Although equal in number and better armed and equipped than the IRA, the Auxiliaries were completely pinned down on the bridge and under the lorries. MacEoin's men were so competently positioned that in order to make a break for the open countryside, the encircled British would have to venture onto the open road where they would be caught in a murderous crossfire. And, even if they survived that and made it into the fields, they could still be seen by several more IRA riflemen. Regular soldiers would have recognised the hopelessness of their position and given up, but the 'Auxies', fearing that their history of excesses against the local population would attract severe reprisals, continued to hold out. MacEoin, knowing that he held the upper hand was content to wait, and Patrick Coughlin, lying beside the IRA leader, voiced his approval of the tactic.

On the far side of the road, however, one man did not agree. As the siege wore on and the sniping continued, Kevin Ryan was becoming more and more impatient waiting for something more decisive to happen. As his frustration grew, he began to openly criticise MacEoin's tactics and tried to persuade the nearest IRA men to charge the Auxiliary position with him. They completely ignored him, although they too were beginning to feel the strain. One man, who had clearly heard enough, told the rebellious Ryan at rifle point that if he didn't shut up he'd shoot him instead of the 'Auxies'. The North Longford Brigade obviously had total confidence in their leader, a fact which only served to increase Ryan's already intense dislike of MacEoin; and seeing the Column commander apparently taking Patrick Coughlin into his confidence caused the Dublin man to extend the range of his anger to include the former Connaught Ranger. And he was prepared to let everyone around know it. The man who had threatened him suggested that if he wasn't satisfied with the way things were being done, he should go and tell MacEoin to his face; and Ryan decided to do just that.

During the next lull in the shooting he called out that he was coming across the road and wanted covering fire. Without waiting for a reply he broke cover and made a dash across the open road. The rest of the IRA men had little choice but to give him covering fire and by some miracle he made it to where MacEoin and Coughlin knelt behind a dry stone wall. In the confusion, however, one of the Auxiliaries saw his chance and made a bid for freedom. Before any of the attacking force could react and shoot him down, he had dashed down the road, into the fields and was lost from sight behind the hedges. Coughlin and two others gave chase but he got clean away and set off to summon British reinforcements.

MacEoin was livid and Coughlin could understand why: his carefully thought out plan was now in tatters. When Ryan again began to shout the odds and label the entire Flying Column and their leader as 'useless bloody country culshies', MacEoin had two of his men disarm the rebel and effectively placed him under arrest. He told Ryan in no uncertain terms that if he caused any further trouble, he would have him shot. In any case, he promised the hothead, he would deal with him later for placing the whole IRA operation in jeopardy.

With the certainty of British reinforcements arriving, something he estimated would take them less than an hour, MacEoin called a council of war of his senior lieutenants and invited Coughlin to attend. The leader spelled out the alternatives: either they had to mount a serious assault to finish off the trapped Auxiliaries or force them to surrender, or they had to abandon the ambush here and now. A direct assault would prove extremely costly in Irish as well as British lives, so there seemed to be little choice but to pack up and go home.

It was then that the experienced Coughlin had an idea. It occurred to him that if the escaped 'Auxie' could have managed to disappear from sight so quickly after gaining the shelter of the fields, a few men should also be able to approach undetected by the same route and outflank the British position. MacEoin agreed that it was worth a try and detailed three men to accompany the former Connaught Ranger.

They started from a point well away from the ambush site and carefully tried to follow the exact route taken by the escaping 'Auxie'. As they neared their objective MacEoin and his men intensified their sniping to cover them. Coughlin's plan worked to such an extent that they reached a point where they had a clear view of a group of the British defenders sheltering behind the opposite parapet of the bridge and opened fire on them. Several on the Auxiliaries were hit, one of them being the officer in charge who was killed outright. With their commander dead, and not knowing whether their comrade had reached safety and summoned reinforcements, the Auxiliaries finally gave up. They had suffered twelve casualties with four men dead and eight wounded. One man on the Irish side had also died and three had been hurt.

Many of the IRA men, remembering the terror tactics of the Auxiliaries, were all set to assault the prisoners but were prevented from doing so by MacEoin. He insisted that they be treated humanely, and ordered some men to fetch water for the British wounded and make them as comfortable as possible. He went so far as to congratulate the Auxiliaries for putting up such a worthy fight. This kind of behaviour was most unusual from either side in the Irish War of Independence where the niceties of The Geneva Convention were rarely, if ever, observed.

It proved to be too much for Kevin Ryan. He broke away from the men holding him, grabbed a rifle and aimed it at one of the prisoners. Patrick Coughlin grabbed him from behind and the shot went wide. Then Coughlin swung Ryan around, hit him on the jaw and knocked him cold.

Before anyone could do anything else one of the IRA men watching the road raised the alarm: British reinforcements were approaching rapidly and in force. MacEoin's concern for the British wounded had almost cost him dearly, but the Flying Column managed to gain the safety of Clonfin Woods and make their escape. They got away with eighteen rifles, twenty revolvers, a Lewis gun and eight hundred rounds of ammunition. British reprisals after the ambush resulted in several farms being burned by the 'Auxies' and one farmer being killed.

After the ambush, MacEoin sent for Patrick Coughlin to tell him that his action had saved the day for the IRA and to thank him for his help. He also told Patrick that there would no longer be any doubt about his willingness to fight for The Cause. But the success of the ambush had raised a problem: he had to send a detailed report to the IRA command in Dublin and he felt that Coughlin should be given credit for his part in the victory, otherwise the report would not be complete. But that would involve exposing Coughlin's secret, and MacEoin was not about to do that without first discussing it with Patrick.

For his part Patrick was certainly not looking for glory, but he had seen enough of MacEoin to know that the Flying Column commander would want to make sure that his report on the action was completely accurate. Something that was, to say the least, unusual in a leader with no formal military training whatsoever.

On a personal level, now that he had seen action, Patrick felt that he had at least partially achieved his objective in escaping and reaching Ireland, and he had done something to honour the memory of James Daly. And having had an opportunity to reflect, he thought it time to consider those who had helped him: knowing more about the real situation made him realise that Michael Flynn in particular had taken some serious risks in putting him in touch with MacEoin. Then there was Kate Steele. To his surprise, Patrick found that he actually cared about what had happened to her.

He told MacEoin that he was free to complete his report as he felt he should, but asked if he could arrange a meeting for him with Michael Flynn before he sent it in. He owed it to Michael to make sure that he was pre-warned.

Sean MacEoin's conduct at Clonfin gained him widespread praise, especially in the United States, where the Irish Republican propaganda machine swung into action; he even received grudging respect from the British Army.

Kevin Ryan, however, got away from Longford and went back to Dublin vowing vengeance on both Sean MacEoin and Patrick Coughlin.

Chapter 27

"You're an extremely lucky man that things have turned out as well as they have, Michael." The speaker was Michael Collins and he was seated with Michael Flynn in the parlour of one of 'The Big Fella's' many secret retreats in Dublin.

"But you know very well that you should have informed me the moment you learned about the escape of one of the Connaught Rangers," he added some severity to his words.

Michael had delivered Sean MacEoin's completed report on the ambush at Clonfin, and had explained in detail how Patrick Coughlin had come to be involved in the action. He had held nothing back and included the parts played by himself, Commander Wilson, the Quinlan brothers and Kate Steele.

"I can see that now," he told Collins, "but at the time things looked a lot different. When I heard about Pat's escape I couldn't do anything except wait and see whether the Quinlans could find him. When they did, sure wasn't he dead set on joining the fight for Ireland with a gun in his hand and trying to somehow honour the memory of his friend, Jim Daly. He went to so much trouble escaping from the British and making his way back home that I couldn't deny him at least the one chance, and I knew that Sean MacEoin would be the man to show him the ropes."

Collins gave him a quizzical look. "And I don't suppose that you thought for one minute about the valuable propaganda opportunity the escape of a Connaught Ranger would provide us with."

"I did," Michael answered truthfully, "and I said as much to Pat. But he wasn't keen on being used as a propaganda tool; all he wanted was to join in the real fight. And with Wilson involved and the talks with your man Cope on the cards, I decided that it might be better to keep Pat's escape as quiet as I could for a while."

Collins stood up as if to add emphasis to his words. "Ah yes, I can see how the thought of disrupting a possible cease-fire would be foremost in your mind. But these decisions are not yours to take, Michael. We are having enough trouble trying to carry on this war against the British without having people running around following their own agendas."

He paced round the room and went on. "And I must say, Michael, that you seem to be taking this desire for a peaceful solution too much to heart. It's beginning to cloud your judgement. You must realise that rushing into a cease-fire without properly considering every single detail would, in the end, do more harm than good. We could easily lose everything we have gained so far. If we fail to achieve freedom this time, all we will be doing is leaving it to the next generation of Irishmen to try and win it for our children in yet another bloody fight with the British."

He resumed his seat, allowed his words to sink in, then modified his tone. "We will leave it at that for now. Over the last few years you have been of great service to The Cause and suffered a great deal for it, but please remember that unless we pull together we will never achieve freedom."

"Point taken," Michael said.

Collins nodded. "I sincerely hope so," he said.

Michael realised that he had been extremely lucky not to have incurred 'The Big Fella's' wrath. Had things not turned out as they had, he might easily have suffered the fate he had warned Kate Steel could befall her. He suspected that holding nothing back and telling Collins the whole truth had helped his case, but he knew that he still had to tread extremely carefully.

The decision to come clean with Collins had been taken when Michael met with Patrick Coughlin and Sean MacEoin in the public house in Ballymahon. MacEoin gave Michael an account of the Clonfin ambush, but he still had to report to the IRA command in Dublin. Before he did that, however, he wanted to warn Michael that the report would include the part Coughlin had played in the action.

The report would inevitably reach Michael Collins, who would want to know exactly who Coughlin was and how he had come to be with the North Longford Brigade.

Patrick had already thought this through carefully. He knew the risk Michael had taken to get him into the fight for Irish independence and he was not prepared to ask his friend to take any further chances; and since arriving back in Ireland he could not fail to notice the high regard people like Sean MacEoin felt for Michael Flynn. So he offered to accompany Michael back to Dublin, tell Collins his story himself and inform him that he was now prepared to go to America; but both Michael and MacEoin disagreed. They felt that it would be unwise to expose Patrick to the possibility of being captured on the journey to Dublin until they were certain that Wilson had not put out a general alert for him. If he were to be arrested while in Michael's company, they would both face the consequences, and it would not do for the former 'Ranger to be arrested before Michael had the opportunity of talking to Collins. MacEoin suggested that Michael deliver his report to Dublin in person and take it directly to Collins rather than the IRA command, so that he would be the first senior Republican leader to learn of the Connaught Ranger's escape and arrival in Ireland.

Before he left for Dublin, Michael was able to reassure a clearly concerned Patrick Coughlin that he had located Kate Steele and that, for the moment, the English girl was safe.

Collins lapsed into silence and re-read MacEoin's report while Michael tried to think of what would happen next. When it was clear that Collins was satisfied that he had gleaned everything he needed from it, Michael asked:

"So, what happens now? Will you be sending Pat to America?"

"I'm not sure yet," Collins replied. "An unwilling representative is not likely to make much of an impression on the Americans."

"Pat told me that he would be willing to go now," said Michael. "I think that he feels he has done most of what he came home to do. He's taken a hand in the fight for Irish freedom and got something back for Jim Daly, and now he has a notion that it might be better all around if he was somewhere the British can't get their hands on him. He has one bit of unfinished business, but sure he can soon settle that and then he'll be ready to go and talk to the Yanks."

Collins was again lost in thought for several minutes. Finally he said, "That may no longer be necessary. You may be surprised to learn that Sean MacEoin's conduct at Clonfin has already become widely known and is generating a great deal of favourable publicity, particularly in America, and the British have been obliged to tone down their condemnation of us over there. Certainly when I met with Alfred Cope earlier today he seemed less disposed to label us as 'terrorists'. I feel that, at present, it may be more beneficial to follow this line rather than cloud the issue by introducing another term into the equation."

"So you'll let Pat stay with Sean over in Longford?"

"No, Michael," answered Collins, "I don't think we will. According to Sean MacEoin this fellow, Coughlin, shows every sign of being an experienced soldier with the ability to think and act quickly. And not only that, Sean thinks that he has a keen military mind, with a good grasp of British infantry tactics. I have a feeling that he could prove to be a useful addition to the staff here in Dublin. We can always send him to America later if need be. How do you think he would react to that?"

"Would he have a choice?" Michael asked.

"No," Collins admitted. "But now, Michael, what about this English girl that Coughlin got involved with. I assume that she is the 'unfinished business' you mentioned earlier."

"She is," Michael said. "It's safe to say that he wouldn't have got anywhere near Ireland if it wasn't for her. Wilson would have had him at Kingstown for sure. Knowing Pat, I'd say that he feels responsible for her because of it."

"Well, I don't like the thought of her running around Ireland looking for him. She could prove to be a distraction we could well do without, and we certainly can't afford to waste too much time on her. What do you think we should do about her?"

"The obvious solution would be to send her back to England, but if the police over there catch her they'll tell Wilson. He knows by now that Pat Coughlin has made it home to Ireland, but if he gets the whole story of how Pat managed it, the British will be able to twist things around and reduce the propaganda value of his escape."

"I must say that I would prefer a more permanent solution." Collins left Michael in no doubt exactly what he meant by that. "But, like you, I fear that if it emerged that we killed an English girl who had helped a Connaught Ranger to escape, all the good publicity generated by Sean MacEoin would be swiftly wiped out. But we have to do something about her. From what I can see she's a strong-willed young woman who is not prepared to listen to advice."

"She's that all right," Michael agreed, "but I think I got through to her. I laid it on the line for her when she went to Killarney, and I'd say that she'd be ready to listen to Pat now. But we'd still have to keep a close eye on her. It would be dangerous to leave her kicking her heels on her own, she'd soon get fed up with that and then God knows what she'd do."

"Do you think that there might be more to Coughlin's feeling for her than gratitude for helping him?"

Michael had thought about this and felt that in spite of their different backgrounds and current situations they could well have developed deeper feelings for each other. He remembered how completely different were the worlds he and his wife, Maureen, had come from, and yet this had not prevented them from falling deeply in love. But he also suspected that Collins was anxious to have some kind of hold over Coughlin and saw Kate as providing it for him.

"It wouldn't surprise me one bit," he said, both in answer to Collins' question, and as a comment on his own private thoughts.

"Very well then," Collins told him. "We'll bring Coughlin back to join the staff here in Dublin, and as he brought this girl here, he can be responsible for her. But make sure that they understand that if there is the slightest hint of her causing trouble, she will have to be permanently removed from the scene. Do I make myself clear?"

"You do," said Michael.

"Where is she now?" Collins asked.

"I have her in hiding at the Ryan's," Michael answered. "But I can't leave her there for much longer or people will be asking questions about her."

Collins appeared startled. "You had better get her out of there now, Michael. Kevin has left Longford and he's swearing to get his own back on both Coughlin and Sean MacEoin for what happened at Clonfin. I haven't decided yet what to do about him, and I want to hear his side of the story before making that decision. And I have to bear in mind that we still have a need for men like Kevin Ryan. But if he finds that girl and learns that she is associated with Coughlin, he is liable to shoot her on the spot; and from the way he's acting, I wouldn't put it past him to start boasting about it."

Chapter 28

Kate could sense the tension her presence was generating in the Ryan household. There was no open hostility but she certainly felt that she was not entirely welcome. The Ryans had been expecting her, but all that Michael Flynn had told them was that she was wanted by the police for helping a friend of his. It was taken for granted that this friend was one of 'the boys' and it would have been out of the question for them to ask who or what he was. As such they were content to put her up for a few days and keep her presence quiet. The head of the house and Michael's father-in-law, Joseph Ryan, was cordial enough and willing to provide sanctuary to someone 'the cops were after', by which he assumed to mean the reviled RIC. The senior Ryan spent his days sitting by the fire in a rudimentary wheelchair having never fully recovered from injuries received in a clash with those same police during the infamous Dublin 'lock out' riots some years before. While he was eager to help The Cause in every way possible, he could not escape the fact that Kate Steele was English and, as such, was not to be fully trusted.

Mrs Ryan, too, was ready to tolerate her guest but had little to say to the 'foreign' girl. The friendliest member of the family was Kathleen, their daughter, with whom Kate was forced to share a bed. When they were alone Kathleen would question Kate about what life was like 'over the water' and was keen to learn about the latest films and fashions.

It was Kate's first contact with what she regarded as an authentic Irish family. It quickly became evident, however, that she had fallen in with people totally dedicated to the Irish Republican cause. What little conversation took place in her presence was dominated by talk of 'The

Troubles' and the war against 'The Brits'. At first she suspected that these were barbed comments meant to imply that she, as an Englishwoman, was somehow personally responsible for all of Ireland's troubles, but she soon came to the conclusion that their whole lives did, in fact, revolve around The Cause. She wondered if Patrick Coughlin was driven by similar sentiments, but the comparison didn't quite stand up to even a cursory examination.

As she looked around her new, and hopefully temporary, surroundings, she was not at all thrown by the confined space and poor furnishings of the tiny terraced house in the Dublin back street; it was in essence almost an exact replica of the tiny terraced house in the Bristol back street where she had grown up. Even the sleeping arrangements were familiar; right up until she had left home for the women's hostel at the Gretna factory, she had shared a bed with one or both of her sisters. That apart, however, she found the lives and customs of the Ryan family strange, and in some instances a complete mystery to her.

And the presence in the house of the little shrine confused and even disturbed her.

A small table covered by a plain white cloth stood against one wall of the single downstairs room. On the wall above the table hung a picture of The Sacred Heart, and on the table itself stood a statue of The Madonna and Child. Flanking the statue were two small black and white photographs in jet black frames. One was of a young man in civilian clothes but wearing a bandolier over his shoulder and carrying a rifle; the second was of a young woman wearing what Kate thought must be a wedding dress. There was also a small china bowl filled with water and she was intrigued to notice that every time Mrs Ryan or Kathleen passed close to the simple shrine, they dipped their fingers in the water and crossed themselves. In the evening she sat in an embarrassed silence while the women knelt and prayed before the shrine. Mr Ryan seemed to pay little heed to the ritual.

Kate knew something of Catholic beliefs and customs from having talked with the Irish navvies at Gretna and, in particular, from her time spent 'walking out' with James Quinlan. So she knew that the Ryan women were honouring the dead, presumably the two young people in the photographs. She did not know who the dead people were but she assumed that they were family members and she was unsure about whether it would be appropriate to enquire.

Eventually, during her second morning with the family when the two women were out, she plucked up the courage to ask Mr Ryan who the couple in the photographs were. Much to her relief he was willing to talk to her about them. The boy was his eldest son and he was obviously extremely proud of him. Joe, named after his father, had been one of the Volunteers in 'The Rising' and had died bravely fighting for Ireland.

"Sure wasn't he one of the boys in the GPO fighting alongside Padraig Pearse himself," he told her proudly.

At this point he went on to tell Kate about his second son, Kevin, who was carrying on the fight as a member of the IRA, and who had already paid the British back for the death of his brother. When it came to the girl, however, all he seemed prepared to say was that she was his daughter who had been murdered by 'them devils' the Black and Tans, 'bad luck to them'. Kate sensed that talking about his daughter upset the crippled man and she did not press him further. But she felt strangely affected by the tragedy that had overtaken this man's family. She felt she should say something comforting but all she could manage was an inadequate expression of sorrow.

Later that night, in the darkness of their room Kate persuaded a reluctant Kathleen to talk about her dead sister, but having heard the story, she almost wished that she had, for once, reined in her curiosity. Maureen Ryan and her husband had been arrested by the 'Tans near Killarney, and in spite of being heavily pregnant, she had been thrown into a prison cell. As a result of her rough treatment she had died in childbirth. A tearful Kathleen went on to explain to Kate that Maureen's husband, Michael Flynn, had been forced to flee to America leaving behind their baby son. Michael was back now but couldn't go to see the little boy for fear of the 'Tans catching him again. Close to tears herself, Kate did her best to comfort the girl. Again, she felt quite inadequate. Offering sympathy in such circumstances was not something she had ever had occasion to become familiar with.

Kathleen eventually dropped off, but Kate had difficulty in getting to sleep and remained awake late into the night. In her short time in Ireland she had witnessed a man being shot down and a woman's home being burned, yet these events, while having a sobering effect at the time, remained as merely fleeting images in her mind. The man at Kingstown had been shot while she was otherwise fully occupied with trying to outwit Commander Wilson; and she may not have even seen the burning cottage had it not been for the reaction of the other passengers on the train.

The story of the tragedies that had befallen the Ryan family were, however, much more immediate. During the war she had seen and been saddened by many instances of bereaved families mourning the loss of someone killed in the fighting, and the death of the Ryan's son, while arousing some sorrow was not a situation with which she was unfamiliar. But the manner of the death of their daughter was something entirely different, and she was deeply affected by it. She remembered seeing propaganda posters during The Great War depicting enemy soldiers ravaging women and bayoneting children, and she had hardly given them a second glance; but now she realised that similar atrocities were part of the reality of life in Ireland. And at last she began to understand what it was that drove men like Michael Flynn and Patrick Coughlin to do the things they did.

So she continued to lie awake and tried to think things through. Understanding more about what was behind Patrick's determination to reach Ireland made her feel glad that she had helped him, but she regretted her selfish attitude and behaviour towards him. More than ever she wanted to meet him again, and not just to make up for her previous lack of courtesy; she also dreamed of how exciting it would be if she could join him in whatever he was doing to help right the wrongs being done to families like the Ryans. To Kate, in her present mood nothing seemed impossible or far-fetched and she was determined to find some way of realising her dream. Michael Flynn would soon be coming to fetch her and when he did she would speak to him. Knowing about the death of his wife enabled her to understand, at least a little, about his behaviour in Killarney and she realised that he had taken a considerable risk in meeting her there. If he was prepared to face dangers like that she might be able to persuade him to take a chance on her and let her help him and Patrick in their fight for justice.

But she could not shake off the uncomfortable feeling that both of these men had been able to gain an insight into what her original motives had been for coming to Ireland. And in reality she had to admit that joining them was no more than a pipe dream.

As she eventually started to drift off to sleep she began to think of Patrick in a much different light. She desperately wanted to see him again and, she realised, it was not because of her dream of joining him in his adventures.

She had just dropped off when she and Kathleen were rudely awoken by Mrs Ryan. Michael Flynn had come to collect her.

Chapter 29

With his delicate assignment of helping to set up talks between Sinn Fein and a senior diplomat from Dublin Castle successfully accomplished, Commander Wilson had time to turn his hand to other matters. Top of his list of priorities was the resumption of his hunt for the escaped Connaught Ranger, Private Coughlin. He sat in the tiny office temporarily assigned to him at 'The Castle' to review his options.

He had come frustratingly close to capturing his quarry at Kingstown and had it not been for the heavy-handed action of the Auxiliary Police, he would have arrested Coughlin and perhaps his accomplice, Kate Steele, as well. But, whether by luck or by design, his quarry had escaped. Michael Flynn had already confirmed that Coughlin was in Ireland and Wilson was certain that the escaped prisoner was by now taking an active part in the war against the forces of The Crown. He was well aware that he could have the Kerry county councillor arrested and, under 'questioning' by the Black and Tans or Auxiliaries, even someone with Flynn's dedication to 'The Cause' would eventually tell them everything they needed to know. And apart from the fact that the very thought of handing anyone over to that sort of treatment was deeply abhorrent to him, he suspected that he would be required to meet and negotiate with Michael Flynn again. In the Commander's opinion, the leaky nature of security at 'The Castle' meant that it would not be long before rumours of talks between British officials and Sinn Fein began to circulate and if, as was likely, this were to cause a problem with the cease-fire negotiations, he and Flynn could well be called in to put things back on track. With Michael Flynn in prison facing trial for God knows what, if indeed he was still alive, that would be impossible, and consequently any hope of a cease-fire could be delayed for months if not for years.

Even without Flynn's help, Wilson felt that he could make an educated guess about where in Ireland Coughlin was hiding. Working out of Dublin Castle gave him access to virtually all the material pertaining to the war against the IRA that circulated in the building. Most of this passed through his hands without a second glance, but because of the unusual circumstances surrounding the IRA ambush at Clonfin, he paid much closer attention to that particular report. The more he studied the file the more he became convinced that there had been someone with some skill as a soldier, certainly someone with a higher level of military experience than would be expected of the usual IRA leader, involved. That someone had managed to turn almost certain failure into success and the name of Private Patrick Coughlin sprang immediately to mind. The escaped Connaught Ranger had already managed to escape and avoid capture for several weeks in England, and had somehow found his way to Ireland albeit with some help from Kate Steele; a feat which required considerable ingenuity and daring to accomplish. With that in mind, there was, in Wilson's view, every reason to believe that Coughlin had been the experienced soldier behind the IRA success at Clonfin.

He also suspected that given the publicity attached to the ambush and the conduct of Sean MacEoin, it would not be long before Patrick Coughlin's participation in the action became known to the IRA leadership in Dublin. Once that happened, it was inevitable that the whole story of the Connaught Ranger's escape would also emerge. Paradoxically the thought provided some comfort. Assuming that it was Coughlin who had turned the tables on the Auxiliaries at Clonfin, he would now become absorbed into the Republican Movement proper and his exploits would also become public knowledge. In which case, and very much to Wilson's relief, having Flynn arrested and interrogated would be a pointless exercise; even if he revealed Coughlin's whereabouts, the fugitive would be quickly spirited away, possibly to America, before the authorities could even come close to laying their hands on him.

Once the secret was out, however, the British Army would make every effort to recapture the escaped mutineer and all the forces available to them in Ireland would be mobilised to help in achieving that end. While Wilson was as anxious as anyone to see the mutineer back behind bars, he feared that should Coughlin be apprehended by the military, his original death sentence would almost certainly be reinstated: senior officers in the British Army were bound to insist that Coughlin be executed, if only to save face. But Wilson realised that the execution of another Connaught Ranger, and especially one who had now taken an active part in the war for Irish Independence, would inflame public opinion in Ireland, and a population who were now fully prepared to welcome a cease-fire could quite easily turn against it. It had been the summary executions carried out after the Easter Rising in 1916 which had turned Irish public opinion solidly in favour of the Republican Movement and totally against Great Britain. All this, however, would mean little to those Members of Parliament and army generals who believed that they could still achieve a military victory in Ireland.

Commander Wilson was prepared to admit to himself that he was developing a grudging respect for Private Coughlin as a person; but to an officer in the Royal Navy, mutiny was the most serious of all offences and, irrespective of his personal assessment of Coughlin's character, a mutineer must never be allowed to get off scot free.

It was a dilemma; and Wilson knew that he would somehow have to resolve it by himself. It would be useless to seek guidance, much less ask for a direct order, from his superiors in London; he had learned enough about political machinations to know how quickly hands could be washed and memories erased.

To further complicate matters there was the question of what to do about the Steele girl who had helped Coughlin. Even if she did not know exactly where the Connaught Ranger was, she was guilty of helping a convicted mutineer to escape, a much more serious crime in the Commander's view than stealing from hotel guests and innkeepers. And, having gained an insight into Coughlin's character, he still had hopes that if he could find her he might be able to flush his principal quarry out. He had a strong feeling that Coughlin would consider that, irrespective of what her motives might have been, he was in debt to the woman who had helped him. But where was she, and how to begin searching for her?

As he sat and thought the problem through, he again leafed through the report on the Clonfin ambush and picked up on an item that he had previously passed over. The IRA man whose impatience had almost cost the ambushers their success had been identified as Kevin Ryan, and the Commander knew that Ryan was Michael Flynn's brother-in-law. So, again, his thoughts turned to Flynn, who seemed to be playing a central role in the affair. Wilson suspected that Flynn knew where Kate Steele was hiding, and it was highly likely that he had helped her to disappear; he was equally sure that Michael would try to keep her well away from active members of the IRA, who would be loath to trust an unknown English girl. He also reasoned that Flynn would not countenance giving up Kate Steele to the Irish police, who might be under pressure to hand her over to the Black and Tans. But the Irishman had indicated that if he found the Steele girl, he would try and persuade her to go back to England.

So assuming that he had found her, the question was where would he be hiding her? The only possible answer to come immediately to mind was Flynn's in-laws, the Ryan family. He suspected that because their son, Kevin, was a known IRA activist, and one high on the authorities' most wanted list, his family's home would be kept under surveillance. When the commander went to check with the intelligence gathering section at 'The Castle' he found that this was indeed the case. And then he found exactly what he was looking for. According to the surveillance report, an unknown couple had visited the Ryans' some days ago; the man left by himself soon afterwards while the woman remained there for two days until the man came back to fetch her. To Wilson's immense disappointment, the couple had not been followed, the watchers had only been directed to look out for Kevin Ryan, but it was confirmation enough that Michael Flynn had located Kate Steele.

Although there was nothing to discuss regarding the meetings between Michael Collins and Alfred Cope, Wilson decided that it was time to talk with Michael Flynn again, but it would take a day or two to set up a meeting. He looked out at the weather and prepared himself for another walk in the rain through Phoenix Park.

***

The meetings between Alfred Cope and Michael Collins dragged on, apparently without any definable progress being made. Commander Wilson was accurate in his assessment of the security at Dublin Castle where Collins' extremely efficient intelligence service ensured that virtually nothing happening there remained a secret for very long. But inevitably, in such an environment, it was not only the IRA leadership who were kept informed, loose talk was the order of the day and although not all of the 'news' emerging from the nerve centre of the British administration was based on fact, enough of the truth leaked out to keep the rumour-mongers and gossipers busy. With this in mind Collins recognised that the time had come for him to report to a wider section of the Republican leadership than the handful of trusted allies he had thus far been keeping informed. A full meeting of the Irish Republican Cabinet was convened, or at least a meeting of those members not currently in prison. The cabinet meeting would be chaired by the *Priomh Aire,* Eamonn de Valera.

After the cabinet meeting Collins met with the man he was increasingly taking into his confidence, Michael Flynn.

"I feared that he might attempt to exert his influence over some members of the cabinet and get them to order me to suspend the talks with Cope," Collins told Michael.

"I'm surprised that he didn't," Michael answered.

"I think that after he accused me of mishandling funds and was forced to withdraw the charge, he has decided to tread more carefully."

"And he had nothing at all to say about you talking to the Brits?" Michael asked.

"Even Dev knows that in this war our most valuable weapon is public opinion, especially in America, but ironically, in Great Britain also; and he's politician enough to know how quickly that can change. He is well aware that if we were to be seen placing obstacles in the way of a possible cease-fire, it could quickly swing against us. So there were no ructions on that score."

Michael knew that there was more to come: he would have been extremely surprised if de Valera had allowed a cabinet meeting to pass without having at least something to say.

Collins confirmed his opinion. "So he went back to his current pet theory that we should abandon ambushes and small scale operations in favour of a major pitched battle. As you are well aware, I'm against this because I don't see how we can possibly win a pitched battle with the British army. We simply haven't the resources. But I suspect that some members now see some advantages in making a concentrated effort as a preliminary to a cease-fire."

"Where does that leave us now, and what can we do about it?" Michael asked.

Collins sighed. "I had to give some ground on this, so I agreed to arrange for a feasibility study. It looks as if I was right to keep your friend, Coughlin, here in Ireland, his input could prove to be very useful to this."

"I'd say that Pat is your man all right," Michael said. "But in the meantime I'll fix up a meeting to tell Commander Wilson that you'll carry on meeting Cope?"

"You may inform the gallant Commander Wilson that the Cabinet of the Irish Republic has directed me to continue meeting with the representative of the British Government," said Collins with a smile.

Michael laughed. "I don't think for one minute that he recognises the Irish Republic, but sure won't I tell him anyway."

"But it won't do any harm to keep them in suspense for a while, so you should also tell him that I intend to take a little time to reflect on the progress made so far before the next meeting. And that's not simply a delaying tactic; as you are well aware by now, Michael, we have to get this right or we could set the Movement back by years."

"All right, I'll go and have a chat with him," Michael said.

As he was leaving a telephone rang in another room and Collins went to answer it. When he returned his expression told Michael that something was very wrong.

"Bad news I'm afraid, Michael," Collins said gravely. "It appears that Sean MacEoin has been arrested at the railway station in Mullingar."

Chapter 30

Kevin Ryan took a long pull from his pint of black porter, wiped his mouth on the sleeve of his trench coat and looked across the small table at his drinking companion.

"Ah sure he'll be no loss at all, Sean," he said. "I'm telling you that MacEoin is nothing but a country culshie with no stomach at all for a fight."

It was getting late in the evening and the curfew was already in force, but they felt quite secure in the tiny back room of this Dublin public house. They would have ample warning should the Black and Tans or the Auxiliaries decide to mount a raid on this known rebel stronghold; and ample time to disappear into the well-hidden cellar and out into the labyrinth of narrow streets that made up the area of the city around the pub, where they would be welcomed into any number of homes should the necessity arise.

"I wouldn't go as far as that, Kevin," the man called Sean replied. "MacEoin has done a lot for The Cause over there in Longford, sure weren't you there yourself when he beat the 'Auxies' at Clonfin."

"I'm telling you, Sean, that bastard MacEoin did nothing at all at Clonfin. All him and the rest of them wanted to do was to sit on their arses until I woke the lazy bastards up."

Ryan was obviously becoming agitated and these days an angry Kevin Ryan could rapidly become completely unpredictable. So O'Connor took his time and drank some of his porter before speaking again.

"Maybe you're right, Kevin, but sure isn't it always a sad day when one of the lads is taken by the Brits."

Kevin was not about to be mollified. "Well you won't catch me crying over MacEoin, bad luck to him, he can rot in a British jail until they hang him for all I care," he said with feeling.

Again O'Connor took his time about replying. "Well anyway 'The Big Fella' wants him rescued and I hear that he gave the job to the Dublin Brigade, so we'll have to take a shot at it. Some new fella is working out a plan."

Ryan stood up as the news gradually sank in. "Jesus Christ, that must be that bastard, Coughlin. Collins must be out of his bloody mind. Connaught Ranger or no Connaught Ranger I wouldn't trust that bugger one bit, or anyone else who spent their whole life in the British army. I'm telling you, Sean, he's a bloody Brit spy and Collins must be blind not to see it."

He sat down before continuing, "And I can't work out what 'The Big Fella" wants with MacEoin anyway. Sure all that eejit can do is let the bloody 'Auxies' go after he has them beat. God knows that's no way to win this war."

"I'm with you there, Kevin." O'Connor had no argument whatsoever with Ryan on the last point. He refrained from asking who Coughlin was, but the mention of the Connaught Rangers made him wary that he might be getting into something way over his head. And given Ryan's current state of mind, prying too deeply could well be dangerous.

"But Collins is the boss," he added, "and sure he'll definitely have something in mind. Maybe MacEoin knows something and 'The Big Fella' is frightened that the Brits will get it out of him."

Ryan's views on that were quite straightforward. "And sure that would take them no time at all."

After breaking away from MacEoin's Longford Brigade, Ryan had returned to Dublin where he received little sympathy from Michael Collins, who sent him to re-join the Dublin Brigade. For someone who had, until recently, been a trusted member of 'The Twelve Apostles', Collins' elite squad of gunmen, this was a perceived slight that Ryan was not likely to forget in a hurry. And he blamed MacEoin and Patrick Coughlin jointly for his troubles. He had convinced himself that they had told Michael Collins a pack of lies and turned 'The Big Fella' against him. And he also felt that his brother-in-law, Michael Flynn, was not entirely blameless: hadn't it been Michael who had brought Coughlin in to join 'the boys' in the first place? He considered suggesting to Collins that the Connaught Ranger be sent to America but then realised that this would take Coughlin out of his reach.

The Dublin Brigade was by far the most active IRA unit in the country and since he re-joined it, Ryan had taken part in several attacks where he had been responsible for adding the deaths of several more 'Tans and 'Auxies' to his growing score. Being involved in frontline action again made him feel better, but he still harboured his grudges. The news of Sean MacEoin's arrest raised his spirits, although he knew that he had to be extremely careful about voicing his opinion on the matter. But he felt he could make an exception of the man sitting opposite him.

"Collins is up to something, Sean, and I wouldn't be one bit surprised to find that MacEoin and this bloody Coughlin are in it with him, and Mick Flynn, too, maybe. If me and you can't be trusted to know what it is, I'm telling you now that I don't like the smell of it."

Sean O'Connor was an old friend. They had fought side by side in The Easter Rising of 1916 and been interned together after the Republican defeat. It was at the internment camp at Fron-goch in Wales that they had first met Michael Flynn. Although O'Connor was not comfortable with the way Ryan was questioning Michael Collins' handling of the situation, he agreed with his friend about how the war against the 'Tans and 'Auxies' should be conducted; he would not have treated British prisoners with the same respect that MacEoin had shown them.

O'Connor stood up and drained his glass. "Well, Kevin, me boy," he said, "it's late enough for the 'Tans to be fed up with trying to enforce the curfew and the buggers will be half asleep. I'll go first and I'll give you the nod if it's all clear."

Ryan shook his head. "I think I'll stop here for a while, Sean. I'm going home in the morning. I want to have a chat with the old fella about all this; he might be a cripple these days but the Da still has his ear to the ground. I'll see you back at the digs tomorrow."

O'Connor's was about to try and talk his friend out of doing something most of 'the boys' would have considered to be foolish but, recognising Ryan's mood, he knew that it would be useless to argue with him. "Well, for Christ's sake be careful Kevin," he said. "Sure don't you know very well the Brits are watching the house."

Ryan held up his hand in a gesture of distain. "They're watching all right, Sean, but sure it's no trouble at all getting past them eejits." For the first time that night a fleeting smile crossed his face. "I'll be going home with the milk in the morning."

Soon after dawn a milkman reined in his horse outside the house two doors down from the Ryans'. He got down from the cart and banged loudly on the door. A highly vocal argument about non-payment erupted between him and the angry householder. Several neighbours, including Kathleen Ryan, came out into the street to complain about the noise at this ungodly hour. The two sleepy, plain-clothed policemen in the upstairs room of a house opposite were drawn into enjoying the fun. More concerned with whether their relief would arrive on time than they were with keeping watch, they allowed Kevin to slip unnoticed from where he was hiding among the milk churns and in through the open door of his parents' house.

An hour later when the street was crowded with an unusually large number of people, all apparently going to work at the same time, Ryan quietly joined them. Having eaten a hearty breakfast prepared by his mother, and receiving her blessing, he got clean away. He had sat by his father's bed and talked over his troubles with him. The chat with old Republican fighter made him more certain than ever that something was in the wind and he was deliberately being kept out of it. That, he imagined, would never have happened a few months ago.

Why would Michael Flynn have asked the Ryans to hide an English girl for him? To Kevin's father, the story that she was 'wanted by the cops' didn't ring true: if she was really on the run from the RIC then there were plenty of people in place to help her without someone like Flynn, who was known to be 'well in' with Michael Collins, being personally involved. To an old hand like Kevin's father, this meant one of two things: either Michael was up to something behind Collins' back, or, much more likely, the 'Big Fella' was actually behind whatever was going on. He also dismissed his wife's assertion that the English tart was Michael's 'floozy'; 'and my poor Maureen not yet cold in her grave'. Both the Ryan men were, however, agreed that nothing would be further from Michael Flynn's mind.

The more Kevin let the problem dwell on his mind, the more he became convinced that Michael and this mysterious woman were both working for Michael Collins, and that all three were 'out to get him'. But he still retained sufficient control of his feelings to heed his father's warning to 'watch out for himself'. He knew that it would be extremely dangerous to voice his suspicions too loudly; in his world a word in the wrong ears could literally be more than your life was worth, and even friends like Sean O'Connor might take exception and turn against him.

So he resolved to keep things to himself for the time being. But he would keep his eyes and ears open, and keep a special eye on Michael Flynn.

Chapter 31

It was once again raining in Phoenix Park, as Wilson had suspected it would be, so he had made arrangements to meet Michael Flynn in the tearoom at the Dublin Zoo which was situated in the park. Due to the weather, very few visitors had chosen to come to look at the animals and they had the place virtually to themselves, so anyone paying them undue attention would be easily spotted.

Before he could bring up the subject of Kate Steele, however, Wilson first had to consider Michael Flynn's account of what had happened at his last meeting with Michael Collins. Not that there was much to think about, when you peeled off all the usual groundless rhetoric it simply meant that Collins wanted time to think. This was not a problem as far as the Commander was concerned: he felt that his man, Cope, would also welcome a short recess to give him an opportunity to report in person to the British Prime Minister. The important point was that the talks would be resumed once both sides had drawn breath. As Michael had suspected, the Royal Navy man was not at all impressed by the idea of Collins being given permission to continue the negotiations by 'The Cabinet of The Irish Republic'.

But when Wilson eventually managed to raise the question of the English girl, he found that Michael was being unusually evasive. It was not at all like the Irishman to use stalling tactics; for one thing he was not particularly adept at it. All Michael was prepared to say was that he suspected the girl had returned to the British mainland. To Wilson this did not ring true, but when he pressed Michael for more information, all he got was: "Leave it with me Commander and I'll see what I can find out."

Michael did not relish being evasive with Wilson, much less blatantly lying to him, principally because the Commander had always been honest with him. But in this instance he had been left with little choice, the situation regarding Kate Steele had changed drastically.

Had he known that in spite of both the weather and their precautions he had been recognised and his meeting with Wilson noted, Michael would have been even less happy as he left the park.

***

Michael had gone to meet Patrick Coughlin as soon as the former Connaught Ranger arrived in Dublin, having travelled from Ballinalee in the back of a lorry loaded with potatoes for the city market. As ordered, he took the former soldier to see Michael Collins straight away. Following the brief introductions, Collins broke the news to Coughlin that Sean MacEoin had been 'taken'.

"Jesus, but that's hard lines all right." Coughlin was clearly saddened by the arrest. Over the past weeks he had come to regard the Longford IRA man as a friend. "And the worst of it is that I never had a chance to say good luck to him. Sure I never even knew that he was coming up to Dublin. If I knew he was coming here I could have come along with him and between the two of us, we might have got away."

"It's one of the lessons you have yet to learn," said Collins. "We never allow our more important people to travel together if we can help it, and we don't make our travel arrangements known to anyone except those directly involved. It's a policy which has served us well. If you had been with Sean, the chances are that you would now be in gaol, too, except in your case you'd be in Portland waiting to face a firing squad. Think about that, Patrick."

"Christ, you're right," was the best Coughlin could manage in reply.

Collins mentioned some of the difficulties that the arrest of MacEoin caused for the conduct of the war. Apart from the problem of finding a new commander for the North Longford Brigade, and Collins was the first to admit that MacEoin would be a difficult man to replace, the arrest had other and perhaps even more serious ramifications. Much of the favourable publicity generated by the victor of Clonfin could now be lost and might even rebound on the Republican Movement. Now that MacEoin was in British hands, there was a real danger that the propaganda advantage would pass to them because they had proved that they were capable of capturing one of the IRA's most prominent leaders.

Collins looked at Michael. "As well as the practical difficulties involved in replacing Sean MacEoin," he said, "this could, of course, also cause us some embarrassment in other areas."

Michael knew that he was referring to the talks with Alfred Cope, and he could see how the Nationalist hand would be weakened by MacEoin's arrest.

'The Big Fella' turned to Coughlin. "This is where you come in Patrick," he said.

He explained to the former Connaught Ranger that he had brought him to Dublin to make the most of his military experience. He felt that Coughlin could make a real contribution to The Cause by helping to develop the IRA's tactics for fighting the regular British Army.

Coughlin was somewhat taken aback. "But sure I never rose above the rank of private soldier," he said. "And sure isn't it true that if there was a lower rank that's where I'd be. What would the likes of me know about tactics?"

Collins dismissed the suggestion. "Don't sell yourself short, Patrick, you proved that you knew what you were doing at Clonfin. But more importantly, you know the British Army and its infantry tactics, and that may be of particular use to us in the near future."

Again Michael could see what Collins was getting at: he was already planning ahead in case Eamonn de Valera got his way and they were forced into fighting a pitched battle with British regular soldiers.

"But perhaps you would like something nice and easy to get you started, and work me out a plan to get Sean MacEoin out of prison," 'The Big Fella' said with a smile.

For once the capture of a senior IRA leader was being kept a closely guarded secret and Collins' intelligence network had not yet been able to let him know in which of Dublin's prisons MacEoin was being held. In all probability it would be Kilmainham Gaol, where the leaders of the Easter Rising had been imprisoned and the subsequent executions carried out; but it was most unusual for Collins not to have that sort of information at his fingertips and he wanted to make certain. In any case 'The Big Fella' was adamant that he wanted the Longford man freed before the British authorities could arrange to put him on trial for treason, which was the charge usually levelled at captured IRA men simply because treason carried the death penalty. In the meantime lodgings had been arranged for Patrick in a 'safe house' in Rathmines.

Michael knew that Patrick was anxious to meet Kate Steele, and he was equally anxious for the meeting to take place without delay. He suspected that by now she would be getting impatient in the house in Kingstown, where he had left her with a strict warning not to venture out until she heard from him. He had opted for Kingstown because he hoped that the memory of the man being shot down by the Auxiliaries when she first arrived there would reinforce his warning; and even if she hadn't listened to his advice he knew the woman who ran the lodging house and she could be trusted to ensure that Kate didn't step out of line. Another reason behind his decision was that in the unlikely event of her agreeing to return to England, it would be a simple matter to smuggle her aboard the steamer for Holyhead. It would not be easy to persuade her to leave Ireland, but Michael hoped that with Patrick's help it might be accomplished.

Michael knew that it would not be wise to keep anything else regarding the English girl away from Collins. He would have preferred to have a word with Patrick beforehand, but he was left with little choice but to bring the subject up while they were still with 'The Big Fella'. He told them what she had said about how some of the things she had seen and heard since she arrived in Ireland had affected her, and how it had made her want to help right some of the injustices she had witnessed.

"What do you think about that, Patrick?" Collins asked.

Coughlin knew that in spite of the debt he felt he owed to Kate, he had to be truthful with Collins. "Well," he replied, "the last I saw of her she was being knocked to the ground by your man, Wilson, to save her from being shot by the 'Auxies'. I don't know what effect seeing that fella being killed and everything else she saw here in Ireland had on her; but I can see how the girl I came to Ireland with would have the notion that running around with a gun in her hand playing Cowboys and Indians would be great gas."

"We obviously can't allow that," said Collins. "But what do you think, Michael? Do you think that there is anything in this sudden desire of hers to help The Cause?"

It took Michael a moment to get over his shock. He had fully expected Collins to totally dismiss the idea of recruiting Kate Steele to The Cause and to order either her immediate execution or return to England.

"I'd say that she was genuinely sorry to hear from the Ryans about what happened to Maureen," he said, "but who knows how long that will last. The one thing I do know is that she'll soon get fed up with sitting around the house on her own. That's why I didn't tell her that I was seeing Pat. If she knew that he was in Dublin she'd be out looking for him. The best thing is still to make her go home to England; from what I can see sure she's well able to keep herself out of the way of the police."

Collins reaction was immediate. "I'm afraid that it's much too late for that now, she knows far too much about us."

Michael mentally kicked himself for not thinking of this. He should have realised that 'The Big Fella' would consider it too late to send her back to England, or hand her over to the Irish authorities, because by now, she would have seen and heard too much. And he had to concede that Collins had a point: apart from Patrick Coughlin, she had met both himself and the Ryan family, and she knew about the safe house in Kingstown. The realisation served to render Collins' next remarks all the more surprising.

"The possibility of getting an English girl to work for us, irrespective of her motives, is one that I cannot dismiss lightly. If it could be arranged, it could prove to be extremely useful. Are we absolutely certain that she is not working for Commander Wilson?"

"From the way Wilson talks about her and from what Pat says, I'd say that the Commander was as surprised as anyone to meet her at

Kingstown," Michael told him. "Commander Wilson would never deliberately plan for a man to be shot just to cause a diversion so that he could talk to her, and sure wasn't it the shooting that let Pat get away from him in the first place."

"Tell me," said Collins, "how much experience does she really have of working in hotels?"

It dawned on Michael what 'The Big Fella' had in mind. "Oh she knows her way around hotels all right," he answered. "Enough to get away with stealing from the guests for a long time, and to do that she'd have to know how to keep her eyes and ears open."

Again Collins thought long and hard before making his mind up. "I feel that this is too good an opportunity to disregard; I have something in mind where an English girl is likely to be more successful than an Irish one," he said. "I want you two to follow this up and see if you can recruit her. You can threaten her with handing her over to the British police, or even lay the alternative on the line for her, if she won't cooperate with us. But a more effective approach in the long run may be to play on her inherent desire for excitement. Then, of course, there are her feelings for you, Patrick. I'll leave it up to both of you, but I don't have to tell you to tread carefully. And make sure she understands that if she agrees to work for us what the consequences would be should she ever be foolish enough to back out."

Significantly, he neglected to tell them to remind Kate that if she agreed to work for him, she would be committing treason, with the certainty of having to face the consequences if she was caught.

***

"Jesus, Mick, but I hope to God we can persuade her to come in with us. I don't like the way Collins said that she knows too much. If she doesn't do what he wants he might even have her shot."

They had just left Collins and Patrick was worried. Michael thought that although it would do nothing to allay his friend's fears, he had to tell Patrick the truth.

"There's no 'might' about it, Pat," he said. "The way 'The Big Fella' sees things she's already a danger to The Cause, and sure he has a point. She could tell the people up at Dublin Castle a hell of a lot about us. And the truth is that working for Collins might still only be a temporary reprieve. She's in the same position as yourself, the death sentence could be reinstated. I don't like it any more than you do but we have to face the facts. Anyway, it will give us time to think of something else."

Coughlin digested this, then had another disturbing thought: "Christ, Mick, he wouldn't expect us to be the ones to shoot her would he?"

"No, Pat," Michael reassured him, "if it comes to that he'll give the job to someone like the brother-in-law, Kevin Ryan."

"From what I saw of him at Clonfin I'd say that Mr Ryan would be happy to do it too," said Patrick. He paused for a minute before carrying on. "I hope to God that she's ready to listen to us now. It's hard to make head or tail of her, Mick, and she's too headstrong for her own good. Maybe she only has herself to blame for the trouble she's in, but there's no real harm in her. I'd hate to see her buried in a ditch after what she did for me, even if it was only to satisfy her own mad notions. And I'll do anything to stop it."

Again they lapsed into silence. Then Patrick gave an ironic laugh. "Jesus Christ, Mick, will you listen to who's talking? Me calling her headstrong, and after the way I've been acting. If it wasn't for me, she might be safe and sound in a jail in England and sure isn't it all my fault that she's not. Have you any ideas at all about what we can do about her?"

"The only thing we can do is persuade her to work for us," Michael answered. "And there's no need for you to be blaming yourself, if she hadn't come to Ireland with you sure she'd only have got herself into some different trouble. Come on, Pat," he added with a laugh, "sure aren't you the grand fella for making the plans. Maybe it's time for you to start earning your pay."

As they set out for Kingstown to see Kate, Michael was again unaware that they were being watched.

Chapter 32

Even after everything that had happened to her, or that she had caused to happen to herself over the year since she had decided to leave home for good, Kate failed to see the irony of being back working in a hotel. But waiting on tables and serving behind the bar in the best hotel in the seaside village of Killiney, just south of Dublin, held the prospect of exhilarating times ahead. As in the hotel in Bournemouth she was involved in something which provided her with the excitement she craved.

She was working for the Irish Republican movement, 'The Cause', as Michael Flynn called it. Not that she fully understood what The Cause actually was, and had she understood it is doubtful if she would have really cared. The only 'cause' she had been interested in up to now was avoiding the police and searching for the man who had so aroused her curiosity, Patrick Coughlin. When she had agreed to join the Irish fight for independence, they had made it clear to her that once she was in there was no way out; but that was something she preferred not to think about for the moment. As far as she was concerned, she was helping Patrick Coughlin in some momentous enterprise. Although she appreciated the inherent dangers of what it was they were involved in, she managed to push these to the back of her mind. What she had taken to heart though, was being told that if things went wrong, Patrick would be one of the first to suffer.

She had been told that her 'contact' would be Michael Flynn who, in spite of what he had told her about his having to be careful in Beaufort, seemed to have complete freedom of movement in Dublin. It would be much nicer if Patrick was the one she was to meet to pass on all the 'intelligence' she managed to gather, but that suggestion had been turned down flat. Their last meeting, the first since she had seen him disappear after his wild dash along the quay at Kingstown, had been at the lodging house where Michael had deposited her in that same the port. She didn't know when she would see Patrick again but she was confident that she would, and in the meantime she consoled herself with the thought that she was helping him in whatever it was that he was trying to achieve, and that had the effect of bringing him closer to her.

***

One evening during the previous week, Michael and Patrick, in line with standard Republican practice, travelled separately to Kingstown. It was well after dark when Michael, by prior agreement, was the first to arrive. After a careful inspection of the area he knocked on the boarding house door. There was the sound of a heavy key in a lock and he was admitted by the landlady. He was shown into the front parlour while she went upstairs to fetch Miss Steele. As long as she was the woman of the house, gentlemen visitors, even men with the standing of Michael Flynn, would not be allowed to visit female guests in their rooms.

When she entered the parlour Kate's face fell, she had hoped that her caller might be Patrick Coughlin. She was, as Michael had thought she would be, thoroughly bored with being kept a virtual prisoner, and her first reaction on seeing Michael was to complain about her treatment at the hands of 'that horrid woman'.

Her complaints drew little sympathy. "By now you should know very well that it's for your own good, Kate," was Michael's only comment.

"But surely it wouldn't hurt her to let me go out for a walk occasionally," she said.

"That's where you're wrong, Kate," he answered. "There could easily be people around who might remember you from the ructions when you got off the boat and report you to the police."

He could see that she had taken this argument on board, but she was still far from being mollified; and he could, to some extent, understand her frustration. What really caused her belligerent attitude, however, was the uncertainty of her current situation. She was no longer the mistress of her own destiny and had no idea what would happen to her next. A girl like her needed something to look forward to, so Michael adopted a different strategy.

"Kate," he said, "sure don't I know very well that you won't take one bit of notice of what I tell you, but there's a fella coming here tonight that you might listen to. Pat Coughlin will be in any minute, and you can tell him all your troubles."

"Patrick is coming here? Tonight?" Her surprise was tinged with pleasure.

Then it was his turn to be surprised when she became quite flustered. She went to the mirror over the fireplace and stood on tiptoe to comb her hair and then straightened her dress.

"Why didn't someone tell me he was coming?" she said crossly. "I look a sight."

It was the first time that Michael had seen her act even remotely like any of the other women he knew, and he realised that her feelings for Pat Coughlin went deeper than she would ever admit to him; or perhaps even to herself.

He found Coughlin waiting in a doorway across the street. They exchanged places and Patrick went into the lodging house, where he found Kate in the parlour still frantically combing her hair. He took off his cap.

"So, Kate," he said, "how are you?"

She fiddled with her comb. "I'm fine, thank you Patrick," she answered. "How are you?"

"Ah sure I'm grand," he said.

There followed an embarrassed silence with neither quite knowing how to continue. He stood with his cap in his hands and she still fiddled with her comb. Patrick, who had at least had some time to prepare, had several things to get off his chest. But as soon as he began, his carefully prepared speech was instantly forgotten.

"I came to say thanks for what you did for me at Kingstown, Kate," he said. "If it wasn't for you, that fella Wilson, would have had me for sure."

"But it was really that poor man who was killed that gave you the chance to get away," she answered.

"Oh he gave me a hand all right, God rest his soul." Patrick crossed himself in the manner Kate had seen Mrs Ryan do. "But sure wasn't it you who kept Wilson busy while I ran away, and if it wasn't for me, you wouldn't be in the fix you are now."

There was another awkward silence while he collected his thoughts. "I would have come back to make sure that you were all right, but sure I couldn't. The truth of it is, Kate, that if I get caught here in Ireland I'll be taken back over the water to face a firing squad."

Kate's shock was evident. She dropped her comb and her hand flew to her mouth. For all her speculation about what had made Patrick come to Ireland, this was something that went beyond anything she had imagined, and it took her a moment to recover.

"Well then, I'm glad that you didn't come back," she heard herself saying, "because if you had been caught I would have blamed myself."

Patrick did not want to frighten Kate, but he desperately wanted her to know why he had not come back to look for her at Kingstown, and the only way he could see of doing it was to tell her at least something about himself and his situation. It was something that had been preying on his mind since the day they arrived in Ireland in such dramatic circumstances, but he had kept his troubles to himself; there was nothing to be gained from bothering others with his personal problems. Now, however, he was much relieved to have the opportunity to give Kate at least some kind of explanation for his behaviour. He didn't want to tell her blatant lies, but he said nothing about the Connaught Rangers or the mutiny; he simply told her that he had deserted to join the fight for Irish freedom and to help right some of the wrongs she herself had witnessed.

Once she had recovered from her shock the questions began to crowd in on her mind, and she was anxious to learn more. But Patrick, sensing her curiosity, cut her off.

"I can't tell you the whole story now but, God willing, someday I might be able to. Believe me, Kate; it would be too dangerous for you to know all about what I'm doing now. Sure don't you know too much already? There are people around who would never take the chance that you wouldn't tell the cops what you know about me. I know that you wouldn't, but sure that wouldn't mean a thing to these fellas."

Kate believed him, and disciplined herself not to press him for answers he was obviously not ready to give. It was not how she had imagined their first meeting since Kingstown would be. The fact that he had not only thanked her for what she had done, but that *he* had also seen fit to apologise for getting *her* into her current predicament had come as a complete surprise. She was deeply affected and she wanted him to know it.

"I'm sorry I've been making things difficult by running around like a fool trying to find you, Patrick," she said. "I had no idea that things in Ireland were as bad as they really are."

Like her, Patrick had fully expected their meeting to take a much different turn; this was a different girl to the one he had met at Wareham and travelled to Ireland with. She was showing him a sense of responsibility he never thought she possessed.

He grinned to lighten the mood. "Ah sure wasn't it Mick Flynn you made things hard for, but don't blame yourself for that because it was me who asked him to look out for you. And if he hadn't found you down in Killarney, Wilson would have caught you for sure. "

"Then I'll have to thank him when I see him, if I ever do see him again," she said.

"Oh, you'll see him, all right. He's still around, freezing to death in a door across the street. I'll tell him to come in now. He has something to say to you."

He went out and crossed the street. As a precaution Michael had changed his position, but he saw Patrick emerge and went across to meet him. Before they went back inside Patrick wanted to hold a short council of war, and Michael looked around anxiously while the former soldier outlined what was on his mind.

"I'd say that trying to do what Collins said and use her thirst for excitement to get her to join us won't work, Mick; she's showing every sign of having come to her senses about the way things are at long last. But if you have to lay it on the line go easy on her, God knows I'd hate to use threats or to frighten her any more."

Michael gave him an old-fashioned look. "I'll do my best to go easy on her, Pat," he said. "I don't like the idea of threatening her either. But we can't play games with 'The Big Fella'. If we don't do what he wants he'll make things hard for the three of us."

When they went in they found Kate in the kitchen helping the landlady to make tea. It was brought into the parlour and the older woman withdrew. The English girl was anxious to have her say before Michael had a chance to tell her what he had in mind.

She turned to him. "I'm sorry that I caused you a lot of trouble, Michael. And thank you for what you and Jack Quinlan did for me in Killarney. Anyway, I know what you're going to say now. You're going to tell me again that the best thing for me to do is to go back to England, and this time I'll do what you say. You can't keep on hiding me, and I'll probably get Patrick into trouble if I stay here. I think I'll go to London, the police won't find me there and I'll make out all right."

She had turned from Michael to Patrick so that her last sentence was addressed directly to him.

Michael and Patrick exchanged glances, and Michael nodded to acknowledge that he understood what his friend had said outside. It was his turn to be surprised by the apparent change in Kate's attitude. He decided that Patrick was right. Trying to get her to work for Collins by stimulating her need for excitement was not going to succeed; he would have to adopt a direct but, he hoped, not overly threatening approach.

"I'm afraid that it's too late for that now Kate," he said gently but firmly. "If you left Ireland now, Pat would have to go with you because they'd know that he helped you and they'd never trust him again. And that would only mean one thing for the both of you. You'd have to go a lot farther than England because you'd have everyone after you over there, the IRA as well as the British Army and the police. And you'd have to pray that it was the cops who found you first."

He felt a twinge of conscience about playing on her obvious special feelings for Patrick. What he had said was true, but it was not the whole truth; if Michael Collins even suspected that she was leaving Ireland with what she knew, she would not live long enough to board the steamer.

It took a few minutes for the reality of her position to sink in. But when it did, both men were impressed by the manner in which she seemed to deal with the horror of her predicament:

"What can I do then?" she asked in a voice that was surprisingly calm. "I can't go home to England and I can't stay here in Ireland, and I don't think that I would like being a long way away from Patrick. So what else is there? Patrick told me that you had something to say to me, Michael. If you are going to suggest a way out of this for me, you had better let me hear it."

Michael decided that it was not a time for beating about the bush. "A few days ago you told me that you would like to do something to help put things right in Ireland. Do you still want to do that?"

"It's true that I've been quite upset by some of the things I've seen here," she answered, "and especially hearing what happened to your wife. So yes, I would like to do something to help, but you'd have to tell me what it is before I could agree."

"I'm not going to tell you much to start with, Kate, just that it would involve using some of the talents you have picked up over the last few years. But to start with, you would have to know what you were letting yourself in for, and I'll leave Pat to fill you in on that. I'll leave the pair of you to it and he'll give me your answer tomorrow."

He got up to leave, but Kate stopped him. "Just two questions Michael," she said. "If I agree would I be helping Patrick with whatever it is he's doing? He risked a lot to come here so it must be important. And what happens if I say no?"

"If you agree you'd be helping all of us, and that means Pat as well. If you say no you'll be on your own, and there'll be nothing more either Pat or I can do to help you." With that, he left.

For much of the remainder of the evening Patrick tried to make it absolutely clear to Kate what working for The Cause actually entailed; and especially the absolute rule that once you joined you could never leave, at least not with your life. But while she listened and seemed to understand the implications, including the fact that if she was discovered and arrested she would be charged with treason, which carried a much more severe penalty than the one she faced for mere theft; he could see, however, that she had already made up her mind. She was adamant that she wanted to accept Michael's solution to her problem. Patrick couldn't be certain about whether it was because she was genuinely keen on helping him, or whether she was again merely satisfying her need for excitement. In the end he gave up and decided that her reasons for agreeing probably contained a little of both. Either way he was certain that she did not possess the level of dedication to The Cause that people like Michael Flynn had and he couldn't blame her for that. But if her main reason for joining The Cause was based on her personal feelings for him, then it added a further complication to his life; one which, however, he was more than willing to bear.

Later, when the landlady looked into the parlour, she found them side by side on the sofa. Kate was fast asleep with her head on his shoulder.

***

Since Victorian times the resort of Killiney had been popular with soldiers and civil servants stationed in Ireland as a place to relax with their families. During the War of Independence it was far enough out of Dublin city and far enough north of the Wicklow mountains to avoid the worst of 'The Troubles'. So soldiers, policemen and workers from centres like Dublin Castle, including native Irishmen and women, still frequented the little seaside town. The IRA had long viewed it as a prime target, but the authorities were alert to the danger and so, a strong military presence was stationed there. There was also the problem that a major attack could well result in the deaths of women and children, and while such niceties never bothered the Black and Tans or Auxiliaries, Collins worried that it could be detrimental to The Cause. He feared that public opinion, not only across the world but also in Ireland itself, would turn against him.

He knew that the biggest hotel in the resort was a favourite haunt of off-duty RIC men, soldiers and workers from all the various administrative centres in Dublin and as such, it contained a goldmine of very valuable information, if only he could find a way of reaching it. Then Kate Steele came to his notice and he spotted an opportunity. Having got Michael Flynn and Patrick Coughlin to recruit her, Collins pulled strings, as only Collins could, and got her a job in the hotel. He reasoned that even if guests had been warned about the dangers of loose talk, they were likely to let their guard drop when being served by an English girl.

Her job was simply to keep her eyes and ears open and report everything she saw and heard. And on her first weekend there she struck gold.

Chapter 33

In Beaufort on the following Sunday afternoon, Jack Quinlan harnessed the pony to the trap and took his mother to visit Michael Flynn's parents at their farm. Annie was especially looking forward to seeing Michael Flynn's baby son who was still being looked after by his grandparents. She would hold the baby for a little while and then she would commiserate with Mrs Flynn about the terrible things happening in Ireland; things that even prevented a father from visiting his infant son. Jack was a regular visitor to the farm where he would pick up the latest news to pass on to Michael, who was extremely loath to involve his family in either his work for The Cause or his troubles with the local Black and Tans. The arrangement whereby Michael's parents brought his son to the Quinlan's cottage, a place Michael could visit in relative safety under His Lordship's protection, was still in force, but whenever it proved difficult for him to get to Beaufort, Jack would go to the farm to pick up the latest news. He would then contact Michael by letter or telegram to an address in Dublin: an address which was changed at regular intervals. It took time, but having direct access to a leading member of the Nationalist Movement would have placed the Beaufort House steward in an impossible position.

Jack usually cycled to the Flynn farm but on this pleasant early spring afternoon, Annie had asked him to take her with him in the trap. As they neared the farm, they were almost run off the narrow country road by a speeding Crossley tender carrying a group of Black and Tans. Jack had heard them coming up behind and pulled off the lane into a gateway. But whether by accident or design, and Jack suspected that it was the latter, the tender veered towards them and only missed the trap by inches. Annie screamed and the pony shied; Jack seethed with anger as laughter and jeers reached him from the disappearing 'Tans.

He forced himself not to let his mother see his frustration and they resumed their journey. But Jack found it disturbing to think that had it been anyone other than him, the 'Tans would not have veered away at the last minute, in which case the trap and its occupants would have been smashed into the ditch. He strongly suspected that the British irregulars had recognised him and decided to give him a reminder of their presence in the area, but they knew that they couldn't run the risk of causing him and his mother serious injury. They would be well aware that deliberately running His Lordship's steward off the road would be an extremely dangerous game for even them to play.

Being in such a privileged position while good friends were bearing the brunt of the brutal tactics adopted by Black and Tans was not something that sat easily on Jack Quinlan's mind. It was something he had spoken to Michael Flynn about, and his old friend did his best to set Jack's mind at rest. Michael reminded him that in spite of not being a member of any of the Republican groups, he had already done more than most to help The Cause. Not least among Jack's contributions, Michael told him, had been his part in setting up the meetings between himself and Commander Wilson, and in helping to find Patrick Coughlin. And, although Michael could not at present go into detail, he was able to reassure Jack that both of these events would eventually prove to be far more valuable in the struggle for Ireland's freedom than simply carrying a gun could ever be.

While Michael's assurances did not set Jack's conscience entirely at rest, he certainly had no ambitions to take an active part in the guerrilla war. He had seen enough blood spilled in Mesopotamia to convince him that he wanted no further part of warfare, guerrilla or otherwise. Jack Quinlan was no coward, he had proved that many times over in the Great War, but he strongly believed that all that useless bloodshed had eventually led to nothing, and certainly not to a better world. There were, however, occasions when he could see no alternative to violence if the excesses of the Black and Tans were to be curbed.

As if to strike a balance, however, he was not altogether comfortable with the tactics of the IRA either and it would have taken a great deal of provocation to entice him to join them. He wondered if he would have felt the same if he had been subjected to an outrage, similar to that suffered by Michael Flynn; would he have shown the same determination in trying to find a peaceful path towards the cause of Irish freedom as his old school friend? It was a question he was glad not to have to answer.

When they finally reached the farm they found another visitor already there: someone who, in Jack's opinion, represented all the worst elements of both factions. Kevin Ryan was sitting at the kitchen table.

Under normal circumstances there would be nothing unusual about an uncle visiting his little nephew, but 'normal circumstances' was not a term which could be confidently applied to Kevin Ryan. He showed no interest whatsoever in the baby Mrs Flynn was bouncing on her knee as she sat by the fire. Jack noted that Kevin sat alone and that Mr Flynn was nowhere in sight. The farmer was presumably outside attending to farm chores, but the only tasks that would traditionally be carried out on a Sunday afternoon were haymaking and milking; but haymaking was still months away and it was as yet much too early in the day for milking. Under normal circumstances, the tradition of Irish hospitality would have made it impossible for the master of the house to leave a visitor, especially a family member albeit by marriage, sitting alone at his kitchen table on a Sunday afternoon. To Jack, it was an indication of the low regard in which Ryan was held by the Flynns.

Annie made directly for Mrs Flynn and the baby and the farmer's wife handed her grandson across to be drooled over by her best friend. For the next several minutes they would be totally oblivious of everything except the child, so Jack had little choice but to join Kevin at the table.

"So, Kevin," he said, "how are you keeping these days?"

"So, Jack," came the answer, "I'm grand, and yourself?"

"Ah sure I'm grand," Jack replied. "You're down to see the wee fella I see."

"I am so," was all that was forthcoming.

There was no open animosity, but the resentment towards him in Ryan's attitude was clearly evident to Jack, and he knew exactly where it stemmed from. Because Jack was a former British soldier currently employed by the English aristocrat who owned Beaufort House, to Kevin's mind he must be regarded as an enemy of The Cause. The fact that several months previously Jack had been instrumental in saving Kevin's life following the failed IRA attack on that same important Englishman, did nothing whatsoever to soften the gunman's feelings towards the Beaufort House steward. If anything it increased his resentment, and he could never bring himself to admit, perhaps even to himself, that he owed his life to Jack Quinlan.

Today, however, they were visitors in another man's kitchen, so Jack tried again to engage Kevin in friendly conversation. "And how is the lad's father? It must be hard on Mick not to be able to see his son."

Kevin seemed to find this somewhat amusing. "Come on now, Jack," he said with a sarcastic laugh, "sure don't you see a lot more of Mick Flynn than I do these days. We move in different circles as you might say."

Jack decided not to pursue the matter further; he considered that to do so would make it all too easy for Kevin's resentment to flare up into open hostility.

"Ah sure maybe you're right." He stood up. "Anyway, I came to see Mick's father, so I'll go and have a chat with him now."

Jack found the farmer in the cowshed, still wearing his Sunday Mass suit and absent-mindedly forking hay into the manger. They exchanged friendly greetings.

"I saw your man, Kevin Ryan, in the kitchen," said Jack. "How long has he been around?"

"He came yesterday," said Mr Flynn, "and God knows how long he'll be stopping."

Jack thoughtfully scratched his chin. "I never saw Kevin Ryan as the sort of a fella who'd come all the way down from Dublin just to see his nephew."

"You're dead right there," the farmer replied. "But I'll tell you, Jack, if it wasn't for him being Maureen's brother, God rest her soul, and Michael's brother-in-law, I'd kick him out this minute."

This caused Jack to issue a word of caution. "I'd say that you'd be well advised to watch out for him, that Ryan is a dangerous man and God knows what he'd do if he's roused."

The farmer's frustration began to show. "But what else can I do, Jack? The only reason I can see for him turning up here is because he's hiding from the Black and Tans, and if they find him here they'll do worse than they did the last time."

The Flynn farmhouse and barn had already been badly damaged by the 'Tans in a spiteful reprisal for their failure to capture Michael, and Jack knew that if they were to get the slightest hint that Kevin Ryan was sheltering there, they would arrest the Flynns and cheerfully raze the entire farm to the ground.

Flynn was obviously worried. "I'm that afraid for the missus and the little fella that I have half a notion to go to the RIC myself and turn him in. But I can't, can I? because if I was to do that, sure I'd have the IRA after me as well, and even that wouldn't stop the 'Tans attacking the farm."

Jack could see the farmer's dilemma. He resolved to do something to help but couldn't immediately think of what. "Wait now 'till I think about it," he said, "but the first thing to do is to get Mrs Flynn and the baby out of the way. I'll take them back to the house with me and Ma, they'll be safe enough there."

"Thanks, Jack," was all a very relieved Mr Flynn could say in reply.

Back in the farmhouse Mrs Flynn began making tea for her visitors. As she busied herself with kettle and teapot, Annie took the baby over to the table to see Kevin.

"Look," she said to the child, "sure isn't it your uncle Kevin who came all the way down from Dublin to see you."

Kevin had no particular argument with Annie Quinlan. His resentment was completely focused on her son, so he felt that he had nothing to lose by being friendly. "He's a grand little fella too Mrs Quinlan," he said, "and sure don't we all think the world of him."

"It's a terrible thing that his father can't be here with him," Annie said sadly. "God help us, but what is the world coming to when a man has to go such lengths just to see his own son."

Kevin thought that this might well be worth following up. "I hear that Mick has to come to your house to see him. Tell me now, when was the last time he was down?"

Annie was glad to find that Kevin seemed ready to chat with her. She could not help but to have heard some of the things people were saying about him, things which, at the moment, seemed hard for her to believe, so she carried on. "Oh he was down a couple of times a while ago. Let me think now, sure wasn't it the same time that Commander Wilson was up at the house."

Kevin felt an unexpected stirring of interest. "Commander Wilson? I never heard of him. Who would he be, Mrs Quinlan?"

"Ah sure isn't he the man my husband was working for when he died at that ammunition factory over there in Scotland," Annie was anxious to explain. "And a real gentleman he is, too, didn't he come all the way to Beaufort to tell me how sorry he was about what happened to Jack's poor father."

Kevin forced himself not to appear too interested. "A Commander you say? He must be a soldier or something."

"Jack told me that he's in the Royal Navy," said Annie, "but over at the factory he was some sort of a policeman."

By now Kevin was having difficulty keeping his excitement under control. Contrary to what Mr Flynn thought, his sole purpose in visiting Beaufort was to try and gain some insight into whatever it was that Michael Flynn was involved in with Patrick Coughlin. From what Annie Quinlan had said, it seemed obvious this Navy man was a British security officer, and the fact that he had been at Beaufort House at the same time that Michael was visiting the Quinlans, seemed to Kevin to go far beyond the bounds of mere coincidence.

"Tell me, Mrs Quinlan, did Mick ever meet with this Commander Wilson if they were at Beaufort together?"

"He might," the unsuspecting Annie replied, "when Michael went up to the house with Jack."

Kevin's mind raced. "Now that I come to think of it I might know this Commander Wilson, is he a tall thin fella with the cut of a gentleman about him?"

"That's him all right," replied Annie.

Before he could question Annie any further, Mrs Flynn came over and began arranging cups, milk and sugar on the table. She was about to go out to call Jack and her husband in for tea, but Kevin volunteered to go instead. They watched him crossing the farmyard and resumed their previous conversation.

Much to Mr Flynn's relief Kevin told him that he had to go back to Dublin that night. "Maybe you could give me a lift as far as the pub in Beaufort, Jack. I left a bike there."

Now that there was no longer any immediate need to take Mrs Flynn and the baby home with them, Jack reluctantly agreed but prayed that there would be no further encounters with the Black and Tans on the way. The journey back to Beaufort was completed in silence, and they dropped Ryan at the pub. He entered by the back door and soon afterwards came out again accompanied by a woman. They cycled together, posing as an innocent couple, by the back roads to Kilorglan, from where Kevin would arrange to be taken safely back to Dublin.

As they resumed their journey home Annie was eager to talk, and to Jack's surprise the baby was not her main topic of conversation.

"Now isn't he the queer one that Kevin Ryan," she said thoughtfully, "he's not one bit like his sister, Lord have mercy on her. One minute I was telling him about Commander Wilson coming to see me, and the next he wants a lift to Beaufort with us. Sure he hardly left us time to drink a cup of tea."

Jack's heart sank. Although he didn't know exactly why, he suspected that Kevin knowing about Wilson's visits to Beaufort did not bode well for whatever Michael and the Commander were involved in. He hoped that he could get a message to his friend in time.

Chapter 34

Commander Wilson had to draw on all of his training as a naval officer and his experience of security work, both of which had taught him the virtue of patience, in order to avoid becoming completely frustrated. Not for the first time since the outbreak of war in 1914, he yearned to be back on the bridge of a British warship, and at this very moment he would have settled for the bridge of any one of His Majesty's ships irrespective of size or type; even service on a river gunboat would have been welcomed. What was dangerously close to driving him to distraction was the thought that every time he felt he had made a breakthrough in his hunt for the mutineer, Private Coughlin, he found himself being sidetracked.

He was convinced that the capture of MacEoin would have left Coughlin rather isolated and exposed out in County Longford, in which case Collins and Michael Flynn would have little choice but to bring their prize new recruit back to Dublin. And here in the city, the Commander felt he stood a much better chance of successfully taking the former 'Ranger alive. By now, Wilson had studied the layout of the city carefully, and using his access to all the intelligence available at 'The Castle', he found that he could make at least some educated guesses about where the IRA were likely to hide their most important men. He was amazed that the bureaucracy at 'The Castle' had prevented anyone else carrying out a similar in-depth assessment. And in spite of what Michael Flynn had told him, he strongly suspected that Kate Steele was still in Ireland. Judging by her behaviour since she left the public house in Wareham, he could not envisage her agreeing to return to England, and assuming he was right, then she would almost certainly be in Dublin, too. The Commander was sure that arresting either one of them would lead him to the other.

But just when he had worked out a plan of action, he was called into a meeting with Alfred Cope who himself had recently returned from meeting with Lloyd George. The outcome of the meeting was that the naval officer turned security man was required to take on yet another role. Much to his annoyance, he was ordered to drop everything else he was doing and work exclusively as an adviser to Alfred Cope in his negotiations with Michael Collins. His part in foiling the Irish Republican plot to disrupt the wartime munitions factory in 1916 still came back to haunt him; that, and his experience since arriving in Ireland in the eyes of his superiors made him an expert in all things Irish. And the fact that he might even be required to accompany Cope and actually meet Collins in person did little to help ease his annoyance.

His first duty now was to contact Michael Flynn and get him to persuade Collins to agree to an expansion of the cease-fire talks to include 'advisers'.

***

"Ah, Michael," Collins greeted his visitor, "what brings you here in such a hurry? I assume that you have come with something from our friend, Commander Wilson."

Michael explained what the British side were proposing and found 'The Big Fella' surprisingly receptive.

Collins smiled. "I can't say that this comes as much of a surprise," he commented. "I've been wondering how long it would be before Lloyd George decided that he had better have a witness to back up Cope's account of what we talk about. To tell you the truth, I was thinking along the same lines myself. Can I take it that you would be willing to act as my, what did Wilson say his role would be? Ah yes, 'adviser'."

Initially Michael wasn't sure whether to be flattered or frightened. He was still an elected Sinn Fein county councillor and although it was almost a year since he had been able to sit in the council chamber in Tralee, as such he was qualified to play an official part in the talks. But he was experienced enough to know that this could well be something of a poisoned chalice: if things went horribly wrong he could well end up as a scapegoat. While he realised that Collins had made his mind up and it would be futile to argue, he needed to make something clear.

"If you want me there, sure of course I'll do it," he said. "But you know very well how I feel about a cease-fire; I think it's our only hope and I have to say that I'll do all I can to bring it about. So I'm not exactly an impartial observer. Maybe you'd do better to take one of them important fellas from the *Dáil*."

"That is precisely the reason why I want you, Michael," Collins answered. "I know where you stand, and I believe that you will be honest with me. The last person I want as an 'adviser' is someone with a hidden agenda or a personal axe to grind. I simply can't afford to keep looking over my shoulder."

Michael was well aware of the kind machinations played out in every political system in the world, and the *Dáil* was no exception, but he couldn't resist commenting:

"And here was I thinking that we were all on the same side."

Collins laughed. "You don't know the half of it, Michael. But you can tell the Commander that we're all set to carry on, so he can go ahead and give us of some possible dates for the next meeting."

***

They were again seated in the private back room of the back-street public house in Dublin, and Sean O'Connor was doing his best to get Kevin Ryan to calm down and look at things more dispassionately.

"Jesus, Kevin," he said, "you're not trying to tell me that Mick Flynn is a traitor to The Cause. You'd have to be very sure of your facts and you'd still have a hard job to get anyone at all to believe it. And you have to be bloody careful about who you say things like that to."

"But sure isn't that exactly what I'm telling you, Sean. I'll bet you anything you like that he met this fella, Commander Wilson, down in

Kerry. And even if he didn't meet him there, I'm certain that it was Wilson I saw him talking to as friendly as you like up in Phoenix Park."

"And you're certain that this Wilson is a Brit security man?" Sean asked.

"For Christ's sake, Sean, what else can he be? Sure wasn't he a Brit security man in the war and you know very well what that means: once a Brit security man, always a Brit security man."

Sean said nothing, he sat and thoughtfully drank from his pint of porter, hoping that Kevin would follow suit and give himself time to think. He knew that of late his friend had become erratic and at times downright unpredictable, but he didn't think that Kevin was so far gone as to be simply imagining everything he was saying. And that was extremely worrying.

But once he had raised a head of steam there was no stopping Ryan. "They're all in it together, Sean, this Wilson, Mick Flynn, and Coughlin – sure don't we know very well that bastard is a Brit spy. And that bloody steward at Beaufort House, Quinlan, as well. I wouldn't trust him for one minute and I'd say that it's his boss, that bloody English lord or whatever he calls himself, who is running the whole show."

Sean thought that his best bet was to play along. "Just supposing for a minute that you're right, Kevin, what can we do about it?"

"The only thing I can do is to go to 'The Big Fella' himself," Kevin answered.

O'Connor was beginning to think that there was actually something in what Ryan was telling him. Underneath all the bitterness Kevin was actually making sense. But he felt that there was still a need for caution.

"We can't do that yet, Kevin. You'd have to have a lot more proof before you can go to Collins with this, and he'd never take your word for it. Anyway, he has enough on his hands with the plan to lift Sean MacEoin out of jail. But if we can get the proof of it, sure won't I go to him with you myself."

"Good man yourself," said Kevin. He leaned forward in a conspiratorial manner. "Listen, Sean, you're well in with some of them fellas in the *Dáil*, and if you had a chat with a few of them we might find out a bit more before we say anything to himself."

O'Connor felt that agreeing to do what Kevin asked would help to keep a lid on things for at least a little while. Then he had a sudden thought. "What about this English girl you said was mixed up in this, where is she now?"

Kevin sat up in interest. "Jesus Christ, you're right there, Sean, sure didn't I forget all about her. They had her in hiding at the house in Kingstown but she's gone now. But if we could get a hold of her it would be dead easy to squeeze all the proof we want out of her."

Chapter 35

Dublin's Mountjoy Jail, nicknamed 'The Joy', was built in 1850 to house convicted prisoners awaiting transportation to Van Dieman's Land. Any convicted felon given longer than a seven year sentence could be transported, and in reality this included people convicted of crimes ranging from petty theft to treason and even murder. By 1921, however, the prison was almost entirely populated by captured IRA men and people accused of being in league with them; and the harsh conditions in the prison had changed little in its seventy year existence. In a world where virtually every crime was deemed to have been committed in furtherance of the Irish fight for independence, there were very few 'non-political' prisoners in either 'The Joy' or Kilmainham Gaol. Among the most distinguished IRA men in 'The Joy' was Sean MacEoin.

The news that an important 'rebel' was being held in Mountjoy was picked up from loose talk by Kate Steele as she served behind the bar at the hotel in Killiney. Collins had been proved right in his assumption that RIC men and British soldiers would be more inclined to let their guard drop in the presence of a barmaid who was so obviously English. On the rare occasions when anyone thought to question the highly unusual presence of an English woman working in the County Dublin resort, she would explain that she had come to Ireland to be with her soldier husband who was stationed here. But unfortunately he had been killed in an ambush by the IRA. The fact that she could provide only the vaguest details about how and where he died did nothing to detract from the authenticity of her story, or from the sympathy it generated. If anything, given the conditions prevailing in Ireland, it served to reinforce it, and the wedding ring she wore completed the picture. Word soon got round among the regular visitors to the hotel and the questions were reduced to a mere few.

Kate revelled in the excitement and intrigue of it all. Even if she realised that a cursory investigation into her background would be enough to send her to 'The Joy' as an IRA spy, she didn't show it.

She had no idea of what was meant by 'The Joy' when she first picked up the remark about the rebel prisoner held there but, in line with her instructions from Michael Flynn, she didn't arouse suspicion by appearing too eager in her search for useful 'intelligence'. Later in the evening she heard the same RIC men talking about a place called Mullingar and reported both snippets of conversation to Michael. It didn't take him long to put two and two together and deduce that Sean MacEoin was being held in Mountjoy and not Kilmainham.

At this point Collins gave Patrick Coughlin instructions to start planning a prison break. Patrick studied layouts of the jail and realised that he would need some more accurate information on precisely where in the labyrinthine old building MacEoin was being held. Even if the prisoner was, as might well be the case, being held in solitary confinement, without accurate information locating him would be akin to looking for a needle in a haystack. But the other prisoners, most of whom knew or would at least recognise MacEoin, would know where in the prison he was incarcerated; and most prisoners were allowed visitors. So it was a simple matter to obtain the information he needed, but the planning process had inevitably been delayed.

The delay caused Michael Collins to put off his next meeting with Alfred Cope; he was banking on a successful prison break to help him regain the ground he had lost due to MacEoin's capture.

***

It was well after midnight when the British Peerless armoured car drove slowly up to the gates of Mountjoy Jail. The Peerless was a heavy unwieldy vehicle, not really a true armoured car but an amalgamation of parts from a collection of vehicles quickly assembled at a time when Britain was short of armoured vehicles. It comprised an armoured body built by Austin Motors mounted on an American

Peerless chassis and powered by a petrol engine from the same company. The body had originally been designed for use by the Russians in the Great War and still featured the twin turrets favoured by them. The armoured body was, however, too short for the chassis so that part of the Peerless lorry was left sticking out at the back, adding to the makeshift appearance of the vehicle. But armed with two .303 Hotchkiss machine guns it could be quite lethal against infantry and was impervious to small arms fire. In Ireland it was mostly employed in escorting convoys of supplies between military bases.

The car which arrived at 'The Joy' in the early hours looked distinctly the worse for wear. A front tyre was shredded and the paintwork on the side and engine cover above the wheel was blackened and blistered. It had obviously seen action in the very recent past.

A British Army officer sporting the three pips of a captain on his shoulders got out of the car and looked warily around the darkened street. The driver at the wheel was fully prepared for an instant retreat and the gunners in the turrets peered warily through the slots in the armour above their machine guns. The captain went to the gate and pulled hard on the chain connected to the guardroom situated inside the prison to summon a sentry. There was the sound of hob-hailed boots on the cobbled yard and a small slit in the gate was opened. The officer from the armoured car urgently explained that they had orders to transfer a prisoner from Mountjoy to Dublin Castle but had been caught in an IRA ambush and suffered some damage to the car on the way. He urgently needed to speak with the orderly officer and in the meantime, he wanted access to the prison so that his men could change the damaged wheel in safety. The sound of gunfire and explosions still echoed across the city and although a nightly occurrence, it lent credibility to the officer's story and the sentry left to fetch the orderly officer.

A regular army lieutenant arrived and inspected the damaged vehicle. Satisfied with what he saw he ordered the gate to be opened and motioned to the driver to bring the car into the prison yard. Once inside, the captain, without consulting the orderly officer, directed the driver to park the car directly outside the guardroom.

The captain ordered his men out of the car. To the orderly officer's surprise five men in uniforms from a variety regiments emerged from a vehicle that normally carried only a crew of four, all carried .303 Lee-Enfield rifles except the driver who wore a holstered revolver. As they emerged they donned steel helmets, fixed bayonets and lined up by the side of their vehicle. A corporal detailed the driver and one man to carry out the necessary repairs and the two gunners were ordered back into the car. The driver and his helper removed the spare wheel which was fixed to the side. They unloaded some tools and began to jack up the front of the car preparatory to changing the wheel. The captain casually lit a cigarette and engaged the lieutenant in conversation, describing their brush with the IRA. To the orderly officer it looked like a well drilled military operation, but he did think to question the captain about the lateness of the hour and the number of men he had brought. He seemed satisfied with the explanation that owing to the importance of the man they were to transfer, 'one couldn't be too careful'. The necessary papers, which obviously contained the identity of the prisoner, were for the orderly officer's eyes only and would be handed over in due course.

To the casual observer the corporal would have appeared to be idly watching the two crew members at work changing the wheel, but a closer inspection would have revealed that he was carefully scrutinising the prison yard. When he was satisfied that the prison had settled back down to its nightly routine following their unexpected arrival, he nodded to the captain who finished his cigarette and ordered the lieutenant to follow him into the guardroom. They disappeared inside and the corporal motioned to his men to set the next part of Patrick Coughlin's plan to rescue Sean MacEoin into motion.

The 'corporal' was Paddy Daly and he had been selected to lead the attempt to break Sean MacEoin out of Mountjoy Jail; the 'captain' was Emmet Dalton, a former British officer wearing his old Great War uniform with the captain's pips added, and who could affect a passable English accent. The other four men were also members of the Dublin Brigade of the IRA and all were volunteers. The armoured car had been captured earlier that evening in an efficiently staged ambush while escorting a rations convoy to a barracks in the city, and two British soldiers had been killed. The damage to the car had not been planned by Coughlin but it proved to be only a minor inconvenience and, in fact, it added an extra element of credibility to the operation.

Patrick had wanted to lead the attack on the prison in person, but this had been vetoed by Michael Collins.

'The Big Fella' had personally picked out Daly to lead the raid and had suggested Dalton be included because of his British Army experience. As leader, it was left to Daly to select the other four members of the party. There were dozens of volunteers, but one particular requirement stood out: at least one man had to be able to drive an armoured car, and the only IRA man he knew who had anything approaching that kind of experience was Kevin Ryan. He was aware that Ryan had never driven an actual armoured vehicle, but he had competently handled a Peerless lorry on which the car was based. Coughlin had specified the Peerless because there were several in service in Dublin and the extra turret provided them with increased firepower. The minute that Ryan heard of the call for volunteers from the Dublin Brigade, he guessed that they were being sought for the attempt to free Sean MacEoin and he was determined to get himself selected. He saw it as an opportunity to get his own back on both MacEoin and Coughlin for what had happened at Clonfin; and his first thought was to make sure that the operation failed. In which case MacEoin would remain in prison and, as the man responsible for planning, Coughlin would have to carry the can. As the plan for the operation unfolded, however, he realised that it would be extremely difficult to sabotage the attempt and get away with it; neither Daly nor Dalton could be regarded as 'eejits'. But this was not a total setback: if the plan actually succeeded, then both MacEoin and Coughlin would have to acknowledge his part in the break-out, and his standing with Michael Collins would, he thought, be restored.

Coughlin strongly objected to Ryan's inclusion, but the operation still required a driver and Collins, although he expressed misgivings, was persuaded to overrule Patrick.

They finished changing the wheel and the 'corporal' motioned to Ryan to get back into the driver's seat and the two gunners to stand ready in the turrets. He and the other man stood by the car primed for instant action. Inside the guardroom, Dalton handed a sheaf of papers to the lieutenant who scanned through them, unaware that they were forged orders for the transfer of the prisoner, Sean MacEoin, from Mountjoy to Dublin Castle. Being a soldier whose responsibility was limited to guarding the prison from outside attack, the orderly officer had little knowledge of such things, so he sent for the senior member of the prison staff on duty. There was a delay while the prison official was located and dragged out of the comfortable camp bed in his office, all the while complaining bitterly about being disturbed at this time of night. As they waited, the corporal of the guard came out from the back of the guardroom with two soldiers and set off with them to relieve the sentries at the main gate. Paddy Daly had already noted that Kevin Ryan was beginning to show signs of impatience and kept drumming his fingers on the steering wheel. Then he spotted Ryan holding his revolver at the ready while the guards were being relieved. He got into the car to prevent the hothead from doing anything rash.

The waiting was beginning to get on everyone's nerves, so, their leader decided that they needed something to take their minds off it. He went into the guardroom to find try and find out what was happening and saw the prison officer scrutinising the papers with the lieutenant. Dalton stood by smoking a cigarette and doing his best to appear unconcerned. The 'captain' explained to his 'corporal' that there would be a slight delay. The 'corporal' reported that repairs had been carried out to the armoured car but they needed to drive around the yard to make sure that it was fully functional in case they were attacked on their way back to 'The Castle'. The 'captain' agreed, the 'corporal' saluted smartly and went outside to explain to the others what was happening. He told them to make a show of thoroughly checking the car. Ryan drove it around the yard and the gunners traversed the turrets. With something to occupy them the men relaxed and when they finished the car was parked just inside the prison gates and facing outwards.

Inside, however, the tension was mounting. The prison official, still grumpy at being disturbed in the middle of the night, decided that he would assert his authority over the British Army officers. Although he could detect nothing seriously wrong with the paperwork, he announced that he intended to telephone Dublin Castle to 'clear up a few points'. This was something that Coughlin had anticipated and as a precaution the telephone lines out of the prison had been cut. When the prison official couldn't get through he shrugged and said that the transfer would now have to wait until his superiors came on duty in the morning. In an effort to get him to change his mind, Dalton began to argue that his orders called for the transfer to be completed before morning, and that there had already been too much of a delay. But while he could pull rank on the lieutenant, he had no authority over the prison official and the man knew it. A heated argument ensued, but the more Dalton threatened to report him for causing an unwarranted delay to such an important military operation, the more the official dug his heels in.

Dalton eventually gave up and went out to hold a council of war with Paddy Daly. The original plan was obviously not going to work and they agreed that more direct action was called for or they would have to simply give up and drive away; assuming that it would now be possible to get away without a fight. But they agreed that they had come too far to turn back. They quickly devised a secondary scheme, informed the others what they had in mind, and set about putting it into action.

The two IRA men went back into the guardroom. They made sure that the door to the quarters at the back of the guardroom where the rest of the guard detail relaxed was closed while they held the lieutenant and prison official at gunpoint and disarmed the army officer. The soldier remained quietly calm, but the prison official began to protest, until threatened by the 'corporal' with a fixed bayonet. Badly frightened, he agreed to conduct them into the prison proper, collect the necessary keys and release Sean MacEoin. Dalton reminded him that if he tried anything too clever they knew exactly where MacEoin's cell was located. The lieutenant said nothing, and because he didn't seem to be at all fazed by his predicament, Dalton considered that he would bear watching. Outside one of their men fell in behind and they began marching their captives across the yard. Ryan had been directed to start the car and keep the engine ticking over and the men in the turrets told to have the Hotchkiss machine-guns ready for action.

Ryan, however, had been bitterly disappointed at not being allowed to go into the prison. When he heard the new plan he desperately wanted to be one of the men to actually release MacEoin, so that he could begin making the sarcastic comments and disparaging remarks he had prepared for the occasion. He had tried to argue but was given short shrift by Dalton, a move which left him seething. As his three colleagues marched in proper military fashion across the yard, his impatience got the better of him; he left his seat in the car and ran after them.

Dalton heard him running across the cobblestones and turned to see who it was. He shouted at Ryan to get back in the car. Daly turned to add his voice to Dalton's. The lieutenant saw his chance; he made a break for it and bolted across the yard blowing a whistle. He was cut down by one of the machine-gunners in the armoured car, but the damage had been done.

The combined effect of the whistle and the gunfire alerted the whole prison. There was nothing for it but to beat a rapid retreat. Dalton got hold of Ryan and pushed him back into the driver's seat; the corporal of the guard roused his men and led them out of the guard room but they were forced back by machine gun fire, leaving one man lying in the doorway; the sentries at the gate were shot down and Paddy Daly and the last IRA man ran to open the gates. Ryan had collected his senses and as he drove out through the gate the last two attackers jumped onto the exposed end of the chassis behind the armoured body and they sped off into the night.

Later the six IRA men changed back into civilian clothes, the two machine guns and ammunition were removed and the armoured car was pushed into the River Liffey with the British uniforms inside. Little was said and Kevin Ryan was pointedly ignored. They dispersed to their various units across the city and Paddy Daly went to break the news of their failure to Michael Collins.

Chapter 36

The failure of the attempt to free Sean MacEoin from 'The Joy' proved to be a severe setback to Michael Collins' plans. And Michael Flynn was deeply nervous about the detrimental effect it appeared to be having on the prospects of negotiating a cease-fire. Instead of being able to exploit the advantage that the successful rescue of such a prominent Republican as MacEoin from a reportedly secure British prison would have given him, Collins knew that at the next several meetings with Alfred Cope he would be forced onto the defensive. Michael feared that Collins, who had always expressed misgivings about a cease-fire, might simply give up any attempt to arrange one. And to add to this he was worried that 'The Big Fella' would lay the blame for the failure squarely at Patrick Coughlin's door.

He asked Collins if this was the case. "No, Michael," Collins answered, "the plan was a sound one. Patrick Coughlin did everything we could expect of him. And so, with one exception, did the men who carried it out. The one thing that Patrick couldn't possibly anticipate was some obstinate minor official deciding to lord it over the British Army."

"And the exception being Kevin Ryan," Michael commented.

"I'm afraid so," Collins replied. "But then I have to take at least some of the blame for that. I know that Paddy and Emmet wanted to take him, but I should never have agreed to it and made them find another driver. There was far too much resting on the success of this operation for me to take a chance on someone like Kevin."

Michael had, by this time, completely lost confidence in his brother-in-law's ability to function rationally. But Kevin was a member of his wife's family and he was loath to do anything that might cause any more heartache for the Ryans. He felt that it would cast a cloud over Maureen's memory; and to add to that, Mr and Mrs Ryan were, after all, his son's grandparents. So he worried that Collins would lose patience with Kevin, and that could only lead to fatal consequences. Even so, he felt compelled to inform Collins of what Jack Quinlan had told him: Ryan had apparently found out about his meeting Wilson at Beaufort House. Collins had been non-committal but Michael knew that he would certainly bear it in mind.

"What will happen to Kevin now?" he asked.

"Until this war is over and Ireland is free, there will always be a need for men with Kevin Ryan's particular talents," Collins told him. "So, for the moment, we will keep him in reserve, but we certainly cannot include him in anything else that requires the virtue of patience."

This all sounded somewhat vague to Michael. His experience, however, told him that he would have to be satisfied with it.

In the early days of the talks with Cope, Collins had indeed been at best lukewarm in his support for a cease-fire. He knew that one would eventually have to be arranged but not, in his view, until after they had run the British forces in Ireland ragged. He was also worried that a truce would rob the movement of their greatest advantage: that of secrecy. As time went by, however, the ability of the IRA to pursue the war began to show signs of weakening. Shortages of arms and ammunition were fast approaching crisis point. They could still mount bombings, raids and ambushes, but for how much longer? Nobody could be certain. They badly needed a breather and the only way to get one was by negotiating a truce, so the talks with Alfred Cope would have to go on. Collins, however, hung on as long as he reasonably could before agreeing to another meeting in the hope that, in the meantime, the IRA could pull off a spectacular success, but it was not to be and the next meeting was eventually arranged.

It was Michael Flynn's first attendance at a meeting since the main protagonists had agreed to the presence of the two 'advisers'. Before the meeting he was briefed by Collins who outlined what had been achieved to date, which Michael found to be disappointingly little. They agreed that for his first meeting with Cope and Wilson,

Michael should not get involved in the arguments unless directly invited to by Collins, and 'The Big Fella' was sure that Wilson would have been given similar instructions. But there seemed to be no clear plan for the conduct of the meeting and little was said about what they eventually expected to achieve. There was one concession, however, that Collins said he would insist on from the British before he would agree to any kind of truce, and that was that the hated Auxiliaries and the Black and Tans must be removed from Ireland. Not only would this remove a real threat to the IRA's chances of success, it would also ensure widespread support for a cease-fire among the Irish people.

In the event Michael came out from his first session as Collins' 'adviser' with a feeling of disillusionment. Rather than being involved in a meaningful discussion about the terms of a cease-fire, he was obliged to sit through what seemed to him a pointless argument between Collins and Alfred Cope.

As soon as they sat down at the table Cope brought up the subject of the 'bungled' attempt to break Sean MacEoin out of Mountjoy Prison. He voiced the opinion that the affair proved that IRA was a spent force and should seriously consider giving up what had become a hopeless fight. Collins countered this by pointing out that it proved nothing of the sort. The IRA had captured a British armoured car, penetrated a supposedly secure British establishment and got away again without a single casualty on their side. As the arguments passed back and forth, Michael had to steel himself not to interrupt and ask when they were going to get down to discussing a truce.

After the meeting, when the 'advisers' were alone, he was surprised to hear Commander Wilson express similar sentiments. Michael was aware that the Englishman was as anxious as himself to see an end to the war, but he wasn't altogether sure why. He knew that like many regular British servicemen, Wilson was deeply unhappy with the conduct of the war by what they called 'the irregulars', but Michael suspected there was more to it than that. When asked, the Commander reiterated that a negotiated truce was the only hope of bringing what he regarded as senseless bloodshed to an end. What he didn't reveal to Michael, however, was that solving the 'Irish

Problem' was also the only way he could see of ever being able to escape from the security service and getting back to sea.

There was something else that Michael was mystified about: to some extent he could understand how Collins had been forced to put up a defence of the IRA, but he failed to see what Cope had expected to gain by continually hammering the point home.

"I'm very afraid," Wilson told Michael, "that following the failure of the IRA to break MacEoin out of prison, certain factions in Whitehall are more convinced than ever that a military solution is possible in Ireland."

In spite of his frustration at the way the meeting had turned out, Michael found himself defending the action at Mountjoy in precisely the way Collins had done.

"But sure how can they make it out to be a victory when they lost four men to none of ours?" He regretted the outburst the minute he uttered it.

"Whether it happens to be true or not is really irrelevant," Wilson replied. "The important thing is that the powers that be in London, who admittedly are quite remote from the real situation here, believe it to be true."

He looked Michael squarely in the face. "And I suppose you realise that you have just put forward exactly the same sort argument we have been listening to all afternoon. It seems to me, Mr Flynn, that as advisers we should try to rise above such things if we are ever going to get these talks back on track."

The remark was enough to bring Michael back to reality. "Point taken, Commander," he said.

The failure to free MacEoin from 'The Joy' was soon to have another adverse effect on Collins' plans, as he explained to Michael on his return from a meeting of the *Dáil*.

"I find it ironic, Michael, that a similarly unrealistic assessment of the outcome of the Mountjoy affair should be held here as in London. Certain members of the *Dáil,* Mr de Valera among them, seem to regard it as a resounding victory for us. All of which lends weight to Dev's pet theory that we should throw all our resources into mounting a decisive effort in an attempt to win the war in one fell swoop."

"But don't they know how scarce those resources are compared to the Brits?" Michael asked.

"Oh they're well aware of that," Collins replied, "but Dev seems to have come up with something he says will help to redress the balance. When you came back from America with him, did you notice a couple of crates being unloaded?"

"I did so," Michael answered. "I saw them being loaded as well but when I asked Dev what was in them he wouldn't let on."

"I'm not surprised," Collins told him, "those crates contained a dozen of the new Thompson sub-machine guns with ammunition, and he has some of the lads in the *Dáil* thinking that they will provide us with the means to defeat the whole British Army."

Chapter 37

Sean O'Connor thought things over as he sat and in the back room of the pub and waited for Kevin Ryan to come in. There was no guarantee that Kevin would actually turn up but O'Connor very much hoped that he would: he had important and disturbing news to discuss with his friend.

There was no denying that, of late, Kevin Ryan had become nothing short of an enigma and was even being regarded as something of an embarrassment within the Dublin Brigade. Word had, of course, got around about what had happened at Mountjoy Jail and the general opinion was that Ryan had not exactly covered himself in glory. In short, the blame for the failure to free the extremely well liked and much respected Sean MacEoin was being placed squarely at Ryan's door. O'Connor also knew that in spite of his impressive previous record of service to the Republican cause, people close to him were rapidly becoming tired of having to listen to Ryan persistently voicing his opinion that some kind of conspiracy was being hatched by Michael Flynn and Patrick Coughlin. He had already warned Ryan of the dangers involved in making groundless assertions of that sort, but it seemed that the warnings had not been heeded. He had to admit that he, too, had begun to harbour similar feelings about Kevin and had seriously thought that, in his own interests, he would do well to break off all contact with the volatile Ryan.

But then some whispered news came his way that might just lend some credibility to Ryan's conspiracy theory. So he waited and hoped that Kevin had not noticed the change in attitude towards him among his old friends and decided to lie low for a while.

Ryan, who was completely oblivious of such things, eventually entered the pub. O'Connor heard him loudly order a pint from the bar on his way through. He came into the back room and sat down. Within a minute or two a girl brought in his porter and left. In certain Dublin public houses men like Kevin Ryan and Sean O'Connor were not expected to pay for their drinks.

"So, Kevin," O'Connor said, "and how are things with you this fine night?"

"Ah sure I'm grand, Sean," Ryan answered. But he had no more time for small talk and came straight to the point: "What's the word from the lads in the *Dáil*?"

In typical Irish manner O'Connor took his time about answering. He leaned back and took a long swig from his porter. When he was ready he leaned forward. "You were right about something going on, Kevin," he said. "And if what I heard is true, it's not good news at all I can tell you."

A few months previously, Ryan would have been happy to play the game in the time-honoured easy-going Irish way and he, too, would have had a drink before resuming the conversation. But the 'new' Kevin had neither the time nor the patience for such traditions.

"For Christ's sake, Sean, leave the bloody porter alone and tell us what they said."

O'Connor had thought long and hard about how to break the news to Ryan. He had himself been shocked and dismayed when he first heard about what was going on behind the scenes, and he was angry that people within the Republican Movement could even contemplate such things. By the time he came to meet Kevin some of his anger had abated but he was still deeply disturbed about the situation. He had no idea about what the effect would be on his drinking companion, with Kevin anything was possible, but he had no option but to come right out with what he had been told by a friend in the *Dáil*.

"From what I heard we are having secret talks with the Brits about a cease-fire."

He fully expected Ryan to immediately fly into an uncontrollable rage at the news, but was amazed to see Kevin sitting in shocked silence for at least a full minute. Ryan, then, began to nod his head and when he spoke his voice was little more than a whisper.

"A cease-fire is it, didn't I tell you Sean, them bastards are all traitors. Wait 'till I tell 'The Big Fella' about this."

O'Connor hesitated, not knowing how his next piece of news would be received. "As far as I know it's Collins himself that's doing the talking, he's meeting some fella called Cope from 'The Castle' to talk about a truce. And I'm told that he has the backing of de Valera and a few more of our top men."

Ryan looked aghast, and then he laughed. "Get away with you, Sean, sure this fella you know in the *Dáil* is only codding you. Nobody at all is talking about a truce."

"It's God's truth, Kevin. They're talking about arranging a bloody cease-fire."

At this Ryan did fly off the handle. He banged the table with such force that the glasses of porter almost toppled over and some of the dark stout flowed onto the floor. Then, just as suddenly, his anger subsided and O'Connor was amazed to see him sitting with his head in his hands seemingly close to tears.

"God help us," he said with feeling. "Michael Collins talking to the bloody Brits about a truce; and with the whole *Dáil* behind him, you say?"

"The whole *Dáil* aren't in it," O'Connor said, "only a few of the lads in what they call the cabinet. It's being kept from the rest of them and the fella that told me wasn't supposed to know anything at all about it. According to him, when they do find out a lot of them will be against it like us."

O'Connor had taken it for granted that Ryan would never accept any sort of truce with the British. He held similar sentiments himself, albeit for different reasons. Ryan, he knew, had come to enjoy the fighting and particularly the killing which, of late, seemed to be his sole reason for living and he cared nothing for anything else; even winning the war had lost any real significance for him. For O'Connor, it was not the war itself that held the attraction. In fact he would like to see an end to the fighting, but only after they had achieved a complete victory over the British forces in Ireland. For generations his family had fostered the dream of a free and independent Ireland and many of his ancestors had died for 'The Cause'. Like Kevin Ryan he had virtually been raised to help bring that dream to fruition but, unlike Kevin, he had not lost sight of the ultimate goal. He was aware that any kind of negotiated truce would inevitably involve compromise, and he believed that making any kind of concession whatsoever to the British would amount to nothing less than a betrayal of his heritage.

"I hope to God that your man in the *Dáil* told the rest of them and they're going to put a stop to it before it goes any further." The thought had a pacifying effect on Ryan.

"Sure didn't I say the exact same thing to him myself," O'Connor asserted. "But the bastard told me he couldn't do a thing about it yet because he doesn't know whether some of them would be for it. The truth of it is that he won't make a move until he knows for sure which side of his bread has the butter on it."

Ryan could hardly believe his ears. "Christ Almighty, what's wrong with him, Sean? Sure there's nobody in all Ireland who would be in favour of a cease-fire."

O'Connor himself was mystified. Why would anyone in the Republican Movement, especially men who had fought the British for over four bloody years since 'The Rising', want to see a cease-fire? In his view all those men and women who had died for The Cause deserved better, and he had said as much to his contact in the *Dáil*. The representative, however, explained that there was more at stake than just the concerns of those who were doing the actual fighting with the IRA; he had been elected to speak for all the people of Ireland, the majority of whom would welcome an early end to the war. O'Connor knew that there was some truth in this and he was prepared to concede that a great many people were totally weary of the endless round of ambushes and reprisals. He could not, however, ever bring himself to accept that any compromise arrangement with Great Britain was going to win Ireland's freedom, and he cited the surrender after 'The Rising' to prove his point. That, he argued, had merely led to a further four years of heartache for the people of Ireland. Only total victory would achieve their ultimate goal.

He knew that putting the argument about what the majority of the people of Ireland might or might not want to Kevin Ryan would be a complete waste of time, and as he didn't totally accept it himself, he didn't bother.

"Ah sure he's a politician these days, Kevin," he said. "He doesn't know who to trust and he's keeping things to himself until he finds out how the land lies, and by that time it might be too late. So he's playing a different kind of a game, and I'd say that he only told me about this is because he thinks I might be the one to do something to put a stop to any talk of a cease-fire for him. And I'll do it, too, if I get half a chance."

Ryan brightened up. "Good man yourself, Sean; between the two of us we'll banjax these bastards. What did you say this fella from 'The Castle' is called?"

"Cope," O'Connor told him.

Ryan slapped the table again but with less force on this occasion. "That's it, Sean me boy, all we have to do is to shoot this fella and the Brits will have nothing more to do with any more talk of a cease-fire."

"I had that notion myself," O'Connor said, "but sure with only the two of us we'd never get anywhere near him."

"But all we have to do is get a few of the lads to help us."

"That's all well and good, Kevin, but we'd have to get half the Dublin Brigade with us and then the news would be out. Collins himself would hear of it and then it would be us that's banjaxed."

Ryan looked dismayed. "God Almighty, are you telling me there's nothing at all we can do about it, Sean?"

"Hold on now, Kevin, sure I'm not saying that at all," O'Connor assured him. "There are some others we might be able to get at. Mick Flynn and some security man from 'The Castle' have the job of fixing up the meetings."

Ryan sat up. "Wilson," he said quietly, "didn't I tell you, Sean, him and Mick Flynn were up to some devilment. Well, this is our chance to fix things for the pair of them."

"Easy now, Kevin," O'Connor cautioned. "We can't shoot Mick Flynn: that would be like doing for 'The Big Fella' himself. We'd have all the boys down on us in no time, and the cease-fire would still go ahead. But this Wilson, now, he's a horse of a different colour. If we were to get him the Brits would see it the same way as killing Cope. And sure nobody at all could blame us for doing in a British security man."

He drank what little of his porter that had not been spilled. "Leave it to me, Kevin," he said, "and I'll think of a way to fix your Mr Wilson for good."

Chapter 38

Kate Steele was still enjoying life at the hotel in Killiney. She enjoyed the jokes and the banter of the clientele, and particularly that of the men released for a short while from the tensions of the war. She was beginning to develop a sense of what might be important from the snippets of conversation she picked up, and she made notes for her weekly report to Michael Flynn. Once a week on her day off she made a trip into Dublin to visit one of the many cinemas in the city. She went to a different cinema every week and the purpose of her visits was not simply to go to the pictures.

Michael always arranged to meet her for a matinee performance because going to an evening showing made it difficult for her to get in and out of the city in time to beat the curfew, and there was less likelihood of her being caught up in IRA activities. Kate would find Michael waiting for her, sometimes outside the cinema and sometimes in the foyer; it depended on how many people were about and where he would appear least conspicuous. To anyone watching they would appear to be sweethearts meeting for a visit to the movies. They would go into the cinema to watch the film, and when the lights went down she would surreptitiously pass him the notes she had made of the 'intelligence' she had picked up during the week. At some time during the show he would go to the toilet, and if he was certain that the coast was clear he would glance through them. When he returned to his seat he would whisper a question or two. By now, Kate would often be absorbed in the film and he would have to nudge her or raise his voice to get her attention. Even during the silent films, their sometimes animated conversation would usually elicit impatient glances from those around them, but he was confident that the other cinemagoers would be too absorbed to pick up anything of much importance from their whispers. She could not help but notice that he never remained sitting any closer to her than was necessary for the exchange of information.

Afterwards, he would walk her to the tram stop or railway station. Usually he would remind her of the danger involved in what she was doing and issue a warning to be extremely careful. Then he would tell her where to meet him next week and walk away. The intrigue of it all excited Kate and the only reason she took any notice of Michael's regular warnings was because it added to the sense of danger. She refused to allow the very real dangers that Michael spoke about to spoil things for her, and the fact that she was committing an act of treason was something she preferred not to think about at all.

Inevitably her natural curiosity caused her to ask him what happened to the information she gave him and if it proved to be useful. Michael simply told her that it was safer not to know; whether safer for her or safer for him he didn't say but she suspected that he was referring to both. The only time she got an inkling of how her information was being used was when she heard some of the off-duty RIC men in the bar talking about a failed IRA assault on Mountjoy prison. The thought of having been somehow involved in such an event gave her an immense thrill; the fact that men had been killed during the raid she pushed to the back of her mind.

Patrick Coughlin, though, was never far from her thoughts and she desperately wanted to know if the information she gave Michael Flynn was passed on to him. Because Patrick had been one of the men to recruit her, she thought that it probably was, and she found herself wishing that she could see him again. She knew that Michael Flynn would never tell her where Patrick was or what he was doing and she decided that the only way to find out was to follow Michael and see where he went after leaving her at the railway station. But the next visit to the city rendered this unnecessary.

Being paid for working at the hotel and having her board included meant that she still had some money left over from what she had stolen from the pub in Wareham. Spring had now really begun to take hold and the weather was pleasantly warm, so she went into Dublin early that day to do some shopping. Time flew by and she was late arriving at the cinema.

Although it was only mid-afternoon, there was a queue to see the latest Hollywood western. Michael Flynn was nowhere to be seen, so, she lingered at the back of the queue until the doors opened and people began to file into the theatre, but still he failed to put in an appearance. She feared that because she was late, and knowing how security-conscious he was, he might well have been and gone. This would mean that Michael's carefully laid plans would have gone awry and she would have to wait for him to contact her by some other means; if, in fact, he ever did. Her heart dropped at the thought of being, once again, cast adrift in Ireland without the slightest chance of ever meeting Patrick again. But there was nothing she could do about it, so she decided that she might as well go and see the film.

She remained in the queue and when she was just inside the cinema doors a man wearing the flat cap and muffler of a Dublin workman dashed across the road to join her. He put his arm around her and held her tightly.

"God help us but sure I nearly didn't make it in time, darlin'," he said in a loud voice. Then he whispered in her ear as if apologising for being late, "Take it easy now, Kate, don't act too surprised. Just pretend to be mad at me for being late."

She almost cried with pleasure when she instantly recognised his voice. "Patrick!" she exclaimed. He gave her a nudge with his elbow and she carried on in a barely audible whisper, "What on earth are you doing here?"

They had reached the pay kiosk so he didn't answer. She felt such a thrill at meeting him again that she didn't mind. He bought two tickets for the stalls. The lights had dimmed and the show was about to start when they entered the auditorium. An usherette led them with her shaded torch to seats near the back. As soon as they were seated, Kate could no longer contain her curiosity, or indeed, her pleasure.

She sat close to him and put her arm through his. "Patrick," she hissed in his ear, "for heaven's sake tell me what you're doing here."

"All in good time, Kate, all in good time," he whispered back. "Sure didn't I nearly have to say 'please' to Mick Flynn to make him let me go to the pictures with you. Wait now 'till Tom Mix has all the rustlers shot and we'll have a chat about it."

She passed him her notes but he merely pocketed them without a glance. Unlike Michael Flynn, he didn't go to the toilet to read them. And, also unlike Michael, he didn't at all mind sitting close to her. She couldn't remember when she had enjoyed a film more, and not because of what was happening on the flickering silent screen. Patrick, too, drew immense pleasure from sitting by her in the darkened cinema. For a little while, at least, he could find relief from the stresses of his part in the fight for Ireland. They sat close together with her arm through his; with the rest of the patrons they cheered the hero and booed the villain; they tapped their feet in time with the piano player as the posse chased the bad men across the screen.

All too soon the show was over. They lingered as long as they could but eventually had to leave the cinema. As they walked arm in arm towards the station where she would catch a train back to Killiney, she told him what she had heard about a failed IRA attack on Mountjoy Prison and she wanted to know if it was anything to do with what she had passed on to Michael Flynn a few weeks earlier.

She had obviously been thoroughly enjoying their visit to the pictures and he hated to introduce a sour note. But it was time to return to the reality of the situation.

"Kate," he said, "I can't tell you anything about that. If people ever got the notion that you might know things like that sure we'd all be in trouble. And to tell you the truth, it would be a lot easier for myself and Mick Flynn if you didn't ask us about these things."

Of late, Patrick had come to regret his part in recruiting her to work for The Cause. He was well aware of the fact that if he and Michael hadn't persuaded her, not that she had taken much persuading, to work for them, Michael Collins would have taken matters out of their hands. Even so he had begun to apply his mind to finding ways of getting her safely out of Collins' clutches. But there was still one more thing he had to ask her to do, and after that he was resolved to finding a way of getting her away from Ireland.

As they neared the station, he asked her to concentrate on gathering information about people who worked in one particular building used by the authorities in Dublin, and what they did there. He left her before they reached the station; although he was sure that he was not, as yet, known to the RIC, it was always wise to take precautions. Before they parted, he almost pleaded with her to be extra careful, and for once she was determined to heed the warning. He told her which cinema to go to the following week and her disappointment was evident when she learned that it would be Michael and not Patrick who would meet her.

She stood on tiptoe and kissed him on the cheek. "Please take care of yourself, too, Patrick."

***

The man watching Michael Flynn to see if he went to meet with Commander Wilson had a fruitless vigil. Michael never left his lodgings all day.

Chapter 39

"Sure isn't that the stupidest thing I ever heard of!" Patrick Coughlin was totally against the proposed action and he didn't particularly care who knew it.

Michael Flynn motioned to him to calm down. "So you think it can't be done, Pat?"

"Oh it could be done, all right. With a whole battalion of Connaught Rangers supported by a battery of 18 pounders, you could do it; with them you could take Dublin Castle itself. But this is a different proposition altogether," Coughlin answered testily.

After outlining what was being proposed by the Republican leadership, Michael Collins had remained silent while they mulled it over in their minds. Coughlin's outburst, however, signalled that it was time for him to intervene. "We will have the whole Dublin Brigade at our disposal, fully five hundred men," he said.

Michael Flynn noted that he had said 'will' and not 'would'. And he knew that the use of the word had been deliberate.

"For a job like this it's not the number of men you have that counts, but how well they're armed," Coughlin argued. "What do our lads have? A few .303 rifles and a handful of revolvers, and none of them with more than half a dozen rounds apiece."

"We will have those brand new Thompson sub-machine guns Mr de Valera brought back from America, and there is plenty of ammunition for them," Collins reminded him.

"How many guns did he bring, and how much ammunition?" Coughlin asked. "And while we're at it, what size magazines do them things have?"

"There are twelve guns with two thousand rounds each. I don't know what kind of magazines they have," Collins answered.

Coughlin took some time collect his thoughts. "Look lads," he said eventually. "These guns are brand spanking new, they didn't come out in time for the war and nobody on this side of the Atlantic Ocean knows anything at all about them, or the best way to deploy them. Did Dev bring any instructions or service manuals with him?"

"Not that I am aware of," Collins said.

"In that case I'd say that the only reason the Yanks gave him the bloody things was for us to try them out in action so that they'd learn something about how effective they are for our kind of fighting. So we'll have to work out the best way to use them by ourselves. At a guess I'd say that they can fire at least five hundred rounds a minute, anything less and they wouldn't be much better than what every army has now. But at that rate of fire two thousand rounds won't last any time at all, and any other type of ammo that we have won't fit. So we'll have to be careful about picking the right men to use them. In the wrong hands they'd do more harm than good. They'd shoot more of our own lads than British soldiers."

As an afterthought he added, "The British don't have them yet, or anything like them, so I'd say that we don't want them to capture any of ours to use against us. And that gives us another problem in deploying them: we'll have to guard the bloody things as well."

At this Michael felt he had to make a point. "And we'll have to keep them well out of the reach of fellas like Kevin Ryan."

Collins held his hand up to end the discussion. "All right Patrick," he said, "you've made your point, for now at least. And if it's any consolation I tend to agree with you. But I'm afraid that the decision has already been made by the Military Council. Mr de Valera has persuaded them that we must make a major effort to try and convince the British that a military victory in Ireland is not possible. These new weapons will come as a complete surprise to the British, and with them they think that this operation can be successfully pulled off."

"They'll only come as a complete surprise if the Yanks haven't told the British that they gave them to us, and I wouldn't put that past them for one minute," said Patrick. "I suppose I'm the military bloody genius who has to work out how to do all this?"

"No, Patrick," Collins assured him. "Because this involves the whole of the Dublin Brigade, they are planning it themselves. What I want from you is your evaluation of what the major problems are and what can go wrong. It's probably too late, but I want to gather as many considered arguments as I can to take to the Council. Who knows, they may yet be in a mood to listen. You've already given me some useful thoughts about using the Thompson guns and you make a valid point about not letting them fall into British hands. Now, is there anything else you can think of?"

Patrick's frustration showed. "Sure didn't I tell you at the start that it's the stupidest thing I ever heard of, and it's hard to think of anything that can't go bloody wrong."

Michael Flynn felt that he needed to bring his friend back to what Collins had asked of him. "Do you think that they can at least get into the building, Pat," he asked.

"Oh they can get in all right, Mick, it's not too heavily defended and sure a few hefty country girls armed with hurley sticks could get in. But getting out again, now that's a horse of different colour altogether. Look at where the bloody place is: it couldn't be any closer to the dead centre of Dublin. Half the British Army, not to mention the 'Tans, the 'Auxies' and the RIC, are no more than a stone's throw away. And in case any of these eejits haven't noticed, sure isn't it standing alongside the bloody River Liffey and it can't be attacked from that side."

As I understand it," said Collins, "the idea is for only a small part of the force to break into the building while the rest of the Brigade form a defensive perimeter."

"Jesus Christ, in that, case sure won't the Army have the whole Dublin Brigade surrounded with troops and armoured cars in no time at all. And it won't take them long to bring up artillery as well if they need it. The first thing the boys will have to do is to capture the bridges and then hold them, or their only way out will be to swim, and you can bet that the Army will be ready for that as well. If I was the British general, I couldn't think of anything I'd rather have."

This outburst was followed by a period of silence. It was eventually broken by Coughlin. "What do they want with that place, anyway? According to Kate there's nothing at all there but a pile of old records. If they want to mount a major attack why don't they hit a barracks or a depot or somewhere that stores arms and ammunition?"

"The thinking behind it," said Collins, "is to disrupt the British administrative system in Ireland by destroying as many of their records as we can, which, in itself, is not a bad idea at all. There are all kinds of administrative functions carried out there including collecting taxes. You must know how the Irish people feel about the taxes they pay being used to help fund a war against them."

"Can't they see that they'd have more chance of doing that with a small group?" Coughlin wanted to know.

"They want to kill two birds with one stone and make a show of force at the same time," Collins replied. "It will show the British how much fight the IRA still has left in it. Again, I can't argue with the sentiment, just the method of achieving it."

"God help us all," said Coughlin.

***

After the meeting with Collins, Patrick was anxious to have a private word with Michael. He wanted to ask for his advice and, if possible, his help in getting Kate Steele out of working for The Cause. He felt a little embarrassed about it because he knew his friend would realise that the request was entirely based on personal feelings, so he began by putting forward a 'tactical' reason for moving Kate out of the Killiney hotel.

"You know very well, Mick, that leaving someone undercover for too long is dangerous, especially someone like Kate who thinks that it's a great gas to be working for us. That means she's sure to get careless and they'll catch her at it before long. I know that it wouldn't worry Collins one bit. The only thing that would bother him about her getting caught is what the 'Tans might get out of her, and you can bet your bottom dollar that he has plans ready to make sure things never go that far. Sure won't he have her shot at the first sign of danger."

Michael gave him a knowing look; he realised that it was worrying about Kate that made Patrick so unusually argumentative when talking to Collins. "I know how you feel about her, Pat, and I'd say that she has her eye on you, too. But I was thinking the same thing myself: she's been on her own down there in that hotel for long enough. The trouble is that 'The Big Fella' thinks she's doing a grand job there and we'd have to give him a good reason before he'd agree to pull her out. He wants her somewhere that he can keep a close watch on her, and like you said, sure 'tis no skin off his nose if she gets caught. Have you any ideas yourself?"

Patrick had thought long and hard about it, and the only answer he could come up with was the tried and tested solution that Irish people had resorted to for generations in times of trouble: emigration, usually to America.

"That wouldn't be so easy, Pat," Michael said. "The minute she left Killiney, Collins would be looking for her. He won't let her run around loose, and he'd find her, too, even in America, if she got that far."

Patrick's frustration surfaced yet again. "So, there's nothing at all we can do?"

"I didn't say that at all Pat," Michael said. "As far as I can see, the only way around this is to get Collins himself to send the pair of you to America, the same way that he sent me over there last year. And there is something in the wind that might give us the chance to do it."

For some time Michael had been anxious to tell Patrick about the ongoing cease-fire negotiations but felt unable to. Now however, with members of the *Dáil* and the cabinet involved, he thought that the negotiations would soon become an open secret and there was no harm in telling someone as trustworthy as Patrick Coughlin. If a truce was eventually arranged, Commander Wilson would be released from his duty as adviser to Alfred Cope, and Michael felt that by this time he knew the Royal Navy man well-enough to believe that Wilson would immediately resume his hunt for Patrick Coughlin; a man he would still regard as a mutineer. He would also be looking for the mutineer's accomplice, Kate Steele. And this time, without the constraints imposed by the cease-fire talks to consider, there would be nothing to prevent the Commander from employing all the resources of the RIC to help him.

In those circumstances Michael told Patrick, Collins might be persuaded to get both him and Kate out of harm's way, for a time at least.

"But ," he cautioned Patrick, "all that will have to wait until after the thing 'The Big Fella' was talking about is settled."

***

Kevin Ryan and Sean O'Connor had to temporarily abandon their plans to be on hand when Michael Flynn next met with Commander Wilson. Wherever and whenever that meeting took place they planned to shoot Wilson and let the British know, if in fact the authorities would be in any doubt, that the IRA had carried out the assassination. Then they planned to explain to Michael Collins that they had caught the British security man in the act of arresting Michael Flynn.

But for the moment, they were under orders to stand ready for a major action with the rest of the Dublin Brigade.

Ryan, however, was not overly disappointed at the temporary postponement to their plans. "Jesus Christ, Sean," he enthused, "the whole bloody Dublin Brigade in one operation! And I hear we'll have a load of new Yank guns. Now they're talking, sure won't we have the Brits running home to their mammies this time, all right; and there'll be no more talk of a cease-fire after that."

"Don't count your chickens yet," O'Connor said. "If we give the Brits too bad a beating, they'll be after a cease-fire worse than before."

Ryan was not convinced. "But sure we'd never agree to it when we're the top dogs, Sean."

"I wouldn't be too sure about that, Kevin," O'Connor counselled, "that's when the bloody politicians will be taking over, and you know yourself that you can't trust them bastards one inch."

But, far from being despondent, Ryan could think only of what it would be like to get his hands on one of 'them new Yank guns'.

Chapter 40

The Dublin Custom House was built by the architect James Gandon in the neoclassical Georgian style and opened in 1791. The four ornate facades incorporated several uniquely Irish features including the fourteen sculptures by Edward Smythe, known as the Riverine Heads. These figures, mounted on keystones above the doors and windows, represented Ireland's thirteen principal rivers and the Atlantic Ocean. As its name suggests, it was originally designed for the collection of customs duty at the Port of Dublin but over the years, the port had moved further downriver so it was no longer suitable for its original purpose. As time went by, the handsome old building was put to several uses, but by 1921 it had become the principal British administrative centre for local government in Ireland. As such, it had nominal authority over all the Irish county councils; but as the vast majority of these, apart from those in the north, were controlled by Sinn Fein, exercising that authority proved to be extremely difficult. Aside from this, however, the building housed some six or seven other unpopular administrative functions, principally the collection of income and other taxes.

Although protected by a British military guard, members of the administrative staff were mostly Irish civilians. In common with all of the other British governmental departments in Ireland, Michael Collins had his spies inside several departments at The Custom House, but he wanted to obtain as complete a picture as possible of what went on there. So, Kate Steele had been directed to gather as much information as she could from anyone working there and relaxing in 'her' hotel.

When Patrick Coughlin gave her the assignment, she sensed that he was not overly happy about what he was asking her to do. Nevertheless, she kept her ears open and dutifully reported everything she heard up to Michael Flynn. Each time she went to the city she desperately hoped that it would be Patrick who would again meet her there, but her hopes were never realised. She would ask Michael how Patrick was and would be reassured: 'ah sure he's grand, Kate, and sure isn't he always asking after you as well'. But he would always refuse to tell her where Patrick was or what he was doing. Recently, though, she had been heartened when he told her to be patient because he was certain things would work out for her and Patrick in the end. And, as always, he warned her to be careful although now, as an added incentive, he added that Patrick had asked him to make sure she heeded the warning.

***

The attack on The Custom House by the Dublin Brigade of the IRA was carried out on 25th May 1921, and was lead by Commandant Oscar Traynor.

Entry was accomplished as easily as Coughlin had predicted it would be: the guards were quickly and quietly overpowered and the IRA men detailed to take over the building entered by twos and threes so as not to arouse suspicion. They spread out through the dozens of offices and herded all the civilian staff into the main hall, where they held them under guard. Strict instructions had been issued, largely at the behest of Michael Collins, to the effect that no civilians were to be harmed. Once they were reasonably sure that all the staff were accounted for, the raiders went back through the offices doused them in paraffin and started fires.

Outside, the rest of the brigade formed a defensive cordon by blocking the surrounding streets. Telephone lines out of the building were cut, and the nearest fire stations were taken over so that experienced help would not be available to put out the fires once the alarm was raised.

But things quickly began to go wrong: an army patrol spotted smoke from the fires and rather than go and investigate the cause himself, the experienced officer-in-charge called up reinforcements. Troops, including Black and Tans and Auxiliaries, arrived from all over Dublin and soon the men surrounding the building were, as Patrick Coughlin had predicted they would be, themselves surrounded.

Inside, the signal to withdraw was prematurely given and some of the fire-raisers dashed outside. In the ensuing confusion, six IRA men were killed and twelve were wounded and, what was even worse for the Dublin Brigade, seventy-five of its members were taken prisoner.

The Thompson sub-machine guns played little part in the action. The men using them had been instructed that for the weapons to have maximum effect they should only be used against groups of enemy soldiers, but the British, aware that the IRA might have set up the two Hotchkiss guns stolen from the armoured car used in the attempt to free Sean MacEoin, refused to bunch up. Several bursts were fired at armoured cars from too great a range and failed to penetrate the armour plating. The sub-machine gunners were also hampered by the fact that they were under strict orders not to let the guns fall into enemy hands. But during the confused withdrawal, when the majority of the surviving attackers had already made their escape, the IRA suffered another and potentially more serious casualty. A man carrying one of the Thompsons became separated from the squad detailed to guard him, or more importantly to guard the sub-machine gun. He was killed by a revolver bullet fired from close range; a shot fired, not by a member of the British forces, but by someone on his own side. The killer got clean away taking the Thompson with him

The Custom House burned for several days, resulting in serious disruption to the British administrative system in Ireland. Unfortunately as well as income tax and county council records, many irreplaceable birth, marriage and death records were also irretrievably lost.

The attack received worldwide publicity and proved to be a propaganda triumph for the Irish Nationalist Cause. But, principally due to lack of ammunition – some men had only four or five rounds each, it turned out to be a military disaster. This was amply reflected in the number of prisoners taken by the British forces. Being out of ammunition many men had no option but to surrender. This level of losses could not be sustained or the IRA would soon become totally ineffective as a viable fighting force.

***

"I suppose," Commander Wilson commented ruefully, "that this is yet one more occasion when both sides will claim victory. Although how anyone can claim the burning of a lovely old building and the destruction of thousands of records as a victory is quite beyond me. Especially with the losses the IRA suffered in achieving it."

"The loss of those records will give the British administrators trying to run Ireland headaches for years," Michael Flynn told him. "But like you said yourself, Commander, it's no use at all you and me arguing the toss about it. Our two men at the negotiation table will be doing all the arguing we'd ever want to hear soon enough, and sure aren't they a lot better at it than we are."

***

"Didn't I tell your man Collins that it was a bloody stupid notion?" Patrick was almost shouting in frustration. "They didn't have to take all those casualties just to burn a bloody house down. And how many prisoners was it the Army took?"

"Seventy-five," Michael answered. "And that's not the worst of it, Pat. The boys lost one of the American guns as well."

"Jesus Christ, Mick!" said Patrick. "One of the Thompsons, how did the British manage to get their hands on that?"

"From what I hear, they didn't," said Michael. "Nobody knows for sure who got it, but I wouldn't put it past someone like Kevin Ryan to shoot one of our own lads to get a hold of one of them things."

***

Because of the casualties it suffered in the attack on The Custom House, the Dublin Brigade was forced to return to its tried and tested tactics of small scale raids, ambushes, bombings and assassinations.

Kevin Ryan and Sean O'Connor were again free to make plans for sabotaging any possibility of a cease-fire being arranged. The watch on Michael Flynn was resumed and soon began to bear fruit.

Chapter 41

The arguments predicted by Michael Flynn and Commander Wilson about who had come out on top in the battle at The Dublin Custom House dominated the next meeting between Collins and Alfred Cope. Michael and the Commander were obliged to sit through yet another soul-destroying bout of claim and counter-claim. From one side came the assertion that the IRA had received such a bloody nose that they should now seriously consider giving up; the other side countered by stating that if the British lost any more of their records they would be forced to concede that Ireland would soon become virtually ungovernable. Much to the disappointment of both 'advisers' the subject of a cease-fire was never raised.

After the meeting however, Collins appeared unusually satisfied with the result. "I think that we made a significant step forward today, Michael."

Michael gave him a decidedly questionable look.

"Look at it this way," Collins went on. "After what I said to Mr Cope about them losing any more of their precious records, they will now be obliged to waste more of their resources protecting every administrative centre in Ireland."

Michael could not resist pointing out that the British seemed to have plenty of resources to waste.

Collins was not to be dissuaded. "That is certainly true Michael, but it does provide us with an opportunity. Guarding buildings robs them of their prime advantage, which is, of course, their freedom of movement. Defenders become static targets so perhaps we can use those Thompsons to good effect after all."

"Has the missing gun turned up yet?" Michael asked.

"Not yet," Collins answered.

"What are the chances that the British have it and are not letting on?"

"That could, of course, be the case," Collins told him, "they might possibly have got their hands on it and there could be all sorts of reasons why they wouldn't want us to know. They certainly haven't mentioned it in any of the reports I've seen. I very much doubt though, that they did capture it. The fact is that our man was shot from the front at close range which, I'm very much afraid, points to the fact that he knew his killer or at least didn't have any reason to suspect him. The British would never have got that close to him without him being able to get off at least one burst. It's really rather a tricky situation because it seems that it could only be one of our own. Have you got any idea about who would be prepared to do something like this?"

Michael suspected that like himself, Collins already considered Kevin Ryan to be the only possible candidate. "I'd say that you have a notion the only one who'd do it is Kevin Ryan?"

"It could be any number of people, but I hate to say that going by his recent behaviour, Kevin has to be the prime suspect. He does, of course, deny it as you would expect, and the problem is that Sean O'Connor is backing him up. He says that he was with Kevin the whole time during the withdrawal and he was never out of his sight. I didn't specifically mention the missing Thompson when I questioned him, because at that stage the fewer people who knew about it the better. And while I am perfectly prepared to accept that in his present state of mind Kevin might lie to me, I have no reason to think that Sean is not telling the truth. I simply can't see what he would have to gain. If he knew that Kevin had done anything untoward I'm sure that he would have told me."

Michael tended to agree. Like most men close to the top of the Republican Movement, he knew O'Connor, not as well as he knew Ryan, but well enough to agree that there was no reason for him to risk deceiving 'The Big Fella'.

"Maybe I should have a word with Kevin's father," Michael offered. "There's always a chance that, if Kevin has the gun, he might hide it at the house. The way he is now he wouldn't care who he puts in danger from the 'Tans. Joe Ryan wouldn't tell on Kevin, even to me, but I might find out something if I could get him talking. All it would take is for him to let on that he knows about the Thompson being lost."

Collins shook his head. "No, Michael, if Kevin has got the gun we don't want to alert him. We have now put the word out that we want the thing back and if that doesn't work, we'll have to take more drastic measures."

Michael didn't ask what was meant by 'more drastic measures'; he felt that he had offered all the help he could and if Collins wanted any more, he certainly wouldn't hesitate to ask. Throughout the exchange about the sub-machine gun, the fact that there had not yet been able to join in any meaningful discussions about a cease-fire had not been far from Michael's mind. And he wanted to see what Collins had to say on the subject.

"After all this, is there any chance of getting down to doing any real talking at all about a cease-fire?"

"As I've said on many occasions Michael," Collins answered, "there will eventually have to be a truce. But there are complications, and this time they are not being caused by actions on our side. There are moves afoot in London which may or may not bring things to a head."

This was something new to Michael, to date all the delays to the cease-fire had stemmed from actions by the IRA. "And what moves would they be?" he asked.

"I've heard that some of the provisions of the 'Government of Ireland Act' are to be implemented," Collins answered.

The 'Better Government of Ireland' Bill was introduced to the House of Commons in December 1919 as an alternative to the failed moves to introduce Home Rule in Ireland, and had been debated on and off for nearly two years. One of its main proposals called for the setting up of separate parliaments in Dublin and Belfast.

"So it's likely that there will be the two parliaments after all," Michael observed. "That'll put the cat amongst the pigeons."

Collins nodded. "It certainly will, Michael, but exactly how? That is the problem. We do, of course, know the bald facts about what is happening, but I should like to have some more detailed information about the thinking behind it. It may well be just a sop to the Unionists, in which case it will probably lose steam like the Home Rule Bill, but if the British Government is really serious, then we may be in for a rough ride."

"Maybe Commander Wilson knows something," Michael said. "He's as anxious as anyone to see a cease-fire and he might be ready to tell me what he knows."

Collins agreed. "That is certainly worth a try."

Michael telephoned Wilson. Collins had been persuaded to allow Michael to use the telephone to contact his opposite number rather than the complicated system of letters he preferred. But he would only sanction its use in one direction: Michael would have to call Wilson; 'The Big Fella' would not countenance anyone connected with the authorities having contact numbers for any of his people.

He found the security man to be surprisingly receptive. "I agree that as advisers to the main participants in the negotiations, we should certainly discuss any matters that may have a bearing on the talks, Mr Flynn."

Michael grinned to himself: even in the most informal situations the Royal Navy man was still not disposed to address someone he knew to be a member of Sinn Fein by his Christian name.

"And I suggest that we do it privately before the next official meeting," Wilson added.

Michael sighed. "Before the next official big argument, you mean, Commander."

"Quite so," said Wilson. "But I think that, assuming you agree, the time has come for us to play a more proactive role and jointly put forward some more constructive proposals."

This sounded very much like music to Michael's ears. "I'm with you there, Commander," he said.

The only difficulty concerned where they should meet. Wilson was reluctant to meet at one of their usual Dublin venues where, for one thing he felt that they were becoming far too exposed, and which also allowed them too little time for anything other than a brief exchange of information. Personally, Michael would have been quite ready to meet on the Commander's home ground in Dublin Castle. He was not, as far as he knew, high on any wanted list in Dublin and he felt that it would be quite safe for him to visit 'The Castle', especially as Wilson would almost certainly provide him with a guarantee of safe conduct. But he realised that Collins would immediately veto such an arrangement, not through any concern for Michael's safety, but because it would be wide open to misinterpretation by those Republicans not in the know; and that meant virtually everybody except a few members of the *Dáil*.

After several suggestions, Wilson came up with what both agreed was a workable solution. "I've been thinking of spending a few days down in Beaufort next week," he said. "I'm told that the fishing there is first class at the moment and I'd like to try my hand. Perhaps it's time you also went down to see your son."

"Sure wasn't I thinking the same thing myself, Commander," Michael commented.

Wilson became more businesslike. "I believe that His Lordship will be willing to accommodate us again. And in my view it might be useful to let him know at least some of what we are about. He is, as you may be aware, extremely keen to see an end to this war, and he has told me categorically that he will do all he can to bring it about. His family have lived here for several generations and he regards Ireland as his real home. He still has many friends in Whitehall and he may have heard something of importance which he might be persuaded to pass on to us, unofficially of course. He would, however, certainly want to know what purpose we intend to put any information to before he would divulge anything. I must warn you that he would require a firm assurance that he would not be named as a source of inside information; and I have to ask you if you are prepared to give him your word on that, and if necessary, to keep what we hear from Mr Collins?"

Michael took a deep breath, but he knew what he had to do. "If it'll get the ball rolling on a cease-fire, I'll do whatever it takes, Commander."

"Very well," said Wilson. "I'll see what can be arranged. Call me back tomorrow."

When he called back, Wilson had already spoken to the owner of Beaufort House and received a favourable response. But Michael had one reservation. Without mentioning names he told the Commander of his suspicion that word had got out about them having previously met in Beaufort. He assured Wilson that he didn't envisage it happening again but that he would, however, like to take extra precautions.

"So I'll have to ask for help from Jack Quinlan. Jack is sure to catch on that there's more to this than me calling in on the people at home, but he won't ask to know what it is. In spite of what happened before, I'd stake my life on us being able to trust him, Commander."

"Very well," replied Wilson.

On Saturday evening, Jack Quinlan picked Michael up from the station in Killarney and he spent the night at the Quinlan cottage. On Sunday, his parents came after Mass and brought his son with them. For a few hours, the real purpose of his visit together with all thoughts of war and even a cease-fire were forgotten. He was amazed at how much the baby had grown; according to Annie Quinlan he would soon be walking, and Michael would give anything to be there to see it. Too soon the time came for his family to leave and he had to kiss his son goodbye. As he watched them leave, he felt his determination grow. He was once more resolved to do everything in his power, short of killing another human being, to help make Ireland free. It was the only fitting memorial he could imagine for his wife, and the only future he wanted for his son.

Chapter 42

Sean O'Connor was becoming increasingly worried. He had lied to Michael Collins when he told 'The Big Fella' that he had been with Kevin Ryan all the time during the withdrawal from The Custom House. If he was found out he knew that he was finished as a member of the IRA and that could mean only one thing: he was already a dead man. At the time he hadn't known why Collins had asked him about being with Kevin, and had lied simply because his friend had asked him to say that they were together the whole time. And, foolishly as it turned out, he hadn't questioned Ryan before agreeing. But he knew that this excuse would carry no weight whatsoever.

It was only afterwards that he heard about the missing Thompson sub-machine gun. That was when an excited Kevin couldn't wait to tell him not only that he had the gun but, to make matters worse, how he had acquired it. His first thought was to try and persuade Ryan to hand it back and say that they had simply found it, but he knew it would be useless: one of 'the boys' had been killed and Collins would not rest until he found out who had pulled the trigger. Asking Ryan to abandon his prize by dumping it in the Liffey would be an equally hopeless gesture; Kevin was so delighted with his new toy that he would die before parting with it. The thought crossed O'Connor's mind that he could do just that: kill Ryan and take the weapon back to Collins. But he realised that would still leave too many questions he would find it difficult to answer, and he was not at all sure that he would be able to convince 'The Big Fella' of his own innocence in the affair.

The die was cast and he had little choice but to throw in his lot with Ryan and hope that what they were about to do for The Cause would exonerate him. But the thought failed to totally allay his fears.

"Jesus Christ, Kevin, I hope to God that we don't make a bags of it," he said anxiously. "Sure didn't we stick our necks out so far with 'The Big Fella' that it'll be dead easy for him to chop the bloody heads off us when he finds out."

"Ah sure the way we planned it there's nothing at all that can go wrong," Ryan replied. "I'm telling you, Sean, we'll show the whole bloody lot of them how to put the Brits on the run. And sure there's nothing else we can do now anyway."

Acceptance of the fact that there was indeed nothing else they could do provided O'Connor with no comfort whatsoever.

Ryan went on, "Listen Sean, according to your man up there in the *Dáil,* the bastards are going to let the Brits get away with setting up that so-called parliament in Belfast, and sure someone has to stand up for Ireland. God help us but the next thing you know they'll be accepting a cease-fire and then where will we be? But I'm telling you, with this godsend from America, we'll put a spoke in their wheel yet."

While O'Connor wholeheartedly agreed with the principle of sabotaging a cease-fire, he was not quite so confident of the method by which they hoped to achieve it.

Their watch on Michael Flynn had failed to lead them to Commander Wilson, so gunning the British security man down in Phoenix Park was not going to be as easy as they first thought. But their watch had borne fruit of a different kind. Instead of following Michael, O'Connor had tailed the girl he met at the cinema, and this led them to revise their plans. They returned to an idea that Ryan had suggested earlier. And now they knew exactly where to find Kate Steele.

***

In Beaufort, after the Flynns had left, Jack Quinlan harnessed the pony to the trap to take Michael back to the railway station in Killarney. On the way, Jack assured his friend that he had managed to set things up exactly as Michael had asked him to. With everyone's attention focused on Michael and the baby, nobody had noticed that Jack had slipped away for an hour after lunch. If he was curious about what he had been asked to do, he was not about to question it. Much to his surprise, His Lordship had taken him aside and told him that this weekend he was to provide Michael Flynn with all the assistance he required and not ask questions. It was obvious that something was up but Jack didn't attempt to find out what. For one thing he was loath to put Michael in the awkward position of having to tell him to mind his own business.

The journey to Killarney passed without incident. To any interested observer, and as usual there were a few of those around, it would appear that Michael had paid a routine visit to see his son. Both sides in the conflict had an interest in Michael Flynn, and when he came to Beaufort both sides kept an eye on him. Over time, however, a set pattern for Michael's visits had been established, and as long as the pattern remained unbroken, both sides did little more than go through the motions. It was almost a year since the Black and Tans had arrested him, an arrest which had led not only to the death of Michael's wife but also, and more importantly in their eyes, to the death of one of their own. So the 'Tans in the Killarney area still considered that they had a score to settle with him. But they had to tread carefully if they wanted to avoid falling foul of the highly influential owner of Beaufort House. While Michael was at Quinlan's cottage, which was within the grounds of his estate, and while he was being ferried to and from Killarney by his steward, Jack Quinlan, His Lordship regarded Michael as being under his protection. It was a highly unusual situation, made more so by the fact that had the RIC or the British Army gathered sufficient evidence to arrest Michael, His Lordship would not have interfered; but he was determined not to be dictated to by the 'irregulars'.

The local IRA was under orders from Collins not to allow Michael to be taken by the 'Tans, but Michael was adamant that he would give himself up before he would be the cause of a gun battle around a crowded railway station. So, Jack would wait and see Michael safely onto his train and at that point, both sides would relax their vigilance. On this occasion, because the June daylight in County Kerry lasted until late in the evening, they delayed their departure from Beaufort, and neither the IRA nor the 'Tans suspected that the pattern was about to be broken.

Michael got on the train and waited until it was just about to leave. He got out again on the opposite side and hid among the parked goods wagons until the coast was clear. By now, the light was failing and he made his way by a circuitous route to Killarney Cathedral. He saw that the pony and trap had been left outside and went in by a side door to where Jack was waiting for him. They exchanged hats and coats; Michael came out by the main doors, got in the trap and drove away. He prayed that anyone watching would mistake him for Jack Quinlan. Jack waited for a little while then went around the building to where he had left his bicycle earlier in the afternoon and pedalled back to Beaufort. He caught up with Michael just as he arrived at the main gates of Beaufort House.

It was essential that on his return to Beaufort, Michael remained out of sight. If he were spotted by servants or estate workers after he had supposedly returned to Dublin, the news would quickly spread through the whole of the Beaufort area. It would raise unwanted interest in why he had returned and the news that he had would very soon reach the ears of the RIC, and inevitably the Black and Tans. The IRA, too, would wonder why they had not been informed and start asking questions. So he was accommodated in a secluded but well appointed fishing lodge by the river, and he spent the night among the rods and tackle.

Commander Wilson arrived early next morning and, after a chat with His Lordship, they went fishing. The gillie had been told that he would not be required that day. He was pleased to be given a day off but was surprised to see the master of the house, and his guest, carrying the well-stocked picnic basket themselves.

His Lordship went fishing but did not wander far from the lodge, partly to act as lookout and partly to be on hand if required.

It came as a great relief to both Michael and Wilson to be able to sit and exchange views away from prying eyes and without the usual time constraints; and just as importantly, away from the sniping indulged in by Collins and Cope. They did not, of course, always agree with each other's reading of the situation, but after a few hours they found enough common ground which they felt would be well worth while putting jointly to the men ultimately responsible for agreeing the terms of a cease-fire. They had, however, to recognise the fact that they had no way of imposing their decisions on the men they worked for, but at least they had something positive to offer.

His Lordship joined them for lunch. Wilson briefly outlined what they had agreed and His Lordship nodded his approval. He then imparted some information in strict confidence which caused Michael and Wilson to alter their plans and wait a week or so before approaching Michael Collins and Alfred Cope.

Before daylight the following morning, Michael was driven by Jack to the town of Kilorglin, which could be reached by a roundabout route through the foothills of the mountains by someone who knew the country well. There he caught a train to Tralee and then back to Dublin. He would, he knew, have to stall Collins when 'The Big Fella' questioned him about how he had got on with Wilson. But he thought that by telling enough of the truth, he could manage to keep Collins sweet for at least a week or two.

And he left Beaufort in a more optimistic mood than he had felt for months.

Chapter 43

It was her day off, and after lunch Kate prepared to go into Dublin to meet Michael Flynn. Now that summer had arrived, she did not look forward to going to afternoon performances at the cinema as much as she had previously done, and today she had very little 'intelligence' to pass on. She had been told to keep her ears open for anything being said about the British Government intending to set up a separate parliament in Belfast, but she had heard nothing. On a lovely day like today she would much prefer to go for a stroll in one of Dublin's parks, but with Patrick Coughlin rather than Michael Flynn. It was not that she didn't like Michael, he was always the perfect gentleman, perhaps too much so, and she could not forget that he had kept her out of Commander Wilson's clutches and introduced her to the fascinating world of espionage. Since her meeting with Patrick at the cinema, however, the attraction of listening in to conversations in the hotel bar had waned; it had been replaced by a longing to see him again and play a more active part in whatever exciting adventures he was engaged in.

She actually considered leaving the hotel and going to look for him, and the thought itself was enough to bring back the old excitement. But by this time she had learned enough about the organisation she was involved with to know that she would never get away with it.

So, she put her brief notes in her purse, which also contained a few items of the stolen jewellery, and after deciding she wouldn't need a coat, she went out to catch the train. She walked along the promenade to catch some of the fresh sea air and watch the people enjoying the summer sunshine. Along the way she was greeted cheerily by a few people who recognised her from the hotel, and even complete strangers smiled and said hello. Once again, she wondered how such friendly and unassuming people could live in such a troubled country. Patrick Coughlin was trying to right the wrongs being perpetrated in Ireland, and to know that she was helping him gave her a feeling of empathy with the people; a feeling she had never experienced before.

At the station, she had the same uncanny feeling: it was almost as if she belonged here. She received a friendly word from the ticket clerk and even one of the several RIC men on duty greeted her by name. Even though she knew that it was almost certainly wishful thinking, she found herself wondering what it would be like to settle down here one day with Patrick.

There were few travellers at this time of day, but as she stood day-dreaming on the platform a man came up and stood beside her. She looked round but didn't recognise him. He stood for a few minutes looking carefully around then spoke quietly:

"Would you by any chance be Miss Steele?"

Kate thought that he was someone who had seen her at the hotel and was trying to pick her up. Once upon a time she might have played along, but with Patrick still at the forefront of her mind she wasn't having any of that. She made a show of looking him over and deciding that she was not impressed with what she saw.

"What if I am?" she said coldly.

"Take it easy, miss, and don't get the wrong idea," he said anxiously, "sure all I want is to give you a message from Mick Flynn."

Kate's surprise showed. "From Michael?" she said.

"Yes, Miss," he replied, "he can't take you to the pictures today. So he wants you to meet him here."

He thrust a piece of paper into her hand. "And sure I'll have make myself scarce now, I don't like the way that bloody copper is looking at me."

She noticed that the RIC man who had greeted her was coming across and she quickly put the paper in the pocket of her summer dress.

"Was that fella bothering you, Miss Steele?" the RIC man asked.

Kate gave him her sweetest smile. "Not really," she said, "he was just trying his luck, but I saw him off."

By now the man had disappeared. "Well if he bothers you again, just let me know," the RIC man told her.

"Thank you, I will," she replied.

She chatted with him for a few minutes and told him that it was her afternoon off and she had decided to go into the city. She said that she had planned to go to the cinema but the weather seemed too nice so, did he have any suggestions about what she should see in Dublin. Rather than suggest places for her to visit he mentioned several areas of the city that she should avoid at all costs. The train came in and he advised her to be careful as he helped her on board. What, she thought, would Michael or Patrick make of her being so friendly with a member of the hated RIC; but she found the policeman to be just as friendly as the other people she had met that day. It was yet another example of the paradox that was Ireland.

On the train she found an empty compartment, settled down and read the note she had been given. The message was surprisingly short: 'Nelson's Pillar at 6 tonight'.

This was something completely new. She could understand him committing nothing more to paper than was absolutely necessary, or having him change the cinema at the last minute would not have surprised her; but asking her to meet him somewhere as public as Nelson's Column in the middle of Sackville Street was a complete deviation from Michael's usual careful routine. She wondered what it was all about and tried to put it to the back of her mind, yet when she reached the city, she was still puzzling over this sudden and totally unexpected alteration to their tried and trusted arrangements. All afternoon she couldn't concentrate on enjoying the summer sights and sounds of Dublin. At the back of her mind was a nagging worry that something was very wrong, and at one point she seriously considered going back to the hotel and waiting for someone to contact her there. But her old curiosity got the better of her and she set off for the meeting at the 'Pillar'.

***

Michael was becoming increasingly worried. He had been waiting around at the cinema until well after the security-conscious Collins would have considered safe, and Kate had still not put in an appearance. She had not been late before except for the one occasion when it was Patrick Coughlin who met her, and he didn't think that it was likely to happen again, at least not to this extent. The only explanation was that she had been seriously delayed, but by what? That gave him real cause for concern. There could be all sorts of possible reasons: illness, hold-ups on the railway or being asked to change her day off. He could try to contact her but this could take some time due to the complexity of another of Collins' ultra-safe communication systems. And if there had been a serious breach in security, trying to reach her could well exacerbate the situation. No matter which way he looked at it he could not shake off the nagging feeling that something had gone seriously wrong; and if it had, he would need to react quickly but cautiously.

The one thing he could be sure of was that she had not been arrested by Commander Wilson. If Wilson was true to his word, and there was no reason to think that he wasn't, the Commander would now be in London.

Michael agonised for a little while and then decided that he had no option but to contact Michael Collins and hope that 'The Big Fella' was available to see him immediately. If he didn't report it, and Kate's disappearance were to have serious ramifications, then he would be in trouble himself for not immediately voicing his concerns. He had already met Collins once in the last couple of days and given him a carefully edited version of what he had discussed with Wilson in Beaufort. That seemed to be well received but he knew that this news would not be quite so palatable to 'The Big Fella'. To add to Michael's worries, Collins had already made it plain what would happen if there were the slightest hint of things going wrong with his 'Killiney operation', and Michael knew that it was no idle threat. But there was little else he could do. If, however, Collins ran true to form he would have someone else in place in Killiney; someone that neither

Michael nor Kate knew about, and so it would be possible for him to check and see if Kate was still at the hotel.

He also wondered if he should say anything to Patrick Coughlin. Knowing how Patrick felt about Kate made Michael wary of telling him anything before he knew more himself, because once Patrick learned she was missing, he was liable to immediately dash off down to Killiney to look for her. And Collins would definitely not stand for that. On the other hand, he was reluctant to keep his friend completely in the dark and then eventually have to break the news to Patrick that Kate had been arrested or worse. He received word that Collins was free to meet him and Michael resolved his dilemma by contacting Patrick and asking him to come along as well. If he told them both at the same time, 'The Big Fella' would be on hand to keep Coughlin in check. As Patrick had been instrumental in getting Kate to work for them, he felt that Collins would not object.

Coughlin arrived while they were waiting to contact Collins' man in Killiney. Michael told him that Kate was missing and that they were making some checks. Collins made it clear to them that they were to do nothing until they heard from him and, in the meantime, they were told to leave as he had other matters to attend to. The 'other matters', Michael suspected, were designed to prevent them from knowing who his contact in Killiney was.

"Jesus, Mick, what in God's name happened to her?" Patrick asked when they were alone.

"I don't know, Pat," Michael answered, "but before you start counting your chickens, it could be something as simple as a cold."

"It could be," said Patrick, "but from the way you're going about this you don't think she has a cold at all, do you, Mick? Or you wouldn't be bothering himself inside there."

Michael decided that the best thing to do was to be straight with him. "To be honest with you, Pat, and God knows why, but I don't think she has a cold or anything else wrong with her. It's the first time she's ever let us down and sure the last time I saw her she was looking grand."

"Christ, didn't I tell you she was there too long and got careless. And God help her if Collins finds her now, he'll have her shot. But I'll tell you this, Mick, if it comes to that he'll have to shoot me first."

"Easy now, Pat," said Michael, "we'll wait for word from Collins before we start jumping to conclusions."

All Patrick wanted to talk about, however, was starting an immediate search for Kate and he came up with several unworkable suggestions. Michael knew that he was merely trying to keep his spirits up so he didn't argue with any of his wild ideas. But when Collins called them back in they knew immediately that the news was not good.

"She left Killiney all right," Collins told them. "She was last seen talking to an RIC man at the station who helped her on to the Dublin train. I've checked and the train came in on time so we must assume that she reached the city. Has she ever done anything like this before Michael?"

"Never," Michael answered. "Was there nothing else at all from Killiney?"

"Only that she had a very short conversation with another man on the station, but he left in a hurry when the RIC man came along. From the way he acted when the policeman approached them, it sounds as if he might well be one of our men, in which case we can discount him. He was probably just attracted to a pretty girl and she saw him off."

"So it looks like your man Wilson has her," Patrick said.

"No," Collins replied. "My information is that Commander Wilson has gone to London. Did you know about that, Michael?"

"He did say that he might go home for a few days," Michael said. "I didn't think anything of it so I didn't tell you. Sure it's not important."

Collins gave him a hard look. "Everything about Commander Wilson is important at the moment. Please remember that too, Michael."

"For Christ's sake!" Patrick wanted to bring them back to more immediate matters. "What are we going to do about Kate? If she's in trouble we'll have to get her out of it."

"We will have to find her certainly," Collins said emphatically. "With what she knows we can't allow her to get into the wrong hands. Now listen, you two, you are to leave this with me. I'll get my people on to it and I don't want you interfering and muddying the water. Do you understand me?"

It was obvious that the meeting was over so all they could do was nod in agreement and leave. Once they were outside, Patrick was determined not to leave things at that, as Michael knew he wouldn't be.

"I'll have to do something, Mick, if he finds her first it'll be the end of her and God knows I'm not going to let him harm one hair of her head. Have you any notions at all about where I can make a start?"

"I think you're right, Pat and I'll help you," Michael said. "I know how you feel about her, and sure I'd hate to see her shot myself. But listen to me now, Pat, 'The Big Fella' knows very well that you won't let sleeping dogs lie and he's liable to have both of us watched."

"I don't care about that," Patrick said, "I'm telling you, Mick, I'll do anything to find her."

"I know, Pat," Michael told him. "But we'll have to be very careful. The thing is, if we were to find her there's a danger that all we'd do is lead Collins straight to her."

"Is there nothing at all we can do?" Patrick waited anxiously for Michael to think of something.

Michael, however, took his time before answering. "The only thing I can think of is that fella at Killiney station," he said. "Collins thought nothing of him but I'm not so sure. If it was one of 'the boys' he wouldn't be hanging around a railway station in front of a load of RIC men, and he'd definitely have more on his mind than talking to the girls. The more I think about it the more I'm certain that he was there for a reason, and the only reason that makes any sense is that he was waiting for Kate. Otherwise, why would he take the risk of talking to her?"

Patrick immediately saw a ray of light at the end of his very dark tunnel and was all for taking immediate action: "Christ, Mick, you might be right. Come on we'll go down there now and find out what happened at the station."

"Hold your horses, Pat," Michael said. "We can't go down there asking questions. We'd be arrested and put in jail before we found out anything at all; that is if Collins didn't catch us at it first. Either way it wouldn't do Kate any good. We'll have to think of another way around it. We'll need help and I can only think of one man who could get away with asking questions of the RIC."

"Who's that?" Patrick asked.

"Commander Wilson," Michael told him.

"Wilson! Christ, Mick, are you out of your mind altogether? If Wilson catches her he'll arrest her as a spy on top of all the other things."

"At least he won't shoot her on sight like Collins will if he finds her," Michael reasoned. "And we'd have at least half a chance of getting her away from him. Anyway, Wilson doesn't know she's a spy, and if we play our cards right there's no reason why he should ever find out."

Patrick was not convinced, so Michael made the position clear. "Look, Pat, it's a case of deciding who you'd rather have finding her: Wilson or Collins. But make your mind up quick before the 'The Big Fella' gets the same notion I had about the man at the station."

***

An afternoon spent wandering aimlessly around the city did nothing to ease Kate's mind. The more she thought about Michael's uncharacteristic change of plan the more disturbed she became. Several more times she thought that giving up and returning to the hotel would be the safest thing for her to do, but deep down she knew that her curiosity wouldn't allow her to. She got to 'The Pillar' in good time and sat on a bench to wait, half in excitement and half in apprehension. The time neared, and then went past, six o'clock and Michael was still nowhere in sight. She began to think that perhaps she was the victim of a cruel joke. Just as she was about to give up and leave she saw a face she recognised. It was the man from the station at Killiney exhibiting the same furtive manner.

"Hello again, Miss," he said. "I have to take you to meet someone."

Kate hesitated. "Who are you?" she asked him bluntly.

"Ah sure I'm nobody at all, Miss," came the reply. "But the fella that sent me to get you is terribly keen to see you and we'll have to be quick now because he can't wait long."

Kate felt a sudden surge of relief mingled with excitement. Remembering what had happened at the cinema it could only be Patrick who could possibly have arranged this.

"Is it Patrick?" she asked.

Sean O'Connor thought fast. The 'fella that sent him' was Kevin Ryan, and he didn't know who this Patrick was, but spotted an opportunity to get her to go with him quietly. He relaxed his grip on the revolver in his coat pocket.

"Ah sure of course it is, Miss, who else would it be."

Chapter 44

Commander Wilson was on his way back to Dublin on the morning sailing from Holyhead to Kingstown having left London some eight hours earlier. The June weather was glorious, the Irish Sea was unusually calm but the sea air was bracing. Having spent a largely sleepless night, he had only managed a few fitful hours on the boat train, he decided to pass the entire voyage outside rather than in the stuffy first-class passenger lounge. He had left London with some highly significant news and he would need to have a clear head when he arrived back in Dublin. But standing on the gently rolling deck brought back his longing to be at sea with the Royal Navy and, once again, he inwardly cursed the day he had allowed himself to be enticed into the cloak and dagger world of security work. Had it not been for the exceptional demands of wartime, he would not have countenanced such a move.

The steamer entered Dublin Bay and turned towards Kingstown. He was now forced to re-focus his thoughts on the problem at hand. How much of what he had learned in London should he pass on to Michael Flynn? It was something that he had been turning over in his mind since his departure from London until he had been distracted by the call of the sea.

Flynn had been partner to the decision made in Beaufort to take up His Lordship's suggestion that the Commander travel to London to meet some people the former government minister was confident would be 'in the know'. His Lordship had given Wilson the names of certain old friends in and around Whitehall who might be able to help him, and he had telephoned ahead to gain the Commander access to them. It helped that some of the names on the list were men who had been instrumental in sending Wilson to Ireland to explore the possibilities of a truce in the first instance. In the event, these men were still anxious to see a quick settlement to 'The Irish Problem' and they had been very forthcoming. Wilson knew that Michael Flynn had taken a serious risk in giving his word that he was prepared to keep any highly sensitive information from Michael Collins, and Wilson trusted the Irishman to keep his word. Under these circumstances Michael was entitled to be fully briefed, but some of the information he had been given was highly confidential, and in the wrong hands could cause severe embarrassment in certain quarters in Whitehall. On a personal level, the Commander realised that by telling Michael Flynn everything, he could be accused of passing state secrets to someone who was in effect an enemy agent. In either case he would be breaking a confidence: something which did not sit easily with a man of Wilson's background and integrity.

By the time they docked, however, he had made up his mind: he could do nothing other than take the same level of risk as his Irish counterpart and tell Flynn everything.

As soon as he reached Dublin he found that one part of his dilemma had already been resolved. News vendors all over the city were loudly proclaiming the news that the separate parliament was to be opened in Belfast on June 22nd, just a few days away. At that point Ireland would be effectively partitioned. But if the fact that the parliament was, at last, to be opened following years of speculation was common knowledge, certain aspects of the way in which the opening would be conducted were not.

Wilson had learned that the Belfast parliament would be opened by the King, George V. This was only to be expected, but it was what the King proposed to say that was at the crux of the problem. George V, against fierce opposition, was determined that his speech would convey an unmistakably conciliatory message; he would extend his hand to all of his Irish subjects and his speech would represent a plea to all of the parties involved to settle their differences peaceably. This approach by the King would undoubtedly upset not only Unionists and Nationalists in equal measure, but also those members of Parliament and British military who still believed that Ireland could be brought to heel by force of arms. More importantly it would, in Wilson's view, compel the British Government to make a meaningful effort to secure peace in Ireland. And the first requirement for that would have to be a truce.

Wilson was sure that it provided the leverage he and Michael Flynn needed to force Alfred Cope and Michael Collins to the negotiation table and compel them to engage in some meaningful discussions. It was news he could not keep from Michael if they were to attain a goal that had hitherto seemed out of reach.

When he reached 'The Castle' there was, as he fully expected there would be, an urgent message from Alfred Cope. He was to go and see his superior the moment he got back from London. He left instructions that if Mr Flynn telephoned he was to be told immediately, even if he was in conference, and made his way to Cope's office. On his way there he was handed an envelope by a member of the security staff.

The envelope was addressed to *Mister Wilson Dublin Castle*. Inside was a single piece of paper with a short handwritten note: *if you want the English girl we will have her at the bridge in Stephens Green at 6 on Thursday morning if you bring the cops she will be shot*

He instructed the guard who had brought the message to find out when it had been delivered and by whom, and went in to meet with Cope. Lloyd George's man wanted his opinion on what bearing the new development in British policy would have on his talks with Michael Collins. Wilson told him that it was bound to have some effect, but it was much too early to predict what that effect might be. While he was speaking to Cope, he imagined Michael Flynn having exactly the same conversation with Collins. The Commander suggested that, for the moment, there was little else they could do but to try and set up a meeting, and he would talk to Michael Flynn about arranging one. But he did express the opinion that Collins would not agree to a meeting until after he had time to analyse the possible ramifications of the events in Belfast. A frustrated Cope could do little but allow Wilson to get on with things.

After leaving Cope he turned his thoughts back to the note. He found that it had been delivered to a sentry at the gate just an hour previously by a boy on a bicycle who had disappeared before anyone thought to question him. Even while working for Cope, Wilson had kept the problem of finding Private Coughlin and Kate Steele in mind, and nothing had happened to change his belief that the Steele girl was still in Ireland. He was equally sure that if he could find her he would find the fugitive Connaught Ranger as well, and he had not the slightest doubt that the girl mentioned in the note was Kate Steele. The Commander had always thought that she was being hidden somewhere by Michael Flynn, but he had to admit that this message did not bear any of the hallmarks he would have associated with Flynn. Nothing about the tone of the message, especially the poor grammar, pointed to it having originated with that particular Irishman. Although the unexpected breakthrough had come completely out of the blue and from a totally unexpected quarter, his first instinct was that it was genuine and he decided that he had to follow it up. Then the significance of the date struck him. Thursday would be the 22nd. So he had to consider the possibility that there was a connection with the events in Belfast; but what exactly the connection was he couldn't imagine.

He was correct about Michael Flynn having a conversation with Collins similar to the one he had just had with Cope; it was one of the first things Michael told him when he telephoned. Wilson outlined what he had learned in London but they urgently needed to meet. The Commander suggested they meet in St Stephen's Green where they could mingle with the Dubliners going for a summer evening stroll in the park. Michael agreed, for the moment unaware that Wilson had a secondary motive for choosing that particular venue. Wilson knew that the bridge mentioned in the note could only be the ornate stone footbridge over the lake in 'The Green' as it was called, and he wanted to check the immediate surroundings prior to deciding how to deal with the mysterious message about the Steele girl.

At first it had not been his intention to say anything to Michael about the note, but on reflection he thought that he should do so. For one thing Flynn might well have some ideas about the authenticity of the message, and secondly, Michael's reaction could well indicate whether he actually knew where the girl was.

The meeting at 'The Green' went well. Michael agreed that if the King's opening speech was delivered in the vein that His Lordship's friends had forecast, then the chances of obtaining a cease-fire were greatly enhanced. They talked over possible ways of maximising the opportunity they had been handed and quickly reached agreement on a way forward.

"Now Mr Flynn," Wilson said as they were about to part. "What do make of this?"

Michael had not been given any warning and his surprise was clearly evident as he read the note. But the reason for his surprise was not the one Wilson had anticipated. He took a minute to recover then took a similar piece of paper from his own pocket and handed it to the Commander.

It was Wilson's turn to be surprised. The message on Michael's note was written in the same hand and read: *if you want the English girl back bring the Connaught Ranger to the bridge in Stephens Green at 6 on Thursday morning.*

Chapter 45

Kate Steele was both figuratively speaking, and in reality, being kept in the dark. The single window of the bedroom had been covered by a rudimentary blackout curtain, and the heavy black cloth was held in place by nails driven into the wooden window frame. In the two days she had been held prisoner there, she had managed to free one of the bottom corners and it provided just enough of a gap to allow in a shaft of summer sunlight and to enable her to see out. Not that there was much of a view, she could only see a small section of the far side of the street, but it was enough for her to deduce that the upstairs bedroom she was being held in was at the front of the house. She thought about enlarging the gap but she still retained sufficient awareness to realise that a larger gap would be discovered and re-sealed; then she would lose what little relief it provided. Even this limited view allowed her to see some of the comings and goings in the street below, which served to relieve the boredom and to some extent, help to allay her fears. She tried calling out to the few passers-by, but if she was heard her calls were ignored. People knew that two of 'the boys' were currently using this particular house, and nobody even so much as glanced up at the window.

Even though she was afraid, very afraid, of the men who held her captive, she tried not to succumb to her fear. She particularly feared the man who continually played with the strange-looking gun. He had told her quite matter-of-factly that he intended to kill her and she believed him. At first she had tried to brazen it out; but when he told her that she would be kept alive only until after he had used her to trap Patrick Coughlin, her resolve had all but broken down.

She had been locked in the room since she met the man she now knew was called Sean, at Nelson's Column. When he had implied that he was taking her to see Patrick she had followed him without further questions. They caught a tram out to the suburbs and walked to a narrow street of terraced houses. The street and the houses reminded her of the street where the Ryan family lived, but she could see that it was not the same one. They reached a house roughly halfway along. He took a key from his pocket and unlocked the door, held it open for her to enter and then locked it again behind them. She found herself standing in a tiny hallway from where a narrow stairway led upwards.

"Where's Patrick?" she asked?

"Upstairs," he answered and motioned for her to go up.

On the landing he pointed to a door on their right. She pushed it open and, as she stood in the doorway, she received a violent push in the back which propelled her into the room. She heard the door close behind her and the key turn in the lock. There was still plenty of daylight left outside but the room was dark. She looked around her but could only make out vague shapes.

"Patrick," she called, "Patrick, where are you?"

There was no reply and she realised that she was alone.

She felt her way along the wall to the door to look for a light switch but there wasn't one. Electricity had not yet reached this far into the Dublin suburbs. As her eyes grew accustomed to the gloom she gradually explored her surroundings and discovered that she was in a sparsely furnished bedroom. There was a single bed, an upright chair and a washstand with a bowl and a jug of water. A not very clean towel hung over the back of the chair. In the corner she found an enamel bucket with a lid and some squares of newspaper. She tried the door and found it securely locked. She banged as hard as she could on the door and stamped her feet on the bare floor demanding to know what was going on but she got no reply. So she sat on the bed to consider her situation.

To begin with she was angry; angry, at first, with the man who had duped her into following him on the pretext that he was taking her to see Patrick; then angry at herself for believing him, when all afternoon her instincts had been telling her that something was seriously wrong. She realised that her curiosity had once again led her into trouble; exactly how much trouble she was soon to find out.

Having locked her in, Sean O'Connor went back downstairs. He opened a bottle of stout and sat down to wait for Kevin Ryan. Ryan had gone home for no other reason than he wanted to show his father his shiny new Thompson sub-machine gun. He carried the gun hidden in a cardboard box tied up with string and bearing address labels to resemble a parcel. But even with the weapon thus concealed he was taking an enormous risk in carrying it at all, especially in broad daylight and to a house that might still be under surveillance. O'Connor had tried to warn him that his disguise as a postman was not at all convincing, and if he was caught with the gun by either the 'Tans or the IRA he was a dead man. But his warnings had fallen on deaf ears. Ryan had grown to regard the gun as a sort of talisman and seemed to believe that while he carried it he was invincible. O'Connor harboured a disturbing thought that Kevin wouldn't really mind being discovered with the gun if it presented him with the opportunity of using it. That was why he had persuaded Ryan to let him get the Steele girl by himself. O'Connor definitely did not like the idea of his volatile colleague taking the gun to somewhere as public as Nelson's Pillar where there were always plenty of RIC men and often 'Tans and 'Auxies' around; and he knew that Ryan would flatly refuse to leave it behind.

He realised that he had to face the fact that Ryan had become totally obsessed with using the sub-machine gun, and was determined that Commander Wilson and the Connaught Ranger would be his first targets. All thoughts about the plan they had worked out, and the reason for to killing Wilson, seemed to have been forgotten.

O'Connor had no compunction whatsoever about killing a British security man; like Ryan he had been involved in the assassinations on Bloody Sunday. And if it were true that the English girl was also a British spy, then he was quite prepared to shoot her as well. As far as the former Connaught Ranger was concerned, he could see that Ryan held a personal grudge against Coughlin and while he failed to see how killing the 'Ranger would help to scupper any moves towards a cease-fire, he knew that it would be foolish, and very possibly fatal, to interfere.

His real concern, however, was that they would now have to shoot Michael Flynn as well. Unless they did so, it would be impossible to claim that they had killed the British security man while he was in the process of arresting Michael after he had been betrayed by the English girl. Left alive to tell the tale, Flynn would simply contradict their story and that would be that. Under those circumstances the British would see no reason to pull out, and the cease-fire negotiations would go ahead. Worse still, there would be 'The Big Fella' to worry about: Collins was bound to mount a full-scale investigation into the death of Michael Flynn which Ryan and O'Connor would have great difficulty in explaining. Added to that, Collins would know who had stolen the Thompson and that would be fatal for everyone concerned, including Sean O'Connor. Trying to persuade Ryan not to use it in the 'operation' would be a complete waste of time and it would in all probability be dangerous to try.

O'Connor kicked himself for not simply walking out and going to Collins when Ryan had insisted on including Coughlin in the plot. He should have realised that the only way to reach the Connaught Ranger was through Michael Flynn.

Now that he had abducted the English girl, however, O'Connor had little choice but to go ahead with the rest of the scheme. But there was still a way in which he could still come out of this alive and perhaps even salvage the plan to sabotage the cease-fire. He would have to tread carefully, however; once Ryan got started with the Thompson nobody would be safe.

Ryan came back just in time to beat the curfew. As well as the parcel containing the Thompson he carried a small shopping bag of food. Before he had even acknowledged O'Connor, he unpacked the gun and carefully checked it over.

Satisfied that the weapon was in perfect working order he turned to his companion. "Did you get the girl?" he asked.

"I did," O'Connor replied. "She's up there in the room now."

"Good man yourself, Sean O'Connor," Ryan enthused. "Did she cause you any trouble?"

"Not a bit," O'Connor assured him. "She got the notion that I was taking her to see somebody called 'Patrick' and she came as quiet as a lamb. She tried to break the door down for a while after I locked her in the room, but she gave that up a while ago."

It was perfectly safe for them to let Kate make as much noise as she liked because it was well known in the neighbourhood that this particular house belonged to 'the boys'. And nobody was prepared to interfere with whatever went on there.

"Patrick?" Ryan said. "Jesus Christ, that'll be that bastard Coughlin. Didn't I tell you that they were all in it together, Sean? And sure if he's sweet on her it'll make the job a lot easier for us."

"It will so," O'Connor agreed. But it added fuel to the feeling that Ryan was more intent on settling his account with Coughlin than he was on assassinating Wilson.

He got up and went out to the back kitchen. "I'll make her a drop of tea and a bite to eat. Sure we don't want her to die of starvation for a while yet."

"You're right there, Sean," Ryan told him. "But don't give her any of that good grub I brought from home, weak tea and dry bread is good enough for the likes of her."

O'Connor prepared a mug of sweet tea and cut some thick slices of bread. He lit a short stub of candle and with the tea and candle in one hand and the bread in the other he started up the stairs. Ryan followed but didn't offer to lend a hand; he was too preoccupied with his Thompson. On the landing, O'Connor placed the tea and food on the floor and went to open the door.

Although frightened at being left alone in the dark, and especially about not knowing what was going to happen to her, Kate was still angry enough to have some fight left in her. When she heard the footsteps on the stairs she thought that it was just the man who had locked her in, so, when the door swung open she was ready. She made a bolt for freedom and barged into O'Connor. She pushed him aside but ran straight into Ryan. He shoved her roughly back into the room and pointed the gun at her.

Somehow she summoned up enough courage to shout at him and demand to be taken back to the hotel in Killiney where she worked.

Ryan slapped her face. "Shut your gob, you British bitch."

Although stung she was determined not let him see how frightened she really was.

"When Patrick hears about this you won't be so sure of yourself!" she yelled. "And who do you think you are anyway?"

He stood back and laughed at her. "Kevin Ryan is who I think I am," he said. "And sure the high and mighty Mister bloody Coughlin will hear about it, all right. Sure won't I tell him myself, one minute before I blow his bloody head off with this."

That shook Kate, but even now she found the determination to fight back. "What makes you think you'll even find Patrick or get a chance to use that silly looking thing?"

He put his face close to hers. "Well now darlin'," he sneered, "won't it be him that finds me when he comes looking for you."

With that he turned and walked off. O'Connor left the food on the washstand. In the process he noticed Kate's purse on the stand and picked it up. He followed Ryan downstairs, taking the candle and purse with him and locking the door behind him. Ryan was still laughing as he went down the stairs. Kate sat on the bed and cried.

O'Connor emptied the purse onto the kitchen table and called Ryan. Along with some money and the pieces of jewellery a small piece of paper with some notes written in it had also dropped out. The notes didn't seem to make any sense but the words 'parliament' and 'Belfast' stood out. It was enough to grab both men's attention.

"There you are, Sean," Ryan said, "didn't I tell you that she was a bloody Brit spy, and Flynn and the rest are in it with her."

O'Connor could find no argument with the girl being exactly what Ryan claimed her to be, but he was still far from convinced that Michael Flynn was 'in it with her'. When Ryan wasn't looking he pocketed the notes; he realised that they might come in handy as evidence if he was ever called on to explain things to 'The Big Fella'.

Chapter 46

After he left Wilson, Michael went to see Coughlin at his lodgings. He was greatly relieved to find that Patrick was not only still there, but in a much less emotional frame of mind. Earlier, when Michael showed him the message about Kate, the former 'Ranger had been ready to explode. His frustration at being unable to do anything positive about finding Kate, and while he was at it, wringing the neck of whoever had abducted her, had been driving him to boiling point. Michael would not have been surprised to find that Patrick was out scouring the streets of Dublin in a futile effort to find her.

While Michael had been meeting with Wilson, however, Patrick had forced himself to accept that flying off the handle and running around to no real purpose was not going to help Kate. What this situation required was some clear-headed rational thinking.

So, on his return, Michael was met by the same cool, calculating Coughlin who had managed to escape from the British Army, avoid capture in England and make his way home to Ireland. He listened intently while Michael told him about Wilson receiving a similar note telling the Commander that if he wanted Kate, he too, was to go to the bridge in St Stephen's Green at 6 am on the 22nd. Patrick took his time to consider the full significance of both Michael and the Englishman getting the same message before commenting.

"Well, there's one thing about it," he said eventually. "We have more of a notion about what we're up against. What does your man Wilson think about it?"

"He thinks it's a trap of some kind," Michael answered, "and I'd say that he's not far wrong."

"That Commander Wilson is no eejit," Patrick said. "It's a trap, all right. And Kate is the bait."

"But what sort of a trap is it, and who's setting it for us?" Michael wanted to know.

"Ah sure that's the easy bit, Mick. There's only one fella I know of that would have it in for me and a British security man at the same time."

"Kevin Ryan," Michael said.

Patrick nodded in agreement. "Kevin Ryan, the very man. I know why he has it in for me; I gave him a fist in the gob at Clonfin. And he knows very well that I'll come looking for Kate. But what would he want with Wilson? Sure there's loads of other British security officers around if he's dead set on shooting one."

"He knows Wilson is looking for Kate as well," Michael said. "He picked up a lot of information down there in Beaufort about me and the Commander."

"But that doesn't tell us what he has against this one Englishman," Patrick argued.

Michael racked his brains and suddenly the truth struck him like a thunderbolt. "Jesus!" – It was not like him to take the Lord's name in vain – "he must have found out about the cease-fire. Kevin Ryan is the last man in Ireland who would want to see a cease-fire, and he thinks if he kills Wilson the British will pull out of the talks."

"What's the situation with the cease-fire?" Patrick wanted to know.

Michael told him that the prospects of a truce were about to receive a significant boost, but couldn't tell him why.

Patrick accepted this without further questions. "I think you might have it there, Mick," he said "Sure hasn't he even worked it to happen on the day they're opening the parliament up in Belfast."

Michael was worried. "We'll have to stop him," he said. "Apart from killing you and Wilson, the way Kevin is these days he'll kill Kate as well, for sure. And he might be right about delaying the chances of a cease-fire as well if he kills Wilson."

"Are you telling me that by killing Wilson the whole cease-fire will be banjaxed?"

"No, not entirely, Pat," Michael answered. "But with the connections Wilson has he'll be a hard man to replace and a lot of the good work he's done lately will be lost. That could hold things up for months and God knows what could happen in the meantime."

Patrick had been thinking. "Ryan has bitten off a hell of a lot to chew on his own; he must have someone helping him."

"That'll be Sean O'Connor," Michael told him. "He stood up for Kevin when Collins suspected him of being the one who stole the Thompson."

"Jesus, I forgot all about the machine gun," Patrick said.

"We don't know for sure that he has it, Pat, but we'll have to assume that he has. And from what I hear about it he could kill everyone with one burst from that thing."

There was also something else on Patrick's mind: it seemed to him that Michael had failed to think it through far enough to realise that he, too, would be in the firing line, and he decided to make the point. "You know that they'll have to get you as well, Mick. They can't leave you alive or you'll spill the beans about the whole thing. So the first thing to say is that you should stay well away from Stephen's Green altogether and leave it all to me and Wilson."

Michael had, however, thought of that. "You're right about them having to kill me as well, Pat, but I don't think any of us should go to Stephen's Green. I'll have a chat with Michael Collins, and sure he'll soon put a stop to their shenanigans."

Patrick shook his head. "Sure didn't I think of that myself, Mick, but what would 'The Big Fella' do? He hasn't found Kate yet, or Ryan and the Thompson either, so there's no guarantee that he'll find them in time now. So what can he do but send a flying column from the Dublin Brigade to Stephen's Green, and if Wilson turns up with the RIC or the army or both there'll be ructions. And that won't do the chances of a cease-fire any good at all. A battle in the middle of Dublin while your man, the King, is opening the parliament up in Belfast is the last thing anyone wants; except, maybe, for Collins himself."

Michael realised that Patrick's assessment of the situation was more accurate than the 'Ranger realised. A pitched battle in Dublin could well be enough to persuade the King to alter the tone of his speech.

But Patrick wasn't finished yet, and it was plain that he was becoming quite agitated about his next point. "Whatever happens, telling Collins is a sure way to get Kate killed. If he doesn't do it the RIC will. And by the same token you'll have to make sure that Wilson doesn't turn up with a whole bloody regiment of Black and Tans, that would get us all killed."

"But what else can we do Pat?"

Coughlin quickly calmed down again. "We'll sit down and think about this before we do anything at all. There's a way around this and if we put our heads together, we'll find it."

***

The loneliness combined with the boredom, and the fear of the unknown, was beginning to tell on Kate. She had now spent one whole day and two whole nights in the darkened room. Even during the long hours of bright midsummer daylight the only break in the gloom came from the tiny gap she had made in the blackout. Her only human contact was with the man called Sean when he came to deliver her bread and tea twice a day; and Ryan when he came to taunt her. When Sean came with the food, Ryan stood on the landing with his gun to prevent her escape. When he told her that his name was Kevin Ryan, she had assumed that he was Michael Flynn's brother-in-law. She didn't think for a minute that Michael was behind her abduction; she was sure that he would do nothing to harm either her or Patrick, but she decided to ask the gunman anyway. He laughed, pointed the gun menacingly at her and told her to mind her own business. Last night she tried to shame him by asking what his sister, Kathleen, and his mother would think about what he was doing to her; he slapped her face again and told her to 'shut her British gob'.

Yesterday, with the heavy blackout curtain in place the room was stifling. She was torn between using what little water she had for freshening up or for drinking. In the end she rationed it out so that she had a little for both and, after another largely sleepless night, she pleaded with Sean to fetch her some more. She feared that he would ask Ryan who would almost certainly have refused, but to her relief he didn't, and brought her a full jug of fresh water. In spite of her meagre diet she was forced to use the enamel bucket and even with the lid on it began to smell in the heat. Having got Sean to bring her the water she asked him to empty it, but he gave her a disdainful look and went away.

At night the room was barely a few degrees cooler than it was by day, but she lay on the bed fully clothed. She fully expected that one or both of them would assault her sexually and she was determined to fight back. She placed the water jug on the floor by the bed to use as a weapon. They never did come in the night but the fear that they might made it difficult to sleep. Had she known more about the culture and customs of Ireland at the time, she would not have been so anxious: Ryan and O'Connor would happily shoot her as a British spy, but because of their Irish catholic upbringing, the thought of raping her would not have entered their heads.

But worst of all was the feeling of hopelessness. She had allowed herself to be used as a lure to trap Patrick and there wasn't a single thing she could do about it.

***

By dawn Patrick had devised a plan and talked it through with Michael. They were hopeful that they had worked out a way of foiling Kevin Ryan's plot to sabotage the cease-fire, rescue Kate and, most importantly, live to tell the tale.

But the scheme was far from foolproof and they would require the cooperation of at least two other men to put it into action; and they had only twenty-four hours to arrange it. Michael went to set the wheels in motion.

Chapter 47

St Stephen's Green Park in Dublin was first enclosed in 1664 when a wall was built around what was then an area of marshland. Over the centuries, as the city expanded to encircle the area, it gradually developed into one of Dublin's best known parks; although it was not opened to the general public until 1880. A feature of the park was an ornamental lake crossed at its narrowest point by a stone footbridge. The park was well wooded and planted with shrubs so there was plenty of cover, particularly around the bridge. Even during the War of Independence, 'The Green', as it was known locally, was well populated by visitors and by people using it as a short cut during the day, and on summer evenings it was a favourite meeting place for Dubliners. But in the early morning it was virtually deserted.

This was not, however, the only reason why Kevin Ryan had chosen it as the ideal place to assassinate Commander Wilson: during the Easter Rising of 1916, the insurgents had occupied 'The Green' and dug defensive trenches. These had been filled in but 'The Green' still held a special significance for those who had fought in 'The Rising'.

After her third night of captivity, Kate was nearing the end of her tether. The previous night, however, she had finally managed to catch a little sleep. When all was quiet downstairs she had moved the washstand over by the door, so that if they came to rape her in the night they would have to push it aside and the noise would wake her. She hoped that it would give her enough of a warning to be prepared. In the morning she planned to move it back before Sean brought her 'breakfast', because if they noticed what she was doing she feared they would remove it altogether.

But this morning she was overtaken by events. The first grey streaks of dawn were just breaking over the city when she heard Sean coming up the stairs. Thinking, at first, that he was going to molest her, she picked up the water jug from the floor and stood ready by the door to hit him with it as he entered. When he pushed the washstand aside, however, she could see that he was carrying a mug of tea together with the rapidly diminishing candle. She was obviously not going to be given any dry bread this morning. Sean seemed not to be bothered by the way the washstand had been moved, and the way she was standing with the jug in her hand. He simply looked at her and put the mug on the stand.

"Drink that quick, and smarten yourself up a bit, you're leaving here this morning." They were the first words he had spoken to her since he had first locked her in the room.

In her tiredness, her first reaction was one of relief at being able to vacate the hot, smelly room. But then Kevin Ryan came in and she realised that today was the day he planned to kill her and Patrick. Something snapped in her mind. She flew at him and tried to hit him with the water jug. He ducked, hit her with his closed fist and knocked her out cold.

"That'll keep the bitch quiet for a while," he said to Sean. "But I hope to God she wakes up in time for me to shut her up for good."

They dumped Kate on the bed and went back downstairs and, although she was still out cold, Sean locked the door behind him as a precaution.

In the dirty, untidy parlour Ryan was in a state of high anticipation. He couldn't wait to use the Thompson in anger. In the month since he had acquired the gun he had never actually fired it, principally because he had only one full magazine and, once that was gone, he knew that it would be impossible for him to lay his hands on any more .45 ammunition. And having to keep it hidden from both the British and the IRA was driving him to distraction. In fact, although they had mounted several successful raids and ambushes since the battle at The Custom House, none of de Valera's Thompsons had been used by the Dublin Brigade. The frustration of having to wait for his chance to fire the gun only added to Ryan's already unstable mental state. O'Connor watched warily as his companion played with the gun, swinging it round, pointing it at imaginary targets and making childish, machine gun like noises. Sean took out his own British service revolver and carefully cleaned and reloaded it.

"Jesus, Sean, sure can't you leave that stupid little popgun at home," Ryan told him. "Haven't I enough firepower here for the two of us."

O'Connor ignored him and went on with what he was doing.

The waiting began to play on Ryan's already frayed nerves. "For Christ's sake, is he coming here at all?"

"Sure won't he be here soon enough now," O'Connor said. "It'll do no good to be there too early, if we spend too long on that bridge the cops or the 'Tans might get the notion that we're not there for the good of our health."

Ryan momentarily brightened up. "I hope a few 'Tans do turn up. Sure with this won't I be able to do for every bloody Black and Tan in all Dublin."

"Don't forget to save up enough ammo to do the main job," O'Connor said.

***

Across the still largely slumbering city, Michael had spent the night at the Sinn Fein safe house where Coughlin lodged. Their landlady prepared them a hearty breakfast while they made careful preparations for what lay ahead of them.

Patrick checked over the .303 Lee Enfield rifle of the type used by the RIC. "Are you sure now that you don't want to go armed, Mick? God knows there'll be more guns on that bridge this morning than there are in Dublin Castle itself."

"In that case, sure one less won't make a blind bit of difference," Michael answered. "But seriously, Pat, I killed one man and after that I swore to God that I'd never kill another."

Patrick nodded his reluctant acceptance. "Well, I'll be on my way."

Michael held out his hand and the former Connaught Ranger shook it.

"Don't be late now," Patrick said. "Sure isn't it bad manners to keep people waiting."

With that he left. Michael said a silent prayer that the trump card they had up their sleeve would arrive in Dublin on time.

***

In Dublin Castle, Commander Wilson had been awake all night, trying to reconcile his personal feelings with his duty. Although not completely happy about having to carry a sidearm, the Royal Navy man decided that today he would have to make an exception. From the wide choice available from 'The Castle' arsenal, he chose a short barrelled .38 Smith and Wesson that would fit easily in his pocket.

As he set out for St Stephen's Green, he still had the uncomfortable feeling that he was allowing his heart to rule his head; and yet again he inwardly cursed himself for getting involved in the treacherous world of security work. He now knew the names of the men behind the message, and because it would be impossible for him to find Ryan and O'Connor on his own before they reached the rendezvous, the simplest way of dealing with the situation would be to alert the RIC; he had already decided that it would be much too risky to involve the 'irregulars'. The police could then lay a counter-trap for the two IRA men in the park and catch them red-handed. This approach would almost certainly result in the deaths of Private Coughlin and the Steele girl, and the Commander wondered if he would be able to live with that. The thought that his duty might require him to do so did little to help.

If, however, he chose to ignore the note and didn't do as instructed, Ryan would simply shoot Coughlin and the girl. But Michael Flynn had told him that he fully intended to be at the bridge at the appointed time to do what he could to help his friend and Kate, and Wilson believed him. It was typical of the man that he would not send his friends into an obvious trap while, he himself, kept safely out of harm's way. Knowing how jittery the RIC were at present, the

Commander realised that everybody involved was in as much danger of being shot by them as by the IRA; and that included Flynn. If Michael were to be killed then everything they had worked for in trying to attain a truce would be lost. And the chance might not come again because, in Wilson's opinion, Flynn was the only one who could keep Michael Collins in check. Then Michael came to him with the argument about what a pitched battle would do to the prospects of a truce, and he realised that he had to think again.

Now the question was, where exactly did his duty lie? After some soul searching, and against his better judgement, he abandoned the idea of alerting the RIC and agreed to go along with the plan outlined by Michael, although it bore all the hallmarks of having been devised by Private Coughlin. He knew that he was being used as the bait in the trap but without his cooperation the plan would fail.

The thought that he could well be heading for his own death did not escape him. But the die was cast and he was placing his life in the hands of a convicted mutineer

***

Kevin Ryan's nerves were almost at breaking point when they heard the sound of a horse and cart coming along the cobbled street. It stopped outside the door and immediately afterwards, the sound of retreating footsteps were heard. O'Connor looked out to check that it actually was Ryan's friend, the milkman, leaving his horse and cart for them.

Satisfied that it was, they went upstairs. The still groggy Kate was bound hand and foot with strong twine and gagged with the dirty towel. She was wrapped in a blanket from the bed and carried downstairs. They removed a couple of the milk churns from the cart and dumped her in the gap. She had recovered well enough to struggle against the restraints, but a sharp kick made her lie quietly. Ryan had discarded his cardboard box and wrapped the Thompson in a piece of sacking so that it could be fired without being unwrapped. But when he checked to see if there were signs of anyone peeping through their curtains, he held it in plain view and brandished it menacingly.

O'Connor frowned at his partner's blatant showing-off but said nothing.

On the milk cart they hid the guns under the driver's seat; Ryan again made sarcastic remarks about O'Connor's choice of weapon and told him that he might as well leave the useless toy at home.

"Anyway, you know what you have to do now, Sean," he said as they set off. O'Connor didn't reply. He knew exactly what he had to do, and it didn't include leaving his revolver behind.

Chapter 48

Commander Wilson was the first to arrive. He stood on the bridge and lit a cigarette. A couple of tired looking RIC men with rifles slung on their shoulders came from the area of the Victorian bandstand. Wilson had heard that it was a favourite spot for policemen to go for a secret smoke during the quiet hours between when the IRA went to bed and the city awoke. Although there was nothing suspicious about the man on the bridge, they felt a need to justify their presence in the park at this time of the morning so they un-slung their rifles and approached him warily. They demanded to see some identification and, when they had inspected Wilson's credentials, they stood back and saluted. Wilson feigned anger; he told them that he was there to meet with an informant and they were to leave the area immediately or they would frighten his man off.

They were making their way to the imposing Fusilier Gate at the north-western corner of 'The Green' to do as they had been ordered when they met another police officer on his way in. Thinking that he was heading for the bandstand, they advised him to watch out for a British security man on the bridge who wanted to be left alone to meet an informer. He thanked them for letting him know, but when they were out of sight, he ignored their warning and made for the bridge.

As he passed Wilson he touched the peak of his cap and said, "The top o' the mornin' to you, sir."

The Commander was plainly annoyed but inwardly he had to smile. It was the first time he had heard the phrase other than in a music hall, even in Ireland. He firmly told the policeman to make himself scarce and the man went away.

The sun was rising and the rays touched the College of Surgeons across 'The Green' when the milk cart rattled up to the eastern entrance. Ryan and O'Connor lifted Kate from among the milk churns and went into the park as if carrying a bundle of some kind. Once inside they removed the blanket, untied her ankles and made her stand up. Once she had gained some control of her cramped legs and with her hands still tied and the gag still in place, they moved under cover of the trees and shrubs towards the bridge. Kate was by now too disoriented and frightened to resist. When they could go no further under cover, Sean looked carefully from behind a tree.

"There's only one of them there yet. It's your man, Wilson, we could get him now and be gone before he hits the ground," he said.

"Jesus no, Sean," Ryan said. "Sure I'm not wasting bullets on one man. Mick Flynn and Coughlin will be here any minute and then we'll have a grand time. I'll mind her while you keep an eye on the road."

O'Connor went to look for Flynn and Coughlin with his worst fears confirmed. Ryan was going to hang this out and mock his victims before killing them. By that time, they would be discovered and lucky to escape with their lives. With this in mind, he reasoned that he would certainly have to put his own back-up plan into action; but the British security man had to die, and the cease-fire negotiations sabotaged before he could implement it. And if the chance came his way he would kill the British female spy as well if Ryan hadn't already done so.

He spotted two figures coming up the road: one he recognised as Michael Flynn, he couldn't make out the other man's face because he had his hat pulled well down; but it had to be Coughlin, a man he had never met.

"They're here," he said as he got back to where Ryan had removed the Thompson from the sack and was tormenting Kate by describing what an efficient killing machine it was. She was trembling with fear; wanting desperately to run but unable to do so.

Ryan moved into the open with the Thompson pointed directly at the bridge. "Bring her," he said over his shoulder to O'Connor.

He marched boldly up to Wilson and waved the gun in his face. O'Connor, pushing Kate in front of him, joined them. The

Commander was determined not to appear at all phased by Ryan's antics. "Good morning to you, Mr Ryan and to you, Miss Steele. So what happens now?"

Ryan was not to be drawn into providing an explanation just yet. "All in good time, Commander, wait a minute now 'till a couple of other fellas get here."

O'Connor felt a pang of anxiety at hearing that the security man knew who Ryan was, and wondered if he had been recognised as well. If his name was passed to the RIC, Collins would soon know, and it was one more reason why Wilson had to be killed. If it were left up to Sean, he would have killed him there and then without further ceremony, but he had to be wary of Ryan and that gun.

Michael and Patrick approached the bridge. "Come in, lads, and shut the door behind you," Ryan said jovially.

When they came up to where Wilson stood, he ordered O'Connor to 'line them up there now, Sean, like good soldiers'. Kate was beginning to struggle against the cord securing her wrists and O'Connor was having difficulty holding her. But he managed to hang on to her as he roughly pushed the other three into a line across the footpath that crossed the bridge.

Michael cast an anxious glance across the lake. He needed to buy some time. "I hope to God you know what you're doing here, Kevin," he said. "That girl there is working for Michael Collins, and he won't want to see her hurt."

Ryan burst out laughing. "Jesus, but that's a good one, Mick: an English girl working for the 'Big Fella'. Wait 'till we tell that to the lads, eh Sean."

Sean was silent. He knew that Ryan was past caring, but he had a disturbing feeling that something was not quite right. Their reaction to being held at gunpoint seemed all wrong for a start.

Ryan walked up to Michael. "I'll tell you who she is, Flynn: she's a bloody British spy and she's working for this bastard security man from Dublin Castle. Well, haven't I fixed enough of their kind before, and now I'm going to do for another one of them."

He turned on Coughlin. "And you as well, you cocky bastard. Just because you're one of the great Connaught Rangers, you think that you're a real clever fella don't you? Well I'll show you how smart you are."

He knocked Patrick's hat off with the barrel of the Thompson, and at this point, things began to go badly wrong for Ryan. He stood back in amazement. "Jesus Christ sure it's not Coughlin at all Sean. It's that bloody Quinlan from down in Beaufort."

He snapped. "Bastards!" he yelled and in a fit of rage he turned the Thompson on the group and squeezed the trigger.

Ryan had never had any training in firing the weapon, or any other sub-machine gun for that matter. And he wouldn't have accepted any advice on the subject even if it had been available. He knew nothing about the Thompson's unique characteristics and had never given a moment's thought to how the gun would behave in unpractised hands. Wilson, who was standing at the end of the line, was hit by the first bullet and was driven backwards by the impact; a split second later the next round merely nicked the top of the bridge parapet as the gun unexpectedly pulled upward and to Ryan's right spewing bullets harmlessly into the air. Caught completely by surprise, he wasted half the magazine on shooting leaves off the trees before he released the trigger. He brought the gun back to bear on his targets but he never got off another shot.

The bullet that killed him was accompanied by the sharp crack of a rifle from across the lake. Kevin Ryan dropped the Thompson and his lifeless body tumbled over the parapet into the water.

Everyone stood momentarily transfixed. Kate, who had worked the gag from her mouth, broke away from O'Connor and screamed. Jack Quinlan put his arms round her to try and calm her down.

Sean O'Connor quickly grasped the situation and realised that someone, he didn't care who, had saved him the trouble shooting Ryan himself, as he had always intended to do. Once Ryan had killed Wilson, and anyone else who got in the way, O'Connor planned to shoot Ryan and take the Thompson back to 'The Big Fella' with the story about how he had captured it; and, if Flynn happened to be still alive, how he saved Michael's life in doing so. The notes found in the girl's purse would add credibility to his story. Now, however, with Wilson already dead there was no need for any further shooting.

He trained his revolver on Michael and Jack and motioned them to stand back while he bent down to retrieve the Thompson. He was now in a position to take it back to Michael Collins.

Then Wilson, who was slumped on the ground with his back against the parapet, moaned and began to stir.

O'Connor stared at him incredulously. "Jesus Christ, he's still alive."

He aimed the revolver at the Englishman, obviously intending to finish him off. A second rifle shot rang out from across the lake and Sean O'Connor was dead before his body touched the ground.

Chapter 49

Patrick Coughlin was worried. As soon as he saw that O'Connor was not going to cause them any further trouble, he rose from his hiding place in the lakeside shrubbery and ran for the bridge. His intention had been to kill Ryan before he had an opportunity to use the Thompson, but Kate, struggling to get away from O'Connor, kept blocking his line of sight thus preventing him from getting a clear shot at the IRA man. Ryan therefore, had managed to get off one burst before he died and Patrick knew that Wilson had been hit. How badly he didn't know, but it would be enough to send his carefully laid plans badly awry.

He knew that the sound of the gunfire would alert the authorities, who would arrive quickly and in force. So as soon as both Ryan and O'Connor had been neutralised, Michael and Jack Quinlan were supposed to beat a hasty retreat and to separate in order to take different exits out of the park. And they each had a carefully rehearsed story ready just in case they were stopped. Patrick had planned to take care of Kate himself. Wearing the RIC uniform, he felt that they could get away in the confusion before anyone wondered what he was doing there, and started asking awkward questions. In the current situation, it was virtually unheard of for a lone RIC man to be on patrol by himself.

But Wilson being hit had changed everything, and as he ran he inwardly cursed himself for his foolish 'top o' the mornin' remark' earlier on the bridge.

Jack had released Kate and was bending over Wilson with an obviously anxious Michael looking on. Even in the uniform she recognised him instantly. "Patrick," she cried and ran to him.

They embraced. "Hush now, darlin'," Patrick said gently. "Sure everything is all right now."

But he knew they had to get away quickly. He noticed that Jack was pressing a couple of folded handkerchiefs over the wound to try and stem the bleeding. "How bad is he, Jack?" he asked.

"He was hit in the shoulder," Jack told him, "and the bullet is still in him. I'm trying to stop the bleeding but if he doesn't get a doctor soon, he'll die."

"All right," he said urgently. "I'll do that and stay with him until the cops arrive. You and Mick get going quick and take Kate with you."

Although he was well aware that there had been no alternative, the shooting of Ryan and O'Connor had affected Michael quite badly. He had been party to the scheme devised by Patrick and he felt responsible for the deaths; and now, as he heard Patrick talking to Jack, he remembered that there was something else he was responsible for. He was the one who had suggested that Jack Quinlan was the only person he knew who could successfully impersonate Patrick Coughlin.

He couldn't allow Jack to take any further risks. "I'll stay with the Commander, Pat," he said. "I know him better than either one of you, and he'll stand up for me when he's able."

"No, Mick," Jack said. "I have this thing working as well as I can and it won't do any good to disturb it. Anyway, sure aren't I covered in blood and how would I explain that to the 'Tans. And anyway if I stop here they won't bother me; sure haven't I the best chance of all of us with His Lordship's letter in my pocket."

Patrick knew that Jack was right about being the best placed to get away; in fact, he had a better chance on his own than with them. And he knew that it would be useless to argue, Jack Quinlan would never leave a wounded man to his fate. Patrick remembered how Jack had risked his own life to help him when he had been wounded in Mesopotamia during the war and, ironically as it turned out, Jack had also once saved Ryan's life following the IRA ambush in Beaufort.

Being involved in violent action had sharpened Patrick's wits, and the instincts developed during many years of soldiering came into play. "He's right, Mick," he said. "He's the best man for this job, and there's a way that we can all still get away with this yet."

He quickly explained what he had in mind and Michael immediately complied. He rolled around in the shrubbery for a minute and then threw a handful of leaves and grass over the already dishevelled Kate. They were then made to march smartly towards the Fusilier's Arch with Patrick urging them on with his rifle and blowing his police whistle. They heard several answering blasts and, just before they reached the arched exit, a group of RIC men led by a sergeant burst into the park. Patrick was relieved to see the two men he had spoken to earlier among their number. He waved and shouted to them and the sergeant halted his men.

Before the sergeant reached them, however, Patrick poked Michael with the rifle. "Bugger off, you and take your floozy with you!" he shouted at them, "and don't let me catch you in The Green again or I'll arrest the pair of you for vagrancy."

Kate had still not recovered enough from the series of shocks she had suffered in the last few hours to fully appreciate what was happening, but Michael grabbed her arm and forced her to run for the park exit, shedding dead leaves and blades of grass.

By the time the any of the RIC men realised what had happened they were gone.

"What the devil is going on here? Someone reported hearing a machine gun!" the sergeant yelled at Patrick.

Patrick ignored him and turned to the two RIC men who clearly recognised him. "The British security man on the bridge was shot by a fella with some sort of a machine gun," he told them. "He's not dead and I have some other fella holding a pad over the wound, but if we don't get a doctor quick he'll be dead."

"That's right, sergeant," one of the officers said. "When we questioned him he said he was waiting for an informer, sure it must be the informer that shot him."

"And I shot the bastard with the machine gun myself," Patrick said proudly. "I think he's done for."

"What do you mean 'you think'?" the sergeant said. "Didn't you make sure?"

"Christ no," Patrick said urgently, "I was too bothered about the security man who was shot."

The sergeant hesitated, he had fallen for IRA tricks in the past, which had almost cost him his life, and he wasn't prepared to rush things. He started to say something but Patrick interrupted him.

"Jesus Christ, sergeant, we'll have to call a doctor quick or a British security man will die, for sure. The bloody 'Tans and 'Auxies' will be here any minute and they'll make sure that we get the blame for it."

The sergeant reacted to that. He dispatched two men to call for urgent medical help, and under the circumstances he thought it wise to tell them to contact Dublin Castle as well. The rest of his men were dispatched to secure the bridge with a warning to be careful 'in case this country culshie didn't kill that bloody machine-gunner'.

"Now, who were those two you let go?" he asked Patrick.

Patrick laughed. "Ah sure they were nobody at all, sergeant. I found them in the bushes and from the look of them I'd say they were there all night trying to make their mothers ashamed of them."

"You bloody eejit! They could be witnesses and you let them escape. I'll have you back milking cows before you can scratch your stupid arse."

"Jesus," Patrick looked shocked. "But wait a minute now and I'll catch them for you, sergeant."

He ran out of the park after Michael and Kate. The sergeant yelled at him to come back, but he was ignored and Patrick Coughlin was soon well out of sight.

Throwing up his arms and swearing blue murder at the eejits being recruited these days, the sergeant made for the bridge where he found one of his men pointing a revolver and shouting at Jack Quinlan, who remained calmly kneeling and holding the blood-soaked swab to Wilson's shoulder. O'Connor's body still lay where he had fallen near the abandoned Thompson.

"All right, what have we here?" he said to the policeman with the revolver.

"This fella won't get up to let me check his identification, Sergeant," the man answered.

Determined to assert his authority, the sergeant kicked Jack on the leg. "Will you get up out of there this minute or I'll have you shot."

Jack looked up at him. "No," he said, "I won't. This man is Commander Wilson from Dublin Castle. He's a member of the British security service and, if I let go of this pad, he'll bleed to death."

"That's right, sergeant," said one of the policemen who had checked Wilson's credentials. "His name was Wilson, sure enough."

"And that's why you shot him, you IRA bastard!" the sergeant yelled at Jack

"For God's sakes," Jack answered, "if I was the one who shot him, would I be here trying to stop him bleeding to death before you and your gang of eejits get a doctor for him?"

The sergeant was having difficulty holding his temper but his instincts warned him to tread carefully. "There's an ambulance on its way and I have alerted 'The Castle'," he said. But he couldn't resist one more try at intimidating Jack. "And how would the likes of you know exactly who he is if you didn't come here to shoot him?"

Jack ignored the question. "In that case," he said, "wouldn't it be a good notion to send a man out to the street to show them where to come? And how I know who he is, is none of your business, sergeant."

The sergeant bristled: he wasn't used to be spoken to like this by mere civilians. But something about Jack's confident manner and his knowledge of who the wounded man was, made him back off.

There was a shout from one of the policemen. "There's another body in the lake, sergeant."

Before the sergeant could react to that, there was a commotion as an army ambulance, escorted by an armoured car, arrived at the park entrance. An army doctor, wearing the pips of a captain on the shoulder of his white coat, was directed onto the bridge closely followed by two stretcher-bearers. The doctor opened his bag and bent over Wilson, who groaned as the pad was gently removed and replaced by a proper swab. Jack got up and stretched his cramped limbs as the doctor worked on the patient assisted by the stretcher-bearers. A further detachment of the RIC arrived and the sergeant was relieved to see that they were led by an inspector he recognised as coming from Dublin Castle. As if by prior agreement, nobody spoke until the doctor was satisfied that Commander Wilson could be moved and had supervised the transfer of the patient onto the stretcher.

"How is he," the inspector asked.

"Too early to tell," the doctor replied. "But I can say one thing with some certainty: if that chap hadn't had the wit to stem the bleeding, the patient would have died by now."

He turned to Jack, who had so far been ignored. "You have seen wounded men before," he said.

"That I have," Jack replied, "too many of them."

As the ambulance, with its escort, was leaving 'The Green', a tender full of Auxiliary Police drove up. Completely ignoring the police they ran into the park. On their arrival, groups of bystanders who had gathered to find out what was happening quickly dispersed. At the bridge the police inspector told the officer in charge of the 'Auxies' that they were too late; the shooting was over and all that was left was to remove the bodies and begin a thorough investigation into what had happened. Neither of these activities were of any interest to them, so after throwing their weight around for a while, the 'Auxies' left.

After a short conference with his sergeant, the inspector eventually turned to Jack. "So," he said, "who are you and what exactly are you doing here? I understand that you know the injured man, Commander Wilson."

"I do so, Inspector," Jack told him. He looked at his bloodstained hands. "If you open my coat you'll find a letter in the inside pocket that'll tell you all about me."

The inspector hesitated as if fearing a trap, but with all his men around he decided that he was perfectly safe. He took the letter from Jack's pocket. It was addressed to 'Commander Wilson' at Dublin Castle and the envelope was still sealed. Again, the inspector hesitated, he was reluctant to do so but could see no alternative to opening it, especially as Jack had as good as invited him to. The single sheet of paper contained a note from the owner of Beaufort House saying that he was happy to comply with Commander Wilson's request to let him have the services of his steward, Quinlan, for a few days. His Lordship wrote that he was sending his man to Dublin by the first available train and was directing him to wait for the Commander to contact him at the Shelbourne Hotel near St Stephens Green.

Without waiting to be asked, Jack took up the story. "I was on my way to the hotel from the station when the shooting started," he told the inspector. "I was heading back the other way when one of your fellas came at me blowing a whistle and pointed a rifle at me. He dragged me onto this bridge and that's when I saw that Commander Wilson was hurt, so, I stayed to help him while your man went for help."

The inspector called the sergeant who verified Jack's story about the RIC man with the rifle, and added that it was this officer who shot the man still lying on the ground, and was presumably also responsible for the body being pulled from the lake. He started to tell the inspector about the man and woman found in the bushes, but the officer stopped him in mid-sentence.

"We will get to the bottom of this back at 'The Castle'," he said. "You finish up here while I check this man's story."

He was inclined to believe that Jack's letter was genuine, but he had heard about the cleverly forged documents used by the IRA at Mountjoy Prison and he decided not to take any chances.

"On second thoughts, sergeant," he added, "I'm taking him to 'The Castle' instead and I'll meet you there later."

If the decision to take him to the seat of British power in Ireland was meant to intimidate Jack so that the policeman could gauge his reaction, it failed, and he knew that the letter was genuine. It had, in fact, been arranged by Wilson as a subtle addition to Coughlin's original plan, once he knew that Quinlan, too, would be involved. Jack didn't make the slightest protest as he was driven under escort to 'The Castle' in the inspector's car. On arrival he was at last allowed to clean the blood from his hands and as much as he could from his clothing. He did his best, but ruefully had to accept the fact that he would need a new best suit. Even within the confines of 'The Castle', the inspector was determined not to let his charge out of his sight until he had irrefutable proof of his identity.

Eventually, he rang Beaufort House and spoke to His Lordship. Jack's reason for being in Dublin was confirmed and the inspector broke the news about Commander Wilson being shot.

He handed the phone to Jack. "He wants a word with you," he said.

Jack spoke to his employer at length; he described Wilson's injury and assured His Lordship that there was a good chance that the Commander would pull through. When he rang off he turned to the inspector.

"He wants me to stop here in Dublin until I have definite news of Commander Wilson," he said. "He has a suite at the Shelbourne Hotel and I'm to use the maid's room there until I go home."

The inspector nodded. "All right," he said. "I'll take you there, but don't leave the hotel because I will want to speak to you again."

'So far so good' Jack thought after the policeman had left him at the hotel reception desk. He had got away with it but he was deeply concerned about the others. There was one more worrying thought: the Shelbourne Hotel was where they had agreed to meet after they had escaped from 'The Green' and, assuming that Michael and Patrick had got clear, he was confident that they would eventually show up there. He prayed that they would not arrive at the same time as the police.

Chapter 50

When Patrick ran out of 'The Green', he had a quick look round for Michael and Kate. They were nowhere in sight. It seemed as if they had managed to get away, but there was no way of making sure that they had. He was sorely tempted to go back and see how Jack was getting on, but decided that by doing so, he could easily be responsible for them both being arrested. Patrick knew about His Lordship's letter to Wilson, and Jack Quinlan was no eejit: he would know how to make the best use of it. By going back himself he would have to face a lot of questions that he would have grave difficulty in answering. So, for the moment, his wisest move was to return to his lodgings and change out of the makeshift RIC uniform; and he had to go quickly as he had just seen the second group of policemen arriving at the 'The Green'.

But that in itself presented problems. Coming across Dublin in the early hours when the streets were virtually deserted was one thing; he simply removed the uniform jacket and cap and in the darkened streets he could pass for an ordinary Dublin workman. Concealing the rifle had been tricky but he managed to hide it in a bundle of firewood. But now that the city was wide awake it was a different matter entirely. In broad daylight, an RIC man on his own would stand out, and Patrick feared that the deficiencies in his uniform could well be noticed. There hadn't been time to obtain an authentic police uniform before going to rescue Kate and the one he wore had been quickly assembled from a number of sources. In the excitement at St Stephen's Green, no one, not even the RIC sergeant, had noticed, but he knew that he couldn't hope to get away with it for much longer. Had he been with Kate as planned, then all eyes would have been on her, but on his own he was vulnerable. Then it occurred to him that he could adopt a similar ruse to the one he had used to help Michael and Kate. He made for the nearest railway line, climbed onto the tracks and walked purposefully along as if on urgent RIC business. When he came to a railway coal yard, he went in on the pretext of searching it, and to his great relief found it to be deserted. He disposed of the policeman's jacket and cap in an empty goods wagon but he was reluctant to get rid of the rifle – Michael Flynn was supposed to hand it back. There was nothing else for it, however, so he hid the Lee-Enfield deep in a clump of furze hoping that it would not be found before Michael could arrange to have it collected. Then he rolled in a pile of coal and emerged looking every inch a hard working coalman. On the tram out to the suburbs he was made to stand on the platform at the back and he laughed inwardly; what would the Regimental Sergeant Major say if he saw one of his usually smartly turned out Connaught Rangers in this state?

Back at his lodgings he washed and changed and sat down to wait. He gave the remains of the uniform to the staunchly Nationalist landlady to dispose of; she later made the most of her good fortune by washing it and taking it to her favourite pawnshop.

He was desperately worried about the others, particularly Kate, but he had to give them time before going to see if any of them had managed to reach the Shelbourne Hotel.

As Michael ran through the Fusilier's Arch with the RIC sergeant's warnings to 'halt' ringing in his ears, he hadn't got far before he was forced to virtually carry the totally confused and exhausted Kate. He spotted the police car rounding the corner by the hotel and led her off in the opposite direction. But he knew that he couldn't go very far before doing something about reviving her. They stopped for a breather and she almost collapsed, but they soon had to move on as they were attracting too much attention. He brushed the leaves and grass from her dress but she still looked a sight, and he had to field several concerned offers of help by saying that she had been badly frightened by the shooting in 'The Green' and he was taking her home.

Across the road, in Dawson Street, stood a large church. St. Anne's was one of the largest Church of Ireland churches in Dublin and, as such, the congregation was drawn from the minority Protestant community. But Michael, a Catholic, was not in a position to worry about that, and in any case, he had no time for religious bigotry no matter from which side of the Christian divide it came. As he led Kate inside, however, from force of habit he genuflected and looked round for a font to dip his finger in prior to crossing himself. Realising his mistake, he sat Kate in a pew at the back to catch her breath.

They had only been there for a matter of minutes when a man in a grey suit, and wearing a clerical collar, entered the church through a door at the side of the altar. He knelt in prayer but, sensing that he was not alone, he turned and saw the couple seated at the back. He rose to his feet and approached them, then, noting Kate's obvious distress, he introduced himself as the vicar and kindly asked if he could be of help. Michael readily accepted and they were led through the door by the altar and out of the church to the vicarage next door, where Kate was handed over to the care of the vicar's matronly housekeeper. The man himself set about making them some tea.

By way of an explanation, Michael, whose upbringing made it difficult for him to lie to a clergyman of any denomination, stuck to his story that the girl, who was English, had been badly frightened by the ructions in 'The Green' not half an hour ago; and she had fallen in her hurry to get away. Whether the vicar believed him or not was a moot point, many far stranger things were happening all around him on a daily basis, so, he didn't question Michael too closely.

When Kate returned, still under the care of the housekeeper, she had washed her hands and face and combed her hair. Her dress had been brushed and the creases smoothed out, and outwardly at least, she looked altogether more presentable. But the signs of her ordeal were still evident in her face which looked pale and drawn. After some tea and a couple of the housekeeper's homemade scones, she gradually recovered enough for Michael to consider that it was safe for them to move on. He wanted to get her as far away from St Stephen's Green as soon and as fast as possible; and he worried that the vicar and his housekeeper could get into trouble if he and Kate were to be found in his vicarage. So, much against the concerned housekeeper's advice, they left and walked away in the direction of Trinity College. He had been tempted to take Kate to the Shelbourne to see if Patrick or Jack had reached there, but realised that it was much too soon yet to risk that.

The original plan had been to take Kate back to the hotel in Killiney. Patrick had reasoned that by now, the people there would be sufficiently concerned about her disappearance to have alerted the RIC, and the easiest way to nip their investigation in the bud was for her to go back there with a plausible story. If she explained that she had been inadvertently caught up in an IRA ambush and been so frightened that she had gone into hiding, there was a pretty good chance that, as an English girl not knowing her way around, she would be believed. She would then give in her notice, explaining that she had seen enough of Ireland and was going home to England.

Patrick believed that, by this time, the English police investigation into her disappearance from the Silent Woman Inn would have run its course and it really was safe for her to go back 'across the water'. He had planned to risk incurring the wrath of Michael Collins and accompany her to London. After seeing her settled there, he would decide whether or not to return to Ireland by himself.

But they hadn't bargained for the severity of Kate's treatment at the hands of Ryan and O'Connor. So, while Michael thought that Patrick's original idea was still the best option, he worried that Kate was still too confused and disoriented to make it work. She was gradually recovering though; enough to ask him what had happened to Patrick, but not enough to face the questioning that would ensue once she reached the Killiney Hotel. She needed more time. They walked slowly to Burgh Quay and sat on a bench by the river looking across at the still smouldering Custom House. Gradually she began to improve; in a small café she ate a reasonable lunch and she seemed to understand what she had to do. The thought of going back to England with Patrick cheered her up and glimpses of the old Kate broke through. Michael felt that she was at last up to the task ahead.

The midday editions of the newspapers were now on the streets and were dominated by accounts of the events in Belfast. The opening of the new parliament was quickly becoming the talk of the city of Dublin. Michael bought a copy, but there was nothing as yet about the content of King George's opening speech.

He accompanied Kate on the train but left her at the station before Killiney, and with a silent prayer that she would be all right, returned to Dublin. Now all he had to do was to find Patrick and Jack.

As he neared the Shelbourne he saw the police car parked outside and an officer standing at the entrance. He guessed that either Jack or Patrick was inside being questioned, but as he turned to leave he almost collided with Patrick Coughlin, so it had to be Jack who was in the hotel. The RIC had, by this time, removed the bodies and completed their investigation, so 'The Green' had returned to normal and it was safe for them to wait there until the police had finished with Jack.

In the hotel the RIC inspector's frustration was beginning to show. His enquiries were leading him nowhere, and if events took their usual course, there would soon be yet another incident involving the IRA, and he would be called away to mount yet another fruitless investigation. And, given the happenings in Belfast, he fully expected 'the boys' to arrange something in reply. But as it was a security man from 'The Castle' who had been hurt in St Stephen's Green, he was expected to come up with at least some answers. Jack Quinlan was his only witness but was being no help whatsoever. Quinlan's description of the mysterious RIC man would have fitted half of the men in the force, and so far it had been impossible to find the elusive rifleman. Every officer's whereabouts at the time of the incident was being checked and so far every single one had been accounted for. There was only one possibility left: the man with the rifle wasn't an RIC officer at all; but if not, who? It was unlikely that he was one of 'the boys' because the two dead men had been identified as known IRA activists. Who then had killed them, and why? The witness also stated that he had not seen the man and woman who were said to have been hiding in the bushes: he had been too concerned about Commander Wilson to take in what was going on around him.

The inspector was not altogether happy with Jack's description of events. But then Quinlan had definitely saved Commander Wilson's life, and his identity as His Lordship's steward had been established beyond doubt. So, the policeman couldn't press too hard. Eventually, he gave up in despair.

Jack breathed a large sigh of relief. His involvement in the affair was largely Commander Wilson's doing. When Michael outlined the scheme to the Commander and persuaded him to go along with it, he had to admit that they were still one man short, and the only man that either of them could think of was Jack Quinlan. Each had his own reasons for not being happy about involving Jack, but there was nobody else, so Wilson rang His Lordship who put the problem to Jack and the steward immediately volunteered.

Michael and Patrick entered the hotel separately and were met by Jack who sent them up to the luxurious surroundings of His Lordship's suite. It was the first time that Patrick and Jack had actually met since the war and they had a lot to catch up on. But there were more important matters to discuss, and before that, Michael had to assure Patrick that Kate was well and back at the Killiney Hotel.

It was unfortunate that Commander Wilson had been hurt, for which Patrick blamed himself, but it was too late to do anything about it now. As Jack was to remain in Dublin to keep His Lordship informed about Wilson's progress, he was in an excellent position to make enquiries at the hospital. They could be thankful that under the circumstances events had turned out so favourably, but a lot still depended on Kate playing her part. Patrick was impatient to take her out of Ireland, but was persuaded by Michael to give her a few days more at the hotel to fully recover.

Gradually Patrick and Jack began to relax and talk over old times. But Michael still had one more important job to do, one that he wasn't at all looking forward to. He had to somehow explain what had happened to Michael Collins.

He couldn't hope to get away with palming 'The Big Fella' off with half truths, so he told Collins everything, but with one exception: he lied and told Collins that he knew nothing about Commander Wilson receiving an identical note to his own from Kevin Ryan. It had come as a complete surprise to find the Englishman at 'The Green'. Michael knew that Patrick would back him up, but lying to 'The Big Fella' was always fraught with danger.

To Michael's great surprise and immense relief, Collins didn't seem too perturbed about the whole incident. Even the deaths of Ryan and O'Connor didn't seem to overly concern him, but he did express his annoyance at the thought of the sub-machine gun falling into RIC hands.

"And this plan was devised by Coughlin within the space of a few hours?" 'The Big Fella' asked.

Michael said that it had.

"Well, Michael," Collins said, "we shall need his particular skills again. We have obviously got to do something in reply to this extremely provocative British action of setting up a separate parliament in The North. I want to see Mr Coughlin immediately."

Michael had known that Collins would plan something in answer to the events in Belfast. But now it looked as if Patrick was to be part of that response, which did not bode well for the former soldier's plans to take Kate back to England.

Chapter 51

From his hospital bed, Commander Wilson could hear the cheers of the Dubliners as General Macready made his way to the Mansion House to finalise the terms of the cease-fire agreement. He felt vindicated by the fact that events in Ireland had moved on apace since the opening of the parliament in Belfast.

The King had, as Wilson had been told he would, made an impassioned appeal for peace, and called upon *".... all Irishmen, to pause, to stretch out the hand of forbearance and conciliation, to forgive and forget, and to join in making for the land they love a new era of peace, contentment and goodwill."* And Wilson knew that the Irishman he now considered to be a friend and who was a regular visitor, Michael Flynn, was equally happy with the outcome. Following The King's speech in Belfast, Lloyd George made a public appeal to Eamonn de Valera proposing a peace conference and offering him safe conduct to London to discuss the proposal. At first the proposal was rejected, but following a second appeal from Lloyd George peace negotiations were begun. When it came down to the actual cease-fire arrangements, however, Commander Wilson, Michael Flynn, Alfred Cope and even Michael Collins had all been sidelined.

For Michael Flynn the cease-fire didn't come a moment too soon. Michael Collins' plans for a major response to the opening of the parliament in Belfast would not now come to fruition. And it meant that Patrick Coughlin was released from helping to plan it. Now that the truce was actually in place, Collins felt exposed; his first priority was to salvage as much of his undercover organisation as he could in case the truce failed. Michael was confident that 'The Big Fella' would now be agreeable to pack Patrick and Kate off to America out of harm's way in case he had further need of them: news that would be most welcome to Kate Steele who was still somewhat marooned at the hotel in Killiney.

Michael, himself, could at last return to County Kerry and resume his place on the county council. And far more importantly, he could go home and be with his growing son.

Jack Quinlan had, as directed by His Lordship, kept an eye on Wilson's progress. He visited the hospital on several occasions, and when he was satisfied that the Commander would make a full recovery, he returned to Beaufort bearing a letter from Wilson to His Lordship. Although Jack was unaware of it until his employer informed him, the letter spelled out how the Beaufort House steward had saved the Commander's life.

As well as being satisfied with the outcome of the peace negotiations, Commander Wilson, who had been assured that he would make a complete recovery from his wound, had something else to look forward to. Because his position as a security man in Ireland was now fully exposed, he could no longer serve there. In which case there was at last a possibility that he might eventually be able to return to duty at sea. But he still had one more task to perform; a task, which following recent events, left him with yet another personal dilemma to resolve.

The escaped mutineer was still at large. And Wilson supposed that now the cease-fire had been arranged and Alfred Cope was no longer involved, he would have to return to hunting the fugitive down. He suspected, however, that even with the truce in place, his political masters would still want him to keep the escape secret and the search low key. Arranging the truce was he realised, only half the battle; maintaining it was likely to prove just as difficult, and the London government would still be anxious not to hand the Irish side what would still be an embarrassing propaganda coup. He hoped that they might even call off the hunt entirely. The more he learned about Private Coughlin, and the more he saw of the situation in Ireland, the more he began to understand the motives behind his escape. As a naval officer, Wilson still could not condone mutiny, and he was sure that the provisions of the cease-fire would not have made provision for the mutineers to be set free. But the character shown by the man himself presented the Commander with an entirely different view of the affair. Coughlin had saved his life by shooting the IRA men when he could have waited until they had finished him off first. That would have meant the that his hunt for the fugitive would be over, and with the political situation being what it was, Coughlin would have been effectively a free man. And Wilson was certain that the thought would have crossed the 'Ranger's mind.

Then there was the question of the Steele girl: she was technically still wanted for theft in England, but he hadn't heard from the Dorset police for months and assumed that they had lost interest in her. What worried him more was that he suspected that she had been helping the IRA and, if so, would now be guilty of the far more serious crime of treason. Did the terms of the cease-fire then extend to her? And, if so, should she be given immunity from arrest like all the others involved in the fight for Irish freedom?

It was Patrick Coughlin, however, who remained uppermost in his mind. The more he thought about him the more Commander Wilson became convinced that it was time for compromise with the man who had saved his life, and who had been prepared to risk arrest to save the girl. According to Michael Flynn, Coughlin had accomplished all he had escaped and come to Ireland to do. He had honoured the memory of his friend in the only way he thought appropriate, and was now intent on leaving the country for good. After some further thought his sense of justice came to the fore. He asked Michael to get Patrick to visit him, without fear of arrest, so that he could talk with him in person.

To begin with the atmosphere was rather strained with neither of them quite knowing what to say, but they gradually relaxed. As he left Patrick extended his hand and Wilson accepted it. He still couldn't condone mutiny, but he was ready to shake the hand of a Connaught Ranger.

Footnote:

Within six months of the cease-fire the Anglo-Irish Treaty had been signed and The Irish Free State established. Following this, on July 31st 1922, the Connaught Rangers were disbanded after over two hundred and thirty years of service to The Crown. The colours, along with those of the other infantry regiments raised in southern Ireland, were laid up at Windsor Castle in the presence of King George V. The surviving men imprisoned for mutiny were released.

Author's Notes and Acknowledgements

This book is a work of fiction albeit based on factual events in Irish history, and it should be regarded as such. It is not intended to be read as an accurate historical account.

Some of the fictional characters are based on members of my own family although, as in my previous books, the family name has been altered. The Irish historical figures apart, all of the other characters are fictional, and any resemblance to any person living or dead is purely coincidental.

As ever, placing fictional characters into real historical events presents certain difficulties and requires the author to apply a degree artistic licence. Michael Flynn, Patrick Coughlin, Kate Steele, Commander Wilson RN, Kevin Ryan and Sean O'Connor are purely fictional, as is 'His Lordship', the owner of Beaufort House. To the best of my knowledge nobody bearing any those names was ever involved in any of the events described in this novel.

This means that the details of certain historical events, the ambush at Clonfin, the raid on Mountjoy Prison and the burning of the Dublin Custom House, have had to be adapted to accommodate them. Thompson sub-machine guns are said to have been used by the IRA but I have not been able to determine exactly where or how.

Sean MacEoin was a real historic figure and his conduct during the action at Clonfin actually did receive universal praise; he later became a senator of the Irish Free State. The men who led the attempt to rescue him from Mountjoy, Emmett Dalton and Paddy Daly, are also based on real people.

The incident taking place on St Stephen's Day is purely fictional.

Alfred Cope, at the behest of the British Prime Minister, Lloyd George, did maintain contact with Michael Collins. But as far as I can ascertain the possibility of a truce was never discussed and, of course, none of my fictional characters were involved. The actual negotiations leading to the ceasefire did not follow the course described here.

I learned my Irish history at school, and from childhood memories of knowing and talking to people who had lived through the period covered in the book. As with the first two books, **'The Last Coachman'** and **'This Bitter Land'**, whenever I needed a reminder or confirmation I turned to **Tim Pat Coogan's 'Ireland in the Twentieth Century'** and **Robert Kee's 'Ireland, a History'.**

I am again grateful to **Donald and Rachel Cameron** for allowing me to set the story in and around **Beaufort House**. Details can be found at: www.beaufortireland.com

Thanks also to **Richard and Denise Bell,** the current landlord and lady of **The Silent Woman** at Cold Harbour in Dorset for allowing me to set part of the story in their public house. www.thesilentwoman.co.uk

St. Anne's Church in Dublin still remains a flourishing place of worship. I am grateful to members of the congregation for showing me round.

Thanks to the staff at **Olympia Publishers** for their help and assistance.

And last but by no means least, a big thank you to my wife, **Shireen**, for her encouragement, help, and support. And to whom this book is dedicated.